Crow Feathers

by

Kathleen Haley

Crow Feathers

Cover Art by *Lisa Dawn MacDonald*

The Wild Rose Press, Inc.
PO Box 708
Adams Basin, NY 14410-0708
Visit us at www.thewildrosepress.com

Publishing History
First Edition, 2025
Trade Paperback ISBN 978-1-5092-6084-3
Digital ISBN 978-1-5092-6085-0

Published in the United States of America

Dedication

To Ethan, who connects me with real worlds when I'm stuck in fictional ones.

Prologue

Ingrid
Four years ago

Dressed all in black, he lay on his belly in the grass pointing a sniper rifle like a member of a special forces team zeroing in on his enemy. All he needed was the fatigues, helmet, and boots. Who or what was his prey?

He jacked a round into the chamber. *Oh God*, now I couldn't make a sound or he'd shoot me too. We were up on a hill overlooking Princeton in a forest I'd played in when I was little. Spying him, I'd crouched down behind a gigantic fallen trunk. I shivered, stifling a gasp as he made a few adjustments, looking through the sights, and steadied his finger over the trigger. Any moment now . . .

Assuming he'd come from the road—as I had—I couldn't remain here without him seeing me on his way back. I thought fast about how I could escape without his noticing my presence.

The tree! Of course. Behind me stood a partially hollow oak my friends and I had made into our hideaway years ago. It had convenient knots on the inside that we used as steps to climb toward a split in its trunk. Best of all, its entrance faced away from the killer's sightline, hidden by a dense bush. Would I still fit inside the space? It'd been at least ten years since I'd

1

tried, and I was mildly claustrophobic. Would the tree hold sturdy, or had it rotted to the point of crumbling under my weight?

My hands were quaking, and beads of sweat trickled down my back and between my breasts. Adrenaline surged through me like a high-voltage current.

As an artist, I was drawn to details even in the midst of danger.

Tilting my head to the side to match the angle of his face, I examined the striking profile of the gunman as he took and held a deep breath. Though he was forty feet away, if I narrowed my eyes and focused, I could just make out his features. His head was huge, the upper half of his face set forward with a broad jutting brow that continued down over a prominent arched nose. The lower half of his face was slightly inset with intelligent lips, a sharp, strong jaw, and the kind of muscular neck that indicated the rest of the body was ripped. His high cheekbones were sculpt-worthy and his medium-length black hair thick to match his bushy, low, dark eyebrows. I couldn't see his eyes.

The shot pierced the air, its echo ricocheting about the trees—my cue to run for the old oak. Though I'm sure my steps cracked the late summer leaves strewn on the forest floor, I didn't hear him running after me. My heart hammered as I scurried behind the bush, nosing my way through the hole in the tree. It must've taken me about ten seconds to get there and secure my hiding place. I climbed up so that if he discovered the hole in the tree, he wouldn't see my feet. It was a tight fit. I got a foothold on the first two knots in the dark hollow trunk—thankfully they were still where they used to be.

Only then did I hear his steps stalking toward me. A plane passed overhead, mercifully covering my labored breathing and the thundering in my chest that I was sure would give me away.

Had he seen me?

By the time the plane had gone, I was able to mute my breaths.

His voice sounded low and gravelly, but calm, from about twenty feet away. As he spoke, did he turn himself about to be heard from all sides?

"You're lucky I had to make sure I hit my target. Be careful that I don't come for you next."

I was trembling so much I almost slipped and lost my foothold. Though his tone held a dangerous edge, it was tinged with what almost sounded like mirth. The raspy cawing of the crows above us cut into the ensuing silence.

"Long blonde hair, tight ass, and an agile body. It'd be a shame to put you in your grave."

I stifled a hitch of my breath. So he *had* seen me!

"Wherever you are, take heed. I'm the best at what I do. And I'd come for you—not that I'd take pleasure from it. If you tell anyone what you've seen, neither the law nor your god will protect you."

Knuckles white, I gripped the tree for dear life. I closed my eyes, praying he'd leave so I could relax my hold.

After another few minutes—minutes that seemed eternal—he said in haunting tones, "Until our paths cross again, my little witness."

Leaves crunched beneath his boots as he retreated into the distance. I listened carefully to discern the direction in which he headed. After waiting another ten minutes, I began to cramp from holding my awkward position for so long. Heaving a breath of relief and jumping down, I slid back out through the hole, dusting myself off. As I adjusted to the light again, my eyes darted around, and I traced a slow circle to make sure he was well and truly gone.

Why had I come here today, of all days, to collect my crow feathers? The birds' molting period would last a few more weeks. That morning, when I'd left home, I'd had no way of knowing I was stepping onto a landmine. I checked my pockets, feeling the collection of four or five different lengths and shapes of feather I'd gathered.

I decided to take the opposite way from the killer to escape the forest. My hands were clammy, my skin bathed in a cold sweat, and my throat dry as a tundra. I ran the two miles, looking behind me every twenty strides. Only once I'd closed the front door behind me, and gulped down a glass of cold water, did my adrenaline ease.

That evening, as my parents and I watched T.V. while preparing dinner, the newscaster reported that the multimillionaire Harry King, resident of Princeton, New Jersey, had been shot dead by the side of his pool by an unidentified shooter. The anchorwoman speculated that one of his many enemies had hired a hitman.

I kept my mouth shut.

Chapter One

Ingrid

He was half an hour late. I scanned the restaurant, a fifties-era Italian place in Hell's Kitchen, not far from the river. A large Italian-American family crowded around a long table, laughing raucously, punctuating the air with shouts, and regaling one another with stories. Their gestures were as loud as their talk. To my left, a bar arced about a wall plastered with signed photographs of Italian-descended celebrities from the last hundred years. Businessmen, couples, and regulars perched on the barstools huddling over drinks and appetizers. Behind me, two-tops and four-tops full of friends and family buzzed with chatter. The soundtrack was, you guessed it, Sinatra.

Having chosen this place, Marvin had ordered us a bottle of champagne in advance. I sat sipping bubbly and praying he'd show up soon so I didn't look like the girl no one wanted to dance with at a party. This would be our third date. I'd met him two weeks ago on a remodeling project for a brownstone in Clinton Hill, Brooklyn. He was the architect, and my firm had sent me to cover the initial floor plans meeting. He'd taken my number and asked me out for drinks. Since then, we'd gone to dinner in Greenwich Village and shared a first kiss. While he was successful, good-looking, and thoughtful, I didn't feel any zings of excitement when I was near him. But he was safe, predictable, and nice.

I took out Jasmine Guillory's latest steamy romance and tried to read so I didn't feel so blatantly alone in a sea of Friday-night revelers. My phone buzzed with a text from Marvin:

—*Sorry, I'll be here till at least 10. The junior architect's model needed to be redone. Project due tomorrow. Stay and enjoy dessert. Happy birthday!*—

What dessert? I hadn't had dinner yet, though I'd lost my appetite. How pathetic was I, all alone and stood up by a date on my birthday? My cheeks burned, and the area behind my eyes stung. But then, when I thought the evening couldn't get any more embarrassing, a waitress glided over holding a small plate with a round chocolate cake, a single candle burning in its middle. *Oh God, everyone's staring.*

"Happy birthday, Miss Pellerin," she chirped, pronouncing my last name the way most people did, to rhyme with "yell her in," even though it was French. She set the cake down and began a chorus of "Happy birthday," as one of the waiters moved closer to back her up. I just about died, wanting to crawl beneath the floor with shame. Soon, everyone in the restaurant joined in, each singer chanting in a different key. More heat seeped into my cheeks as I tried to hold it together. Not only was I their charity case, but I had to look delighted and grateful.

"Make a wish!" the waitress warbled.

I humored my audience, blowing out the candle and pasting on a smile as everyone clapped.

An elderly woman in the Italian party chimed, loud and clear, "Is she all alone on her birthday?"

"If she is, she has a lot of champagne to drink," a man in the group observed.

Another woman clucked sympathetically. "So pretty too. Do you think she's been stood up?"

Jesus, I just need to get out of here.

What a mistake to have agreed to a date with Marvin when I might've scheduled tonight with Andrea instead! Now my best friend was out on her own date that I didn't want to interrupt. Downing the rest of my glass of champagne, I packed up my novel and pocketed my phone, rising and reaching for my jacket.

Just then, the atmosphere in the room shifted. A colossal, electrifying presence filled the space, shrinking the restaurant to the size of a pea and sucking up all the air, including what was in my lungs. A dark, Herculean figure stood to my left, making me freeze mid-movement. Without looking at his face, I sensed the man's rugged attractiveness in his broad shoulders and iron-clad chest and arms. He must've towered eight inches above my five foot seven.

"Is this seat taken?" His voice was throaty and warm, wrapping itself around me like a velvet glove and squeezing out my remaining breath.

Swallowing, I raised my eyes to his. Deep-set and searingly intense, they were emerald green and ringed with silvery flecks that sparkled like diamonds. Lost in his gaze, I shook my head slightly.

He pulled out my chair, and I sank down, mesmerized by his face. Taken alone, no one of his features screamed handsome. But taken all together, he was devastating. The suit he wore stretched to accommodate his ripped chest, arms, and thighs, fitting him like a second skin. He oozed power, wealth, and sex in a rough, intimidating package. A slight smile curved his lips as he folded himself into the seat opposite me and removed his jacket, hanging it on a nearby hook.

The waitress returned with a second champagne flute. "I see your date made it! Would you like to see some menus?"

A laugh gurgled from my throat at the absurdity. Drinks, dessert, now dinner. A no-show date, and then a magnetic stranger. The abyss of humiliation to the height of exhilaration. Everything was upside down. But there was no way I could leave, now that this force had stepped into my sphere. I remained glued to the spot.

The waitress rattled off a few specials, but I took in nothing over the buzzing in my ears.

The stranger seemed to detect my bemusement. "We'll take all four specials. And a bottle of the Bricco delle Viole Barolo."

My heart rate slowed at last as the buzzing died down and I registered my situation. "I can't stay," I blurted.

His low eyebrows lifted slightly. "Why not?"

"My date…" I faltered.

Giving a ghost of a smile, he leaned in on his corded forearms, which strained against his button-down shirt. "Your date isn't here. I am."

"It's just that he might not like it." I fiddled with my napkin.

He sipped his water. "What he likes is immaterial. He missed his chance. He's clearly an idiot of the first order."

His self-assurance matched his larger-than-life

aura. Ticked off as I was at Marvin's neglect, I didn't bother defending him.

"How did you know I like fish?" I found myself focusing on the one detail I'd gleaned from the specials.

He smirked. "I gambled."

My gaze dropped to the sexy wisps of dark hair at the opening of his shirt. "It's my favorite."

His eyes flashed. "Good." He sat back in his chair, surveying me like a hawk at midday. I flushed under his predatory gaze, secretly enjoying it. "What do you do?"

My brow arched at his directness. "I'm an interior designer."

"Do you love it?"

I cocked my head. "It's what I've known I'd do ever since I got to college."

"You didn't answer my question."

I sighed, deciding to be honest. "If I could, I'd make art all day instead of designing and decorating other people's spaces. The pressure and politics of the business sometimes get to me. But art doesn't pay. Nor does teaching it."

Our waitress arrived, pouring our wine. We clinked glasses.

"Happy birthday." His green eyes sparkled.

The intensity of his gaze heated me like a fire pit. "Thank you."

He sipped his wine. "What kind of art do you make?"

A flutter arose in my stomach from thinking about my passion. "Oil paintings and sculptures."

"Realistic or abstract?"

"Both. But mostly realistic." His flattering focus made me forget we were talking all about me. "What do you do?"

His gravelly voice was impossibly seductive. "Foreign exchange trading."

"Oh! Isn't that pretty risky?"

His lips twitched. "That's one reason I do it. It also makes billions."

I let my mouth slack. "Wow. You must be really good at it."

He hitched a shoulder. "I've got strategies. And a team of people working for me so we cover all the markets."

"So what's your main life ambition?" I figured I'd match his boldness. The energy that sizzled and crackled around him had ignited something in me. Small talk simply wouldn't do.

His brows drew down. "Three goals. Build a strong road cycling team that races internationally, sharpen my chess skills, and sail around the world."

"If you've got billions, what's holding you back?" I asked before I could stop myself.

He glowered at the votive candle on the table. "Family problems."

I cleared my throat. "Oh, um, are you married?"

He looked up at me intently, narrowing his eyes. "No. I have siblings."

When he didn't elaborate, I took a gulp of wine. The waitress brought out dishes of cioppino and crab toasts with lemon aioli. The seafood and citrus smells made me suddenly ravenous.

"*Mangia, mangia*, as they say," he urged, mirth lacing his voice.

We ate in silence until we'd finished everything. The waitress cleared our dishes, replacing them with fried calamari and squash blossoms and whole grilled branzino.

My mouth watered at the spread. "Do you come here often?"

His low rumble of laughter relaxed all my muscles. "Isn't that my line? I've been here enough times to know whatever they serve will be exceptional."

He was right. The branzino burst with flavor and the crispy squid and zucchini were fresh and tasty.

"This is the kind of place that makes me wish I were a food critic," I said between bites.

"It's never too late." He helped me to some more fish.

I grimaced. "I can already see how that would end. I'd soon be changing my wardrobe for extra-large clothes."

A lopsided grin tugged at the corner of his mouth. "I believe critics sample the food rather than finishing it."

I laughed. "And that's why I'm not joining their fraternity. I lack the discipline."

Chapter Two

Liam

Her laugh revealed straight, gleaming white teeth. It lit up her whole face like an explosion of fireworks. Though her voluptuous body initially drew me in, what held me captive up close was the gentle curve of her chin. Droopy eyelids gave her brown eyes an aristocratic air that her arched nose enhanced. Apple cheekbones and a broad forehead made her face irresistible. By now, I'd memorized the unique shape of her expressive lips. She'd pulled her thick dark-blonde hair back into a graceful twist at the nape of her neck.

I was no poet—and certainly no artist—but watching her, I suddenly understood why people write poems and paint. To capture her kind of pure beauty.

I'd only dropped into the restaurant because the owner was an old acquaintance—read, mob connection—and I liked to stay in the loop. Now, especially with my younger brother Rory snapping at my heels, I had to watch my back and keep my ear to the ground. Giuseppe, the owner, assured me that, so far as he'd heard, no one had come sniffing into my past in the last few months. He gave me a rundown of recently locked-up mafiosi and, equally important, those who'd been released.

I couldn't believe my luck when the woman I'd

spotted an hour ago—and hardly taken my eyes off of since—looked as if she'd given up on her no-show jackass date. I'd have approached her sooner if Giuseppe hadn't been talking my ear off about skyrocketing housing prices in his native Jersey City. I owed it to him to listen, after all the intel he'd given me so freely.

"Where are you from?" I asked her once our plates had been replaced with dessert menus.

"Princeton. You?"

"The opposite of Princeton." I crooked a smile. "South Bronx."

"Hey, you're a billionaire. I'm a lowly interior designer. Which one of us local kids made good?" She spoke without a trace of resentment, only good humor.

I tipped back the last of my wine. "Did you go to Princeton for school?"

"Brown. I studied visual art. What about you?"

"I got an online associate degree in mechanical engineering while serving in the Marines." I scanned the dessert menu.

Her eyes flared. "The Marines! What was your MOS?"

"Intelligence specialist." I reveled in her admiring gaze.

"How long did you serve?" Her cheeks flushing, she sipped her water.

I sat back in my chair, thoroughly enjoying the turn the conversation had taken. "Eight years."

As she leaned in, I saw literal stars in her eyes. "What rank were you?"

"Captain."

Our waitress drifted over, asking what we'd like

for dessert. I looked across at the gorgeous woman whose name I still didn't know. "See anything you like? Something worthy of the birthday girl?"

She smiled shyly. "Well, the chocolate pudding sounds good…"

I was pleased she wanted to draw out our conversation. "We'll take one of those and two glasses of the moscato rosa."

When our waitress left, she said, "You really know your Italian wines. At least, I assume that's what you ordered."

My eyes dipped to her lips. "So, which birthday is this?"

She pretended to take offense. "Don't you know the two things you're never supposed to ask a woman?"

"What kind of vibrator she uses and who she really fantasizes about?"

She laughed. "Okay, four things." She tipped her head to the side. "You seem to have a lot of experience."

"Is that accusation or doubt I detect in your tone?" I ran my tongue along the inside of my cheek.

She caught my gesture, her eyes twinkling. "Accusation. Definitely accusation."

"In that case, I plead guilty." Our waitress placed the wine glasses and dessert before us, and I raised my glass. "Happy twenty-fifth, *mademoiselle*."

Her nostrils flared with amusement. "*Merci, monsieur*. Do you say that to all the ladies with birthdays?"

I raked my gaze over her plump tits and delicate collarbone. "Only to those who can pull off twenty-five."

In a coquettish tone, she dodged the bullet. "As a matter of fact, my dad's French." She took a bite of chocolate budino, closing her eyes and humming over its taste.

Her purr, together with her lips closing around the dessert, made my dick twitch.

"Where in France is he from?"

"Lyon."

I took a sip of wine. "Beautiful town, with phenomenal cuisine."

Surprise tinged her features. "You've been?"

I nodded. "I have a friend who lives in Nice."

She pouted adorably. "Of course you do. And I'm betting you have a driver waiting around the corner."

It was my turn to take mock offense. "Do I look as if I'd let some asshole drive me everywhere like a castrated pretty boy?"

She put down her fork, drinking me in. "No. Come to think of it. You look like the type to drive a Maserati."

"Good guess."

"Seriously?"

"I'd be happy to give you a lift home in it."

"Can I drive?" She batted her eyelashes.

"Nice try." I took a bite of pudding, holding her gaze. "Maybe on our tenth date."

She tilted her head. "Was this our first?"

I ran my thumb over my lower lip. "This was the prequel to our first."

Her lips widened in a grin. "If *this* is the prequel, I'll buy the whole series."

My jaw tensed. I figured now was as good a time as any to set things straight. "So no more dates with jerks who stand you up?" I felt protective of her already. Okay, maybe a little possessive too.

As if on cue, her phone buzzed with a text. I caught the name "Marvin" on the screen. As she glanced at it, I clenched my fist under the table, drinking some water to cool me down.

She tucked her phone away, drawing her lips into a straight line.

"How long have you been dating the guy?" Not that it was any of my business.

Without meeting my gaze, she fiddled with the gold band on her right ring finger. "We've only been on two dates. I've known him for a couple of weeks. We met on a project. He's the architect."

Fine. Staking my claim could wait till next time. "You know I want to see you again, right?"

Her eyes flickered with what looked like excitement. "But we haven't even finished tonight."

I threw back my head and laughed. "I need to sketch out book one of the series."

****

It was a biting April evening saturated with the scent of coming rain. Walking her to my car, I pressed a hand into her lower back, and she leaned into me. Once more, my dick sprang to attention. *Down, boy. It hasn't been* that *long.*

"So are we going to talk about the elephant in the room?" she murmured against my arm.

"Which elephant would that be?" I knew exactly what she meant.

She placed a hand above my belt. "The fact that we still don't know each other's names."

I chuckled. "There must be a reason why we

haven't asked yet. Maybe we both like an element of mystery and suspense." I'd paid cash at the restaurant, so she hadn't gotten to sneak a peek at a credit card receipt or signature.

To my surprise, she owned, "As a matter of fact, I do like danger—very much."

I stopped dead. Was she hinting at what I thought? I turned to her, searching her eyes, which glowed soft beneath the streetlamps, a whiff of submission emanating from her. Never one to hesitate in high-stakes gambling, I decided to do a test. Capturing her wrist, I pulled her arm to the small of her back while cupping her throat. Her breath hitched, and her pupils dilated until nothing remained of her irises. Her chest heaved and her lips parted, letting out little puffs of air. My hand shifted to her nape, immobilizing her as I leaned into her ear, breathing heavily. The goosebumps that sprouted on her neck and her suppleness in my arms told me everything I needed to know.

I spoke low in her ear. "How much danger?"

Her throat bobbed, a tremor moving through her body. "I haven't had a chance to find out."

Correct answer. "Would you like to find out tonight?"

She nodded.

Game on.

Chapter Three

Ingrid

I'd signaled to him what I liked, but that didn't mean I wasn't going to fight. After all, that was part of what I fantasized about—though I'd never been able to act on it. When we crossed the threshold of my apartment and he pinned my wrists behind my back, preventing me from flicking on the light, I stomped on his foot with my pointed heel and wrestled against his hand, biting down on his bicep. I was genuinely pissed that he'd taken away my control with such assurance.

"Careful," he purred without missing a beat as he pulled me snugly into him. "Two can play at that game." His indulgent tone told me he was delighted with my feistiness. His unrattled demeanor and the way he harnessed my own energy against me, flooded my sheath and drummed up steady pulsations in my clit.

"I lift weights," I declared into the darkness.

"So do I." I felt his smile against my temple.

"Watch out—I'll knee you in the balls."

He laughed. "I look forward to seeing you try." He cupped my throat, freeing my arms. But when I grabbed his hand to pull it off me, he held it firm as granite while pulling a silk tie from his pocket. While I kicked backward at his shins and clawed at his hips, he secured my wrists in front in a one-handed tie, pulling me into him. I admired his deftness, suspecting this wasn't his first rodeo. "First, you should know that I'd never hurt a woman. What I do, I do to arouse either or both of us. Second, you should tell me your safe word, for when you feel things are going too far."

His authoritative tone subdued me more than his calm actions.

"I've never done this before," I admitted.

"But you've thought about it."

"Yes. Lots." I reflected. "What about 'jackrabbit'?"

He nodded into my cheek. "Now, we have a problem."

"What's that?"

"I've tied you up. But you're going to strip for me." He scooped me up and carried me down the two steps into my living room, seeming perfectly comfortable in the dark, in my home. Somehow I found that unbearably hot. As if he'd read my mind, he said, "This is nothing compared to some of the things my unit did in pitch-blackness out in the field."

Wow. This man was something else. In the heat of our skirmish, I'd momentarily forgotten how impressive he was.

He stood me dead center in the room, circling me once like a lion homing in on its prey. Then, turning on a lamp, he took a seat on the sofa eight feet away, crossing an ankle over his knee. I noted the sizeable bulge tenting his pants. "Take off your clothes."

"But…" I waved my wrists.

A wicked grin slid up his face. "Do what you can."

"Or what?" I angled my chin defiantly.

His gaze sliced to the broom in the corner of the kitchen, and I followed his line of sight.

"You wouldn't."

He chuckled darkly, leaning back with his arms resting on the sofa. "I would. In fact, I hope you fail—or disobey my instructions."

I found quickly that this was a lesson in humility and humiliation. My heels I could toe off easily enough. And I was able, with great effort, to cinch down my thigh-high stockings.

He tsked. "When you do that, turn around."

"Why?"

"Don't ask questions." Then he added, "The rear view is stunning."

I obeyed, finishing removing my nylons, to the sound of his contented grunts behind me. These noises and being subjected this way aroused me to the point where, if I could touch my clit, I'd explode. I rubbed my wrists against my pleasure nub.

"Unh-unh," he chided. "Not unless you want to be punished. Turn around."

When I'd done so, I tried to figure out how to deal with my dress, which was a bright pink figure-hugging faux-wraparound that hung just above the knees. Normally, I would pull it above my head. Not only could I not grasp the hem with my hands tied, but I had no way of getting out of the sleeves. I shot a helpless look at my tormentor.

He arched a brow. "You've missed an item you can remove."

A blush seeped into my cheeks. My panties, of course. It took awhile, but I managed to ease them down enough to step out of them.

"Bend over. Touch your toes," he commanded.

I doubled over, holding the position while he

slowly rose from the sofa. He prowled around me so closely that I felt the scorching heat of his muscle-bound body. At some point in the proceedings, he'd taken off his jacket and rolled his sleeves up to reveal ungodly-strong forearms. He was lethally powerful. Standing behind me, he slunk up the clingy fabric of my dress, inch by torturous inch, uncovering my ass.

"This ass." He cupped my cheeks, giving them a firm squeeze. "All night I've been waiting to do this." His thumb traveled to my butthole, circling it suggestively. My breathing became jagged. "And this." Clamping an arm around my hip to anchor me, he gave me a vicious spank. I yelped, leaking more arousal from my channel. He followed this up with three more whacks, rubbing his hand around my ass cheek and soothing away the sting. I'd never felt such exquisite pain. I instantly craved more. "My handprints look good on your skin."

"What was that for?" I gasped.

"For fighting me when we came in the door." Then he tacked on, almost as an afterthought, "And for looking so sexy in the restaurant, when I couldn't do anything about it."

I longed for him to do the same on the other side of my butt to even things up. "Will you, um, do the other one?"

He chuffed a laugh. "Not yet. First, it's time to get you completely naked. Stand up."

With astonishing rapidity, he unfastened the knot, freeing my hands. Then he pulled off my dress and shucked my bra. He wheeled me around so I stood, like his double bass, with my back against his chest. He cradled my throat while skating his palm along my breastplate, down my belly toward my heat. I wriggled delightedly, whimpering my pleasure. He scooped each breast, swirling its nipple with a feathery touch and pinching it. I moaned, lolling my head back into his strong shoulder and closing my eyes to savor his touch. His fingers traced delicate patterns above my mound, which I'd shaved bare. Even the lightest hints of movement there had me thrusting involuntarily against his hand.

"Do you have any idea how insanely beautiful you are?" His voice was a husky baritone. "Curvaceous body, lovely face, fascinating mind, fiery spirit, untapped desire. You're going to be fun to tame."

His words and touch made me shiver with anticipation. "Please!" I cried.

"Please tame you? With pleasure."

I didn't expect what came next. He nudged my legs a few feet apart with his knee and then slapped my pussy with several sharp smacks. I convulsed with the contact of the last one, wailing uncontrollably as I pitched over the edge of an intense orgasm. I nearly crumpled like a push puppet, but he anchored me, slinging me in his arms and stalking toward my bedroom.

How in the world did he know his way around so well?

Once again, as if he could read my mind, he said, "Habit from training. When you enter a place, make sure you note all the entrances and exits that people who want to kill you may come through."

He lowered me to the bed, flipping me on my belly.

"Kneel, with your arms flat above your head."

By now I'd seen that following his commands led to pleasure, so I obeyed without hesitation.

I waited in this position as he cast away his clothes. Sneaking a peek over my shoulder, I gasped at the thick erection that bobbed against his pelvis. It was at once an extension of him and its own being, splendid in its potency and promise.

He read the need in my expression. "If you're a good girl, you may have some. And I may even let you come."

That was a new one for me. "Let me come? You don't get to control my orgasms."

He pounced on me like a tiger, his body encompassing me from behind and his hand grasping the back of my neck, pressing me into the bed. I was suddenly on fire again as he whispered in the shell of my ear, "Let's get this straight, little one. You belong to me. Your mind, your body, your pussy. That means your orgasms belong to me too. I am your sole source of pleasure. You beg for it, and—if you've been good, and if I feel in the mood—I *might* give it. Understand?"

As I hesitated, he unpinned my hair and wound it around his fist, pulling my head back. Halfway to coming right then and there, I nodded. "Yes, I understand."

Chapter Four

Liam

I'd rendered her pliant to my will several times. She was learning quickly. I would have to relish these early moments of torture and punishment before she became so obedient that they grew more infrequent. I could always come up with arbitrary reasons to punish her.

Listen to me. I was already seeing this as a long-term relationship. And my dick hadn't even dipped into her yet. But I knew she'd be tight, silky, and warm.

I might not feel like saying goodbye to this one. She felt like mine—all mine. And I wanted to use the fuck out of her.

It took all the restraint I could muster to prime her pussy for what I was about to do. Licking my way from her anus to her clit, I sampled her juices. Her pussy was like a ripe, dripping peach.

She moaned, tilting her hips into my face. "Oh, God, please!"

"You want my cock, baby?"

"Yes!"

I used the element of surprise to excite her again. Leaning back to get good leverage, I thwacked her left butt cheek, the one I'd neglected earlier. She yowled and then groaned with pleasure. Increasing the pressure,

I repeated this with three more spanks in quick succession. Then I rubbed gently, smoothing out the pain and turning it from tingling to warmth. Her formerly pale ass now had pretty patterns of my handprints tattooing the smooth skin. Shame these would only last half an hour or so. I'd have to be sure to renew them in our next round.

Slicking my fingers over her divide, I caught up her nectar and rubbed it into her asshole. She clenched up immediately.

"Don't worry, baby. I won't fuck your ass yet. I just want you to feel how nice it can be." I inserted my fingertip slowly into her anus, and then removed it. "Relax. Breathe in."

Her ribcage expanded.

"Now exhale."

As her lungs collapsed, I pressed my finger in several inches. Holding it there, I massaged her clit.

"Ahhh!" she cried. "I'm going to come."

"You see how effective it is." I removed my fingers. "But you don't come yet, little one. Not till I say you may."

"Oh, *please*!!" she mewled.

The helpless, pleading sound made me lose control. My dick had waited long enough. Using my teeth, I tore open a condom package and sheathed myself in record time. I'd decided I was going to give her a rough version of myself and see if she could take it. After all, she had her safe word.

Straddling her hips, I eased into her and withdrew, gradually gaining ground with each push. My thrusts picked up speed as I found my rhythm.

"Oh, baby, your pussy is so snug and perfect."

God, this felt good. I was on top of the world. I could do anything, control everything, make miracles happen. All I needed was to ram my cock into this warm place that was made for me and me only. As my cock swelled with more blood, I grew so hot I could've floated up into the ether. Then I began to melt as the swift pounding possessed me like a demon.

"Fuck, baby, I'm coming. I want you to come with me." Snaking my arm around her pelvis, I swirled my fingers over her clit.

"Oh, *God!*" She screamed, contracting into me while my balls tightened. I bellowed, feeling the release that was like nothing else. I continued to pump into her as her walls squeezed out more come, the aftershocks of my climax hitting me.

I pulled out, disposing of the condom, and returned to the bed, spooning her. Our breaths came raggedly, and our bodies were slick as eels.

"What's your name?" she asked when our heart rates had slowed.

I brushed hair from her face. "Why ask now?"

"I realized I wanted to call out your name when I came. But all I could say was 'God.'"

"That'll do just fine."

She elbowed me in the chest. "Cocky bastard."

"That works too."

She twisted, laughing up at me. That's when I realized I hadn't yet kissed those shapely lips. I leaned in, telling her with my eyes what I intended. Cupping her cheek, I nudged her lips open with my tongue. She hummed, pressing her lips to mine, her tongue flitting into my mouth before waiting for mine to sweep hers. I invaded it wolfishly, pillaging her like claimed territory. My grunts dissolved into groans as I tasted the wine we'd drunk earlier and the chocolate she'd eaten, plus an earthy taste that was all her. It was a long, layered kiss, the perfect mix of sweet, savory, and spicy.

When our mouths separated, she giggled. "Yet another thing we did upside down tonight. We had crazy-wild sex and then kissed. And I still don't know your name."

"Liam, baby. Liam Stauner."

"Oh, that's lovely." She threaded her fingers through my hair—such an intimate gesture, and so tender. "Liam."

My fingers skittered down her belly to her pussy. She rocked into me and groaned, confirming that she was ready for another round. "Tell me yours."

"Ingrid. Ingrid Pellerin."

"Where's your mom from, Ingrid?"

"Louisville, Kentucky."

"So you're half French, half American."

"Yeah. And they met in the middle, at Columbia. Mom took an English class that Dad was TA'ing." She traced my eyebrows with fascination. "They're so bushy. I love them."

I drew my brows down menacingly.

She exploded in laughter. "The big bad wolf!"

"Believe it, little one. I'm coming for you now."

She squealed, trying to escape. But I held her fast, turning her over onto my lap and delivering a few swift smacks to her rear. This time, instead of soothing the sting, I bit each of her cheeks, as a wolf would do.

****

We finally dropped off to sleep in the small hours.

When I awoke at 9, Ingrid was in the shower. I joined her there, nailing her against the wall and riding her with her legs wrapped around my hips. Diving into her as if she were the Mariana Trench, I brought us both to a peak in a few minutes.

We'd just rinsed the soap off of each other when, hearing my phone ring, I stepped out.

It was a member of the flight crew, confirming my noon departure. Saturday was a particularly busy day for private jets at the smaller New York-area airports. Donning my suit, I decided to shave on the plane. Now, where were my keys?

Remembering I'd stripped in a hurry last night, I looked under the bed. As I fumbled around under the nightstand, my wrist knocked it off kilter, shaking out a book from the upper shelf.

It fell open to a page with two black crow feathers taped in it. But the feathers weren't what caught my attention. It was the words, handwritten in all caps in black ink:

"August 30, 2018. I SAW A MURDER TODAY. THE KILLER HAD AN UNFORGETTABLE PROFILE. I HID IN THE OAK TREE SO HE DIDN'T FIND ME. BUT HE SAW ME FROM THE BACK. HE THREATENED MY LIFE IF I TALKED. NOW I'M AFRAID TO MENTION IT TO ANYONE. BUT I DON'T KNOW IF I'M DOING THE RIGHT THING BY NOT TELLING THE POLICE. CROWS WERE MOLTING EVERYWHERE. THESE ARE TWO FEATHERS TO REMEMBER THIS SCARIEST OF DAYS."

Fuck. August 30, 2018. Princeton. The blonde witness. My last job. And the one I always regretted

taking. Not so much because there'd been a witness—
though that had been alarming in its own right. But
because it was so close to home. If police were going to
trace the killing back to its source, they could more
easily find me nearby in New York. Usually, I made a
point of parachuting into jobs and leaving after I'd
gotten paid. But this multimillionaire douchebag had it
coming. He abused his wife and got her addicted to
painkillers. Vinny Casale wanted him dead for other
reasons, but these were what justified the murder for
my conscience.

Being a naturally untrusting bastard, I kept my
cards close, my enemies closer, and my secrets damn
near up my butt like a drug smuggler. Some people
called my mistrust of the human race in general
"paranoia." But my upbringing had a lot to do with it.
Now, as I heard the shower turn off, I swiftly debated
what I should do.

One, I didn't know if Ingrid had told anyone about
the killing. So not only was she a loose end, but she'd
potentially leaked my involvement to others.

Two, my brother Rory, self-appointed judge, jury,
and executioner, was on the warpath looking for just
this kind of evidence to lock me away.

Three, in my experience, a threat could only hold
for so long before it needed to be refreshed. Maybe,
after four years, it was time to renew my intimidation of
Ingrid.

Four, did I mention I was a paranoid bastard? This
didn't sit well at all. Not at all.

Five, I was in a hurry and didn't have time to
interrogate Ingrid now.

Six, unlike most people, I didn't care if I broke the

law to get what I wanted.

Based on all these givens, I made a quick decision. I strode into the bathroom.

Chapter Five

Ingrid

Standing in front of the mirror, I was rummaging through my nightbag for tweezers, when a black figure surging from behind frightened the bejeezus out of me. I jumped a foot high and screamed. The look on Liam's face was—I've never seen such a look in real life before. It was the way I imagined Jack the Ripper or any other serial killer looking. In all honesty, I barely recognized him as the same man who'd just made me orgasm ten times in as many hours. His eyes were a frigid chasm-green, reminding me of the waters of the Great Lakes in the dead of winter. The set of his mouth was more grim and determined than that of an executioner. His nostrils flared as if adrenaline coursed in the very cilia of his nose. The veins in his hands popped out like Frankenstein's.

I had a towel around my chest. With a flick of his thumb and forefinger, he unhooked the towel, letting it drop to my feet and exposing my naked body. He never broke his lethal gaze.

Then he swirled me in a tight hold, trapping me like a caged bird, one arm across my collarbone, the other around my pelvis.

This would've been the sexiest moment of my life—if it hadn't been the most frightening.

"So, my little witness. I find you at last."

I blenched. That voice—*that voice!* Saying "my little witness" in that sinister tone. The day flooded back to me, and chills shot down my arms, deafening drums pounding my ears. The crows, the loud gunshot, the tree. All indelibly burned in my memory. And still, even in this terrifying moment, my pussy began to throb, as though it sensed action. God, I was screwed up.

An unhinged smile grazed his lips. "You remember me now, don't you?"

My eyes went wide, and my throat worked on a swallow.

His fingers moved to my throat, squeezing my airway. "You haven't known all along and merely been playing me, have you?"

To the best of my ability, I shook my head.

He brushed his thumb back and forth along the column of my throat. "You may or may not be telling the truth. But I'm sure you remember that promise I made to you then."

I nodded, my traitorous sheath sopping wet and my nipples pebbling. Apparently, my erogenous zones hadn't gotten the memo that I was about to die.

He relaxed his hold, so he could skate his fingers over my parts, as though taking inventory. He started with my cheekbones, tracing them with his fingertips as if shaping them from clay. Then he moved to my jaw, tilting it from side to side to examine it in the mirror from different angles. Next, he held each breast as one holds a brandy snifter in a cigar lounge, decadently. He traced my abs with just as much leisure, causing me to pulsate between my thighs in anticipation of what might come next. He drew a maddening horseshoe pattern above my groin and down my inner thighs, skirting my sex altogether. It was blissful torment, but my survival instinct kicked in and I just barely suppressed a moan.

As if to rub in how utterly he held me in his thrall, he tapped my clit once. I bucked like a startled deer, crying out from the sweet agony of it. I would almost die right now, just to have his fingers inside me, making me come. Having held my breath for nearly a minute, I may even have been on the verge of climax.

"You'll do nicely, my little witness," he declared. "I'll take you for my own. It was bound to happen at some point. I'll just hasten the process."

My jaw hung open and my stomach did a hectic series of flips. "Wh-what are you talking about?"

"I'm taking you where no one will find you. Where you'll be completely under my control twenty-four seven. Absolutely in my power." His sadistic smile infiltrated my pores and shot through my bloodstream like quicksilver. "The way we both like it."

"N-no. I need to stay here. I c-can't go on a vacation. I have no t-time." My teeth chattered, and a cold vise gripped my midsection.

"Vacation?" A furrow creased his brow. "No, my little caged bird. You'll be at my beck and call, trying to convince me to trust you." His eyes narrowed, and a malevolent grin tilted his lips. "But then, you like a little pain."

I shook my head again. "I have three projects—"

"I'll bring your laptop and phone. I may even let you use them occasionally—under my supervision, of course." He slammed his palm against my ass and I spasmed, my leaking pussy hungrier than ever. "Now.

We're going to find your passport and pack you all the essentials you'll need for an indefinite stay—birth control pills especially. I plan on taking you bare from now on."

He yanked me back into him again, sinking his fingers in my heat and groaning. He licked my arousal off of each, one by one. I was so mesmerized by the sight, so turned on, that for a moment I couldn't remember why I should be alarmed. Then I caught the diabolical cast of his features in the mirror—transforming him suddenly into Mr. Hyde—and I tried to escape.

But I was like a doll in his powerful arms, a plaything, kicking, thrashing, punching every which way, trying to bite whatever flesh I could get between my teeth. Feeling the rumble of laughter in his belly, I realized my struggle was futile. As I tried to scream, he clamped his large hand over my mouth.

Before I knew it, he'd whipped out one of my own scarves and secured my wrists with it, tying another scarf around my ankles. Then, like a prisoner on a chain gang, I found myself tethered by a third scarf to the bottom of the radiator in my bedroom.

He seemed to enjoy the whole situation. He dangled a scarf before me as a toreador baits a bull. "Am I going to need to gag you, my little witness? Or will you keep absolutely still while I pack your things?"

I shook my head, an angry tear escaping my eye. "I'll be quiet. But first, I want to ask you—"

"Shh." He held up two fingers to my lips as though lighting a cigarette for me. "I'll let you ask all the questions you like. Once we've gotten out of here. For now, time is of the essence."

Heartened by his softer tone, and seeing glimpses of the lover I'd known for the last twelve hours, I nodded.

"Take a seat, little captive. You'll be more comfortable."

Though my pride dictated that I stand, if anything, just to disobey him, I really was so shaken that sinking into the chair he provided felt like a momentary reprieve from the ugliness.

He snapped his fingers. "Passport?"

I shook my head. "You said not to speak."

He roared with laughter. "That's grounds for punishment later, my little rebel. You'll speak when I direct a question your way."

"It's in the drawer over there."

"Suitcase?"

"In the closet."

For the next fifteen minutes, he darted around, gathering seven or eight of my most summery dresses from the closet and a few pairs of sandals and heels. He riffled through my t-shirt and shorts drawer, choosing a few according to some selection process known only to him. Scavenging through my underwear drawer, he picked out some G-strings, thongs, and matching lace bras, holding them up to appraise each one.

"Mmm, I look forward to ripping these off you."

I managed to scoff. "Not going to happen."

His raised index finger signaled a warning. "Not a peep from you, little crow feather." Then he smiled his smug smile. "Hate sex is the best, after all."

Disappearing into the bathroom with one of my smaller bags, he emerged a few minutes later with literally everything but the bathroom sink.

He snapped his fingers near my ears. I must've fallen into a daze. "Laptop and phone?"

"On the bar counter in the kitchen." A despairing tear rolled down my cheek, splashing my breast. This was really happening. And there was nothing I could do about it. Unless…

When Liam came back into the bedroom, zipping up the suitcase, I made one last-ditch effort to reason with him.

"You have my word I won't tell a soul about what happened—that I *haven't* told a soul about what happened." I tried to sound as dispassionate as possible, though it was tough under duress.

Without meeting my eye, he untied one of the scarves. "I can't trust you."

"But what do you hope to gain by taking me away?"

"A certain amount of time halfway across the world, in the middle of the ocean, ought to instill the fear of God—meaning me, of course—in you." His lips twitched.

I took another tack. "You can't do this. It's kidnapping."

An evil grin curled the corners of his mouth. "I can do whatever I want. Now let's get you dressed."

Once my hands were free, I attempted to slap his face. But he caught my hand, pressing my fingers to his lips while holding my gaze. He took the tip of each finger in his mouth, one by one, nipping on it before releasing it.

Curse my treacherous sex for pulsing as I watched him.

"Careful, little one. That will get a big punishment

when I'm next doling them out." Smirking, he slapped my ass. "Now, get dressed."

"You have no right—"

He grabbed my chin in his large palm. The gesture was at once brutal and intimate, controlling and arousing. "Sweetheart, if I give myself the right, I have it."

"You're vile," I spat.

Holding my body against his, he ran his fingers from my neck to my hardened nipples, which he circled and strummed before moving to my drenched pussy. I shuddered with the delicious torture of his deft but light touch. "Your body, at least, likes my vileness."

A deep blush scorched my cheeks. My body was indeed a foul traitor.

In a wobbly voice, I asked, "Where are we going?"

"Paradise."

Chapter Six

Liam

She'd been good—surprisingly good—from the time I bundled her into the car to the moment of take-off. I'd told her if she behaved, I wouldn't resort to using duct tape. Of course, I probably wouldn't have gone that far, but the art of torture lay in implanting ideas in the subject's brain and playing on them. And I derived a sadistic pleasure in watching her pupils turn to pinpricks of fear—probably since most people associated duct tape with serial killers. Just thinking back on that image put me at half-mast. I was a sick fuck.

I adjusted my pants, glancing around the plane.

Traveling with us were my best friend Guy Travis, who handily doubled as my lawyer-of-leisure, three servants, my financial advisor Stephen and his wife Barbara, one of my traders—a nonchalant young hacker named Bryn—and his nutty platinum-haired girlfriend Connie, who sported a rocker chic vibe.

I'd told Guy the whole story of Ingrid. Even if he weren't my best friend, as my lawyer, he was sworn to secrecy. To Stephen, Bryn, and the three servants I'd introduced Ingrid as my new girlfriend. Not that they needed explanations. They would do whatever I told them, since I paid them all well.

Guy was the most condescending, brilliant, refined prick Mother Nature had ever had incestuous thoughts of while creating. For this reason, she'd bestowed the boyish good looks and charm to preserve him in a perpetual Dorian-Gray time capsule, even though, like me, he was thirty-two. No woman was good enough for Guy; thus, he toyed with them and cast them aside on an almost bi-weekly basis. He'd fucked his way through most of Manhattan's socialites and a good chunk of the most beautiful, successful single working women the City had to offer. Recently he'd begun finding his pleasures further afield—in Toronto, Washington, D.C., Miami, and even as far west as Chicago. Celebrities flocked to him like moths to a flame, and he was a sought-after guest at any select gathering across the Continental U.S.—not that he'd venture further west than Chicago. The party usually came to Guy.

Guy was the type to have a driver and to keep him waiting for long periods of time. Independently wealthy from a trust, he didn't need money, so he only took on law cases he found intriguing enough to hold his interest. He had somewhat long, wavy chestnut locks, golden-brown eyes, and angular features that were viewed as the pinnacle of elegance. He stood an inch shorter than I, with leaner muscles and graceful fingers. His long lashes were the kicker, though. Woman after woman protested enviously over those lashes.

"About time for lunch, isn't it?" Guy yawned, stretching his long limbs and unfolding himself from his seat.

"May I?" Ingrid asked sweetly.

"May you what?" It was hard to remember to be

pissed at her and mistrust her when she looked so angelic.

"Stretch too? Use the bathroom? Have some lunch?"

Since I could hear her stomach rumbling as we'd prepared for take-off, I felt guilty starving her for so long. It was now almost 1, and we'd gotten up four hours ago. Now I wished I'd marked her in some way—given her a hickey or spread my come all over her—so other men would look at her and know she was mine. I needed to remember to buy a choker necklace in Fiji and make her wear it everywhere. One with a tiny lock and key.

I encircled her wrist with my thumb and forefinger, bolting both our gazes to the gesture. "I've got you at 40,000 feet. You're not going anywhere. Make yourself comfortable. It's another fifteen hours before we land."

Without thinking, I laid a tender kiss on her lips. I could tell by the way her body stiffened that the kiss surprised her as much as it did me. But after a few seconds, she melted into it, allowing her tongue to tangle with mine. She tasted deliciously of fennel from the toothpaste she'd used that morning.

She looked with puzzlement into my eyes. "At any given moment, I can't tell whether you're going to kill me or fuck me."

I chucked her under the chin. "Let's keep it that way. Remember, it's in my power to do both."

She tilted her head. "I thought you didn't hurt women."

"You're not 'women.' You're my woman." The answer was completely irrational, but it wasn't a very rational day for me, all things considered.

Thankfully, she didn't probe further.

I spent the next half-hour looking at stocks and checking up on companies that had done mergers and acquisitions over the last day. Catching Bryn's eye, I beckoned him over to help me figure out a strategy for the upcoming days' trading on the London and New York markets.

I was just getting hungry when I heard giggling interspersed with Guy's low voice. Black rage leached into my veins. Surging from my seat, I stalked back to the dining area, where Guy was performing some of his card tricks with Ingrid on a leather sofa, glasses of champagne and plates of sashimi on the table in front of them. Well, wasn't this cozy. I wanted to murder someone, and that someone was Guy. But I tried to play it cool, knowing I'd just provoke him even more if I lost it.

I whistled tunelessly, pouring some champagne and snagging a piece of sashimi.

"Hullo, old chap." Guy adopted his most irritating mannerism—that of the old British school mate. "Penny for your thoughts?"

I scowled. "Take a wild guess."

He pretended to consider this, looking as if butter wouldn't melt in his mouth. "Since your face looks like thunder, I have to assume one of two things. Either the market has crashed, or someone has stolen your girl."

Seething, I took a step closer, balling my free fist. "And I have to assume, since you mention it, that you don't particularly care about that pretty face of yours."

Guy tutted affably, ignoring my threat. "Sometimes abductions are rescue operations, and sometimes they're the spark that ignites a war. Which is yours, old man?"

Livid, I took a few deep breaths before saying or doing something I'd regret. "Neither," I ground out.

He cocked his head. "A third option doesn't exist in the realm of abductions, old sport. You're either righting the apple cart by stealing back what's yours, or you're upsetting the cart by starting a Trojan war."

Ingrid followed our exchange avidly, a fact that pissed me off even more. Before Guy, I was pretty sure she'd thought I was invincible. Now he was poking more holes in me than the Titanic, and doing it with a confounded smirk on his face.

"Are you speaking as a criminal defense lawyer? Or as a friend?" I gritted, still towering over him as though height alone could win the argument.

He tossed a sashimi in his mouth. "As a potential rival, if you must know."

"What?" I couldn't believe I'd heard right.

He shrugged. "Ingrid, here, has excellent taste in art, speaks three languages, and is a talented sculptor and painter. She also has a devilish sense of humor."

My brows slammed down. "How do you know all that?"

"Conversation, photos of art she's exhibited that we pulled up on my phone. Naturally, she was hampered in showing me her pieces, since she doesn't have access to her own phone."

I couldn't tell whether Guy was trying to make me jealous or make me appreciate Ingrid more—or both. He seemed to be chiding me for strong-arming her. He also seemed to be vaguely concerned about the legal ramifications of what I'd done this morning. I resisted the impulse to scoop Ingrid up, whisk her back to one of the sleeping areas, and fuck her loudly enough that the whole plane would know she was mine. That could wait till later. My mind was flying all over the place. "You do know she's not to be trusted—until proven otherwise."

Guy gave me a cool stare that usually slayed ninety percent of the world's population, but left me unperturbed. "So, can't be trusted enough with a phone, but can be trusted enough to sleep with. How's that working out for you, old chap?" He chomped a clump of wakame.

I straightened. "That is none of your business, Guy."

"Well, as I say, it is. Both as your legal council and as a man interested in Ingrid."

I called his bluff. "Since when do you move in on another man's territory—you, who have a plethora of willing options when it comes to women?"

He spoke in his most condescending voice. "There are one point five million single women in New York City, Liam. This one understandably flew under my radar—until you brought her in my sights."

Something occurred to me. "Are you saying that because I've abd—kidn—taken her away against her will, I can't have her, whereas because you've done nothing illegal, she's available to you?"

"Bingo, old chap."

Barely able to contain my rage, I set my glass on a table. "How do you figure that?" If it'd been anyone but Guy, by now I would've ripped out his balls and used them to choke the life out of him.

"Just the basic premise we started with. You don't trust her. No relationship can be built on a foundation of mistrust and survive for long."

I snarled, "Thanks, Dr. Phil. I haven't noticed you having many relationships that lasted longer than a few weeks in the last ten years or so."

He shrugged. "Not for lack of trying. But this one—Ingrid—just might hold my interest."

That did it. I flew at him, pulling him by the tie until his face turned purple. "Have a death wish today, *old man*?"

Ingrid wedged herself between us, laying her hands on the wrist that held Guy's tie and pleading softly, "Liam, please. He doesn't mean it. He and I were just looking at pictures, and he said you should see my art for yourself."

My subconscious registered that this was by far the more likely scenario—that Guy had wanted to goad me so I'd appreciate Ingrid more. Stealing girls wasn't his style. We had a code of brothers that went way back to our Catholic high school in the Bronx, where we'd protected each other against the bullies. Giving him a final tug, I released him, and he fell back onto the sofa with a choke and a sputter.

Guy was wise not to lean on the legal repercussions with me. He knew I gave zero fucks for the law—never had. It was one of the reasons I'd joined the military, specifically, the most hard-core branch. Because I wanted to be above the law. Police were just paramilitary—wannabe military. On separating from the Marines, I'd kept all kinds of weaponry no civilians were allowed to own and few law enforcement officers were authorized to use. And then there was Ned Raymond, the cop who'd wrongfully put my dad behind bars for eight years, where my dad had been killed before the date of his release. What kind of justice was that?

I took another deep breath, closing my eyes and willing the past to retreat into the recesses of my memory. Too much pain, too much trauma. *Keep it together for the present. Now is here. Now is everything.*

If only I could believe that.

Chapter Seven

Ingrid

An hour later, gazing out the window of the plane with Liam sitting beside me, I was divided. Half of me wanted to send signals to the crew—who, I suspected, were in the dark about my abduction—and raise a stink that would at least cause Liam a headache, even if it failed to achieve anything of consequence. That same half plotted ways I could escape once we touched ground. I envisioned screaming at the top of my lungs so everyone in the vicinity would know I was being held captive against my will. That half of me hated Liam and was furious with him for ripping me from my life in New York—my friends, family, and work. I wanted to rebel against him for thinking he could uproot me and get away with it. I also feared the man who could so easily flout the law, knowing he could follow through with his threats anytime he chose.

The other half of me—the immoral, irresponsible side—said to hell with society's dictums. If Liam wanted to abduct me and claim me as his own, wasn't this a sexual reality to beat all fantasies? He was possessing me as I'd always dreamed of being claimed by a man. And the sex last night had been off the charts. Unfortunately, the danger of thinking this way lay in his long-term intentions. What if I got attached and he never saw me as anything more than a plaything? I'd end up with a broken heart when he grew tired of me.

And I could easily see the danger of falling in love with Liam. He was psychologically, emotionally, and physically one of the strongest men I'd ever met. To have gone from an upbringing in the South Bronx to making billions required intelligence, grit, and determination. Last night, even when I was trying my best to hurt him, he'd refused to touch a hair on my head. And he'd insisted I have a safe word. He handled me as if I were made of papier-mâché rather than flesh. To be a captain in the Marines, he must also be an excellent leader and extremely courageous. And, as the mind-reading moments last night had shown, he was highly attuned to me. He had a sharp and ready sense of humor, and he obviously respected women. He was a ball of fire—brilliant, self-assured, and proud.

But—and this was a big but—he was a murderer. The killing I witnessed may not have been his first or his last.

And he had trust issues that went deep. Whether because he was naturally untrusting or his past had made him so, he couldn't see what the rest of the world saw—that I was honest and his friend was loyal. His unwillingness to let me go suggested he was slow to forgive and vengeful. Would it be possible to convince a man like this of my innocence and loyalty? Even if we did manage to have a romantic relationship, wouldn't he be too jealous to allow me the kind of freedom I needed?

No, Guy was right. There was too much mistrust at the core of whatever Liam and I had for it to work long-term. For that reason, I needed to protect my heart. And to that end, I needed to resist having sex with him.

"Are you warm enough?" Liam's throaty voice broke in on my thoughts. He unfolded one of the alpaca blankets the crew provided.

I must've been shivering. "Thank you."

He bent over me, covering my shoulders and tucking the blanket into the sides of the seat as though he were swaddling me. I hadn't expected such a cherishing and protecting gesture. Tears sprang to my eyes, but now that my arms were under the blanket, I had no way of brushing them off. Oh, God, why was I crying? It must've been the onrush of dozens of emotions that had been riding high all day. Liam leaned over, using the pad of his thumb to catch the drops trickling along my nose. Concern etched his features.

"What is it, baby? Do you want some hot tea? A shot of whisky? You want to lie down? Tell me what you need, and it's yours." He spoke with such conviction, I was sure if I'd asked for the *Mona Lisa*, he would've arranged to have it stolen for me.

Everything but your freedom, a warning voice reminded me.

"Can we talk?" I sniffled.

Producing a clean cotton handkerchief from his jacket pocket, he gently wiped my nose and dabbed my cheeks. The intimacy of the act recalled many of the things we'd done together the night before. Heat bloomed in my cheeks.

"Of course." He pulled down one of the fold-up side seats so he could sit directly in front of me, his knees touching mine and his sparkling viridian eyes warmly intent on me.

"Where are we going?" I'd wondered this since

he'd tied me up and packed my things.

He planted his large, warm hands on my thighs. "Verau. It's an island one hundred miles to the southeast of Fiji that I bought a little over a year ago."

My eyes bulged. "You *bought* it? Why?"

A smile tugged at the corners of his mouth. "Why not? It's a slice of paradise. No developers had touched it. It's the perfect size for training a cycling team—ten miles long and six miles wide. I built my own private fortress there, a place where friends and family can gather according to our own laws. It has private beaches, coral reefs, golden sands, a tropical maritime climate, and proximity to Fiji, where we get supplies and staff. Twenty-three members of my domestic staff come from Fiji and the surrounding islands. My boat brings provisions once a week. We have water purification systems, a large generator, even a sewage treatment plant. I paved a few roads—notably, the twenty-eight-mile ring road around the coast and the runway for private jets. This is the first time I'll have seen the completed mansion, though."

Suddenly, excitement supplanted my fears and worries. "Tell me about the mansion."

His eyes glinted with enthusiasm. "I brought in a Japanese architect, since I wanted the house to harmonize with the natural surroundings. It's all wood and glass, with a cypress roof shaped after a Shinto shrine. The large rectangular main building is flanked by four smaller blocks, or modules, all surrounded by wooden porches accessible by small bridges. The floors all have tatami mats, except for the pinewood in the kitchens and dining rooms and tiles in the bathrooms. But I haven't seen the house since they finished it."

"Has it been decorated?" My heart raced as I thought of the potential for the interior of such a place.

He shook his head. "I had a few basic items shipped in—tempurpedic floor mattresses in the Japanese style for all the bedrooms, fixtures for the kitchens and bathrooms, chairs, tables, and cookware. It's extremely minimalistic at this point."

Wow. What an opportunity. I was practically salivating. "Do you *want* to decorate it?"

"I've decided to proceed slowly only once I've seen it as a whole. But one purpose of this trip was to bring some memorabilia to start the decorating process." He grinned, his eyes dancing as he no doubt read my eagerness. "I can see the prospect of an undecorated house, to an interior designer, is like a blank canvas to a painter."

"You could say that." I licked my lips. "Do you want to keep Asian accents throughout?"

He slowly thumbed my lips, sparking brushfires in my core. "I've always preferred Japanese minimalism, and the views of the surrounding landscape are the real stars of the show."

"What about art?"

"I'm open to collecting it organically over upcoming years. I don't feel the need to rush. And I don't want to clutter the place." He gazed off into the middle distance.

I recognized the look. "But there are a few pieces you already have in mind to showcase?"

"Yes. I brought them on this trip."

"Will this be your main residence?" I had unconsciously gone into professional mode, asking all the questions I'd ask a new client.

He brushed a few strands of hair off my face. "I'll probably always split my time between New York and Verau. But I want it to be my main secondary residence."

"The natural light must be unbelievable," I mused.

"All the simulations suggested as much."

"How many square feet?" I braced myself.

"Fifty thousand."

I still couldn't keep my jaw from dropping. "Holy cow. That's half of Downton Abbey. How many people do you plan to entertain?"

He hitched a shoulder. "Supposing I want to hold a chess tournament at the same time the cycling team is in residence and my friends are visiting, I guess fifty or so."

His phone rang. Frowning when he saw the caller, he stood, moving away to take the call. This must be one of the newer private jets that could use satellite links to connect to Wi-Fi data. I wondered where my impounded phone was, and when—if—I'd be allowed to use it to call into work and talk to Andrea and Mom.

Liam's brows shot up, and his tone grew more intense as he punctuated his words with gestures. He paced in circles, clearly unnerved by something. Then I heard, very distinctly, "Get in there. Do whatever you need to do. See her. Talk to her. You know I'm good for whatever it costs. Oh, and Ralph. If you need backup, let me know."

Soon after, he killed the call, raking his hand through his hair and staring out the window. Then he spun on his heel and strode back to the bar.

Curiosity and concern drove me to rise and follow him.

Chapter Eight

Liam

Ralph had found her at last. After ten years. Since finishing my first tour, I had several private investigators searching for my younger sister Gretchen and her daughter Katrina. But the news wasn't good. Ralph had spotted Gretchen while she was out walking, and he'd spied Katrina separately with a group of teens. Both had entered a cult compound near the small town of Sinclair, Indiana. The cult, United Spirits, occupied a converted former Ford plant. Ralph was researching the group as we spoke. He reported that the compound had decent security and was difficult to breach.

Gretchen and her baby had disappeared from Bay Ridge, Brooklyn, twelve years ago, when my sister was seventeen. She'd just given birth to Katrina, and her Seventh Day Adventist foster family had condemned her choice to have a baby out of wedlock and parent as a single mother. The baby's father had neither wanted the child nor offered to help support it. The last time I'd seen her, she was being bullied at school for her pregnancy, and her foster parents wanted nothing more to do with her. It was a hard time for me to help beyond sending money, since I was on active duty as a scout sniper, without the necessary time to devote to her well-being.

I still felt guilty about not being there for her when she needed me. All these years I'd hoped to make it up by finding Gretchen and bringing her and Katrina to live with me. It made sense that she'd be susceptible to the persuasions of a cult; she'd always had low self-esteem and was virtually alone in the world when she'd disappeared.

"Good news or bad?" Ingrid's soft voice sounded at my elbow.

I blew out a long breath. "Both. You want a drink?"

She nodded. "Please."

I poured her some of the fifteen-year-old Springbank Scotch, topping up my own glass. I took a seat on the sofa, patting the space next to me.

She sat down. "What's the good part?"

I side-eyed her. What harm could it do? She wasn't going anywhere or talking to anyone—not on my watch. And my watch would continue indefinitely. "My PI found my sister Gretchen and her daughter. They've been missing for twelve years."

Her eyes went wide. "Where did he find them?"

"That's the bad part. A doomsday cult has her in its clutches, and it doesn't look easy to infiltrate." I tossed back some whisky.

"Are they both healthy and...sane?" She swallowed nervously.

I shook my head. "Hard to say. He called me as soon as he'd seen them. But they weren't together."

She placed a hand on my arm. "I'm sorry. You must've been consumed with worry all these years—fearing the worst, and imagining all kinds of things."

I scrubbed my jaw. "In truth, I thought she might

be…dead."

She looked into my eyes with the sweetest expression. "Is there anything I can do to help?"

I raised her hand to my mouth, kissing her palm and holding her eye. "How about sex?"

Her mouth fell open. "Your sister and niece have been found in a cult, and you want to have sex?"

Taking her whisky and placing our drinks on the side table, I crowded in on her, tracing her delicate collarbone with my thumb. She smelled of the rosemary-mint soap we'd used this morning, and a native lemony scent. Sliding my palm to her nape, I found the small hairs upraised on her skin and goose pimples sprouting. I raked my hand through her hair, tugging it so her whole scalp would tingle. Her pink lips parted, her pupils dilating as she panted out little puffs of breath. I brought my lips to within an inch of hers. "Admit you need me, little captive. Admit you're dying for my touch."

As she blinked slowly, her brow furrowed, and I read the conflict in her expression. Her body wanted to submit to me, but her mind didn't want to lose the single shred of power she still had in our dynamic—her ability to veto sex. In the face of her internal rebellion, I decided I was going to conquer her completely. My iron will and hardened cock dictated that her own will be curbed within the half-hour.

I bit her lower lip, dragging my teeth along its edge and sucking its full flesh. She let out a little moan that made my dick stand to attention. I swooped on her mouth, my tongue preying on hers as I caressed her round, pert breast through her shirt. When she wove her hands around my neck, I pulled her onto my lap so she straddled me.

Hearing one of the servants shuffling into the dining area, I barked, "Out! Draw the curtain. We're not to be disturbed."

"Yes, sir." Warren, my jack-of-all-trades, scurried out, locking the curtain on the side.

Ingrid drew back, the wrinkle in her brow returning. "If you can fuck me, you can trust me."

The little rebel thought she could bargain using her own desire for currency. Too bad it didn't work that way. But her pluck made me want her even more. I turned, shifting her onto the sofa and pulling her to the edge as I hiked up her dress. Shunting her legs apart, I stroked up her inner thighs, from her knees to her heat.

She clawed the sofa, releasing jagged catches of breath.

"No, my little slave. You have to earn my trust." I drew my middle finger lightly along her divide through her panties.

"*Unh*. But you had *my* trust right from the start. That's why I brought you to my apartment." Her voice was hoarse with lust.

I was going to make her voice crack from screaming.

I kissed her pussy through the nylon barrier, causing her to writhe. Palming her belly, I held her down, playing with the ridge of her panties. "Do you wish you hadn't?" My tone was straight from Hades.

She shuddered. I tore her panties down the middle, leaving them crotchless and exposing her beautiful pussy.

"Hmm, my little witness? Do you wish I'd never found out who you were?"

Her conflicted expression told me she realized this was a test. Saying "yes" would leave open the possibility that she planned to turn me in. Saying "no" would bring her closer to my side.

I thumbed the edges of her opening, prying her lips apart and breathing cool breath into her hot channel. Her whole body rippled with shockwaves.

"No," she finally said. "No, I don't wish that."

I was going to make her mean that.

I fluttered my tongue against her clit, flirting with it. She cried out, her hips bucking.

I flicked it with the back of my middle finger, and she practically sang.

When I sucked it, she let out a moan that came from middle earth.

Making my tongue into a point, I drilled into her as deep as I could go. Then I dipped in a finger, curling it up to find her G-spot. Her groans told me I'd hit the mark. I stroked it while teasing her clit with my thumb. Then I withdrew, sucking her clit, before diving back in to play with her hot spot. As I repeated this a few times, her fingers dug into the couch and she arched her chest.

"Oh, oh, Liam! Oh, God. Liam!" Her head thrashed about, and she screamed, grabbing my hair and pulling me into her as her hungry pussy ate my tongue, spilling savory come onto my lips.

I kissed her ravenously, painting her lips and tongue with her own juices. Then I swung her up on the couch so she lay beneath me, her thighs girding my hips. Unbuckling, I wrenched down my pants and boxer briefs to free my swollen cock.

"Bare, my little crow feather."

She nodded.

"Keep your eyes open and on me."

"Okay."

"Remember, you don't come till I give you permission."

"Yes."

I teased her slit with my tip. "Yes, what?"

"Yes, Liam."

I nestled my crown into her opening. "Are you dying for me, little rebel?"

"Yes, Liam!" The vehemence in her tone made my tip eject more pre-cum.

As I thrust in all the way, she gasped, digging her fingernails into my back and swiveling her hips around my shaft. I slid out and stabbed her again, touching bottom. Then I pounded her ferociously, taking out all my anxiety over my sister's situation on Ingrid's pussy. But from her heedless moans, I knew she loved my punishing strokes.

I paused, murmuring over her mouth, "You want me to stop, little one?"

Her eyes widened. "No! No, please."

I smiled.

"Okay, baby, when I've counted down from three, I want you to come."

I leaned forward so my cock grazed her clit each time it entered and exited.

In her ear, I whispered, "*Three*."

She groaned, twisting and gyrating.

"*Two*."

I could feel the walls closing in on my cock.

"*One*."

As I grunted, releasing, she yowled, contracting. It felt like the most beautiful pairing of elements in nature. I pumped in and out a few times so she could milk my cock with her after-squeezes. I pulled her close to me, spooning her.

All may not have been right with the world…but at the moment it sure as hell felt like it.

Chapter Nine

Ingrid

He had quelled me with kindness. I didn't mean to cave, but his sweet gestures and the sad situation with his sister and niece had softened me, weakening my resolve. Now I awoke to find one of his arms banding my waist and the other cradling my head. We must've fallen asleep on the sofa. I was startled to find that though the cabin was frigid, I was warm. His body must've been generating thousands of calories just lying there.

I twisted to look at his sleeping face. Being a painter, I was fascinated with perspective. Whether from a change in angle, a contrast with a nearby object, or an effect of light, the same subject could become something entirely different depending on how you looked at it. Now, more than ever, I realized that perception was subjective. I had first met Liam when I was dejected on my birthday—then I had imbued him with all the heroic qualities of a Titan. Later, when he was subduing me and controlling my bliss, he appeared as a lion tamer. When he surprised me in the bathroom this morning, he was the prince of darkness. Now, asleep, he wore the softest, calmest expression—the sleeping version of the ancient Roman statue of Augustus addressing his troops in the field.

I started to wriggle out of his grasp.

"Where do you think you're going?" he mumbled, clamping me more tightly to him.

"To find some underwear," I squeaked.

"No, you're not." The arm beneath my head folded inward to hold my chest in place, while the other hand roved to my groin, causing me to jackknife into him with delight. "This pussy is mine, and I intend to put it to good use."

When he spoke like that, it made my sex weep.

"You use odd intimidation tactics," I teased. "One would almost mistake them for love."

"Did I mention that your ass is also mine?" He placed his finger at the threshold of my tight hole, and I immediately clenched up. "That's right, my little witness. I can ass-fuck you, and deny you an orgasm, pounding the truth out of you while claiming your soul."

"You're a sadist." I writhed against the arm that snaked around me.

"All the best inquisitors are." Sinking two fingers in my slit, he soon made it impossible for me to think of anything beyond pleasure.

****

When we emerged from the dining area, my cheeks blazed under the knowing glances of everyone in the main cabin. Liam and I hadn't exactly been quiet, and we'd commandeered that space for several hours. Being pantyless under my dress made me feel at once vulnerable and turned on by the slightest things, like Liam's hand on my ass or his finger grazing my nipple.

As we passed Guy, who was reading an honest-to-God newspaper, he commented, without looking up,

"The turbulence has finally died down."

Liam smirked. "Just think what the weather must be like on the ground."

"I'd rather not." Guy sniffed, taking a sip of brandy.

I wished like anything I could take a shower, but freshening up in the lavatory would have to do. After washing my face, taming my unruly waves somewhat, and applying a little fresh mascara, I returned to find Liam in the middle of a chess game with a man who looked to be in his early seventies.

Without glancing up from the board, Liam said, "Ingrid, meet Federico, a chess master who'll be a permanent resident of the island."

Federico tipped his Fedora, winking at me. "Signora."

I sat on the fold-up seat to watch them. "Are you from Italy?"

"Buenos Aires." He took one of Liam's knights. "I am servant to Signor Stauner."

Liam leaned back, surveying the board. "In this case, the servant is the master, and the master the apprentice."

The waiflike blonde who wore torn black jeans came over and took my vacant seat. "You're Ingrid? I'm Connie."

I grasped her offered hand.

The guy with the shaved head and black glasses introduced himself as Bryn, taking a seat on my other side. "I saw some of your art on Pinterest and Facebook. Your sculptures are sick."

I flushed. "Thanks. It's been awhile since I had time to start a new study. Are you two friends of

Liam?"

Bryn crunched on an ice cube from his coke. "I trade for him—and do the occasional hacking job on the side."

Connie snickered. "And the frequent *hack* job."

Bryn shrugged. "No one cares about quality anymore. Speed is the bottom line."

As Federico pondered a move, Liam said, "Bryn, did you manage to get into the cult's compound?"

Bryn shook his head. "It looks like a nonstarter. No IP addresses in the whole area."

"No phones *or* computers?" Liam's face darkened. "It's worse than a prison."

"If your man Ralph can smuggle in a couple of wires, we can listen in." Bryn tipped back the rest of his drink.

Liam moved out his rook. "They may strip-search newcomers—supposing he does get that far."

Federico gave the slightest of grunts, capturing Liam's bishop. "Focus, Signore."

"Surely what can be lured in can be lured back out," said Connie. "If Ralph can meet with Gretchen or Katrina, he may be able to persuade them to leave."

Bryn stood. "Yeah, but that takes time, and Ralph may not have enough."

****

An hour before we were due to land, I concocted a plan. I wasn't wholeheartedly behind it, and I only half-believed it might work. But I had to give it my best shot.

When Liam went to use the lavatory fifteen minutes before we landed, I tucked my sweater down under my seat. After we'd landed, as everyone gathered their luggage, I took my time so that we might be the last ones off.

But everyone deferred to Liam, waiting for him to deplane first, and Liam wasn't going anywhere without me. So I tried to walk as slowly as possible once we'd descended the steps, to give all the passengers enough time to clear the exit.

I patted my bag, looking confused. "Oh, shoot. I forgot my sweater! I must've left it. Be back in a moment." I turned and set off at a run back to the plane, my heart skittering. When I didn't hear steps behind me, I began to hope that my ruse might work.

Entering the plane panting, I spoke low to the flight attendant, a willowy woman with curly red hair, and either the pilot or co-pilot, a short man with cropped brown hair. "I've been kidnapped. The man I rode next to—" I didn't dare gesture out to the tarmac, for fear of calling attention to my mission—"abducted me against my will. Please, can you let the authorities know that I'm here? Or maybe you can take me back when you turn around? My name is Ingrid Pellerin."

The flight attendant, whose badge read, "Maggie," smiled. "Ingrid, it's a pleasure to meet you. I believe you left your sweater behind." She handed me my sweater.

My jaw slacked. "But you'll notify someone about me, right?" I turned to the pilot/co-pilot, reading his badge. "Mike, will you please tell the police?"

He laughed. "Have a nice stay here in Verau, Ingrid. We hope to see you on another flight."

Was I in an alternative universe? Was everyone around me insane, or was I the insane one?

The other pilot came out rubbing his hands

together. "Let's get going, Mags, Mike. I'm starving."

And then the penny dropped. Not only were they employed by Liam and probably staying at his place, but they'd likely been paid to keep quiet. My disappointment plummeted like a brick to the bottom of my stomach. Preceding the crew, I sullenly trudged down the steps, not looking up as I arrived at the bottom. I was too ashamed of my naïveté and readiness to believe the best of people.

Liam's large hand clapped on the back of my neck, and he shepherded me toward a waiting Jeep. His gravelly voice hinted at amusement. "Did you have a nice chat with my crew?"

I scowled. "They're too mercenary for my tastes."

He leaned in, speaking low in my ear. "Frowning doesn't become you, little rebel. Let's see that smile of yours."

"You want me to smile on command too?" I grumbled.

"I can certainly *make* you smile." I could hear his cocky grin without looking at him. He opened the passenger door to the Jeep, tilting my chin up so I was forced to meet his gaze. "Though after your little stunt, I'm not sure you deserve it. Punishment, yes, pleasure, no."

As he drove us along a narrow road, I took in the scenery for the first time. Though the sun had set a few hours ago, even under the cloak of night I could tell the landscape was breathtaking. A midnight-blue sky silhouetted coconut palms and umbrella pines, a nearly full moon rose over the eastern horizon, and dark, forested hills softly undulated on the inland side. In the background, the gentle lap of waves on the shore lulled me into a calmer frame of mind. I imagined it would be hard to remain anxious in an island paradise like this.

As we rounded a bend, I sighted the house. *Oh. My. GOD.* The moonlit water beyond shone through the large windows, creating the effect of a jack-o'-lantern winking at us. The swooping shrine-like rooftops of two outbuildings to the side of the front entrance led the eye in elegantly curving stages to the central roof of the main building. As Liam had suggested, the main block in the middle of the central rectangular structure replicated on a large scale the module-like smaller buildings surrounding it. A traditional Shinto gateway stood over a broad gravel path that connected the large car park to the gardens. I couldn't wait to explore tomorrow. My favorite style of garden was the Japanese rock tsukiyama.

I must've looked ecstatic because watching me Liam broke out in a broad smile. "What do you think?"

"It's extraordinary. Enchanting." I breathed the fresh night air. "I can't wait to see inside."

Chapter Ten

Liam

The builders had done a first-rate job, as had the interior design team. All the inside doors slid on tracks and were made of latticework frames with translucent paper panes. I'd requested that only the northern and southern sides of the house—the shorter ends—have windows in the same shoji style. The long western and eastern sides featured picture windows that allowed the light of the rising and setting sun to travel through the house unobstructed. I loved the clean feeling of the tatami mats beneath my feet, their inimitable grassy smell, and their simplicity.

"Take your pick of slippers or flip-flops," I told Ingrid after she'd toed off her sandals in the anteroom.

She spotted the wall of colorful kimonos. "Don't tell me, like those traditional hotels in Japan, you have a hot tub—"

"Six. And a sauna, waterfall pool, and infinity pool. Do you want to soak in the tub?"

She gaped. "That's a rhetorical question, right?"

"Come on." I took her hand, leading her through the large open-concept main space, which elicited her gasps, and through several corridors to one of the master suites. Seru had brought our luggage in. "Take off your clothes."

She laughed. "You say it so differently from the way you barked it the other night."

"The result is the same."

She cocked her head. "I don't think so."

I gripped her ass, pulling her to me. "All right, then, how's this?" I dropped my voice to its most menacing and authoritative pitch. *"Take off your clothes."*

A tremor traveled through her from head to toe, as she gulped. "Yes, that'll produce the same effect."

I arched an eyebrow. "Well? Do I need to spank you to have my orders followed?"

She started, a sly gleam lighting her eye. "Yes, Captain."

The little vixen. I swatted her ass.

I eyed her as she undressed, enjoying her sinuous contours from all angles, the full waves of hair that fell past her shoulders. Shedding my own clothes in record time, I scooped her up and carried her outside to the pinewood porch. As I pretended I was going to dump her into the tub, she screamed, gripping my neck tightly. My dick went ramrod straight.

"Put me down! I don't trust you."

"No, my little crow feather? I don't think you have much choice. We're in my world now."

But I set her down.

The night was a perfect seventy degrees, since it was the middle of Verau's autumn season. This hot tub offered views of the brilliant southern-hemisphere constellations Dorado and Mensa, the pale moon serenely rising in the east, and Mars and Saturn blazing high overhead. To replicate the hot springs experience, I'd had the tub temperature set at the upper end of what a person could tolerate.

Before we climbed into the tub, Ingrid gasped.

"What is it?" I coiled an arm around her.

"That beautiful wispy cloud!" She pointed to a hazy spiral galaxy low in the southwestern sky.

"That's the LMC—Large Magellanic Cloud. It's a satellite galaxy of the Milky Way."

She arced her head to take in the entire sky. "Wow. I've never been south of the equator. I never realized how much I take our northern star configuration for granted."

"Look more closely and you'll notice a few constellations we have up North, only they'll look slightly different here."

I waited for her to register them. "Oh—there's Orion, I think. And Cassiopeia. And the Big Dipper upside down! Everything's so clear."

"On the opposite end of the house, you can see the Southern Cross."

Limb by limb we eased into the water, Ingrid's groans of pleasure swelling my dick to mammoth proportions.

Straddling my hips to sit in my lap, she murmured into my neck, "When can I call Andrea, Mom, and my work?"

Cunning little temptress. Her supple breasts pressed irresistibly into my chest, and her soft arms draped like silk over my shoulders. Her alluring pussy kissed the base of my cock.

"When we get out of the tub, I'll let you text your friend and mom—though I'll read your messages before you send them. When you call your work tomorrow, you'll tell them you won't be able to come in for several weeks, as a close friend has died and you have to handle the aftermath. You can work remotely during certain hours, but your laptop's Wi-Fi will be disabled. Every email you receive and send on one of our computers will be monitored by me or Bryn."

She gazed at me solemnly. "What about Zoom meetings?"

"You can conduct three a week for work, but with me in the room. I won't hesitate to take you out of a meeting if you step out of line." I cupped her jaw, halfway between wanting to insert my dick between her gorgeous lips and wanting to spank her till her ass was raw. Either way, I had an urge to assert my dominance, to remind her I ruled this domain and she was my slave to do with as I chose.

Widening her eyes, she appeared to decipher the thoughts written across my face. "You can't keep me here indefinitely."

"I can keep you long enough."

"Long enough for what?" she probed.

"To discipline you. To be sure of you." I was deliberately vague, since I hadn't thought through my actions or their consequences. All I knew was that my need to have her in my thrall was visceral, like no other need I'd ever known. I wanted to infiltrate her mind, heart, and soul, ruining her for anyone else. For the first time in over a day, I wondered if subconsciously this had been the main reason I'd brought her to the island—even above my mistrust.

I couldn't say what it was about Ingrid that made me so hell-bent on keeping her. She reminded me of a pure white rose with spiraling inner petals. Though strong, fierce, and smart, she was made to be captured, held, possessed. Pleasing her pleased me. Taming such a spirited, breathtaking creature would be my greatest accomplishment—above any rescue operation I'd done while in service, above any contract hit I'd completed, above amassing unlimited wealth. I wanted to be her sole source of happiness and pain, her reason to live and breathe, her god.

Her gentle voice broke into my thoughts. "Will you get away with it?"

Interesting way of asking a question I'd put to myself a few times. I'd wondered *how* I would get away with it, what made me think I *could* get away with it. Having billions of dollars and numerous lackeys at my beck didn't hurt. My inborn self-assurance also helped. Kissing my way from her forehead and along the top of her nose to her mouth, I said into her lips, "I think I will."

I pressed her pillowy lips to mine, savoring their tender ripeness. As our tongues meshed, I moved her hips back and forth, grinding her into my erection. Lifting her up, I impaled her on my cock, embedding myself in her tight, velveteen-soft pussy to the pleasing sound of her burbling. "Oh, baby, you were made for me."

"Liam, you won't kill me, will you?" Her lost, plaintive tone and the strategic timing of her question told me she meant it.

I smiled indulgently. "Not tonight, little crow feather, not tonight."

****

"Tell me about your friend, Andrea," I said, holding Ingrid in my arms on the low bed in our room. "What will you need to tell her so she doesn't worry?"

"A damn good story. Because she knows me like a sister. I'm an only child, so every close friend I make is like a sibling."

My grip tightened around her shoulders. "You don't have any close male friends, do you?"

"Armen," she said.

My jaw flexed. "Who's he?"

She laughed. "I thought we were talking about Andrea."

"Now we're talking about Armen."

"He's gay," she said, somewhat to my relief.

"He doesn't swing for both teams?" I wanted to cover all bases.

"No. Decidedly not. He's Armenian."

I didn't care if he was Uzbekistani. I just cared about his sexuality.

"All right, Armen can stay. Back to Andrea."

She gazed up at the ceiling. "We met in ninth grade and played soccer together all four years of high school. Even though she went to Rutgers and I went to Brown, we saw each other almost every weekend through college. We shared an apartment in Manhattan when I got my internship and she got her job as assistant editor for Promontory Press in SoHo."

"So she's smart."

"Whip-smart. You can't pull the wool over Andrea's eyes. In fact, I've never dared to try. She always says that being Black in America requires you to have a sixth sense and three-sixty vision. I believe she has those to the nth degree. If you let me have my phone, I can show you pictures of her. She's gorgeous."

I reached over into my bag and unzipped the pocket where I'd hidden Ingrid's phone. "Straight to the photo, and then hand it back."

She saluted me. "Yes, Captain."

For some reason, whenever she said that, it made me sprout a chub—if I didn't already have one.

She brought up a picture of a beautiful caramel-skinned, doe-eyed woman with full lips and a mesmeric smile.

"Is she single?" I asked, scanning her high cheekbones and medium-length, curly hair.

"Like me, she's dating. Despite her qualities, success has been spotty and tenuous."

I threw her phone across the room, leaning over her and cupping her cheeks. "You're not dating, Ingrid. Not anymore. Before texting anyone else, you're going to text that jerk-off who stood you up and say you're no longer interested. You're taken. Understood?"

She nodded slowly. "But I have to be diplomatic. He *is* the architect on my project."

"That's *all* he is henceforth." I caressed the outer curve of her wavy silhouette. "Are there any other men I need to deal with?"

She moaned and shuddered beneath my touch. I felt like a virtuoso cellist, her body was so responsive. "My dad."

A Frenchman. Probably super protective of his only daughter. "Let's handle your mom and Andrea first. Then we'll deal with your dad."

Chapter Eleven

Ingrid

An hour later, I composed a text to Andrea:—Hey D, how was your date with Pez-in-Boots? Did he dispense any candy? My date with Marvin was a flop, but I've been whisked away to an island paradise by another guy I met. I'm here for a while. Will keep texting every day to let you know I'm alive and well. Working remotely. Love you tons!—

Liam frowned at the text. "Is 'D' code for something? Why 'Pez-in-Boots'?"

I laughed. "'D' for Drea. She calls him 'Pez-in-Boots' because he's well-endowed and wears boots everywhere. You know the fairy tale 'Puss in Boots,' right?"

He pursed his lips. "Vaguely. Aren't there too many holes in your message? Too many loose ends that will leave her asking questions?"

I shot him an incredulous look. "There are a lot of holes in the situation that would leave *anyone* asking questions. I'm doing damage control the best way I know how, by treating it lightly. She knows I'm super adventurous and free-wheeling."

"About that." He scrubbed his jaw. "Do you usually bring strangers up to your apartment and have sex with them?"

The irony of that question irritated me. "Excuse me, but it's thanks to my open, trusting, fearless nature that you're in my life at all."

"You didn't answer my question, Ingrid," he said tightly.

I flung my arms wide in exasperation. "What are you asking, Liam? How many men have I slept with? When was the last time I had sex? How many relationships have I had?"

When his deep green eyes bored into mine, I realized he wanted all the answers.

I huffed, "If I answer those questions, will you answer them about *yourself*?"

He nodded. "Of course, little rose."

His sweet response partly disarmed me. I blew out a tense breath. "All right. I've slept with eight men." I ignored the way his body stiffened next to mine and continued. "I've had five serious relationships, including the two I had in college. The most serious was with a man I nearly married at age twenty-five, after we'd dated for two years. That was three years ago. The last time I had sex was six months ago. I never date casually. You were the only man I had sex with on a first date."

I flashed him a challenging look.

He blinked slowly. "That wasn't a first date. It was a prequel date."

I snorted. "Okay. Fine."

He cupped my bare ass. "What happened with the guy you were going to marry?"

"Adrian? He was too jealous. His paranoia ruined everything. He made up the craziest scenarios out of the slightest evidence that had no bearing on reality. His obsession and inability to trust finally became too much, and I broke up with him." I scrunched up the cotton duvet beneath us.

"Hmm. I sense there's a lot more behind that story." He caught my hand and kissed my fingertips one by one.

I was enthralled by the sight. "Can I send the text to Andrea?"

He took my phone, tapped in the code, and hit send.

"Your turn," I said.

A mischievous gleam fired his eye. "How many men have I slept with? Zero, as it happens."

"Smartass." I pinched his pectorals, which, like his abdomen, were as firm as semi-fired clay.

"Ingrid, I'm four years older than you. I've slept with a lot of women. I'm not saying how many. I last had sex about a week before I met you. I've been in three serious relationships." He traced the cleft between my butt cheeks, hovering above my asshole.

I was suddenly ragingly jealous. My mouth set in a tight line. "Whom did you have sex with just before we met?"

He trailed his fingers over my perineum, turning me into a puddle between my thighs. "A woman named Caroline. We had a casual arrangement."

"And do you still have a 'casual arrangement' with her?" My indignation made me disregard the desire pooling beneath his fingers.

"When you send off a text to the architect, I'll send one off to Caroline to break things off. How does that sound?" he said in suave tones.

I nodded. "Have you ever..." I dreaded asking.

"Done the sort of things we did the other night?"

"Never with such a responsive woman." His answer was the perfect balance of tactful, honest, and gentlemanly, and it silenced me.

When my phone buzzed, I reached for it. But Liam was too quick. He opened up the text from Andrea, holding it up so we both could read it: —Ingrid, if you think that's enough to satisfy me, you've got another think coming. CALL ME!!!— A series of eggplants and palm tree emojis followed. Then another text:— Until you call me, I'll assume you've been kidnapped by a serial killer. I *will* go to the police.—

"Can I call her?" I asked Liam. "I promise I won't mention your name or where we are."

He shook his head, typing out, "I haven't been kidnapped by a serial killer. But he is richer than Croesus. I'm fine. Trust me. I will text you every day." He held it up for my inspection.

I grunted. "Fine. Send it. But she's going to call."

Sure enough, no sooner had he shot off the text, than Andrea called. She left a groggy, disgruntled voicemail: "Ingrid, pick up. It's six a.m. on Sunday morning. Now, after your texts, I can't get back to sleep. Texts like that could be written under coercion. You'd better call or tell me what's going on. You know I don't leave suspicious stuff like this alone. And no, Pez-in-Boots did not dispense candy. He's looking for an open relationship. *Next*."

I laughed. Andrea always said that when she was moving on to greener pastures in the dating world. It was so comforting to hear her voice that for a moment I thought I was back in New York. Then I remembered I had to deal with Mom.

"If you let me call my mom, I promise I won't diverge from what I told Andrea," I told Liam. "I can't text her with something like this. It will also reassure Andrea, since she and Mom talk."

To my surprise, he nodded. "You only get one set of parents."

He looked so sad, I laced my fingers with his. "Where are your parents?"

"Dead." Like his tone, his eyes were flat and spiritless.

"Oh. I'm sorry. What happened?"

He whacked me on the butt, making me jump. "No more confidences now, little witness. Call your mom. Put her on speaker. Make it good, or I'll end the call."

Mom picked up after the second ring. "Ingrid, love, we were just talking about you. How are you?"

I cleared my throat. "I'm good, Mom. Are you and Dad going shooting today?"

Liam's eyebrows jumped, and I smiled at his assumption that I meant firing a gun. When not preparing for his law classes or writing articles, Dad was an expert photographer who used real cameras. He and Mom called it "going shooting" when they drove around scoping out good subjects.

As always on the weekend days she shared with Dad, Mom was cheerful. "Yes, we're driving to Bucks County, Pennsylvania in a few minutes. Dad wants to shoot barns and silos. Will you be seeing Andrea?"

Catching Liam's stern look, I swallowed, trying to gather courage. I adopted a chipper tone. "Actually, Mom, I went on a trip. I met a man named Grigoriy who has a house on an island in the Indian Ocean—one of the Maldives. So I'm staying with him for a few weeks. I'll work remotely from here."

I'd just finished *The Brothers Karamazov* a week ago, so the name Grigoriy was on my mind. At Liam's puzzled look, I shrugged.

It really hurt to lie to Mom. First off, I was a terrible liar. Second, the last time I'd lied to my parents—when I was thirteen—my lie had severely backfired. I'd learned my lesson then. Third, I hated being dishonest with people I loved and respected, who deserved only the truth. But I justified all this by telling myself that this was a temporary fix—that I'd make it up to both Mom and Andrea, eventually.

Mom's long silence didn't bode well. "Grigoriy? You've never mentioned him before. A house in the Maldives? Working remotely? This doesn't sound good, Ingrid. Maybe I should put Dad on the phone."

Worse and worse. "No, Mom, it's fine—"

Dad's voice crackled over the speaker, his French accent palpable. "Ingrid? Where are you?"

I braced myself for a full interrogation. "I'm working remotely from an island in the Maldives for a few weeks. I'm staying with a man named Grigoriy."

"Grigoriy who?"

I thought quickly. "Grigoriy Davidov. He comes from Moscow."

Ever the analytical law professor, Dad fired off the questions so quickly, I had to keep my wits about me to reply. "How did you meet him?"

"In a café…in Chelsea." God, if I were Pinocchio, my nose would've toppled me by now.

"How long ago?" Dad pressed on relentlessly.

"About two months ago." A quaver shook my voice.

"Why haven't we heard about him?"

"Um, he's a private man, and I didn't want to jinx the relationship by telling everyone about it, only to have it go south." I cast my eyes to the ceiling, praying that if the gods were frowning on me now, they wouldn't strike me dead with lightning bolts.

"What does he do for a living?" Disapproval and doubt seeped through Dad's voice.

"He's a very successful real estate developer." That came from a magazine I'd read on the flight.

Liam looked amused now.

"Why now, Ingrid? You don't have enough vacation time." Dad's logic was airtight.

I gulped. "My firm is expanding their E-Design services, and they want me to take over a few of the E-Design clients. I would be working remotely anyway, and I needed a break from all the office politics." This lie would have me burning in hell, if my boss had anything to say about it. He loathed E-Design and all it stood for.

"Do you love this man?" Again, a logical question, based on my odd behavior.

My cheeks burned, and I turned away so I didn't have to meet Liam's eyes. "Um, yes!" I tried to sound enthusiastic and lovestruck. "Yes, I do."

"Put him on the phone."

Shit. I'd said Grigoriy came from Moscow. Liam probably couldn't do a Russian accent. "Uh, he's actually asleep now. The time difference and the travel have taken their toll on us both. Maybe another time, Dad." My voice was unsteady.

"Send us pictures of you and Grigoriy—and the island. We want to know you're okay, darling." Dad's voice was softer now, though his request was lawyerly enough. He wanted proof that would set him at ease.

"Okay. I will, Dad. Big hugs to you and Mom." I found myself tearing up. They both loved me so much. All they'd ever cared about was my happiness.

When we'd ended the call, I felt psychologically and physically spent. That's when I realized I'd only had three hours of sleep since Saturday morning.

Heaving a frustrated sigh, I tossed the phone on the mattress between me and Liam and sank back onto the pillow.

"You made me lie to my parents." Tears pricked my eyes, as I turned away from Liam. "They'll never trust me again when they learn the truth."

"I'm sorry." His voice was gentle. "I can see you're very close. For what it's worth, I'm grateful to you for doing that. You're brave and strong, Ingrid." In lower tones, he murmured, "And too good for me."

In my wiped and fragile state, all I could feel was shame at having betrayed those I loved. For what? Of course, I was coerced into lying so Liam wouldn't kill me. But there was more to it than that. I felt additional pressure to succeed in my deceit.

I wanted to think it was for more than sex. I wanted to believe it was for a chance at love.

Chapter Twelve

Liam

I lay awake long after her steady breaths told me she'd drifted off to sleep. Listening to those who loved her was like hearing character witnesses testify in court. I could tell a great deal about Ingrid from what her friend and parents had said. They trusted her completely, expecting from her nothing less than the same openness and honesty they showed her. Her parents set an example of deep love, not just between each other but toward Ingrid. Her friend clearly cared for her just as much. Someone so loved must be truly deserving of that love and capable of loving with her whole heart.

Andrea's loyalty suggested Ingrid was loyal too. Then there was the way Ingrid had talked to her parents—with tremendous honor and respect. Her father's tone had softened once he'd confirmed that she'd made her decision based on love. Honesty, openness, trust, loyalty, honor, respect, and love. These were strong values, too rare and precious to take for granted or trample heedlessly. They were worthy of reverence.

I'd been floored by Ingrid's bravery, strength, and resourcefulness. It was visibly painful for her to deceive Andrea and her parents, and it went against everything she held dear. Despite this, she'd held up our bargain with courage, fabricating plausible ad hoc lies before a tough tribunal.

Why had she done this? It couldn't have been just fear that motivated her to violate her deepest principles. Granted, hate and fear—or mistrust—were the two motivations I understood best from my own lived experiences. But Ingrid had led a sheltered life and was unaccustomed to living in fear. Those who had no need to fear had the luxury of hope.

Hope. Her father had it in his voice when he'd asked Ingrid if she loved the man she'd gone off with so boldly and recklessly. It showed in Ingrid's face the night under the streetlamp when I'd asked her if she wanted to find out how much danger she liked. Without hope, she wouldn't have been bold and reckless enough to let a near-stranger come to her place and do what I did to her.

All this time, I'd assumed Ingrid was too trusting. But maybe she had something I didn't have that I could now afford. What would it mean to have hope? For starters, it would probably entail not assigning bad motives to people. And then, it would likely involve looking forward instead of constantly looking back. And this was the hardest thing to envision—believing in oneself. Because until I believed in myself, I couldn't believe in others.

Being proud, stubborn, and determined, I'd always admired Julius Caesar's decision to cross the Rubicon and his declaration, on the other side, that the die was cast. *Iacta alea est.* It was my motto during the flight to the island. I hoped the events I'd set in motion justified my decision to steal Ingrid away. Should there be a fallout on the scale of the Roman civil wars, I'd have to back up my rationale with every weapon in my arsenal.

****

"Where are you going?" The duvet muffled her groggy voice.

"Out for a ride." I rooted around for a t-shirt in my luggage.

"What time is it?" She sat up, letting her breasts pop free of the covers—succulent tits I'd gladly have milked for breakfast.

I tugged the shirt over my head. "A little after eight."

She rubbed her eyes. "Can I come?"

I was pleased she wanted to join an excursion that was likely to be a daily routine for me. "Sure. There are at least thirty bikes out there. We'll find one that fits you."

Twenty minutes later, in a small outbuilding devoted exclusively to bikes, I claimed my favorite racer, finding a gleaming white hybrid for Ingrid. We rolled silently along the track that led to the ring road, circling clockwise around the northern tip of the island toward a sequestered beach. As I recalled, this stretch of sand had a small cove covered by arching rock formations and filled with all manner of beautiful fish.

"Oh, look!" Ingrid pointed delightedly at a family of brown quails that scampered across a dirt clearing. "Five little ones and their mother. I wonder if they've had breakfast."

The sky was so high and translucent, it glowed. Now the teal sea had claimed its highest point on the white-sanded beach, its waves lashing the rim of vegetation that crawled up to the palms.

"The shelling here must be beyond belief." Ingrid stooped to pick up a purple-and-white speckled, spiraled conical shell. "I suppose it's better to wait till low tide to beachcomb."

Leaving our bikes by the road, we strolled toward the inlet I remembered. I led Ingrid along the rocks to an entrance where we ducked to emerge in a cool, darkened cave. Sure enough, in this cove, schools of white-striped neon-orange fish swished about making mouths at us from beneath the clear water.

"They're beautiful," Ingrid murmured. "Is this a good place to swim?"

"Here you'd want to wait till the tide has gone out a little. Especially if you're at all claustrophobic. But yes, if you like not having to fight the waves, this is ideal."

"It'd be a perfect spot to ride to for a morning swim to beat the heat," she mused.

Removing our shoes, we wandered along the beach in the low-rolling waves that were already retreating.

"This is the most gorgeous place I've ever been on earth," Ingrid declared.

"Have you visited other planets?" I reached down and splashed her.

She shrieked, giving me a little push. "Are you always this good at bursting people's bubbles?"

I captured her wrists behind her back, holding her by the nape while I took her mouth in a carnal kiss. As our lips disjoined, I said, "If I don't do it, someone else will."

She leaned into me. "I'd rather it be you."

****

By the time we'd ridden the perimeter of the

island, I was famished. I assumed Ingrid was too. We didn't bother showering but headed into the main dining room, where Char, our Thai cook, had laid out an assortment of hot and cold dishes. I homed in on the miso soup, savory Japanese pancakes, and breakfast bowls of rice topped with eggs, raw fish, pickled plums, seaweed, and sesame seeds. For those preferring a more Western menu, options included omelets, waffles, rice porridge, bacon, and sausages.

Jesse, the head gardener who'd come with us yesterday, breezed through, brandishing a rasher and mug of coffee as he headed out to inspect the three large vegetable gardens on the southwestern side of the property. Warren, the wiry jack-of-all-trades, was devouring three plates of a variety of foods, slugging coffee in between bites, and chattering to Barbara about a cruise ship that had just skirted the island to the east. Ma'afu, a middle-aged Fijian fisherman, looked done in and ravenous from a shift that had begun at 2 a.m. and just ended. At the far end of the table, Federico was already deep into a game of chess with the fourteen-year-old Epeli, son of Tima, the Fijian cook. Maggie, Mike, and Stuart, the flight crew, were huddled together gossiping about airlines that were about to go bust or had gone bust and been resurrected.

Guy sauntered through in a crisp white tropical wool suit with a half-lined jacket and tan suede shoes, surveying the breakfast spread with disdain and pouring himself a cup of jasmine tea.

"Too good for food or coffee?" I gnashed a piece of salmon. "What do you live on?"

"Tima is preparing me some wakame and brown rice with tofu." Easing himself into a chair, he crossed one elegant leg over the other, observing the servants down his nose. Guy deplored the fact that I had them eat at my table with the rest of the guests. "Coffee makes hummingbirds of our hearts."

"You don't eat fish?" It was news to me that Guy had gone vegetarian.

He fixed his cool gaze on me. "For lunch and dinner, my good man. Not for the first meal of the day."

Ingrid laid a hand on my arm. "I have to call into work."

Guy smirked. "The real world rains on your parade, I see."

"This choric commentary is becoming a bad habit, Guy." I stood. "I recommend getting laid. It helps take your mind off of other people's business."

He sipped his tea. "Other people's business *is* a lawyer's business."

I patted his shoulder. "Give your advice to those you overcharge by the hour, not those who suffer it for free."

I led Ingrid to our room. She looked extremely nervous as we entered. "Simon may fire me. Failing that, Liz may demote me. And no matter what Asher won't speak to me again."

I cupped her shoulders. "Remember. Make it sound as if you're doing *them* a favor."

I placed the call and put it on speaker.

A nasal voice blared forth. "Ingrid?"

"Hello, Simon. How are you?"

"*Anh*, I've been better. We had a double birthday party today. Maura and I are only just getting to sit down after ten hours of blow-up funhouses, clowns, and dancing beagles."

"I'm sorry to bother you on a Sunday night. You see, a close friend of mine died suddenly this weekend."

Simon clucked sympathetically. "I'm sorry for your loss, Ingrid."

"Thank you." She squeezed her eyes tight. "Unfortunately, my friend had no one in the world but me, and I'm her executor. So I'll need to see to things like taking care of her body, arranging for a service, and settling the estate."

He sighed beneficently. "Ah, death. The simplest human event, yet the most complex of human affairs."

"Er, yes. Well, I may need to take a few weeks off to sort all of this out."

Silence. Long, drawn-out, and excruciating.

She went on. "Of course, I'm happy to work remotely to make sure none of my projects are delayed."

"Doesn't your friend have anyone else who can take care of her affairs?" he snapped.

Ingrid's brow furrowed. "No, I really am the only person who can handle them. She had no family."

Simon gusted out an exasperated breath. "Ingrid, I'd understand if you need to take maternity leave, or mental health leave. Or leave to care for your husband or a child. But I'm quite sure the death of a friend isn't in your contract."

"Well, this friend was like a sibling to me. And she was utterly alone in the world. She left a complicated estate with all sorts of insolvency that requires formal probate." Ingrid paced about. "And there are all her worldly possessions to be sorted through. And people to notify."

"If she was so alone in the world, whom can you possibly have to notify?" Simon sniped.

"Acquaintances, colleagues, members of her church…the garden club." Ingrid threw up her hand and rolled her eyes. I could see it'd now become a matter of principle to her that she win this battle with her boss. I was thoroughly impressed with her pluck and verve.

"Garden club," Simon snorted. "Let the garden club handle her affairs, then. Ingrid, you can't simply take off a few weeks without notice. Now, if you'd informed me, say, two weeks ago that your friend was going to die, I might've been able to carve out the time."

"But as I said, it was a sudden death. No one could've known. And if you could carve out the time two weeks ago, surely you can do so now?" She stalked to the window, looking out at the ocean.

He heaved another put-upon sigh. "If we let you work remotely, Ingrid, we'd have to let everyone work remotely. Then what kind of an in-person firm would we have? We'd be no better than an E-Design firm. Do you really want to dilute our product in this way?"

Ingrid's voice took on a sharp edge. "I don't think that if you let me work remotely for a few weeks, out of consideration for my loss of a virtual sister, that we'll be diluting the firm's product in any way. I will make sure that the clients on my projects are one hundred percent satisfied." She sat down in a chair, gnawing her thumbnail.

"Asher won't like it. Neither will Liz. I doubt Renée will approve."

She clenched her teeth. "If you tell them it's happening, they'll defer to you, Simon."

"Don't be surprised if no one acknowledges you in meetings. After all, you'll just be a face on the screen. They'll be at the table," he said in snippy tones.

"All right, I'll turn off my video *and* mute myself. I'll just listen in. Thank you for being so understanding, Simon. You're paving the way for more compassionate workplaces."

He harrumphed. "I'm never one to be a pioneer. It's the people who follow the pioneers who cash in."

"I'll see you tomorrow, Simon. Have a good rest of your evening."

By the time they'd ended the call, I was panting to rip off Ingrid's clothes. She'd shown so much spine and spunk during that exchange that I found myself taking notes on how to neutralize pricks. I couldn't wait to drill into her and drive her wild.

I took her hand, pulling her off the chair. "Shower together, my little warrior?"

Her lips curved in a mischievous smile. "Ah, the shower, such a simple human event, and such a complex human affair!"

Chapter Thirteen

Rory

Now that my brother Liam had left town, I had free rein to investigate his latest criminal activities. My research was purely personal, since the D.A.'s office would've seen it as a conflict of interest for me to pursue my own family. From my PI, Wright, I knew Liam was building a New York-based cycling team, searching for our sister, and looking to purchase a yacht. I also knew he'd flown out on his private jet on Saturday to Verau. But when Wright said he'd seen Liam go into Alfredo's Italian Restaurant Friday evening and leave three hours later with a beautiful woman, I had a gut feeling that I might find a nugget, or at least a kernel, of something relating to his past. Alfredo's owner, Luigi, had strong mob connections, and I knew Liam's contracts to kill had come from several mob bosses.

I chose Wednesday, Luigi's day to visit his mother in Westchester, and likely a quieter day at the restaurant. Waltzing up to the bar, I took a seat and ordered a beer. The bartender was a strapping twenty-something with a buzz cut and a few tattoos creeping down his neck and one arm. I found out his name was Ellery.

"You work weekends here, Ellery?" I asked in a

casual tone.

"Yeah. I'm trying to get as many hours as I can at this point." He wiped down the bar counter. "Saving up for a new car."

I slipped a fifty-dollar bill halfway under my napkin, so it peeked at Ellery invitingly. "I don't suppose you worked Friday?"

He nodded, eyeing the fifty. "Busiest night we had. We were understaffed."

"Did you happen to see this man?" I held up a picture of the *Forbes* magazine cover photo from a year ago. Liam had balls—I'd give him that. For a former hitman to put himself in the spotlight like that, he had to. "He's my brother."

Ellery's face split into a wide grin. "I can see the resemblance. He was here talking to Luigi for about an hour at the bar. He joined a woman for dinner."

I decided not to ask him just yet about what Luigi and Liam had talked about. I didn't want to push Ellery too far too fast.

"Any idea who the woman was?" I sipped my beer.

Ellery looked thoughtful. "As a matter of fact, it was her birthday, and I heard Ginnie, one of our servers, say, 'Happy birthday, Miss Pellerin.' I remember the name because a guy had called in beforehand to have a bottle of champagne served to her. It's an unusual name. What was her first name?" His forehead crinkled and he closed his eyes. "It started with an 'I.' Indigo or something like that."

I wrote out the last name on a napkin, showing it to him. "Spelled like that?"

"Mm-hmm. Could be."

I folded the napkin into my jacket pocket. "What

did she look like?"

Ellery tilted his head. "About five foot seven, blonde hair, brown eyes, I think. Hourglass figure. Very attractive."

"And they left together?"

"Yeah."

"Any chance you overheard what my brother was asking Luigi?"

Ellery shook his head. "It was too busy and loud for me to catch anything. Anyway, it might cost me my job if I talk about the boss's business."

I stood. "Thanks, Ellery."

Back in my car, I searched for "I. Pellerin" in New York. One listing came up, at an address in Yorkville. Driving there, I parked across from the apartment building, a five-story pre-war yellow-brick affair. As I rang the buzzer for apartment G for the fourth time, I got lucky as an elderly woman with two cat carriers edged out the door.

I caught the door, stepping inside and smiling disarmingly at her. "Just visiting a friend."

"Elevator's broken," she grunted. "Again."

Directly to the left of the door, in the mail area, Ingrid Pellerin's mailbox was crammed with mail, and a package addressed to her lay on the floor. The package felt like a paperback book. I examined the sender: Andrea Carpel. The return address was Promontory Press in SoHo. A faint lead, but a lead nonetheless.

Climbing to the third floor and knocking a few times on apartment G, I established that she was either asleep or not at home. A piece of paper had been partially slipped under the door. I eased it out and unfolded it. It read, "Saturday, April 23, 2022. The water will be shut off in all apartments from 11 a.m. to 4 p.m. on Monday, April 25. We apologize for this inconvenience.—Roberts Management."

So she hadn't been in her apartment since this notice had been left, five days ago. That jibed with the load of mail she hadn't picked up. Was it a coincidence that she'd left the restaurant with my brother the night before? I didn't think so. This could be the nugget I was looking for.

Glancing at my watch, I found it was 4:55. I called Promontory Press and asked for Andrea Carpel. I was switched over.

"Andrea Carpel speaking." Her voice was low, warm, and smooth as honey.

I went out on a limb. "Hello, Ms. Carpel, I'm concerned about a friend of yours, Ingrid Pellerin. She hasn't been in her apartment since Saturday."

"Who is this?" Andrea's voice took on a sharp edge.

"Rory Stauner. I'm a prosecuting attorney at the D.A.'s office. Can I meet you somewhere? A café or bar?"

"Meet me at Fanelli's in half an hour. I'm wearing a black skirt suit with green heels."

****

I wasn't expecting the chic, stunningly beautiful Black woman who waited at the corner of the bar scrolling through her phone. Her air of quiet confidence and poise set her apart from the hubbub around her.

Stepping toward her with my hand extended, I smiled. "Ms. Carpel? Rory Stauner."

She had a firm grip.

I handed over my card, taking a seat on the barstool beside her. Glancing at the cocktail menu, I ordered a Vieux Carré.

She sipped her white wine. "What do you know about Ingrid?"

Her tone mixed suppressed anxiety, curiosity, and caution. So she knew Ingrid well—or at least, well enough to care about her.

I leaned one forearm on the bar, facing her. "I have reason to believe she may be missing since Saturday. I wondered if you'd been in touch with her."

"Are you asking in the interest of finding Ingrid or who she's with?" Her chocolate-brown eyes held my gaze.

I nodded. "Both."

Her nostrils flared, the only sign that she was alarmed. "She's texted a few times since Sunday morning, saying she'd been whisked away to an island paradise by some guy. She keeps saying she's fine, but doesn't give any details. Frankly, I've been suspicious she's communicating under duress, since she doesn't answer or return any of my calls." She frowned into her wine. "I was going to call her mom this evening to see if she knows anything more."

"So you and Ingrid are close?"

"We've been best friends for fourteen years—half our lives."

"Does spontaneously taking off to an island halfway across the world with a stranger seem like something Ingrid would do?" I sipped my cocktail.

"How do you know where the island is?" Andrea asked cagily.

"I have reason to believe that she's with my

brother, Liam Stauner, on his island near Fiji." I watched her reaction closely. She gave a slight start, her eyes widening.

"To answer your question, yes, and no." Andrea turned her wine glass around. "She's adventurous and trusting by nature. But for her to suddenly fly to Fiji with a guy she barely knows, leaving her work, friends, and family in the dark—that's extreme, even for Ingrid. She cares about her work. And she usually confides in me about everything. But she's gone almost completely radio-silent for the last five days."

"In your gut, does it seem as if she may have been coerced?" I asked in dispassionate tones.

Andrea's throat bobbed, as she looked down at my drink. "I think it's possible." Then her eyes cut back to mine. "If you're right, is she safe with your brother?"

Since I wanted Andrea to cooperate fully, I decided to give her more information.

"That depends on the reason he took her with him." I pried a brandied cherry off the toothpick in my drink. "He's not the sort to coerce a woman for sex. If my assumptions are correct, it's far more likely she knows something that would incriminate him. He's probably trying to convince her to keep quiet. Since it's in my interests for Ingrid to divulge whatever she knows, I have to convince her otherwise. This is where you come in."

Her brows shot up. "What can I do?"

"Two things. First, don't mention to Ingrid or her mom that we had this talk. My brother is probably monitoring every communication. There's no telling what he might do to Ingrid if he suspected her kidnap had become general knowledge. Second, would you be willing to come with me to the island, and persuade your friend to speak truthfully about everything she knows?"

"But you said it was 'his island.' Why would he let you come, knowing who you are—if, as you say, he's taken Ingrid against her will?" This woman was razor-sharp. She had intuited that my brother's and my relationship was purely antagonistic.

"I'll strike a bargain with him: either he lets me come to ask him a few questions about another crime he has knowledge of, and I'll overlook the kidnapping of Ingrid; or I'll call in the FBI. If you can convince Ingrid to talk, then I'll gather evidence for two crimes at the same time. And we'll leave with Ingrid."

"Why not just turn the case over to the FBI now?" she submitted.

Frankness seemed to be the best policy with this woman. "I'm looking to run for office as a state representative. The sooner I lock my brother behind bars, the cleaner I'll look. I'm conducting this investigation on the down-low, since it's a conflict of interest for an ADA to investigate a family member. Any evidence I find, I'll hand over to the state or the FBI. But this is also personal. I've had my brother in my sights for years now."

I didn't mention the reason I had a vendetta against Liam, and Andrea didn't ask.

She tilted her head. "Why would he let me come, if he wants to keep Ingrid's abduction under wraps?"

"He won't know, until you're there, that you're coming."

She mulled this over for a moment.

"When would we go?" She drained her drink,

uncrossing her legs.

"Can you take a few days off work three weeks from tomorrow? It will take me that long to get the arrangement in place with the Fiji police. I can email you the confirmation code associated with your ticket and the itinerary. We'll take a boat from Fiji to Verau." I tipped back the last of my cocktail.

She nodded. "I have some vacation time. But how do we know he won't keep us hostage?"

"My office will know where we are. So will the Fijian police. Liam won't risk it." *I hope he won't.* I spoke with more confidence than I felt. I was like one of those chess players who tries a desperate gambit at the eleventh hour in hopes of success. I stood, dropping some cash on the counter. "Do you have a card, Ms. Carpel?"

She handed me one.

I nodded. "I'll be in touch."

Chapter Fourteen

Liam

At my instruction, Bryn had hacked into various databases that revealed Ingrid to be squeaky clean. She didn't have so much as a D.U.I. or parking ticket. Andrea Carpel, her best friend, was an editor for a press. Ingrid's father was a Princeton law professor and her mother a dance instructor. This all tallied with my growing sense of her innocence and integrity.

When we'd been on the island a week, I finally asked her what had brought her to the forest that day four years ago. We were lounging on the porch looking out toward the sea.

She gazed off at a pleasure boat half a mile away. "Ever since I was little, I gathered crow feathers there in late summer. That spot was where my friends and I played hide-and-seek. We liked the way it was set back from the road, but had the best views into town. And of course we were fascinated by the hollow oak tree."

"How much did you see of me—from a distance and then when I came closer to you?" With each response, I was basking in Ingrid's honesty.

"I couldn't see you at all when I was in the tree. Earlier, I saw the rough outline of your face. But I didn't recognize you till the morning you came into the bathroom and spoke in the same tone you used in the forest." She shivered. "Then my two perspectives on your face blended into the same image."

"Is that what you're working on in the studio now?"

Ingrid had been sculpting in the art studio for the last few days. She was incredibly talented, as I'd found this morning, stumbling on a life-sized clay bust of my head and shoulders. It conveyed a super-charged dynamism and ferocity I didn't know I had till I saw it reflected through her work. The look in my likeness's eyes was cruel, savage, and otherworldly.

She nodded. "I guess I'm destined never to be able to exhibit this piece. There's something liberating about that."

"Who says you won't be able to? An art show might be in order, after you've created enough pieces. Show me pictures of the work you have." I passed her the phone.

She opened up a gallery of various oil paintings—landscapes, portraits, and still lifes—and sculptures she'd made since her first sculpting class at age eight in summer camp. I lingered long and appreciatively on a painting of the Adirondacks as seen from a cabin near Lake Placid. The sheer number of shades of green was extraordinary. I also admired the still life of white lilies and black-eyed Susans in an antique porcelain vase perched on a blue-and-white tablecloth. The last photo was a clay sculpture of a crow, painted black, his intelligent eyes gleaming watchfully.

"Where do you keep them?" I enlarged the crow to examine it in more detail.

"Mostly in my parents' basement in Princeton. But I have a few pieces in my closet and on the walls of my

Kathleen Haley

apartment."

I raised her hand to examine her delicate fingers. "You have a lot of skill in these hands, Ingrid. You could probably sell your artworks for a hefty price."

"Maybe every third one would be good enough to exhibit or sell," she amended modestly. "But I'm not sure it would sustain me."

"Have you ever thought of owning your own gallery and exhibiting your pieces alongside other artists' works?" I set her phone on the table.

She sipped some water. "If I had twenty grand to spare, I might risk it. At least New York City has high traffic and plenty of capital, though rents are steep."

"Would you have enough time to make your own art if you ran a gallery?" I suddenly became fascinated with the idea as an investment.

"I suppose I could hire people to run it while I'm creating." She turned to me, smiling. "Isn't it boring hearing about my idle pipe dreams?"

"Far from it." I kissed the back of her hand. "Dreams are often much closer to reality than we think." What would it be like to make her fantasy come true? Her glowing smile and musical laughter would be priceless rewards. But first I needed to make sure she was mine.

She became sober. "Can I ask you a question?"

"You may, my little rose."

"Was that the only contract killing you ever did?" She met my eyes unflinchingly.

"Yes," I lied, as much for her sake as mine. In fact, starting with the cop who'd caused my dad's death, I'd killed nine men over a two-year stint as a hitman. But considering she was here on the island because she

100

knew about one of those jobs, I wasn't about to compound her involvement. "Don't ask any more questions about that, Ingrid. The less you know, the better."

She looked skeptical, as though she knew I wasn't telling the truth. Then she switched topics. "When are you going to show me the items you brought to decorate this place?"

"Now, if you like." I rose from the lounger.

She followed me to the room with the bags that contained my collectibles, art, and memorabilia. Some I'd picked up on my travels across Asia, Europe, and Latin America. Some were vestiges of childhood, like the photographs of my parents, grandparents, siblings, and foster family. Ingrid's gaze alighted immediately on a well-worn picture of Gretchen at age seventeen holding a newborn Katrina. She'd sent it to me when I was stationed in Beaufort, South Carolina.

"Your sister looks so much like you," she exclaimed. "She's beautiful."

She caught sight of a picture of me, Rory, and Gretchen when we were eleven, nine, and eight, respectively. "You're the oldest. What's your brother's name?"

"Rory."

"Are you close?"

I laughed. "The opposite. He's made me his sworn enemy."

"Why?"

"Sit in my lap, and I'll tell you." I took a seat, opening my arms to receive her. She nestled her ass over my dick, hardening me instantly. As I spoke, I caressed her curves and teased her sensitive points, winding her tight so I could unloose her at my will. "Gretchen, Rory, and I were raised by our parents, John and Sibyl. John was an independent cannabis grower with a license to sell. He had a plot near our home in the South Bronx. Naturally, he was a phenomenon in our local area—everyone knew him as John Jay. He did well enough that Sibyl didn't have to work."

I held her firm breasts in my hands, drawing light circles around her nipples through her bra and shirt. "When I was eight, Sibyl lost my baby sister Ella. She rolled off a high counter when Sibyl wasn't watching— the impact killed her. Sibyl spiraled into alcoholism and depression that became progressively worse over the years."

Ingrid twisted to meet my eyes, sadness haunting hers. "That's awful. I'm so sorry. That must've scarred everyone in your family."

I cupped her throat, sliding my hand down into the top of her shirt as I brushed her inner thighs. She let out a hollow moan. "A local cop, Ned Raymond, had it in for my father because Ned's son, Charlie, had gotten hooked on speed, cocaine, and heroin. Ned blamed John because he'd sold Charlie his first pot when he was seventeen. Charlie had a fake ID."

Shoving up Ingrid's skirt, I traced my fingers around her heat, moving steadily closer to her groin. I spoke directly into her ear, making her quake. "John had several indoor pot-growing facilities across the Bronx. The nearest was a few blocks away from our house, and on Ned's beat. One evening, when I was eleven, one of the facilities burned down, along with a warehouse next to it that didn't belong to my father. During the investigation, it was alleged that John had burned his facility down for the insurance money. Two cans of gasoline were found in a dumpster not far from the site, and they were covered with John's fingerprints. Ned testified that he'd seen John heading back to the facility after hours, and John didn't have an alibi to disprove Ned's statement. They believed the cop."

Ingrid's breath hitched as I reached under her panties and plunged two fingers in her dripping pussy. "Ultimately, John got eight years in prison for arson and insurance fraud. But our whole family knew he never would've burned down his pot. He saw plants as living beings, and he was a gentle person. I knew Ned had set him up—had probably lit the fire himself or had someone else light it, and stolen the gas cans from the back of John's truck or the premises."

I yanked down Ingrid's panties and pumped my fingers in and out, adding a third. She closed her eyes, groaning and writhing. I was determined that she would associate this story with pleasure rather than pain, since it was so painful for me to remember. "Once my dad went to prison, Sibyl's alcoholism did her in. She was comatose, asleep, or in need of a drink at all times, and she refused to seek treatment. Finally, after a year of trying to care for everyone myself and failing miserably, I reported the situation to a social worker. Sibyl was placed in a rehab facility and Gretchen, Rory, and I were put in three different foster families across the city. I was still in the South Bronx, Rory was in Bed-Stuy in Brooklyn, and Gretchen was in Bay Ridge. A year later, when Sibyl lied her way out of rehab, she died from an overdose."

All this time, I'd been working Ingrid's pussy up to a frenzied pitch, massaging her clit while I thrust my fingers in and out. Now she came, yelping as she gripped my arms, her head tossing from side to side. When she recovered, her eyes sprang open and she looked at me in disbelief. "You just made me come while telling me about your mom's death!"

I shrugged. "It's better than making you cry. I certainly don't want tears from my story." I held up my come-soaked fingers to Ingrid's nose. "Inhale, my little captive. Then suck."

She obeyed, making my cock hard as a crowbar. I lifted her, setting her in the chair while I unbuckled and slid down my shorts and boxer briefs. Then I placed her back on my lap, feeding my length into her from beneath. Silky smooth heat swallowed me whole, and I held her hips, bouncing her up and down on my shaft. As I fell into a rhythm slamming Ingrid over my dick, she began to wail, the walls of her pussy closing in on me like exquisite torture chambers. I groaned, releasing into her, while she crumpled, a rag doll in my grasp.

When my breathing returned to normal, I continued my story. "During the last year of John's prison stint, my senior year of high school, he was knifed to death by his bipolar cellmate." Ingrid gasped, stroking my neck and arm. I didn't share with her my bitterness and hatred of the justice system—or my determination to have revenge on Ned Raymond and the fallout of that vengeance.

Now I felt ready to answer her original question— why Rory hated my guts. "Rory was placed in the worst of the three foster homes. He blamed me for everything. For telling the social worker about Sibyl, for the three of us getting separated, for his crappy foster family, and for Sibyl's death. He became a prosecutor five years ago just so he could hold the Sword of Damocles over the heads of men like me. And now he thinks vengeance will soon be his."

"What do you mean?" She wove her fingers through my hair.

"He wrote me an email this week saying he has evidence to put me away for a long time. He said if I let him come here and I give him a statement, he could have the sentence reduced and he'll overlook your kidnapping. If I don't agree, he'll set the Feds on me and they'll deal more harshly with my case." I brushed her slicked hair away from her flushed face. She looked incomparably beautiful in her halo of post-coital bliss.

"How does he know you took me away?" She straightened in my arms, I couldn't tell whether from eagerness to be freed or concern over my being found out. Possibly both.

"He didn't tell me. I imagine he's had me followed at various points."I pulled her tightly to me, gazing into her warm cinnamon eyes. "I'm not afraid to let him come here. I don't believe he really has anything on me. I'm only too glad to show him I have nothing to fear. But if he comes, what will you do, my little crow feather?"

She flushed. "I have to try to leave if I can. I have to tell the truth if anyone asks me."

I nodded, stroking her hair. "That's what I thought. I'll keep you locked up and guarded in one of the outbuildings while he's here. He probably won't stay more than a few days. It's my island. Rory has no jurisdiction to search it." I kissed her temple, gliding my hand from her chest to her crotch. She trembled like a mouse in my palm. "Your body knows I'm your master. Soon your heart and mind will know too."

Chapter Fifteen

Ingrid

I first began to suspect the cook, Char, when I returned from the bathroom to the dining room one evening and spied her flirting with Liam while replenishing his wine glass. She threw her head back and flashed gleaming teeth as she laughed at something he'd said. Hovering on the perimeter, I took her in more closely. She had a model's body, with rangy limbs, angular hips, and square shoulders. Why hadn't I noticed her perfect golden complexion, sheeny black locks, and high cheekbones before? And why hadn't I seen the familiar looks she cast his way, as though they'd already been intimate in the not-too-distant past? When she caught my gaze, her eyes shaded to a murderous hue and her smile dripped venom. She placed a proprietary hand on the back of Liam's chair, signaling she considered him hers.

Jealousy beat a drum solo in my veins as I stacked her qualities against mine.

Yes, they'd definitely fucked. But when? And why was she still here, to taunt me every time she brought heaping dishes out of the kitchen or came to remove the empty ones? I observed their interactions for several days after that, masochistically gathering damning evidence of their closeness. Surely since knowing me,

Liam had been faithful? We'd had sex five, sometimes six, times a day. Even imagining he'd *thought* of Char when we were together had me breathing fire. I needed to confront him. By the end of the week, I had practically ground my teeth down to a fine powder.

As we walked on the beach that Saturday—our beach, near the cove—I blurted, "Have you and Char fucked?"

He jerked slightly, his brow furrowing. Then he coiled his arm around my waist. When I tried to wriggle free, he penned me in with both arms, holding me fast. Turning me, he cupped my chin, fixing me with his most intense gaze. "When I first came to survey the land and talk with the architect and designers, nearly a year ago, I hired Char and a few others to cater for the construction crew."

"And she catered to you," I finished acidly, pushing against his chest.

"We did have a fling that lasted while I was here," he admitted, not loosening his grasp on me.

"How long?" I demanded tightly.

"A month." He must've seen the fury boiling up from my depths and blowing like steam from my nose and ears, because he hastened to add, "But it was always only meant to be short-term. When I left, I told her we were finished for good."

"She didn't get the memo." I writhed against his arms again, to no avail. "She looks at me as if I'm yellow fever, or last year's Twitter posting."

"I kept her on the staff because she's such a phenomenal cook. You've tasted her dishes."

"And you've tasted her," I retorted.

His brow creased. "I promised her when we had

our fling that I wouldn't let the personal arena interfere with the professional. I kept my word by letting her stay on, even when I brought you here."

"Wasn't that noble of you? Especially considering how I begged to accompany you."

He chuckled. "You are so hot when you're pissed, my little she-devil. I'm going to fuck you hard."

I hauled off and kicked him hard in the shin. I would've kneed his balls, but he was holding me too tightly.

"You'll be lucky if I speak to you after this, much less let you fuck me." I tried to duck out of his embrace, but it was no-go. "Let me go."

He crashed his lips to mine, turning my protests into mews as he braided our tongues, driving me insane with his assertive strokes. His musky, masculine taste weakened my knees. Just as I gave myself over to his sweeping tongue, it retreated in a tantalizing act of denial. I whimpered at the loss.

Withdrawing his lips, he smiled, tracing my jawbone. "You'll fuck me, little one, for as long as I want you. You're always ready—as you should be."

Realizing he was right, I resisted the urge to cry from the embarrassment. I tilted my chin high. "You won't humiliate me by keeping her in your kitchen. You can keep me as a lover *or* her as a cook. Not both."

He crooked two fingers under my chin, his eyes glinting wickedly. "I keep you as my pet." He studied me for a moment. "I'll give Char her month's notice and have her work in the vegetable garden for her remaining time. Your paths won't cross again."

"But you'll still give her her full cook's wages, right? And severance pay?" Even in the midst of my jealous fit, I couldn't help feeling guilty that I was ousting a member of the staff, when jobs were so hard to come by.

His emerald eyes sparkled. "I'll give her whatever you want me to. I'll give her a bonus, if you like."

"Just to tide her over till she finds another job."

He kissed me passionately, caressing the back of my neck and winding my hair about his fist as I loved. Before I knew it, my back was in the sand and he had tugged down my shorts and panties, shedding his own shorts and boxer briefs. He knew I was drenched without even confirming. His cock slid in, stabbing me repeatedly with what I needed most and drawing out my ecstatic cries. I was so completely his it made me almost black out.

God, I'm a goner. How much longer would I have control of my own heart? Or did I still?

****

One morning not long after that, a large boat I didn't recognize pulled in to Liam's dock. Unlike the fishing boats around here, it had an English name painted on its sparkling white side—*The Esmeralda.* Liam had just set out on his long ride, following the interior hills of the island, but for once I hadn't gone with him, as I wanted to capture the dawn and post-dawn moments on my phone.

As I heard the English cadences of the voices filtering from the dock, a crazy notion streaked through my brain. Instinct kicked in, and I saw my opportunity for freedom.

Without thinking things through, I raced down the jetty, my flip-flops slapping the wood slats as my heart pounded in my chest.

I flailed my arms in the universal signal of distress, waiting till I'd reached a man who I assumed was the captain—a bushy black-bearded, stocky fellow—in conference with one of Liam's servants, whom I recognized but whose name escaped me. Both men broke off their talk to survey me curiously.

"Please!" I huffed out. "Take me with you. I'm being held captive against my will on this island by Liam Stauner, the owner—"

The captain actually *winked* at me. "You must be the young lady Mr. Stauner brought here a few weeks ago. We've heard about you around the islands."

My heart stuttered, and I blinked rapidly. *No.* Surely this didn't mean he wouldn't help me. He just didn't have the full picture yet.

Though nonplussed, I forged on. "Can you bring me to the nearest airport? I'll pay you back for your troub—"

The captain threw back his head and let out a peal of laughter. "That's good. Where's that going to get you, my dear, without a passport? The airport officials would simply detain you until Mr. Stauner sent someone to collect you." He wiped a tear from his eye with the corner of his sleeve, as if this were the best joke he'd heard in a while. "Anyway, he isn't a man to be trifled with." He arched a brow. "I certainly won't be the one to try."

"*Please.* I'll pay you well. Bring me to any village or town." My tone had grown frantic, as time was of the essence. Liam's servant had already gone back inside, maybe to report my escape attempt and send someone to find Liam. I was nearer to getting away than I'd ever been. Yes, I'd been happy lately, but this whiff of the outside world tempted me too strongly for me to resist. I laid a hand on the man's arm. "Captain, I beg you."

The captain cleared his throat awkwardly, his eyes darting to something behind me.

Pricklings skittered from my scalp down my spine, and intense heat rolled through me like a brushfire.

A momentous presence confiscated the air around us as a gritty voice commandeered the dock.

Liam was here in his full godlike glory, his tone assured. "Captain Whittier, always a pleasure. I apologize for her outburst."

My heart sank, even as a bolt of electricity zinged through my bloodstream.

The captain took a step back, tipping his hat to Liam. "Mr. Stauner, it's no trouble at all."

I rushed forward to climb onto the captain's boat, but a pair of strong arms wrapped around me from behind, holding me in place with ease. My internal war worsened as part of me yearned to give in and part wanted to see this decision through to the end.

I kicked, screamed, clawed, and punched, getting nowhere in my fight.

"Let me go!" I hollered.

The captain backed away. "I'll be on my way. Give my regards to Josefa."

"I will," Liam replied calmly, as if I weren't thrashing in his hold.

The next thing I knew he'd thrown me over his shoulder, and his large hand connected with my butt cheek. Though I wore thin cotton shorts, his spank still stung like the devil. Yet my sex throbbed with want, and my body craved more. Striding toward the house, he cracked his palm against the other buttock. Delicious pain radiated from the point of impact through my nerve endings, lighting my center on fire.

My traitorous body welcomes the enemy.

"Have you forgotten who owns you, little captive?" He punctuated his question with another sharp swat. "It seems you need reminding."

Though disappointment and embarrassment flooded me, I wasn't in the mood to cave. "I'm *not* your captive. You *don't* own me."

He chuckled darkly. "Don't I though? We'll see."

Damn him for smelling like the fresh outdoors, the woods, and the sea. In vain, I tried not to inhale his scent, which would intoxicate me into submission.

The servants we passed averted their eyes or nodded respectfully to Liam as he marched us through the house. Though I'd stopped crying out, I continued to struggle, beating my fists against his granite back.

On entering our room, he stooped to retrieve something in a drawer.

He set me on my feet, spinning me so my back was to his chest. His hot breath tickled my ear as he held me close, causing mini-explosions to erupt in my groin.

The lethal edge to his tone left no doubt he meant every word. "You have a choice, little spitfire. You can be locked up in here until you give in to me, or you can give in now. If you choose to be locked up, you'll have only bread and water, no company, and no access to anything outside this room." One hand cupped my mons, and the other my throat. My sheath was swollen, and my hardened nipples ached painfully. I cursed my body for responding so eagerly to his touch. "Or you can skip straight to submitting."

A swallow worked its way down my throat beneath

his callused fingers. "If I submit, what then?"

The sensual smile in his voice made smoke rings of anticipation swirl through my insides. "Then we cut right to your punishment."

I lifted my chin in defiance. Submitting now gave me more agency than giving in after being cowed into submission. "I'll take it now."

His fingers closed more snugly on my throat. "That's my good girl."

His praise fanned a million sparks in my core.

"What are you being punished for, Ingrid?"

I struggled to think straight, with his blistering heat encasing me. "For—for trying to escape."

He stroked my neck as if rewarding me with his caress. "And what else?"

My sole concern now was to please him. "I don't know."

"For touching another man." His voice dropped an octave. "And for denying that you're mine. By the time we're finished, you won't think of doing any of these things again." He took a step back. "Strip."

Beneath his scorching gaze, I pulled my t-shirt over my head.

While undressing, I tried to see what he had in his hand, but he kept me facing away from it.

When I was completely naked, he sloped his palm along the curve of my waist. "Bend facedown lengthwise over the trunk with your arms above your head."

The trunk was an old sea chest that stood about twenty inches high at the base of the bed. I knelt and hinged at the hips, draping my torso and arms over the three-foot-long chest.

Using ropes, he fastened my wrists snugly to the corner O-rings at one end of the trunk. Then he tied my ankles with another rope so they were about fourteen inches apart. Gliding two fingers up my slit to my crack, he collected my arousal.

He held his digits to my lips. "Smell and suck, Ingrid. Taste how much being at my mercy turns you on."

Heat flamed my cheeks, and my pussy wept more as I licked my juices from his dripping fingers and tasted my own salty tang.

"You belong to me for as long as I choose to keep you." The rumble of his throaty voice vibrated from my chest to my core, warming and thrilling me at once.

He kneaded, patted, and rubbed my butt cheeks as if priming them. Then a light swish of leather strands brushed my buttocks and upper thighs. *Swish, swish.* The strokes warmed my skin without hurting. As he continued to strike me softly with these tails, pleasure wound around me like a silk stole, relaxing my muscles.

Pausing, he leaned over, caging me from behind with his powerful trunk. "Now that you're warmed up, here's your punishment."

Oh no.

I stiffened, bracing myself as I heard him take a step back. A flick of sharp needles stung my backside, making me jump and gasp. Tears pricked my eyes as I slammed them shut.

"This is a light flogger." He struck me with the falls again, this time in a different spot. Searing pain spread out from the point of impact, and I yelped. "You're going to count six more strokes on each cheek and six on each hamstring. Starting now."

Beneath the surface of my tingling skin, arousal pulsed through my veins.

When he struck me, I croaked, "*One!*"

I was already getting used to the sting.

"*Two!*" I cried as he dealt the next blow.

My rebellion had unleashed the dangerous, sadistic beast within him.

As he continued to flail me, the heat from the scourge's tails made me feel as if I were levitating like a helium balloon. Pleasure like what I'd felt during the warm-up—but an order of magnitude higher—swelled within my center.

Even the burn when he flogged my upper thighs converted into euphoria. But it was a bliss built of expectation. I longed for him to complete my pleasure, to touch me off like a firecracker.

When I'd called out the last of the hamstring strokes, he wrapped the tails around my throat like a collar, extending my neck. "Now, Ingrid, who owns you?"

Tears streaked my cheeks, and snot clogged my throat. "You do."This truth rang through every cell of my body.

His gravelly voice penetrated my core and set it humming. "What are you to me?"

"Your captive."

"What else?" He tugged on my flogger-collar, making me crane my neck more.

"Your slave." I didn't say it to please him. Pain, pleasure, and all-consuming need pushed the words out. And they were too true to leave me humiliated. He was my god, and I would bow to him whenever he demanded it.

"Repeat. As my property, you can expect me to use you any way, any time."

"As your property, I can expect you to use me any way, any time," I incanted. The savage way he gripped my throat was nearly enough to make me come then and there.

Malice and possession laced his tone. "Now, little slave, beg for release."

His cruel dominance fueled the flames climbing between my thighs.

My pride had flown out the window with the first stroke of the flogger tails.

My pussy clenched in anticipation. "Please…will you give me release?"

Still pulling my neck back with the flogger, he shed his shorts. "I might."

As I pressed myself into the trunk, he stabbed me with his throbbing weapon, filling me completely. I moaned and arched my back.

Gripping my waist, he pounded me with brutal strokes, whipping up the hot pleasure simmering in my depths. The burn as his hips slapped against my raw buttocks only ratcheted up the heat.

"Oh, *oh*! I'm going to—"

"Come now, little captive." Pulling out, he slammed home.

His command tipped me over the boiling point, and I erupted, spilling around him. My moans scored the air as scalding waves of bliss rolled over me. His rigid girth continued to swell and pump, wringing out my climax till there was nothing left. He released my throat, letting me collapse over the trunk, spent and unable to feel.

Time passed—I didn't know how much—and somehow my ropes were untied. At some point. I was carried in his strong arms to a chair and sat in his lap. I buried my head in his solid chest as he stroked my hair and kissed my tears away. His tender care finished the job of making me his. Disciplining then cherishing me, he owned me thoroughly.

This time I had no room left to worry about losing control of my heart, my mind, my anything. Liam had conquered every corner of me, staked his claim in every last nook and cranny.

****

By the time we'd been three weeks on the island, our days had fallen into a pleasant but erotic routine. Every morning began with Liam taking me however he chose. He made me sleep naked so he could enjoy every part of me at whim, during the night, or upon waking.

Mondays, Wednesdays, and Fridays, Liam and I rode our cycling circuit, stopping at the cove and returning in time for breakfast. Tuesday and Thursday mornings, I rode alone to the cove for a swim, after which Liam picked me up on the bike and rolled back with me the way I'd come. On those days, Liam followed a more intense training route that incorporated the inland hills. On Saturday mornings we worked out in the gym, an open room suffused with natural light in the southern outbuilding.

Sundays we "slept" in—meaning, fucked longer, more intensely, and in more positions. Liam often tied me up in various ways and teased me for upwards of an hour before giving me release. He used a flogger, a curtain rod, a belt, and his bare hands on my backside, riddling me with marks that declared how utterly he possessed me. He gagged, blindfolded, and trussed me, making me feel thoroughly used and *thing*ed. The longer, harder, and more painful the build-up, the more earth-shattering my climax.

Every day there was the raucous communal breakfast table that combined guests, servants, colleagues, and friends—sometimes as many as thirty. One of the carpenters, Waisake, had replaced Char as co-chef to Tima. There even seemed to be some behind-the-scenes flirtation between the two cooks. The food tasted just as good, if not better.

After having sex in the shower, Liam and I changed and moved to our joint workspace, a room on the eastern side of the same end of the main building—down a few corridors from our bedroom. The light there burst joyously through the picture window, which presented views of the S-curve in the beach, the sequestered palm grove, the brown swifts swooping for lunch, and the lovely winding rock path leading down to it all. Through the open window wafted the scent of gardenias and frangipanis. For four hours Liam traded while I designed, wrote emails, researched, and drew up lists and budgets for my clients. Liam vetted my emails before enabling my Wi-Fi, allowing me to send them all at once, sometime around 3:30—which was 11:30 the previous night in New York.

Then he shoved me up on his desk facedown and plowed into me or ate me out on my back with my legs spread-eagled across his papers. It was a good thing we were the only ones at that end of the house, since my unbridled screams pealed through the air, matching the harsh *kreeah* cries of the jaegers dipping over the ocean.

Afternoon tea followed, with a mixture of sweets and savory items expertly crafted by Tima and Waisake: smoked salmon sandwiched between delicately de-crusted pieces of crème fraîche-laden white bread with thin slabs of cucumber and dill; scones with clotted cream and jam; square glazed tea cakes; and marzipan-covered princess cake. An assortment of Indian teas accompanied this spread, with thick, fresh sweet cream and cubes of Fijian raw sugar. Hungry comers drifted in and out for an hour-and-a-half during teatime.

Two more hours of work, until the gloaming crept into our office and the moon rose from the eastern horizon. Then before dinner, I always sought Liam out, my estrogen levels high as I pranced in my bra and panties, giving him a tease worthy of a burlesque star. Sometimes we had a half-hour to soak in the hot tub.

Dinners were late—around 9, after the European fashion. Everyone had a special seat at the table. Liam sat at one end, with me and Guy seated on either side of him. Bryn sat to my right, with Connie next to him, followed by Stephen, and then Barbara. Then Federico, Maggie, Stuart, and so onto the end, where Jesse, the head gardener, sat. Then more servants all the way up to the empty seat next to Guy. Everyone had their habitual seat of choice.

Liam chaffed Guy no end about the empty place beside him. It was where Guy's "corpse bride" used to sit; the spot saved for the murdered Banquo; Guy's soul in thirty years' time when he still hadn't settled down; the place where women's hopes came to die. At each of

Liam's salvos, Guy fired off scathing comebacks that sent the room into gales of laughter. The two friends fed on one another's antagonism and nastiness like cannibalistic piranhas. If I'd had to guess who would win in a gladiatorial fight, I'd have said Liam. But in a battle of wits, Guy would probably steal the prize.

After dinner, some of us would loll on the terrace overlooking the ocean, watching the early fishing boats emerge or the occasional cruise ship sail by. Guy and Liam usually had nightcaps, often joined by Bryn and Federico—who held off from drinking as long as a chess game was in the offing. If it was a chess night, Liam and Federico faced off sober, Guy doing his best to distract Liam so he got dusted by his master. I sketched faces, hands, postures, and gestures, as studies for sculptures and paintings. Guy's was a particularly pleasing sketch to execute, since his chiseled features cut like knives and his mobile lips presented a challenge to capture.

At night, Guy always played DJ, using the smart speakers and his phone. He never featured the same style of music twice on any given evening, and even the pieces he cued up were anything but standard for their genre. Patti Labelle, Nat "King" Cole, Albert Ammonds, Franz Schubert, Alicia Keys, Ritchie Valenz, Santana, Chris Stapleton, and Snoop Dogg had been the order of tonight's artists so far. But it was the tip of the iceberg of Guy's 800,000 tracks in fifty-two different genres.

"What's the news on Gretchen and Katrina?" Bryn swirled his snifter of cognac.

Liam leaned back in his chair, closing his eyes. "Ralph hoped to spot a pattern in the times they're let out of the compound, but it seems to be completely random. So nabbing them while they're walking isn't an option. Ralph and two other PIs, Claude and Rodrigo, attempted overt entry to the compound by claiming they wanted to join the cult. Apparently, they didn't do a convincing enough job, and were turned away by some of the leader's underlings. Then the three of them tried to bribe various guards. When that didn't work, they tried to create a distraction. The guards freaked out and drew guns in a way that suggested they were untrained in the use of weapons. Dangerous and sloppy."

"So what's the next strategy?" asked Connie.

Liam shrugged. "Posing as FBI agents with a fake search warrant and coming armed to the gills, with bulletproof vests, ready for a showdown. I'll join in." He said all this as though he were going on a trout fishing excursion.

"When are you leaving?" I asked.

He opened one eye, regarding me with amusement. "Are you eager to see me go?"

In truth, I dreaded his absence more than I'd admit.

"Fear not. I'll take care of anything she needs." Guy drained his glass of Scotch, clearly hoping to get a rise out of Liam.

Liam's voice was taut as a drum. "I'll take you with me, Guy. We may need your services if we get hauled into the clink."

"Let me come," I said. "I can talk to Gretchen and Katrina as one of their sex. I may be able to persuade them to come willingly."

Guy nodded. "Wisdom crieth without; she uttereth her voice in the streets. You should heed her, my friend."

Liam closed his eyes again, speaking in a low voice that brooked no dissent. "My woman doesn't belong anywhere near gunfire."

That night, like every night, Liam ripped off all my clothes before we even entered our room, crowding me against the wall and yoking his hips with my thighs, making me feel as if the greatest purpose in life was to be fucked by him—to please him and be pleasured.

Chapter Sixteen

Liam

Rory would arrive tomorrow evening around 8 on a boat from Fiji. I had Ingrid pleasantly ensconced in a series of rooms in the northern outbuilding, stationing two hefty security guards outside her corridor and porch—the only exits. I planned to visit her sporadically to make sure she wanted for nothing—and to enjoy her.

To render her pliant, I had denied her sex for two days. My plan worked in spades. This evening, when I went in to visit her, she dropped to her knees and unbuckled my shorts, looking up at me reverently as she wrapped her delicate fingers around my cock. Her lips were ripe cherries, her eyes lust-clouded ponds. The sight of her tongue swirling my crown, her sweet mouth kissing my tip and licking the pre-cum off my head, made me dizzy. After a lazy suck that took in half of me, she withdrew, making me gasp for her warmth again. Running her tongue along the veiny underside of my cock, she hollowed out her cheeks, creating a tight, narrow channel that swallowed me whole.

As my dick met the back of her throat, I groaned, taking hold of her head. "Oh, baby. That feels incredible. Keep going."

She glided her tongue back and forth along my

base as she sucked upwards, shifting me into the pocket of her cheek. I was spellbound by the sight of her going to work. She fell into a rhythm, pumping in and out as she alternately massaged my balls and pressed her finger in my anus, stimulating my prostate.

"Oh, fuck yeah, Ingrid."

I began to help things along, thrusting at full tilt into her as she held steady and took my brutal jabs that went deep. The more tears ran down her cheeks and the more desperate her choking sounds, the more my dick swelled. It was fucking bliss to hit the back of her throat and feel it reject me. My hips jerked from side to side, and I pulled out to the edge. "Baby, I'm going to come in your mouth, and I want you to hold it for ten counts before swallowing."

She gave a brief nod, blinking slowly. What a beautiful, obedient little sex kitten. She existed to cater to my wishes, and I was king of the world. I stabbed into her, hitting the back of her throat and juddering as I exploded. *Fuck*, that was cathartic. Watching her, I slowly pulled back, counting down aloud from ten. She held on, sliding my come across her palate. At *one*, she swallowed, making my essence a part of her.

I flopped down on the mattress, heaving a sigh of contentment. She draped her luscious body over me, fitting her head into the groove between my chin and chest.

I stroked her soft hair. "You missed me."

She nodded, her tone dreamy. "Very much. You won't stay away so long again, will you?"

"Not if you behave." I trailed my index finger down her belly toward her opening. She squirmed, making little purring sounds. "Rory comes tomorrow evening. I'll come see you after he's arrived, if you don't make a sound."

"I won't."

I cupped her pussy. "You stayed naked for me all afternoon?"

"Yes."

I slicked my middle finger with her juices. "Good girl. You must be hungry for me then."

Her throat bobbed.

Suddenly I was ravenous for her pussy. I dropped kisses along her neck to her shoulder and licked my way to her nipple. Suckling it, I bit down, tugging and elongating it until she squealed. Then I grazed it with my finger, eliciting her moans. I repeated this on the other nipple, in reverse order. She arched her chest under my mouth, placing her hands on my shoulders and giving a little push.

I chuckled. "All in good time, Ingrid."

Feathering her belly with my lips, I breathed hot air along her skin, my hands parting her thighs. I proceeded to give her the slowest, most teasing oral I'd ever given. I savored her like a smorgasbord of delicacies.

"Oh, Liam! Liam, *please*! I want more! Now! Please. I need you so much."

The more desperately she cried out and begged for it, the more leisurely I went along, breaking one rhythm or pattern to switch it up and start a new one. Sometimes I'd insert two fingers while sucking her clit. Sometimes I'd alternate thrusting in my tongue and flicking her clit with my tongue's tip. Other times I'd bat her clit with my finger, swirl it with my tongue, and drill deep into her while brushing her clit with my thumb. Her hips jumped, gyrated, and juddered. She was so crazed and bothered by the end, that her body was like a swarming hornet's nest.

My tongue was deeply embedded within her while my thumb swirled her sensitive nub. She squeezed me, spasming as she let out a long and loud scream. I leaned over and kissed her with her nectar still dripping from my lips. Blushing like a rosebud in May, with beads of sweat dewing her brow, she was hands down the most beautiful creature I'd ever seen. My engorged cock strained against her soft belly.

I flipped her onto her side, scissoring her legs and encircling her waist and shoulders as I sank my girth into her pussy from behind. We rocked and ground our hips together as I stroked her, splaying my hands all over her breasts, belly, and hips. As her croaks became cries, I pulled out, paused, and rammed in deep, bringing us both over the edge. I felt as if I'd passed out, it was such an intense release.

"Will you stay with me tonight?" she asked in a small, breathless voice.

"Not tonight." Discipline required that I keep my distance. She needed to long for me and feel in her bones that I was her master. There would be time enough, after Rory had left, to enjoy my tamed bird. I lifted her chin with my middle finger. "Tomorrow evening, as soon as you've finished your dinner, I want you to strip and kneel on all fours with your ass facing the door. Wait in that position for me until I come."

"Yes, Liam."

Her meekness aroused me again, and I slapped her ass. "Let's practice."

****

Knowing Rory was going to be here in an hour made me unexpectedly nervous. The last time I'd seen him had been awkward as hell. It was about a year ago at a charity event for crumbling Bronx public schools that needed an infusion of cash. If I'd known he was going to be there, I probably wouldn't have gone. Some director of education thought it'd be funny to bring Rory and me together and remind us we're brothers. He'd practically clasped our hands together like a priest at a wedding ceremony.

I suspected Rory was envious of me for my billions, amassed so quickly and effortlessly. But I knew that since I'd picked off Ned Raymond—my first illegal kill, accomplished two months after leaving the service—he'd suspected me of murder. He knew how much I hated that cocksucker and sought vengeance. For some reason, Rory never felt the same way about the guy who framed our father. I always thought it was ironic how I had gone into the military to be above and beyond the law, while Rory had become an assistant district attorney to enforce the law. *My* choice was a reaction against Ned Raymond. Rory's was a reaction against me.

I paced around the living room glancing out at the nearly-full moon, which reminded me that it'd been a month since we'd arrived on the island.

From his armchair by the open sliding doors that led to the porch, Guy tsked. "Pacing is one step away from wringing your hands and wailing for your demon lover. It's getting more and more like an Edward Gorey illustration here by the minute. Have some brandy to take off the edge." He lifted his snifter by way of example.

"How you still have a working liver is anyone's guess." I raked a hand through my hair, still stalking without purpose.

"Over the years I've seasoned it like a well-tenderized piece of meat." He swirled the liquor in his glass. "Which unnerves you more? The prospect of getting caught for one or more of the killings, or the prospect of losing Ingrid?"

"Neither," I snapped. Though, if I were honest, I'd have to answer at this point, *losing Ingrid.* "He's bluffing. Rory doesn't have anything on me."

"If you're so sure of that, why'd you let him come?" Guy tilted the glass to his lips.

"Why do you think? To show him I don't give a damn about his antics. To disarm him." I made my way to the bar, pouring a glass of Scotch and downing it in two gulps. It burned like hell. Pain was just what I needed right then. "Think about the choreography of all this. *He's* coming to me. If he really had something, he'd make *me* come to him."

"Can you be trusted not to say anything incriminating?" Guy steepled his fingers, resting his elbows on the armrests. "Because I wouldn't characterize your current state of mind as sang-froid, exactly."

"Maybe I ought to have Sione strip-search him when he arrives. Check for wires." I poured more Scotch, taking it across to the chair beside Guy. A former pro wrestler, Sione was one of the six-foot-six Tongan security guards currently watching over Ingrid.

"No, old man. Assume he's wired and be on your best behavior. Not that any of that sort of evidence would be admissible in court. But it might convince an

FBI agent to take on the case and dig for more." Guy looked out at the black ocean. "Are they using the northern or southern docks?"

"I told him to come to the southern one, since it's more brightly lit." My mind was only half on Guy's words.

"Then I believe we have a guest—guests?"

I sprang up, adrenaline surging through me. "Let's go."

Guy examined his well-manicured fingernails. "It's so very bourgeois to dispense with a butler, my dear man."

I grabbed his arm. "While you debate the pros and cons of the Russian Revolution, our guest is waiting. Come on."

We strode—well, I strode, Guy sauntered—toward the dock, which shone with several bright white lights. As we approached, I stopped dead in my tracks. Three people climbed off the boat. Rory, I recognized. The third figure was the Fijian captain.

But the middle figure took me completely off guard.

Chapter Seventeen

Guy

Since Liam's jaw had plummeted somewhere beneath the earth's crust, rendering him momentarily incapable of shaping words, I stepped forward to do the honors. Granted, my own composure was somewhat shaken by this vision of loveliness. But I'd been trained in tough schools.

"I wasn't aware that the price of a plane ticket included a princess," I opened, bowing slightly. I took the lovely's hand, kissing the back of it. Her pearly teeth glowed in the marina lights as she flashed me a dazzling smile. "The airlines must be improving their services."

She cocked her head, drinking me in through lush, curly eyelashes that gave mine a run for their money. "I thought this place wasn't for real. Now I'm beginning to wonder about the people too."

I liked her wit. This didn't bode well. Nothing was so dangerous as a witty, beautiful woman with charm enough to slay the Queen.

"You echo my thoughts exactly," I said, without releasing her hand.

A pretty flush suffused her cheeks. "I see old-world courtesy is making a comeback."

"If it pleases you, it's worth resurrecting." My eyes

lingered in the depths of hers.

Rory broke in on our enchanting tête-à-tête. "Guy, I see you're still fond of the ladies."

"One lady holds my interest."

The enchantress giggled. "At least we know where you stand."

Liam finally levered his jaw back in place. "Why doesn't everyone come inside?" He slapped a hundred-dollar bill in the captain's palm. "If you wouldn't mind taking these two bags, I'll get the others."

I tutted as we advanced, two by two, toward the house, with the captain trailing behind. "Once again, dear boy, the lack of lackeys is telling." I turned to the princess. "He has his servants eat at the table with everyone else. As if we were in a nineteenth-century Bowery boardinghouse."

Her perfectly arched eyebrows lifted. "That's very democratic and commendable."

"I'm of the opinion that servants prefer to respect their employers. If everyone's a guest, what's special about being a guest?"

She nodded. "There is something to that. Value lies in rarity."

"Rarity isn't something a woman like you needs to worry about."

She let out a chuff of laughter. "And yet, it's all a matter of perspective, isn't it?"

"Elaborate, princess."

She shrugged. "One person's glass bead is another person's gold nugget."

"A striking New World analogy."

"That's right, you're of the old world, aren't you?" she teased.

I was smitten.

Apparently one of the servants had gotten wind of the arrival of guests and decided to do his job, sallying forth to help the captain and Liam with the bags. After directing them where to go, Liam turned back to us.

"Introductions are in order, I believe." He shot Rory a pointed look. "Andrea, I've admired your picture. I'm Liam. This is Guy."

"Where's Ingrid?" Andrea withheld her hand from Liam's.

I coughed.

Liam turned beet red.

Rory rocked on his heels, a grin curving his lips. "A veritable truth serum. Pun intended."

"She's...in the other part of the house." Liam rubbed behind his ear. He wasn't prepared for this line of attack.

"Can I see her?" Andrea squared her shoulders.

Liam put his hands in his pockets. "Maybe tomorrow."

"What's wrong with now?" Her eyes blazed as fiercely as an Amazon warrior's.

I could've told her that my good friend didn't like to be destabilized—didn't like to have anything chip away at his absolute control.

"She'll see you tomorrow, Andrea," Liam spoke with more assurance than I could've mustered in the face of such spirit.

Andrea turned to me. "Is she all right?"

I gave her an encouraging half-smile. "We've been singing to Simon and Garfunkel beneath the Southern Cross."

She tilted her head. "If that's code for something,

you'd better spill."

Liam chuckled. "Guy means he's a good DJ. You'll see the Southern Cross constellation from your bedroom."

Andrea gave a low whistle. "And here I thought we were discussing Ingrid. Liam, you'd better have her safe, sound, and happy, or I'll fry your genitals for breakfast."

"Nice to know what would be on the menu if I hadn't been decent to her," he quipped.

She narrowed her eyes. "Just know I'm watching you, moneybags." She was struck by something. "She isn't doped, is she? You're not going to try to sober her up?"

Liam turned to me. "Guy, reassure her. You're the one with the voluble tongue."

"This is a drug-free zone, princess. Excepting booze, of course."

Rory waltzed over to the bar and helped himself to some cognac. "Speaking of which, I could do with a little wetting of my whistle. Andrea, care for something?"

Liam took the cognac bottle out of his brother's hand, fixing him with a stare worthy of a twelve-year-old boy snatching back his BB Gun. "I'll do the honors. You both take a seat."

I loosened my collar. "Is it just me, or is it hot in here?"

When we'd all taken seats, drinks in hand, Andrea said, "Just so you know, Liam, not only the D.A.'s office in New York but the Fijian police know our whereabouts."

Liam spluttered as his drink went down his

windpipe. "Ah, good to know that."

"And Rory has thoroughly briefed me for when I see Ingrid." Andrea knocked back a hefty gulp of cognac.

Liam started like a colt. "What's that supposed to mean?"

She tilted her chin up. "Wouldn't you like to know."

He squinted. "As a matter of fact, I would. After all, you haven't seen her *yet*."

You're a ballsier man than I am, Gunga Din.

"What I believe Liam is trying to say," I began, "is that while of course, we're all friends, there's no denying a certain undercurrent of hostility. Thus the need for some of us to be on the defensive."

Rory chuckled. "Guy Travis, ever the suave spokesman of criminals."

"It's worth bearing in mind, Counselor Stauner, that everyone has a constitutional right to a fair trial." I sipped my cognac.

Rory sat back, comfortably crossing an ankle over a knee. "Let's begin that trial right now, shall we?"

Liam's nostrils pulsated. "Who would we try first?"

Rory angled his head to the side. "I don't know, brother. Maybe the man who's committed between five and ten murders, depending on whom you ask? Maybe the man who can be charged with conspiracy to commit murder in all those cases? Maybe the man who kidnapped a woman and is holding her captive on his private island? Maybe the man who keeps illegal weapons in his own personal arsenal? That man might be a good place to start."

Liam threw back his whisky. "If only I believed you really sought justice, Rory. You have an agenda just like all the rest of them. And the wheels of your justice are rusty, crooked, and falling off their axles. How far would you go to bring me down, I wonder? After all, you've dedicated the better part of your adult life to this cause. Some people would question your sanity."

Rory snorted. "Cynics and criminals always resort to the same two arguments. First, they claim that because the system is flawed, it's no good. A fallacy that holds no weight, since we see that anarchy results as soon as we remove the system altogether. Second, they claim that because the judge and jury are human and fallible, they're not fit to condemn anyone. Then who is fit? Vigilantes? Spare me your self-appointed legal authorities."

"Who appointed *you* judge, jury, and executioner, Rory?" Liam demanded. "I don't see your warrants. I don't see any evidence. And I certainly don't see a badge."

"Tut, tut, brother. The evidence, as you said earlier, is, quote, 'in the other part of the house.' And thereby hangs a tale." Rory swallowed a draft of cognac.

"And what is that supposed to mean?" Liam's brows drew down to a point.

"Make of it what you will." Rory jiggled his foot.

Liam stood. "I don't think either of you realizes just what tenuous ground you're on. I've let you on my private property. But I can just as easily escort you *off* that property. So I suggest you play nice. I won't be threatened or coerced by anyone. Now, I'm not feeling as charitable as I was earlier." He turned to Andrea.

"Ingrid may not appear tomorrow. Or the next day. She won't appear until you both play nice. And even then, it may be under my supervision." He clapped, calling out. Surprisingly, for once, the servant came. "Seru, show Andrea and Rory to their rooms."

I rose, placing a hand of comfort on Andrea's lower back. "Fear not, princess. All will be well tomorrow. Poke the lion and expect a roar. If you need anything during the night—anything at all—I'm in the next corridor over."

She moved toward the door, her eyes shooting daggers at Liam. "As ye sow, so shall ye reap, Liam."

Chapter Eighteen

Ingrid

It was late when Liam came in. As I heard the door slide open, I scurried into the position he'd commanded.

Flicking on the low lamp, he groaned. "Such beauty. Such submission. Such sweetness."

His nearness lit bonfires within me, and his voice made me melt. When Liam was in the room, the world looked different—like the technicolor version of an old black-and-white film. Hearing the swish of fabric, I swiveled my head. He was on his knees surveying my ass, his palms hovering over my butt cheeks. I faced forward again, expecting him to cup them.

Instead, he gave my right cheek a sharp whack. I flinched, whimpering. He thwacked it again, four more times. Tears bathed my cheeks to the sound of my moans. After leaving a few seconds of zinging pain, he rubbed out the sting. My pussy leaked arousal. He was the conqueror of all my senses, the giver of pleasure and pain. His power gave meaning to everything.

He whopped my left cheek six times rapidly, before palming it as though applying salve. He slicked his fingers in my channel, grunting his satisfaction at my wetness.

An angry energy zapped from him, and each of his

movements had a sharpness more intense than his usual controlled precision.

"Is everything all right, Liam?"

Pressing me down onto my chest, my ass still up in the air, he slid into me, slowly stroking my pussy.

"It is now," he murmured, continuing steady and gentle.

"What happened? Was it Rory?"

He sped up his pace, pounding me with his usual relentlessness. God, he felt good, filling me and bringing me friction, his balls slapping at my divide. "Yes, Rory."

When he reached around my hip to press my clit, I detonated, howling into the duvet. I took him with me, his groans scoring his own explosion. He crumpled on top of me so that we were one heap of sweat, flesh, and warmth.

We breathed a space.

"Ingrid."

"Hmm?"

"Am I a monster?"

I had to think about that one. "Sometimes. But you're not a perpetual monster, no. Not an *essential* monster. You just have monster moments."

"And do the non-monster moments redeem the monster ones, in your view?"

Again, I quieted. "I don't think the monster moments need redeeming."

He kissed along my cheek toward my mouth, rolling us so we faced each other on our sides. He took my mouth in the sweetest, most tender kiss he'd ever given me. It was soft, warm, and slow, and it breathed hope. He caressed my cheeks, ears, and neck, brushing his knuckles against my temple.

"If you were given the chance to leave me, would you, my little witness?"

I gazed into his emerald eyes that cut like diamonds. "I don't think I could," I confessed, tearing up at the very thought. My voice wobbled and my lips quivered. "Could you send me away?"

He shook his head without hesitation. "No, my little rose. I'm bound to you for as long as you're bound to me."

I thought about that. He meant either that as long as I didn't bail he wouldn't bail, or that we were bound to each other for as long as we were bound to anything. There was something fragile about the statement either way—as if he didn't dare commit beyond the here and now.

"What if I remain bound to you forever?" I suggested.

He slid our hands so we palmed each other. "Then I'll be bound to you forever."

We watched our hands move together in small arcs between our bodies.

"Would you rather be imprisoned by me or free without me?" he asked.

"Imprisoned by you," I said, unwavering. Suddenly I was sure, and the words felt right.

"What if the world wants to set you free?" He laced our fingers together.

"You're the world. If you don't want to set me free, then I don't want to be set free."

"What makes me the world, Ingrid?"

"Because you're Liam. I'm yours."

He traced my eyebrows. "Then I put the choice to

you, my little crow feather. Would you like me to set you free tomorrow so you can choose whether I really am the world? Other people are going to try to convince you to escape your captivity and fly into the wild again."

"You're not afraid that if I speak, you'll be captured?"

He shook his head. "I'm bound to you, remember? For as long as you're bound to me. I'm already captive to you. So why would I fear being captured?"

Tears rolled down my cheeks, soaking the pillow. "I choose to convince them that you *are* the world. And after I have, I'll come back to live in captivity with you."

****

He stayed with me that night. Each time I thought he had fallen asleep, he'd turn in a different position, adjust the pillow, or breathe in an irregular way that told me he'd not yet found slumber.

I couldn't drop off either. Why was he letting me out of my confinement? As long as I belonged to him, had given my freedom to him, my life was simple, rounded off, complete.

He was giving me this choice for one of two reasons. Either he was no longer obsessed with me, or he trusted me at last. But he only gave me the choice after I'd said that he was the world to me and that I was his. So that must mean he trusted me not only as his witness but as his captive. He might still be obsessed. *For as long as you're bound to me, I'm bound to you.* He wasn't afraid I'd tell the authorities what I'd seen. Did this mean he didn't fear the consequences of his arrest? Or he didn't think he would be turned in?

I suspected he didn't know the answers to these questions any more than I. It was as if we'd both been through an earthquake and were still assessing the damages.

At some point we must've drifted off, because daylight bathed the room, and Liam's back gently heaved, his steady breaths and relaxed limbs suggesting he was deep in a dreamless sleep. Not wishing to disturb him, I slipped out of bed and donned my workout clothes. Today was our gym day. I was excited to lift weights in the sunny room where the ocean breezes wafted through from one side, and the tropical forest scents blew in from the other. Thinking I would ask Waisake or Tima to make me a cup of coffee, I slid open the door that led to the corridor.

Mafu, one of the Tongan security guards, stirred on his mat on the floor. "Good morning, Miss," he mumbled. "Is Mr. Stauner still in there?"

"Yes," I said. "I was just going to get coffee in the kitchen."

He scrambled to his feet. "I can't let you go without Mr. Stauner's permission, Miss."

"I don't want to wake him yet, Mafu."

He shook his head. "It's my orders, Miss."

"You have my word, Mafu. He said I could go."

"Let her go," said a woman's voice from down the corridor.

Turning, I blinked to find Andrea, of all people, dressed as if she was ready for island action. Her hair was pulled back in a clip, her bright yellow tee-shirt and lime-green shorts lighting up the hallway. Her eyes blazed, and her expression was determined. She was gorgeous and bursting with life—but how in the world was she here?

"Drea!" I rushed to hug her, but Mafu inserted himself between us.

"No visitors until Mr. Stauner allows it." He placidly held out a sturdy arm to block Andrea from advancing.

Andrea scoffed. "Is Mr. Stauner God now?"

Liam's gritty voice sounded behind me. "You'd do well to remember it, Andrea."

His warm, solid arm slunk around my waist, reminding me that I was caught between two realities. One in which Liam was indeed God. The other in which he was an offender. But I knew which reality I wanted to be a part of for good.

Andrea crossed her arms over her chest. "Cut the arrogant crap, Liam. If you were God, you wouldn't be afraid of letting Ingrid out of her gilded cage."

"She's free to go," he said to Mafu, without, however, easing his hold on me. He murmured in my ear, "You remember everything we said. Our fates are inextricably bound together. I won't let you go if you don't let me go."

I tilted my face up to see his sparkling eyes, nuzzling my cheek against the stubble of his chin. "Never."

How could I when he had become everything to me?

Chapter Nineteen

Ingrid

Andrea and I strolled along a dirt path that had been formed by thousands of island visitors over the years. It paralleled the strand before cutting inland and winding up over a series of hills. I had never explored this path beyond the palm grove, since Liam and I rode our bikes on the paved roads. Sometimes a lush canopy of trees covered us and other times we were completely exposed. The roar of the ocean waves retreated to a murmur as we began to cut our way up a slope through a forest of palms, hibiscus, eucalyptus, and papaya trees.

"What is that flower we keep seeing?" Andrea stopped, indicating a splash of fuchsia growing on reedy spindles.

"Liam says it's a bamboo orchid."

"It's exquisite." She fingered the delicate petals. "I can't believe the beauty of this place."

"I know. Wait'll you see some of the inlets, the exotic fish, and the ripe fruits. Oh, and the Japanese garden! I've got to show you that when we get home."

She swamped me in a hug. "Sweetie, you just called it 'home.'"

It felt so good to be in Andrea's arms. "It is home now."

She disconnected us, searching my eyes for a long moment. "You love him, don't you?"

I blushed by way of an answer. I knew it didn't look good for me to have fallen for Liam.

"But, hon, he's a contract hitman who kidnapped you."

"The man he killed abused his wife. He had lots of enemies who probably would've done it if Liam hadn't."

Andrea shook her head. "No, Ingrid. He's killed anywhere between five and ten men. Rory will show you the pictures and police reports. He has an arsenal filled with illegal weapons. And he took you away, *against your will*."

"Ten men?" Suddenly I lost my breath and strength, sitting down on a rock. Had Liam lied when he said that was his only killing? Suddenly it made more sense why he'd huddled me away all this time.

Andrea took a seat on a rock next to me. "That's right. Over a two-year period. That's three to five murders a year. Liam is a professional, and the mob bosses who hired him knew he could deliver."

I swallowed. "Mob bosses?"

She nodded. "Rory said he started his killing career by murdering a cop."

"Ned Raymond?" I remembered Liam's story from a few weeks ago.

Andrea tucked a leg under her. "I don't know his name, but Liam had it in for him since he was young. Something to do with Liam and Rory's father going to prison."

"That's the man. But he framed Liam's father, indirectly causing his death and directly causing his family to break up." My voice shook, I was so keen to justify Liam's action.

She regarded me intently. "He's a serial murderer, Ingrid. And he's good at it."

"No." Tears sprang to my eyes. "If it's true, there must've been good reasons for him to kill those other men."

She placed a hand on my arm. "Honey, you've heard of Stockholm Syndrome?"

"Of course." I'd often thought about it while on the island. "But my feelings for Liam aren't a coping mechanism in response to my captivity."

Andrea looked doubtful. "No? Because the fact that you kept this whole situation a secret from me suggests you thought I'd frown upon it. And I do."

"Liam knew you're like a sister to me and that I couldn't hide anything from you."

She grew angry. "See, that's just fucked up. He's been censoring your texts and calls—and probably your emails, am I right?"

I nodded. "But there's a reason for that."

"You mean a reason beyond the fact that he's a criminal and a possessive prick?" she snapped.

Even hearing her call him that made my pussy pulsate. "I guess I like his possessiveness—and his prickishness. But yes, there is another reason."

She waited expectantly.

"I can't tell you, D."

"Rory said there must be some reason beyond sex that he brought you to the island. You can tell me, sweetie." Her tone became gentle and soothing.

"But you'll tell Rory." I gazed at the azure sea through the pines. "No, I can't share it with anyone, not even you. He might get put away. His brother is out for blood."

"Rory's a good man, Ingrid. Liam's the one who sheds blood."

"He did in the past. He doesn't anymore." I spoke with more conviction than I felt.

"How do you know?"

I didn't know, but I made up a good reason. "He's earned billions from trading. He doesn't need to kill for hire." But I made a private note to ask Liam why he lied to me, why he was a hitman, and when he'd done his last job. Did he kill only bad men who had themselves committed heinous crimes?

Andrea read my questions in my face. "Do you really trust him to tell you the truth when you do ask him, Ingrid? He's got to be an expert liar, with his past. In order to get away with multiple murders, he has to be strategic and cunning."

"In not telling me anything, he said he was trying to protect me." Even as I said it, I realized my defense of Liam sounded flimsy.

"Yeah, that right there says a lot." Andrea looked up as a small bird with a striking robin-blue neck fluttered past and up onto a branch. "Protecting you from whom? The mob maybe? Family and friends of the men he killed?"

I threw up my hands in frustration. "Oh, D, does it really matter what's in his past? He's a good man. He did two tours in the Marines and became a captain. He pulled himself out of a tough childhood to get to where he is now. He's a great employer—his people love him. He's not just sitting back and enjoying his wealth—he has meaningful aspirations. He's been looking for his sister and niece for twelve years and he's about to go in and rescue them from a cult compound—" I clapped a hand over my mouth, flushing. "*Please* don't say anything about that to Rory, Drea."

She reached over, squeezing my hand. "Don't worry, Ingrid. I'm not here to talk about Liam's future crimes—only his past and present ones. Which brings us back to why you're here."

"Can we walk again?" I stood, needing to get some oxygen to my brain.

She sprang up, and our steps fell into rhythm. "So we've established that he brought you here against your will."

"I won't admit that while Rory's in the room. Wait, you're not wired, are you?" I jokingly moved to pat Andrea down, and she laughed, nudging me in the shoulder.

"What does he plan to do with you, sweetie?" She side-eyed me. "He can't keep you away from your family, friends, job, and home indefinitely."

We passed a tree that seemed to be sprouting red tulips from its leaves. I stopped to admire the luscious flowers.

"Maybe once he trusts me, we can have a normal relationship back in New York."

"So you admit you have an *abnormal* one here. That's a start." Her breath caught as we crested the hill where stunning views of the ocean opened on all sides. "Jesus, this place is *amazing*."

Our path was flanked by low-lying yellow flowers that looked like daisies. "See that craggy outcrop down there? That's Liam's and my cove. It's my favorite place to swim and collect shells. You and I can ride there tomorrow."

She smiled affectionately. "You really love it here, don't you?"

"Who wouldn't? And Liam has been nothing but thoughtful and generous." I blushed.

Her smile grew sly. "Hmm. I take it the sex is hot."

"God, Drea. I never thought it could be this good. I've become an addict." Even thinking of last night had my thighs tingling and the back of my neck prickling.

"You're not worried you're thinking with your pussy? Maybe it's lust—not love?" She dipped her head at me.

"Last night when we were baring our souls, I realized I never want to spend one day away from Liam. I love him, D. I can't imagine life without him."

She spoke softly. "But you haven't really spent time with him off his island, honey. Of course he's going to look good in paradise—in his own paradise. But what about in the real world? What if you find out he really is the psychotic, obsessive control freak he looks like from Rory's and my perspective? This could be just infatuation. Sorry, I have to play devil's advocate."

"He's *my* psychotic, obsessive control freak." I grew wet just thinking of those aspects of Liam. "As long as the law doesn't catch up with him, I don't mind."

We were meandering south along a ridge that was still largely exposed.

Andrea grew grave. "Of course, the bottom line is your long-term happiness, Ingrid. But I wonder if you can be happy with someone who's never paid the price for his crimes and who doesn't allow you complete freedom."

"I believe—I hope—we can come to an understanding about my freedom. A compromise that lets him be possessive without being too overbearing. A life arrangement akin to having a safe word." I kicked a dense pine cone so it skittered along into the brush.

"And you're not afraid he's just using you for sex? What are his feelings for you?"

I looked down at the wispy grasses blowing in the breeze beside the path. "I don't know. I think he trusts me more now. I know he's obsessed with keeping me close. He does a lot of little things that show how much he thinks of *me*. Like when he housed me in the outbuilding the last few days, he had Tima and Waisake make all my favorite breakfast and dinner items specially. He remembered what they were, and he brought them to me himself. He genuinely enjoys taking care of me." I chose not to mention his aftercare rituals after especially rough sex. "When I fell from my bike last week, he dressed all my wounds with the skill of an army medic. And he set me up in the studio and had a boatload of art supplies delivered the first week I was here. But above all, he listens to me and responds to what I say with an intensity I've never known. I can't believe that someone with that kind of laser focus would be anything less than committed to a person he spends so much time with. Liam's a man of extremes. There's nothing lukewarm about him."

Andrea expelled a long breath. "So you feel there's something intrinsic about you, *Ingrid Pellerin*, that captivates him above all other women. That it wasn't simply that circumstance threw you in his way—and that you guys have incredible sex."

She had homed in on my main insecurity. "Honestly, I don't know, D. I guess that is something that being out in the real world would tell me. But just as he's intense, he's observant. I'm sure he hasn't missed any of the honest qualities I've shown him. He knows I work hard, exercise hard, love my art, love people, and try to be kind."

She looked thoughtful. "That's not too shabby a foundation for love." She turned to me. "But if he really loved you, he would've let you see me."

"He did. Last night he gave me the choice of coming out today." I didn't mention that he hadn't told me about Andrea's arrival.

Her lips set in a grim line. "He may have done that under duress. We did pressure him last night."

I shrugged. "It still cost him a lot to do it, I know. That's what counts."

Andrea laughed. "You'd fight to the death for this man, Ingrid."

"He's worth fighting for," I maintained.

We started trekking down the path that I hoped would bring us back out onto the dirt road that skirted the paved one.

"Don't you miss New York?" Andrea asked.

I picked a pretty blue periwinkle and twirled it in my hand. "Surprisingly, not really. I like working remotely—not having to deal with the office intrigues of Simon, Liz, Asher, and Renée. The island has everything I want. Except you, Dad, Mom, and a few other friends."

"What about cinema, live shows, bars, *people*?" Andrea suggested.

"We're fitting out Liam's movie room. You've

probably seen the ocean-facing terrace. The staff converts it into a dance floor, game area, and bar every night. And the Verau community—small as it is and centered around this house—is wonderful. Liam involves the servants in everything and pays them handsomely, so of course they show him loyalty." I cast her a sidelong glance. "Have I convinced you yet?"

Her eyes twinkled. "Convinced me that…?"

"That life is good here, that I'm happy, that Liam is special, and that your Stockholm Syndrome theory is wide of the mark?"

She bumped shoulders with me. "You'd make a damn good saleswoman, Ingrid."

Chapter Twenty

Liam

Talking to Rory over breakfast confirmed that he had only a bunch of weak circumstantial evidence and hearsay about my killings. Stuff like the testimony of a convicted mobster who'd seen me getting paid by a boss for one of my jobs. Or the fact that Rory could trace the sniper bullets used in five of my murders to the same rifle, and that I'd been photographed at a shooting range using the same type of weapon. Or that an ex-con remembered hearing a phone conversation where my name was mentioned in connection with a job. Rory was clearly grasping at straws by using my kidnapping of Ingrid to get at me.

But I didn't like the whiff of desperation that emanated from my brother. Being an obsessive type myself, I recognized the quality in others. Rory was obsessed with putting me behind bars. Look what *my* obsession had made *me* do: hunt down and kill the cop who caused my father's death; meticulously research and brutally execute the murder of eight other men; and steal Ingrid away and keep her hostage.

Rory's voice cut into my thoughts. "Ingrid, where were you on the afternoon of August 30, 2018?" His tone was casual and smooth as caramel.

Ingrid was like a deer in headlights. Her hand shot

to her mouth, her eyes bugged out, and she gasped, dropping her fork with a clatter. Silence spread over the table like thick fog. It couldn't have been clearer that she knew something.

Had she said anything to her friend, and had Andrea spilled the beans to Rory?

"Hmm? I can see that date definitely rings a bell with you." He examined her shrewdly. "What happened?"

"N-nothing. That is, I don't remember. I'd have to look in my journal." She clasped her trembling hands together under the table. I covered them with my hand, choosing to believe the best of Ingrid rather than the worst. Her reaction suggested Rory's questions were coming out of left field.

"Where is your journal?" Rory sipped his coffee.

Ingrid's eyes darted to mine. "I don't know."

Ingrid knew I'd impounded the journal, locking it in a safe here in the house.

Rory's eyes jumped between us. "Mmm-hmm. Fascinating."

"Brother," I sneered, "if this is your normal mode of cross-examination, you should request a refund for your three years at Harvard Law."

"Ingrid, I'm sure you're familiar with the expression 'murder will out.'" Rory tapped his index finger on the table. "My brother knows the saying well. So well that he's tied up all the loose ends he can to make sure it never applies to him. Some of his knots, however, are a little sloppy. If you're a sloppy knot, Ingrid, the time to do something about it is now. Because no murderer can sleep easily while his loose ends remain alive to tell a tale."

Blenching, Ingrid gulped and looked down at her plate.

"The law will protect you, Ingrid. If you saw something in Princeton that day, unburden yourself to me or a member of law enforcement. Not only will we work swiftly to bring my brother to justice, but we'll protect you in the process." He pushed his glasses up his nose, screwing his focus to her eyes. "But you need to act today. My brother may tell you he doesn't kill women...but there's a first for everything. I would hate for you to be that first."

I slammed a fist down, causing everything on the table to rattle. "Rory, get out of here. You're frightening my girlfriend."

The bastard ignored me, raising his eyebrows suggestively. "You're next, Ingrid. The man who's committed a number of cold-blooded murders, abducted you, amassed a stash of illegal weapons, and flown off the handle at a few innocent questions is capable of anything."

"No," Ingrid quavered. "He would never hurt me."

"How do you know?" the snake persisted.

"Because hurting me would hurt him," she said with more conviction.

"What about others?" Rory probed. "Do you want to have it on your conscience when he hurts others because you've allowed him to go free?"

"If he hurt others in the past, he's helping others now." Fearless, she met his eyes. "And it's not up to me to bring him to justice."

Bravo, my fine orator.

Rory leaned in, undaunted. "Ingrid, you may be holding out for love from my brother. You may think him capable of that emotion. But he's a ruthless, vengeful, selfish serial killer. Love requires selflessness, trust, warmth, and forgiveness. My brother has none of those qualities—nor will he ever. He's using you for his own purposes. Flip the script, Ingrid. Do it now, while you can. He has nothing on you. *You* have everything on him."

My little warrior tilted her chin up. "I'm sorry you have so little faith in your own brother. I'm confident that if he wants to change, he can. Sometimes change takes a little push from someone who believes in you. I'm happy to be that someone for Liam."

I could have wept, she was so heartfelt in her eloquence. I squeezed her hand under the table.

Rory narrowed his eyes. "Brainwashing and intimidation work wonders. If you want to have a conversation alone, Ingrid, I'm here for another three days." He slid his card across to her, for all the world as though we were in a police station.

She regarded the card as if it were a slug, leaving it on the table. "Thank you, but I have nothing further to say."

"Andrea has my contact info." Rory stood, directing one last portentous look at my girlfriend. "Remember, Ingrid, spending time in paradise can lull one into a false sense of security. It can warp our sense of time and weaken our moral fiber. What seems possible now—holidaying on this island in the lap of luxury—isn't always possible. Infatuations may fade. Relationships may not stand the test of the real world. What's certain is that the law, justice, and society await you at home, to remind you of your moral responsibility. This bubble of bliss will be broken. I'm here to prepare you for that certainty and to offer my help and protection."

I gave mock applause. "A fine peroration, counselor. At least your closing speeches partly justify your hefty law school loans. Now I suggest you scram and make the most of this 'bubble of bliss' while you can. Show us you're capable of going into vacation mode, despite all evidence to the contrary."

If I'd had any doubts earlier about Ingrid's loyalty to me, her replies to my brother dispelled them.

When Rory retired to his room, a collective sigh of relief settled over the table.

Guy opened the buttons of his jacket. "This house is rapidly becoming a nexus for mock trials. If we advertise in the *Fiji Times*, we can make a pretty penny from admission."

I poured more coffee into my cup. "Guy, you must be the only remaining soul on earth who still reads newspapers."

"Well, then, use Titter, or Instagrab...or Facedown."

Andrea snort-laughed. "Please tell me you did that on purpose."

Guy looked surprised. "Did what?"

"The porno versions of social media."

With a straight face, he said, "If I confessed I don't know the *non*-porno versions, would that disappoint you?"

She erupted in laughter. "I expected nothing less."

As he settled back in his chair, crossing his legs, I saw he was moving from clowning to playboy mode. "Then you know either the depths of my ignorance or the shallowness of my tastes."

She looked askance at him. "I suspect the shallow taste bit is a little overdone."

"But not the ignorant part?"

"No, I think you've downplayed that."

Guy's broad smile seeped across his face. "A Daniel come to judgement!"

I rose, leaving them to their foreplay-banter, and placed a hand on the small of Ingrid's back. "Come with me."

Giving a small wave to Andrea and Guy, she lit up from within at my invitation, every feature glowing and her entire body humming. Knowing I had that effect on her made my dick throb and my heart trip. I led her out to the terrace and down the stone path toward one of the Japanese rock gardens.

We strolled over the swirling river-like paths of sedimentary gravel, past triads of volcanic rocks set in Buddha formations and misshapen mountains. Here and there a red pine or Japanese maple lent muted color to the restrained landscape. At the top of one of the stone bridges, Ingrid halted.

"This is my favorite spot in all the gardens." She held out both palms. "I guess a zen believer would say there's a special energy at this point. Maybe so. I just love the views."

I brought us to a stone bench sheltered by a black pine and separated from the Japanese pagoda by a bubbling stream.

We sat in silence, taking in the peace, beauty, and harmony of the setting.

"Ingrid, I'm taking you to Suva for a day trip on Monday. Guy and Andrea will come with us, but I want us to have some time alone as well."

She dipped her chin, looking up at me through her lashes in what I recognized as her teasing vibe. "Would this be our first date?"

I laughed. "Yes. At last."

"Is there a special occasion?"

"I want to buy you a few things." I took her hand. "And for you to feel what we would be like in the real world, as a couple."

"Is this because of what Rory said at the table?"

I laced our fingers together. "Partly. But also because the arrival of Rory and Andrea reminds me that we have been locked in a bubble. And I think it's time we did something romantic."

"I find a lot of the daily things we do romantic."

I kissed her fingertips. "I'm glad. But I'm sure you'll love Fiji."

"You know, I didn't tell Andrea anything."

I smiled. "I do know. Rory figured out all those things on his own.

She hesitated, as though weighing whether to say more. "Liam?"

"Yes, sweetheart."

She swallowed, visibly gathering courage. "Why didn't you tell me about all those murders?"

I scrubbed my jaw. "I didn't want you to think ill of me."

"How many were there really?"

I mumbled, "Nine."

Her eyes widened briefly before she collected herself. "When was your last one?"

I kept my eyes trained on hers. "The one you witnessed."

"How did you happen to get into—uh, hitting?"

159

I had to be brutally honest with her now. "After I killed Ned Raymond and got away with it, word spread through mob circles that I was the person to contact for a job. Once I'd gotten a taste for planning out a kill and executing it, I found I liked it."

She shuddered. "Did you have any criteria for the jobs you accepted?"

I knew what she was asking. "Yes. I only took out people who had themselves killed others."

Her shoulders relaxed. "Oh. That's something."

I chuckled. "It was one bright spot in an otherwise dark profession."

"Do you believe in vigilantism?"

I ran my tongue over my lower lip. "Only when the law fails us."

"So you stand by your first murder."

"I do."

"Do you regret the others?"

That was an excellent question, and one I didn't have an answer to. "I don't know. I know why I did them—for the adrenaline rush, the challenge, and the feeling of power. And I can't exactly change who I was. They were all evil men without a conscience. So I don't know what regretting the jobs would mean."

She nodded. "Thank you for being honest."

I pulled her face to mine for a kiss. "It was easier than I thought it would be."

Her expression mixed flirtation with innocence. "Are you going to kill me now, Liam?"

As I bit her jaw, she squealed. "Not just yet, little crow feather."

Chapter Twenty-One

Ingrid

That night we had our first terrace party with Andrea. Rory bowed out after dinner, citing jet lag and "work-related matters" as reasons not to join us.

"Frankly," said Guy as he cued up a playlist, "holding a party with him present would be like having sex on a church pew."

"Which would make it more distasteful—the fear of getting caught or the discomfort?" Liam coiled his arm around my back as we leaned against the railing, drinks in hand.

"The nearness of the confessional," Guy drawled. "I like to keep my sinning and repenting separate."

Liam arched an eyebrow. "I wasn't aware you did any repenting."

Guy shrugged off his jacket. "Sinning in haste, I repent at great leisure. I have yet to accomplish it."

As the driving rhythms of AC/DC's "Back in Black" blared out, Andrea and I started strutting and stomping to the beats. Liam, Guy, Bryn, and Connie joined us, soon followed by Stephen, Barbara, Epeli, and the flight crew. Federico produced a cigar, lighting it on a candle in the middle of one of the tables and settling back in his chair to watch us. Eventually, Sione, Ma'afu, Waisake, Tima, Seru, and Jesse drifted onto our dance floor. The almost-full moon had reached its zenith in the sky, adding pale luminosity to the candlelight and lamps from inside the house that shone on the terrace.

"You dance like you're about to tip over at any moment!" Andrea told Guy over a guitar solo.

Indeed, Guy did have a pretty hilarious way of dancing. He clearly didn't give a damn about conventional moves, jerking and tilting on the off beats, and stumbling rather than stepping. Yet somehow his style looked like the epitome of cool.

"Help keep me upright, princess." He held out his arms to her.

She laughed, accepting his hands as The Doors' "Roadhouse Blues" came on. "Only because it's this song. I can't wait to see how you ruin it."

The howling harmonica, the clanging piano, the steady guitars, and Jim Morrison's hoarse voice swelled the scene, making everyone dip and sway in time. As I'd discovered a few weeks before during one of our first parties, Liam was a phenomenal dancer. His moves were assertive, confident, and controlled—just like him. I loved being led by him. He spun me out, whirled me back into him, rocked me snugly against his chest, and then flung me out again, his animal energy keeping us constantly joined. Dancing with him was like being bathed in liquid fire. Heat flared within me and without, revving my soul and body.

A slow song came on, Michael Jackson's "Man in the Mirror." Liam pulled me in close, as I nestled my cheek against his chest, my arms resting on his shoulders while he girded my waist. Somehow I could tell Liam was listening to the lyrics. *Make that change.*

His hand glided up my bare back, and he cupped my head, turning me so our lips joined in a downy kiss.

He whispered into my mouth, "You know it."

Little Richard's "Rip It Up" set everyone bopping, swinging, and twisting in the old rock 'n' roll dance style. Wrapped in Liam's arms, slightly buzzed and surrounded by friends and great music, I'd never been so happy. The soft night breeze fanned our cheeks, and the briny ocean scents pervaded the air.

After a few hours of dancing, many of us had grown hungry again. Anticipating this, Waisake and Tima had laid out cold cuts, cheeses, and baguettes on the table. Tima had opened various bottles of heavy Rhone reds, pouring glasses for everyone. Guy's playlist moved to jazz standards played by 1940s bebop artists like Thelonius Monk and Bud Powell.

"Mr. Stauner, I will leave Heneli, Seru, and Epeli to clean up, okay?" Tima asked.

"Yes, go to bed, Tima. You too, Waisake. Thank you both."

Guests and servants crowded around low tables on the terrace chomping into hunks of bread, meat, and cheese.

"What gets you up in the morning, enchantress?" Guy asked Andrea between bites.

Andrea and I looked at each other and burst out laughing. Guy never asked a question in a normal way. He always managed to sound leagues away from the real world. Seeing that he was extremely taken with Andrea, I'd been trying to think of ways to persuade her to stay on a little longer beyond Tuesday and encourage their connection, which seemed to go both ways. They had an undeniable spark that I suspected might lead to an explosion.

"The prospect of conversing with gifted authors, reading good work, and promoting books we've published." Andrea sipped her wine.

"And what is your greatest ambition?" Guy's eyes glowed softly in the candlelight as he stared, transfixed, at Andrea.

She blushed under his intense gaze. "You mean beyond living in Paris for a year?"

Guy chuckled. "That can be arranged."

Her eyes widened before she snapped out of it and laughed, heaping a piece of bread with slices of prosciutto. "I love writing. I wish I had the time to devote to a few projects of my own. I think I might be able to shape them into something publishable."

"What sort of projects?" He propped his chin on the crook of his thumb and forefinger.

"My grandmother's memoir, for starters. Before she died, I recorded more than twenty hours of stories and jokes she told, prompted by a series of questions I asked. She came from Marion, Alabama, marrying my dad's father and moving up to Detroit in the 1950s. She was a schoolteacher. Her maiden name was Edna Lynn Lacey."

"Edna Lynn Lacey." Guy rolled it over his tongue like fine brandy. "Soon to be a household name among those who devour biographies. What else do you have up your sleeve, wordspinner?"

"I have a collection of children's stories I need to polish and expand on. They're inspired by my nieces and nephews." As she smiled at me, I winked back. She knew I adored her stories. One of our dreams was for me to illustrate them with oils.

"Ah, a beloved aunt." Guy's tone was surprisingly reverent. I wouldn't have thought the rich playboy in him would've warmed so readily to Andrea's domestic role. "She often means more to a child than his parents."

Liam turned his wine glass around on the table. "Guy speaks from personal experience."

Andrea started. "You were raised by your aunt?"

Guy gazed into the candle. "My parents left me in the care of Aunt Helen, my mom's sister, when I was nine."

This was more autobiographical information than I'd heard from Guy in the whole month of knowing him.

Andrea leaned her forearms on the table. "What did your parents do?"

"My father was a diplomat, and my mother a socialite." Guy took a leisurely sip of wine. "They weren't the sort to let a child cramp their style."

Andrea's brows drew down. "They sound delightful."

Guy's eyes glinted as they met hers. "Their most delightful moment was when they entrusted me to Helen."

Liam crossed his legs. "And when they entrusted you with your father's trust."

Guy's face darkened. "A salve for their conscience."

"Are they no longer with us?" Andrea asked gently.

Guy shook his head. "Father died of a stroke two years ago, and Mother died in a car accident a couple of years before that." He coughed. "Et in arcadia ego, and all that." He straightened, taking a restorative draft of wine and crooking a smile. "But Aunt Helen is well and thriving."

Andrea placed a sympathetic hand on Guy's arm. "I'm glad you still have her."

I nudged her. "Drea, I'll bet your stories would resonate with Guy. Especially the one about the beekeeper and the drought."

Guy's smile turned wicked. "If that's allegorical, I must see it."

****

Late the next morning, Liam, Guy, Andrea, and I rode our bikes to the cove for a swim. Since Guy had never ventured out riding with me and Liam, I took this as an irrefutable sign that he was smitten with Andrea.

"This place is spooky," Andrea remarked before we climbed in to join the fish.

I'd never thought of it before. "How so?"

"Just looking out at the ocean through that small gap, knowing the tide could rise high enough to drown you. The eerie quiet. Those fishermen eyeing us without seeming to look." Andrea indicated the white boat about a quarter of a mile offshore. Sure enough, the men turned their heads away when we glanced at them.

I laughed. "D, you should write the story of a haunting that takes place on Verau. I'll illustrate it with skulls and buried treasure."

"Fishermen are a part of life on Verau," Liam said, pulling me in the water. "Our own fishermen know all the other captains and crews across the islands within a hundred-mile radius. They all gather at a couple of pubs in Fiji and Vanua Levu to trade stories of catches, weather, and clients."

"They're allowed to fish in your waters?" Andrea sat swinging her legs in the water below the knees.

"These aren't private waters." Liam hitched my hips around his waist in the sea, holding my backside with his large forearm and cradling my head with his hand. "They could fish right next to my piers if they wanted."

Guy sat down next to Andrea. "Shall we brave the water together, princess?"

Their chemistry was palpable. I suddenly had a vision of them standing together in formal attire. Guy's agile body would fill out a tux like an old Hollywood movie star, while Andrea's sultry curves would draw hundreds of admiring stares in an off-shoulder, figure-hugging, flared cobalt number. When they sailed through the room, they would move as one person.

Andrea shivered. "I guess we'd better get it over with."

"One—two—three!" Guy slid into the water, and Andrea laughed, slipping in after him like an eel.

Several times in the course of our swim, I caught Guy gazing at Andrea with lust-darkened eyes. I wondered if she knew how much he longed to kiss her.

After our swim, we meandered along the beach collecting shells. When we reached home, Andrea and I agreed to meet, after our showers, at the central stairway leading up to the art studio.

Twenty minutes later, I was showing her my work.

"Holy shit, Ingrid." Andrea surveyed my finished, fired bust of Liam. "This is amazing. You've made him look like a demon-god."

I saw only the truth.

"I also started a painting of you—from sketches I did in New York." I led her to a canvas in the corner, where I'd mixed startling colors to capture the shine in Andrea's features and personality.

"Wow." Andrea shifted her torso to catch the painting at different angles. "It's like really good kaleidoscopic graffiti. You've made me look like a bantu queen."

"You *are* a bantu queen." I wrapped my arm around her waist. "I'm going to put the Williamsburg Bridge behind you, since you live in the Lower East Side."

"Make it a stormy sky. I love New York in a storm."

"Done." I led her over to one of my workbenches. "I come here for several hours every weekend day. The light in here is unbelievable."

She plopped down on a high stool. "Looking up Guy on the internet, I found a shit-ton of stuff."

"Good or bad?" I headed over to the clay slabs, thinking I'd start a sculpture of the pelicans we often saw dipping into the lagoon on the southern side of the island.

She laughed. "All ambivalent. Just as I would've expected. Even in interviews for glossy tabloids, he manages to undercut himself by sounding rakish and off-limits. He doesn't need to practice law—he's a millionaire from his family trust—but he does it for fun and to keep busy. Though he pitches himself as looking for romance, he breezes through women like a mistral, breaking hearts just as coldly. While everyone seeks his endorsement, the only people he'll give the time of day to are hair care products."

"He does have lovely hair." I removed the plastic film from a new chunk of clay and jumped back. "Oh!"

"What is it?"

"That's odd. Look at this."

Andrea rounded the workbench. We were looking at a six- by four- by three-inch empty space where a block of clay had been removed from the corner of the large new slab. It'd been cut out precisely, with a scalpel, as I could tell from the clean marks on the remaining clay.

"Does anyone else use clay around here?" she asked.

I shook my head. "Not that I'm aware of. No one comes up here."

"Maybe the people who sent it took out a piece." She squished some clay between her fingers. "God, this is so therapeutic. I see why you're such a calm person."

"Sorry, back to Guy." I cut out a large chunk of clay and threw it onto the table. "Would you consider having a fling with him?"

Andrea lowered her voice. "Well, I wouldn't *not* consider it."

I cracked up. "He'd better watch out. You're made of much stronger stuff than the women he's probably used to."

She tossed her hair behind her shoulder. "Judging from pictures of his past dates online, I'm not his type at all."

I cocked my head. "Isn't a gorgeous, sexy, brilliant woman every man's type?"

She laughed. "Oh, Ingrid. If only your brain were in half the men of New York, I wouldn't be single right now."

Chapter Twenty-Two

Liam

Returning from the shooting range early that evening, I caught sight of Rory and Char deep in conversation outside one of the vegetable gardens. An unlikely pairing if ever I'd seen one. An instinct told me to hide behind a clump of palms and observe them. They spoke with surprising familiarity, Char nodding as if she was taking directions. She twisted a little to point toward one of the front outbuildings. What could they possibly have to talk about? Char slipped something into Rory's palm, looking around furtively, before turning on her heel back to the outbuilding where she stayed. Waiting until they'd separated, I made my way through the zen garden, deep in thought.

Their manner didn't suggest they were fucking. But it did hint at an agreement of some sort. Now, what might that be? Char had two more weeks before she left. She'd taken the news of her impending dismissal in stride, as though she half expected it. She seemed grateful for the time, severance, and bonus. I offered her a good reference for her next position.

Ingrid, Andrea, and Guy greeted me in the living room.

"Where've you been?" Ingrid stood on tiptoes to kiss me, winding her arms around my waist. Fuck, I'd missed her smell.

"Target practice."

"What type of gun?" Andrea's tone was arch.

"Beretta M9." I devoured Ingrid's mouth, feeling all the more insatiable because we'd forgone our midday sex.

"Afraid you'll grow rusty?" Andrea's eyes and voice brimmed with suspicion.

I flashed her a wolfish smile. "Like anything, you use it or lose it."

"Planning on using it anytime soon?" Andrea prodded.

I tilted my head. "If I have to."

That shut her up.

"Is everyone ready to go to Suva early tomorrow?" Swooping Ingrid up in my arms I carried her to the couch, settling her in my lap. She was as soft and responsive as a lovebird and ten times as adorable. Damn, I was a lucky bastard. "Josefa will take us at eight sharp."

"We'll be a regular Manet painting," Guy observed, popping a grape in his mouth.

Andrea sat down in the armchair opposite him. "I can't wait to get gifts for my family."

"You'll find, enchantress, that I'm an excellent shopper. Feel free to avail yourself of my services." His tone suggested those weren't the only services on offer.

"He shops too!" Andrea's eyes flared. "You're a unicorn among men."

"Touch my horn and you'll have good luck." His lips twitched.

Andrea rolled her eyes. "I walked right into that one, didn't I?"

"If you're waiting for an endorsement from me," I said, tweaking Ingrid's earlobe, "I can guarantee Guy will never let you pay for anything, he has excellent taste in cheeses, and he'll always arrive half an hour late so you have plenty of time to finish dressing."

"Thank you, my good man. I can take it from here," Guy sniffed. "Miss Carpel, may I have the honor of escorting you through the streets of Suva tomorrow?"

Andrea smiled sweetly. "Mr. Travis, the honor would be all mine."

Ingrid and I were definitely cutting out soon after we touched harbor in Suva.

****

The boat ride was choppy from the strong winds. An unusual storm was due to come in tomorrow, even though it was late May. Our captain, Josefa, had a handsome face plastered in dark tattoos, his bronzed, muscular shoulders and chest telling just as many stories in ink.

"Much as I love your company, Josefa," I said, "I have a helicopter on order for the island as soon as I can clear and pave more land. Two hours in a boat versus half an hour in a helo—you can guess which one appeals. Especially when someone's sick and needs to reach Dr. Leong in Suva."

"Mmm, Dr. Leong is a good doctor," Josefa commented. "Very wise."

"We're paying him a visit this afternoon." I held fast to a pole as a large wave slammed into the side of the boat.

"Ah, tell him I said hello—and his wife!" Unflappable, Josefa steered us like a blade through the tumultuous waters.

With less than 94,000 inhabitants, Suva was more of a large town than a city. Blending traditional Fijian architecture, modern structures, and Victorian buildings, the city wove many cultures together. The population comprised chiefly indigenous Pacific groups, but a lot of South Asian and East Asian people had settled here as well, and most everyone spoke English. The downtown shopping district was walkable and not far from where Josefa dropped us.

As we wandered down one of the sidewalks covered with an awning to protect street sellers' goods from rain, I noticed everyone smiling at Ingrid—men, women, and children, of all ethnicities and ages. I turned to find the reason why: she wore a broad, infectious beam of a smile that lit up anyone who saw her, and her sparkling eyes dazzled. Older island men with white stubble spoke in friendly tones to greet her and ask how she was. Toddlers stared, swiveled their heads, and waved. Even tired mothers who seemed unlikely candidates for sunniness broke out in a slow, unguarded smile, their eyes regaining a spark.

I was floored by her contagious life force.

"What are you smiling at, Ingrid?" I asked.

"The world—life—people. They're all so wonderful," she replied. "And this is already an incredible day."

I laughed. "What makes it so incredible?"

"Here the four of us are—two unlikely pairs—in the capital of Fiji, with the whole day ahead to explore. And there's so much diversity and energy here, it's as if we're inside a cross-section of the globe." Her radiant, generous smile illuminated me, melting my insides. Her very step was full of bounce. This woman was like no one else.

"You're not the sort to take things for granted, Ingrid." I turned us so I could kiss her. "Maybe that's why everyone smiles back at you—because you're so grateful."

Andrea and Guy, who were walking behind us, muttered at something off to our left, and Ingrid and I followed their gaze.

Street artists were not only displaying their works in an open market, but were, in some cases, making the art spontaneously on the pavement, wooden panels, canvases, and other surfaces, while onlookers gathered to drop money in their baskets. The four of us made a beeline toward the long esplanade where the market was held.

Musicians played Fijian songs that combined elements of Indian music, Reggae, and Polynesian music. One artist, painted all in silver, was doing such an expert imitation of a statue that birds were landing on his head and shoulders. A young woman made five-minute spray paintings that virtuosically captured her customers in portrait form. Another man was tracing wax on eggs and dyeing them. An older island man beckoned us (meaning Ingrid) over to use his huge chalk on a large blocked-off segment of sidewalk where he'd started an ocean scene. Ingrid oohed and ahhed over the marine creatures he'd drawn so far—octopus, sailfish, dolphins, and tuna. She knelt down, drawing various underwater plants, starfish, and a treasure chest. Delighted, the man exclaimed over her work, while Guy and I dropped a couple of fifties in his basket.

Guy and I got caught up talking to a shriveled,

white-haired woman who collared us to tell a long story about her granddaughter—at least, I think that's who she was babbling on about—and a cruise ship she'd worked on that sailed around the world. When I told her about my own plans to do the same, but on a yacht, that really got her going. I could tell after a while that Guy was getting antsy, so I finally interrupted the woman and apologized that we had to go.

By the time I looked back at the chalk artist, he was handing chalk to a young girl, and Ingrid and Andrea were nowhere to be found. *Fuck.*

I did a quick three-sixty scope of the street fair, focusing on the near and far ground. But no sign of the women. What the hell? My heart hammered and my palms grew sweaty. My first thought, crazy as it was, was that Rory had snatched Ingrid. That image nauseated me. My next thought, even more frightening, was that Ingrid had run away. This idea dropped a lead weight to the bottom of my belly, sending my pulse into high gear. *No way am I going down without a fight. Not after everything I've done to keep her till now.*

"Excuse me," I said to the chalk artist, mustering as much control as I could. "Did you see where those two women went? The ones I was with?"

He pointed toward a park at the far end of the esplanade. "There was a little child." When he offered no further explanation, I said to Guy, "Wait here, in case they come back. I'll head down to the other end."

My eight years of military training had taught me not to panic under pressure. But if ever there was a time when my nature wanted to rebel against that training, it was now. I couldn't lose Ingrid. She meant the world to me.

Shouldering my way through groups of people, I strode toward the tall pines in the distance. At least the two women were together—had either one of them disappeared on her own, I would've been more anxious. They couldn't have gotten that far, or had the old woman bent our ear long enough for us to lose our companions? And why the fuck hadn't they told us where they were going?

Emerging in the spacious green park, I darted a glance to every corner. In one area, women in bright island dresses pushed strollers, and a large family group sat picnicking on the grass. No Ingrid or Andrea there. In another section, young men and women played an ultimate frisbee game. No Ingrid there either. Another quadrant revealed runners, a few people taking pictures, and a gaggle of women standing around a bench laden with shopping bags. The last corner of the park was full of dogs—big and small—dancing and leaping. Something told me this was the direction to head in.

I stopped one of the dog owners, a squat middle-aged woman with cropped hair, and asked her if she'd seen two women with a small child.

She pointed down a less-trafficked street. "They went that way. They were with my neighbor's cousin."

Somehow that reassured me. Then I saw Andrea coming out of the street back toward the park, her eyes fixed in the direction of the street fair.

"Andrea!" I called. She didn't hear me till I'd sprinted closer. "Where's Ingrid?"

Andrea stopped. "I left her back at the house. She had to wait till the kid's older sister came back. I wanted to go back and find you guys."

"What the hell happened?" Worry and puzzlement

made me ornery.

"A little girl, Nia, was wandering around the street fair wailing for Lani. Ingrid took Nia's hand and told her to lead her to Lani. I followed to make sure everything was okay. When we got to that group of dog owners over there, one of them said Nia lived up that block. She sent one of her cousins to show us. But the front door was locked and the bell seemed to be broken. When we went around the back, a scary guard dog lunged at us—on a chain, thank God. But still pretty frightening. So Ingrid and Nia went to sit in the front, since Nia said her sister was coming back soon and could let her in. That's when I said I'd go find you guys."

I exhaled long and slowly, raking my hand through my hair. "Shit, Andrea. Why didn't you guys tell us where you were going before you went off?"

Andrea shook her head. "I didn't have time— Ingrid had already taken off. She was so worried that the little girl was hurt or abandoned. She's at the pink and yellow house on the left-hand side. You'll see her and Nia sitting out front. Where's Guy?"

"He's where you last saw him, waiting for us. Go tell him where I am. You guys stay there." Surging toward the residential street, I stalked down the middle so I could more easily pick out Ingrid.

I came upon the house exactly where Andrea said it would be, but there was no sign of Ingrid or a little girl out front. Deciding to try it, I scaled the steps to the front door and rang the bell. Then I remembered it didn't work, so I rapped my knuckles loudly on the door.

A minute later Ingrid opened the door, surprise

177

splashed across her features.

"What are you doing here, Ingrid?" I barked.

"Lani—Nia's older sister—just got home. I was saying goodbye." She gestured behind her.

A little freckled girl ran up, her arms outstretched. "Goodbye, Ingrid. Thank you." Ingrid stooped, wrapping her in a hug.

A girl who was probably no older than fifteen or sixteen came out into the hallway. "Thanks again, Ingrid. That's not the first time I've lost people at that street fair."

Ingrid smiled, indicating the general direction of the market. "There's a lot going on all at once there. Nice to meet you both. Bye, Nia!"

Seeing how unruffled she was by this whole incident made me even more livid.

We trooped down the steps in silence to the street before I exploded. "What the fuck, Ingrid? You took off without telling us you were leaving, and then you step in to have a chat with the kid's sister? Don't you realize people are worried about you? *I* was worried about you."

"I didn't mean to make you worry. I thought Lani would be somewhere nearby. I had no idea it would take so long to reunite Nia with her family. But I didn't want to just leave her." She looked up at me pleadingly. "You must see I had no choice."

I shook my head. "You had tunnel vision, Ingrid. I've seen you like that when you're sculpting. You don't even hear me when I come up behind you."

Tears flecked her eyes. "I can't help it. I'm overly focused. When I'm doing something I love, I have one thing in my line of sight and one thing only. I'm sorry."

I placed a hand on the back of her neck, steering us back toward the street fair. "Next time, when you want to take off, tell me. Kid or no kid. I don't want to lose you again."

"You wouldn't here," she asserted, opening her palms. "Fiji is so safe and friendly. People know each other."

I set my lips in a grim line. "You can't trust anyone, Ingrid."

"I trusted you." Her tone was mild, but her eyes flashed.

"That's different," I snapped.

"If anything, it was worse."

I groaned. "Look, Ingrid, I don't want to change your nature. But I can't change who I am either. I'm protective, possessive, and distrustful."

"Well, if I can love who you are, why can't you love who I am?" She blushed, her hand flying to her mouth. It was clear she hadn't meant to drop the L-word.

I turned her, holding her arms. "Just don't leave my side." I ran the pad of my thumb over her lips slowly. "I'm going to punish you for this, my little wanderer."

As her eyes flared, I caught the fine hairs on her neck standing on end in response to my threat.

Chapter Twenty-Three

Liam

Our foray into the real world was shaking me up. Looking down at Ingrid, I could tell she was shaken too—no doubt by my anger. No fucking way was I going to separate my skin from hers for the rest of the day. Whether I had my hands on her neck, ass, waist, or arm, I needed contact. I needed to feel her pulse, her hot breath, the warm blood circulating in her veins. Shepherding her back to the street fair, I smelled the intoxicating scent of sagebrush, citrus, and mint wafting from her skin and hair. I wanted to taste her sweat and saliva.

Pulling her over to the side of a shop, I nailed her against the wall, pinning her hands to her sides and ravaging her mouth. I bit her lips, sucked her tongue, and swiped her palate, encroaching on every corner of her. Dragging my tongue down her jaw to her neck and clavicle, I took her skin in my teeth. I wanted to leave marks that would tell everyone she belonged to me. She moaned, closing her eyes and arching her hips to be closer to mine.

I scooted back, making her writhe with longing, while keeping her hands pinioned to the building. "I'm going to strap you later, my little captive, for making me worry."

Her eyes blinked open. "If you worry, it means you care—a lot."

The urge to admit the truth—to myself and her—overwhelmed me. Laying fervent kisses on her forehead, nose, and lips, I let down my guard a little. "I do. More and more by the minute."

If I was honest, this trip might've been too much too soon. It came directly in the wake of Rory and Andrea's onslaught of my fortress, which forced secrets out into the open that should've remained hidden a while longer. I had only just tested the waters of giving Ingrid more freedom, and now I'd thrown us both out into the wide ocean as though we were Olympic swimmers.

But then, I'd done this so we could discover who we were as a couple in the world. Ironically, I'd learned how much I cared about Ingrid when she was separated from me. No wonder I was so shaken—learning hurt. As I knew from the way they broke you down in the military and built you back up again to their specifications. Self-knowledge that was worth anything never came without pain.

Guy's eyes lit up with a warm glow when he saw Ingrid. That's when I realized how fond of her he was. "I hear the local Fijians lured you away with one of their wee bairns. If they offered you food too, I can't say I blame you for heeding their Siren call. Their hospitality is better than Liam's." He shot me a reproachful glare.

"Guy, you're no better than a parasite of the old Roman comedy," I remarked.

"A pescatarian parasite," he corrected. "While you two were fraternizing with the locals, I found a pleasant restaurant for our lunch."

As if on cue, my stomach growled. "Lead the way."

Guy's lunch place, down a few blocks and around a corner, was located in a large thatched building made of vesi timbers in the traditional Fijian style. Beneath its loft ceiling, long communal tables of teak spilled over with hungry groups of tourists, locals, and shoppers who kept up a steady drone of babble. In the middle of the restaurant, a Lovo—an underground oven slow-cooking meats and fish in banana leaves—pitched smoke upwards to a hole in the roof. The fresh smells and popularity told me this was indeed the place to eat.

The host, a weary, bedraggled bald man, gestured with resignation to the full restaurant behind him. Handing him a fifty-dollar bill, I said, "Bring out another table."

Pocketing the fifty, he livened up, weaving his way to the back and consulting with a waiter.

Five minutes later, the four of us sat around what seemed to be an outdoor terrace table that had been brought to the front.

"Are we fueling for shopping, touristy stuff, or visiting people?" Andrea inquired, scanning the menu.

"All of the above, princess." Guy put down his menu.

"Then I'm going to get a starter too. Any recommendations?" She looked confident that Guy would know what to get.

"Any dietary restrictions or dislikes?" He leaned into her, draping an arm over her chair back.

Her flirtatious smile suggested she welcomed his come-ons. "I'm not too partial to eggplant, artichokes, or radishes."

Guy smirked. "I think I can warm you to eggplant. Otherwise, you're in luck, because the Fijians don't use those vegetables much." Brushing her arm, he pointed out a few items on the menu, as they murmured over possible selections.

Meanwhile, I kept an arm around Ingrid's shoulder. She'd become a visceral need, a source of electricity to power me on and keep me charged. "Do you know what you'd like?"

She nodded. "I'm starving. It's all that sea air in the boat, I think."

Soon the table was spread with Nama (sea grapes that tasted like caviar), coconut curry with Fijian asparagus over rice, Palusami (beef, coconut milk, and taro leaves), Rourou (chilied, creamed taro leaves and tuna cooked in the Lovo), Kokoda (ceviche made with Mahi-mahi), pakapaka sashimi, Wai tom donu (whole barbecued snapper with papaya, kumquat, and coriander), and spicy fish suruwa with rice (an Indian curry).

The waiter brought us four cups of kava—a peppery drink like a muddy tea that acted as a mild sedative on the central nervous system. We raised our cups. Taking a sip of the moderately hot mixture, Andrea and Ingrid both made faces.

"This is...different," said Andrea.

"Different good?" Guy asked.

"Um, it's very tingly." She took another sip. "But I kind of like it."

"It's like nothing I've ever tasted before." Ingrid inhaled before sipping again. "It's making my lips and tongue a little numb. After a few more cups of this, a dentist could operate on me and I'd feel nothing."

I palmed her back. "Fijian friends and family drink kava whenever they get together. There's a whole ritual to the kava ceremony."

"So when do you all plan on returning to New York?" Andrea helped herself to suruwa.

"Who said anything about leaving?" Guy spooned coconut curry onto his plate. "We're working on keeping you here."

She sighed. "Honestly, I'd love that. It's everything you hear about honeymoons in Bora Bora—and more."

"Have you used your hot tub yet?" Ingrid lifted a forkful of sea grapes to her lips.

Andrea nodded. "Last night, for the first time. I've never felt so relaxed as when I climbed out. I drifted off into the soundest sleep."

"I know of other things that can get you off to sleep," Guy murmured.

Andrea nudged him, her lips quirking. "Wouldn't those same things keep me up?"

"You wouldn't miss your sleep." He shot her a cocky grin. "You did say you'd like the full honeymoon experience."

She laughed, blushing as her eyes darted between me and Ingrid. "You've got all the discretion of a tabloid hack."

He lifted her hand, kissing its back. "We're among friends, enchantress. They know my intentions."

"Those intentions seem to be generally directed at any single woman." I had to hand it to Andrea, she shot from the hip.

Guy's eyebrows lifted. "You do yourself a great injustice. A fox with wit, intelligence, poise, and charm is hardly common. Add to that a heart of gold and you have an extremely fatal combination."

The last part seemed to throw Andrea off balance. I let them continue their mating dance, as I turned to Ingrid. "Are you prepared to shop after this? I'm taking you to some clothing and shoe boutiques, and then to a jeweler."

She beamed. "Wow, what's the occasion?"

I hemmed. "Our first date."

"After a first date like this, you'll have a lot of work to build up to a climax in your series," she teased.

"The series may have very few episodes." I sipped my kava, holding her gaze.

"Then I'd like to savor each episode." As she fed me a bite of tuna with her fingers, I curled my tongue around her fingertips, nipping their soft pads.

Chapter Twenty-Four

Ingrid

After lunch, Andrea and Guy left to explore the sights, agreeing to meet us at Dr. Leong's house in four hours. Since the incident at this morning's street fair, Liam had been extra touchy-feely. Being in love with him and naturally affectionate, I basked in his tenderness the way a plant soaks up sunshine. I sensed he was turning a corner in his feelings—as if his obsession for me might be growing into affection.

The first place we visited looked like a rundown cellphone store from the front. I looked in puzzlement at Liam, who pushed a buzzer beside the metal grill of the outside door.

A woman's voice chimed, "Yes?"

"Stauner."

When the mechanism released, Liam ushered me through the inner door. I was shocked to find a sleek, finely appointed interior filled with elegant clothes and overseen by a smartly dressed petite Asian woman who'd pulled her hair back in a glossy chignon.

"Mr. Stauner, Ms. Pellerin, welcome. I'm Cynthia." The woman bowed slightly. "If there's anything I can put aside for you, please let me know."

This was the most exclusive shopping experience I'd ever had. Each time I lingered over an item on the racks, Liam would nod at Cynthia, and she'd pull it in my size, taking it back to the dressing room. By the time I'd picked out a series of skirts, dresses, shirts, shorts, and pants, we had collected enough for two hours' worth of trying on.

"I thought you wanted us to have experience in the 'real world,'" I joked to Liam. "This is more like experience in a real billionaire's world."

"Tell me you hate it after we've walked out with half the shop." Gripping my nape, he dragged his teeth along my lower lip, making me moan.

Like the shop, the dressing room was devoted to us. Cynthia left us to our plush couch, three-way mirrors, and cozy armchairs. As soon as I'd stripped to my panties, preparing to try on one of the dresses, Liam encircled me from behind, surrounding me with his scorching heat.

His lips feathered my temple as he cupped my throat. He held my breasts, thumbing my erect nipples. His fingers skated over my belly and along my inner thighs, drawing my whimpers. I closed my eyes, leaning back into his chest.

"Open, little rosebud. I want you to watch as I take you."

He bent me over an ottoman in front of the mirror, planting my hands on the cushion and tilting my head so I could see everything. His sun-toughened skin, aquiline nose, and fierce expression made him look like a beast, while from beneath his huge, strong body, I peeped out like a helpless lamb. But my trembling was from desire. I was a lamb wet for her captor.

Mesmerized, I watched as he stripped his shirt, shorts, and boxer briefs, revealing legs like metal girders, rippling abs, and a magnificent cock. He tugged off my panties, dipping his fingers in my channel and licking them one by one.

He took me slowly at first, his eyes fixed on mine in the mirror as his girth disappeared in my sheath. Slicking his thumb over my wetness, he plunged it into my asshole, filling me completely. Oh God, poor Cynthia was in for a loud concert. As Liam sped up his thrusts, riding my hips like a rodeo champion, I felt the burning of the fuse leading to my explosion.

"Oh, *oh, Liam*—" I shouted, coming with the force of cannon fire. The sight of him buried deep in me triggered more contractions that brought him with me over a second crest. My limbs sagged, and I breathed jaggedly, as his trunk blanketed me, his hands covering mine.

"What will Cynthia think?" I whispered hoarsely, as if my yelps hadn't already filled the boutique.

"She's paid not to think." Liam's low gritty voice rumbled in my ear.

The first dress I tried on was an all-leather fawn-colored low-cut figure-hugging mini-dress with a halter strap that reached a few inches above the knees. A tan zipper ran from the base of my cleavage all the way to the bottom of the dress. The color and snug fit made me look completely naked.

"Oh, fuck yeah, Ingrid." Liam circled me like a predator, smacking my ass. "Next is a nice tight collar with a chain I can pull from the back."

I giggled. "I don't know where I could wear this."

He unzipped the front partway, sliding his hand in to palm one of my breasts. "You'll be with me when you wear this." He devoured my lips with a feral kiss.

When Liam said things like that, my pussy drizzled. I loved belonging to him completely.

Next was a black lace-lined pencil skirt with a back slit and matching lace crop top in a sweetheart cut that revealed my midriff.

Liam gave a long, low wolf whistle. "Very fuckable. We're batting a thousand, Ingrid."

Then I tried on an A-line square-neck, strappy cotton sundress in white splashed with bright tropical flowers. I felt so fresh, sweet, and alive, I wanted to wear it out of the store.

"That's as you as a dress could be," Liam pronounced. "Put that aside for when we leave."

Liam brought out a formal floor-length sapphire-blue satin dress with a long slit up the thigh in front. He laced up the dress from the back, cupping my ass lovingly as he did so.

"Mmm-hmm," he hummed, groping my waist and hips. "That's a definite yes."

Tight white low-rise boot-cut jeans followed, which I paired with a long-waisted boat-neck cotton turquoise cap-sleeved shirt.

"This is perfect for our terrace parties." I turned to see my butt in the mirror.

"Don't bother to check. You look edible from the back too." Liam sat back in his chair, crossing his legs.

Next, I tried on a burnt-umber short-sleeved one-piece cotton romper with short shorts that buttoned down the front.

Liam was speechless, his eyes bugging out.

"You like it?" I laughed.

"*Like* it? I want to destroy it. Or destroy you in it. Whichever comes first."

I never knew trying on clothes could be such a sexually charged experience. I reveled in seeing myself through Liam's eyes, wanting to make love to my own body.

An hour later, the last thing I tried on was a lime-green rayon dress with midlength sleeves that just barely cleared my butt and had a plunge neckline that dove to my waist, holding up my breasts with a subtle underwire that crossed the cutout over my breastplate. I was pleased with how it accentuated every curve.

"Your hot legs go on forever in this dress." Liam surged from his seat, running his fingers along the back of my thighs. His mammoth bulge speared my butt. Before I knew it, my panties were off again and he'd shoved my back against the mirror, hitching my thighs around his waist. In a flash his cock was out and he'd rammed it into me as he closed his teeth around the column of my throat. It didn't take more than a few minutes before I was crying out from the ecstasy of the tidal wave that slammed into me. As we panted, perspiring together, Liam said, "We'll take this dress too."

"How will we get out the door with all the bags?"

Liam waved this off. "I'll have them deliver everything to the boat. Josefa has plenty of space below deck. Now on to the lingerie boutique and then to buy some shoes. Put on that lovely sundress."

In my crisp bright dress, I felt like new as we emerged on the street. Seizing Liam's hand, I twirled around, pirouetting on the ball of my sandal. He laughed, pulling me close and kissing my cheek.

"Thank you, Liam."

"I love spoiling you, Ingrid."

"I've been working on a present for you too." I traced his Adam's apple. My gift would be a service rather than a good.

"Come on. Let's find some sexy underwear for you." He tugged me down a few side streets to another ugly storefront.

Again, we were the only people in the place, and the saleswoman was expecting us. After half an hour of trying on panties, bras, teddies, and corsets of lace, cotton, nylon, and silk, I'd filled another large shopping bag with purchases. I couldn't wait to wear the pink corset for Liam later.

The shoe store was a fifteen-minute walk from the lingerie boutique.

"Is your energy flagging, Ingrid? We can always hold off on shoes." Liam held my hand.

"No, no. I want to find some shoes to go with the green dress." I could barely wait to see what his next boutique offered.

A beautiful young island woman welcomed us, gesturing toward the shelves. I salivated at the sight of several of them—silvery strappy high-heel sandals, black satin stilettos, turquoise pointed-toe high-heel pumps, nude suede heels, brown peep-toe high-heel booties with ankle platform wedges, and white high-heel sandals with a cage around the ankle.

"We'll take all of them," Liam said to the saleswoman after I'd tried on a selection.

"I'll need another four suitcases to take all of this back to New York." I was thinking vaguely of the future, not of anything imminent.

Liam didn't say anything, his face inscrutable.

When we emerged in the street, he said, "Do you

have enough left in the tank for the jeweler's?"

I'd forgotten he had planned for this too. "You've bought me so much, Liam. I don't need jewelry."

He cupped my jaw, brushing my cheek with his thumb. "Since I met you I've wanted to put a choker around your neck. And a ring on your right ring finger."

When he put it like that, how could I say no?

The jeweler made me feel uncomfortable as soon as we stepped in his shop. I saw the way his eyes drifted southwards, lingering on my breasts and journeying along the contours of my waist and hips to settle just above my knees. He oozed perviness.

Liam must've felt it too, because he leaned closer to the man and said, very distinctly, "Do we need to take our business elsewhere, or are you going to keep your focus on my girlfriend's face?"

The man snapped out of it. "Of course, sir. How can I help you?"

"I'd like to see your choker necklaces."

Being a man of decision, Liam fixed on one necklace right away, and that one was perfect. Three cords of hundreds of diamond-bright square crystals undulated in a circle with twenty-four jet stones embedded in them. The black-and-white combination was devastatingly elegant, making me feel like Grace Kelly.

"This back clasp is too complex for me to undo myself," I noted.

"That's the idea, my little slave." He trailed the back of his finger around the top edge of the choker. Then, crooking his finger in the choker, he pulled it so my back slammed into his front.

I shivered, realizing I was drenched again. Wearing

a choker around my neck was like going pantyless for Liam. It turned me on knowing I was doing it for him, so he could claim me as his at any moment.

"But what shall we do for a ring?" he said, quoting one of my favorite children's poems, "The Owl and the Pussycat."

I laughed, pointing to one in the case. "That one is very pretty."

The jeweler removed my selection. "This, madam, is a tiger's eye with yellow sapphire set in eighteen-karat gold settings. It would match your hair and eyes."

I fingered the smooth round stone offset by a crinkly gold oval edge. When Liam slipped it on my finger, my breath hitched. It was absolutely perfect. I turned my hand, so the golds and browns caught the light at different angles.

"We'll take it." Liam counted out a stack of hundreds, sliding them across the counter.

He left the choker and ring on. I wondered what Andrea would say when she saw how I was decked out.

Chapter Twenty-Five

Andrea

Guy was every bit as good a shopper as he'd billed himself. For hours we meandered among street vendors and small markets selling wood carvings, jewelry, island clothing, pottery, and touristy knickknacks like magnets, placemats, and keychains. I bought something for everyone back home—my sister Vanessa and her family, my brother Chris and his family, my parents, aunts, uncles, and nine cousins, my friends Rick and Stephanie, and my coworkers. After three hours, Guy and I trundled along like old wheezing Fords, our bags flapping on our arms.

As we traipsed along a street lined with Victorian storefronts and restaurants, I said, "Is Liam solid?"

"For that question, princess, I'll need to take the weight off. Let's go sit by the sea wall." Guy bobbed his head toward a spot about a hundred yards away, where we had a glimpse of the ocean.

I appreciated how seriously he was taking my question.

Five minutes later, we had settled on a bench overlooking the sea, beside a walkway where tourists and locals strolled and exercised. Black-winged seabirds skimmed over the surface of the water, and boats of all sizes pulled in and out of the port. Though the wind continued strong as this morning, the air was a perfect seventy-five degrees.

"Liam is a complex man." Guy surveyed me with his deep honey-brown eyes. "He inspires complete loyalty in anyone who comes to know him well—soldiers, officers, friends, coworkers, servants. That loyalty is based on his generosity, courage, and compassion."

"Compassion?" I arched an eyebrow.

Still solemn, Guy gave a brief nod. "As soon as he left the Marines, he volunteered as a court-appointed special advocate at a receiving home in New Jersey to represent neglected and abused children. While his own foster care experience was decent, he wanted to ensure that other children were safely and happily placed."

I remained dubious. "All this while working as a hitman? Many of the men he killed had children."

"That's where the 'complex' part comes in." Guy rolled up his sleeves, exposing brawny forearms. They weren't jacked, but they were naturally lean and shapely. I liked that about Guy's whole physique. He clearly worked out, but in moderation, and he obviously had a fast metabolism. "He's slow to trust people, he doubts himself, and he's obsessive."

"Obsessive about what?" I probed.

He shrugged. "Whatever matters to him—jobs, justice…Ingrid."

"That's the part I don't get." I lifted a foot onto the bench, clasping my hands around my knee. "Ingrid loves him. He's got Ingrid. So why doesn't he lighten up a little?"

Guy shook his head. "He's afraid to hope that she could love him. He doesn't believe in himself enough to think it's possible. And that prevents him from completely trusting her."

His assessment seemed spot-on, just from what I'd read of Ingrid and Liam's dynamic over the last few days.

"Do you think his obsession could be getting in the way of his having a normal relationship with her?" I posed.

"They're well-matched in several areas." He rested his arms on the bench top, his right arm wrapping behind my back. My neck prickled, and heat seeped from my belly to my sex. His hand was so near my arm. Was he going to close the arm-hold? If he did, I wouldn't hesitate to lean into him. "One of those areas is how they enjoy having an abnormal relationship—or, as I prefer to call it, extra-ordinary."

"Well, then, could his obsession be keeping him from falling in love with her?" When I turned back to Guy, his eyes dipped to my lips. I flushed beneath his gaze, biting my lower lip. His eyes followed the movement, his pupils expanding.

"It's possible," Guy conceded. "But when it comes to a woman like Ingrid, I don't see him lasting long against love."

That was heartening.

My voice lowered. "So, getting back to my original question, would he ever hurt her?"

"Not intentionally." Guy blinked, as if realizing he'd left out an essential part of his answer. "Certainly not physically."

I nodded. "Okay, from your endorsement, I'll hold off on siccing the dogs on him. I can't say I *like* him. But I'll try to wrap my head around why Ingrid does."

Guy's lips curved up at the corners. "Your frankness, loyalty, and love for Ingrid speak volumes for your character."

I matched his smile. "I could say the same of you, with Liam."

That's when I felt it. His fingers traced a subtle arc along the skin of my upper arm, making me shiver. Instinctively I edged closer, wanting more of his touch, craving his lips. I lowered my leg from the bench, resting my hands on my thighs.

His free hand palmed my cheek, his thumb brushing my cheekbone. Gently but firmly he pressed his lips to mine, his tongue summoning my tongue to play. From the back of my throat, a little hum escaped as our tongues meshed. His other hand cradled the nape of my neck, activating some of my most sensitive nerves. I tasted papaya, coconut, and kava on his breath, as if he'd selected the best flavors from our lunch to linger in his mouth. His skin smelled of grass, pine, and sea salt.

As our lips separated, a smile slunk up the side of his face. His eyes had darkened to stormy midnight pools.

"What is it?" I whispered.

"Just an idea I had." He kissed me again, this time taking my mouth more assertively, as though claiming it.

Between my thighs, a steady pulse arose. I twisted my torso so I could slide my hands up his chest, feeling its solidity and hardness beneath his shirt. *Mmm-hmm*, this man had quite a body under his elegant clothes. I had a vision of tearing off his button-down shirt so all the buttons scattered every which way. I remembered, from the morning before at the cove, the trail of light-brown hair that traveled from his eight-pack down into his swim trunks. I wanted to lick along those V-lines, grazing those hairs with my palm.

When we came up for oxygen, Guy murmured, "Tonight is a full moon."

I laughed. "Are you going to turn into a werewolf?"

"You'll find out at midnight."

****

We arrived outside Dr. Leong's house after Ingrid and Liam. *Holy shit*, Ingrid looked incredible. She was glowing, with an extra film of happiness surrounding her. I'd never seen her so ebullient and energized—and she was plenty of both those things in her normal mode.

I took her hands, lifting them up. "Your new dress is stunning, Ingrid. Whoa, what's this?" I zeroed in on the gorgeous sapphire ring she wore. "And *this*?" She had a jet-and-crystal choker around her neck. "Liam, did you buy up the entire island?"

"We had to condense everything into a few hours, so we covered all bases." Liam looked proud and pleased with his handiwork.

"Don't be shocked when you see the dozens of bags in the boat, Drea." Ingrid drew our arms together into a dance position, her right arm behind my waist and her left holding mine in the air. As she raised her left hand to spin me, I laughed, following her lead. "I see you and Guy got up to mischief."

I blushed, at first thinking it was written all over our faces that we'd kissed. But then I saw her eyeing our many bags. "Oh, yeah. I had to buy more than three dozen gifts. Now I need a new suitcase to fit everything in."

"You can take mine. I can always get another." Her face fell. "Drea, I really think you should stay longer and extend your ticket. You just got over jet lag."

"I wish I could. But Cleo and Rudra will have to pick up the slack if I stay any longer. I can't do that to them." I hugged her. "We still have another twenty hours. We'll make the most of them."

We sat for a couple of hours having tea with a gentlemanly Malaysian doctor and his wife. Dr. Leong had apparently gone to high school with Guy and Liam, and was a well-respected man in Suva. Afterward, we headed back to the boat, where Josefa was napping in the stern, a wool coat draped over his trunk. Liam nudged him awake, and we took off back to Verau. The whole boat ride back, Ingrid and I chatted about Armen's successful bakery in Astoria, Rick and Stephanie's upcoming wedding in Florida, Chris's daughter Dina's upcoming sixth birthday party, and a fundraiser Ingrid's mom was organizing for her dance school.

When Guy and Liam fell to talking at the other end of the boat, Ingrid placed her hand on my arm, leaning closer. "D, did you and Guy kiss?"

I chuckled. "You know me so well, sweetie. Does it show that much?"

She clapped her hands together. "I knew it. You guys look so right together."

"Well, it was just a couple of kisses." But I knew what was coming tonight.

She laughed. "Kissing is a prelude to other things. And you both share the same hot tub…"

I'd considered that too.

"So is the famous playboy an amazing kisser?" Her voice brimmed with excitement.

"He knows what he's doing. It actually surprised me a little. He puts on that whole detached-from-the-world act when he's fiercely animalistic. I'm curious to see just how carnal he can be." I tingled, remembering the way his tongue swept my mouth and his teeth took my lips.

Ingrid's eyes grew dreamy. "I can't wait till tomorrow's breakfast. We'll have to sit at the other end of the table from the men so we can talk."

Chapter Twenty-Six

Guy

I let the women chatter away, knowing they were likely discussing me and Andrea at the sea wall. My plan was now fully formed for how I'd keep Andrea on the island for at least as long as Ingrid and Liam were here. Call me wily and underhanded, but I knew she'd appreciate my sleight of hand after her initial shock. Surprise was of the essence.

Now to the appetizer on the menu: the seduction.

Shopping with Andrea, I'd seen her eyes light up at a chocolate shop window, but she'd exercised discipline in passing it by. While she was buying a few trinkets for her niece and nephew, I'd dipped into the store and bought a box of assorted truffles. The shopkeeper obligingly labeled the chocolate flavors on a sheet of paper, inserting it under the lid of the box. I deliberately chose the more exotic—chile mango, ginger, cinnamon, espresso, kahlua, passion fruit, and so forth. Again, the element of surprise was everything.

As we disembarked and various servants came out to carry in the shopping bags, I seized Andrea's hand, leading her to a stone bench bathed in moonlight that was at the edge of our shared porch. Over the sea, the moon had just risen—a gigantic, porous, coppery globe.

I kissed her in the moonlight, her warm skin

beautifully reflecting the lights of the house and the moon. Her little moans and mewls half-engorged my cock.

"Do you enjoy playing games?" I nuzzled her jaw, kissing my way down her neck.

"Depends on the game." She yipped as I nibbled her collarbone.

"For instance, a game involving you, me, and some very good chocolate?" I caressed her waist reverently. This woman was the most curvaceous, delectable sight I'd seen in a long time—possibly ever.

"Mmm, that sounds delicious. How do you play?"

"The rules are simple, really." I planed her back down to her fabulous ass, tracing an unbelievable S-curve. "It's a blind taste test. I blindfold you and feed you bites of various chocolates. Each time you guess a flavor correctly, I feed you another. Each time you guess wrong, I get to remove an item of your clothing."

"A one-sided strip tease *and* a blind taste test. Hmm." She paused the briefest of moments. "I like it."

"Do you trust me?" I said it softly into her ear, noting the shiver that passed from her scalp to her fingers.

She nodded, looking eager to get started. "I do."

"Prepare to be fed, princess."

And I meant that in every sense.

Leading Andrea to my room, I switched on a lamp, gesturing for her to take a seat on an ottoman. In my, shall we say, rather vast experience, mood was everything. Producing a dark silk scarf from my drawer, I held it up for her inspection. When she nodded, I fastened it securely around her head over her eyes.

"Are you comfortable?"

"Yes. Perfectly."

I pulled my own seat close, my thighs bracketing her legs. I held up the first chocolate to her nose, wafting it beneath her nostrils like a fine cigar. Leaning in, I poised the chocolate at the threshold of her silky lips. My eyes dropped to the top button of her blouse as she inhaled deeply to smell the chocolaty aromas. Her heaving breasts left my mouth parched. "Open."

She parted her pouty lips, and I fed her a bite of the bonbon.

"Mmm, that's *good*. It's…mango, I think?"

I took a bite of the chocolate, holding it between my teeth, and brought my lips close enough to hers that we traded breaths. "Close—but not quite. It's passionfruit."

While the game was my idea, it was incredibly distracting—and far more provocative than I'd anticipated.

Her disappointment quickly morphed into clear arousal. Her features relaxed, her nostrils flared, and goosebumps shot up her arms. "What are you going to take off first?"

I slunk my hand over her luscious breasts, tracing her erect nipples through her shirt. "Your shirt."

Unbuttoning her top, I eased off the green silk that had tantalized me all day as I'd imagined what lay beneath. A black lace bra greeted my hungry eyes. *Oh, yes, this is fun.*

"Are you ready for the next chocolate, or would you like a sip of water first?"

"Water, please."

After she'd sipped some, we passed on to the next delicacy. I repeated what I'd done before, allowing her to smell before tasting. Watching her lips part to receive what I fed her was rapidly becoming my favorite sight. As her straight, white teeth took the chocolate, I imagined them biting my chest. She allowed the treat to melt on her tongue the way my cock would soon. When her tongue darted out to clear a crumb from her lip, my dick throbbed.

"Oh, that's ginger! Mmm, can I have some more of that?"

I fed her a little more. "You guessed correctly, enchantress. Allow me to give you some more water." *I'll manage to have some fun out of this too.*

She nodded.

Holding the glass to her lips, I tipped it a little more than necessary, causing water to spill down her chin and clavicle. Her shoulders hitched in surprise at the cold liquid.

"I'll take care of you." Dipping my tongue in the tantalizing groove between her breasts, I licked my way up her chest, swerving to nick her clavicle with my teeth. As I lapped up every last driblet of water from her sweet skin, I basked in the scent of lavender and juniper that emanated from her pores.

"*Unnhh*," she groaned beneath the ministrations of my tongue, her thighs clenching as I pulled away.

My hardened cock strained against my pants.

"On to the next." I produced another bonbon from the box, hypnotized as her irresistible teeth and lips closed around it.

This one stymied her. "Pepper of some kind—or spice. And some fruit. I'll guess peach."

I bit into it, brushing her lips so that she opened to receive it. My tongue tangoed with hers during the transaction.

"You decide if you guessed closely enough. It was chile mango." I smiled with satisfaction when her features indicated she was ready to judge against herself.

She shook her head. "No. I was way off base."

My hands roamed lazily to the waistband of her skirt. "This must go. Stand."

She obeyed, and I unzipped it from the back, helping her shimmy out of the skirt. *Ah, that round, plump, tight ass.* My hands molded themselves to her cheeks, squeezing the two perfect globes. Seeing that the elastic of her panties was twisted, I decided to seize another opportunity before feeding her the next chocolate.

"Allow me to straighten a kink in your panties. If I may . . ." Inserting two fingers at the top of her thigh, I ran my hand up through her underwear to her belly button. There my fingers lingered a moment, tickling and teasing her navel. Her thighs pulled together around my forearm, making my dick jerk up. "Open wide for me, fair one." As I slid my hand down, I caught sight of a beautiful black patch of hair nestling between her legs. *Ah, the pleasure garden of my dreams.*

I wafted another chocolate beneath her nose. As I fed it to her, I ran the pad of my thumb along her lower lip, pressing into its pillowiness.

"Oh! That's a liquor. I know it." She scrunched up her nose adorably. "Bailey's Irish cream?"

"Try again." I fed her the rest.

She shook her head, swallowing the piece. "That's my best guess."

"Kahlúa." I trailed my fingers along her breastplate

toward her bra, which had a front clasp opening. "This is the next casualty."

She opened her arms so I could shuck off her bra, her firm, round breasts springing free. I salivated with the need to lick the darkened haloes around her alert nipples. Circling her nipples with my thumbs, I took each in my teeth, tugging until she cried out. Then I soothed the pain with soft brushes of my fingers and warm breaths. She moaned, lolling her head back.

"Try your best. I'd hate to think you're letting me win." Actually, that idea made my already impatient cock drill a hole in my boxer briefs.

I produced another chocolate, fairly confident she wouldn't guess this one.

"Mmm, that's weird but good." She let it drift over her tongue, breathing in deeply. Damn, this game was hot. *She* was hot. "Is it mint?"

I fed her the last bite, decadently swirling my tongue with hers. "Lemongrass."

"Oh! Never in a million years would I have guessed that." Swallowing, she bit her lip. "I guess there's only one thing left for you to take off."

I pulled her to a standing position, crushing her lips with mine and pillaging her mouth. All the flavors she'd just sampled lingered on her tongue. I lapped them up, together with her own aromas.

I slowly tugged down her panties, sloping my hands along her inner thighs. She trembled from head to toe.

Stepping behind her, I spoke low in her ear. "Now, sorceress, we have two options. You can keep your blindfold on, or I can remove it."

Her throat bobbed. "I want to see your body…but I

love feeling all my other senses keenly when I can't see. And I love the way you have all the power now. I guess…leave it on."

I smirked. "We can always do it differently in round two." I lifted her in my arms, laying her on her back on the bed. Then I stripped in record time, keeping my eyes trained on her breathtaking body. She was a goddess, as I'd known that first night when she arrived. She was so confident of her sexiness, so at home in her own skin. I loved that she'd trusted me with all the power. "Spread your legs wide."

Now, the soup course.

My tongue leisurely roamed along her divide, flicking her clit. She cried out, spasming. Parting her labia with my thumbs, I exposed her throbbing pussy to the air, curling a finger up to her sensitive spot.

"*Ohh, God, yeess!*" she moaned.

I left her breathing a space as I drew my tongue along her slit and played with her clit—batting it, tweaking it, swirling it, flipping it. With each touch, she jerked and gyrated, begging for more. Then I fluttered my tongue against her bud while sinking two fingers in her pussy, rubbing against her G-spot as I did the same to her pleasure nub.

"*Please,* Guy!"

I removed my tongue and fingers for a few seconds. Then, alternating thrusting my tongue in and sucking her clit, I brought her to the brink, withdrawing my tongue altogether.

Wounded my heart is, but with the eyes of a lady.

"Please! I'm almost there!"

Yes, princess, all in good time. My tongue slowly, lightly circled her bundle of nerves, drawing out her torment. After a long moment, I plunged three fingers in her heat, swirling her clit with my tongue, and she erupted like a volcano, wailing and digging her fingernails into the bedspread. She bucked her hips into my face, spilling her juices over my tongue and lips. Mmm, she tasted like fine blue point oysters. I kissed her lips rubbing her come into her tongue so she could share her own nectar with me.

Fisting my cock, I pumped it a few times and sheathed it, rolling the condom all the way to the base. Reaching down, I untied her blindfold, and she blinked up at me with her soulful eyes.

Now, for the entrée.

I slid into her pussy, feeling her tight walls grabbing at every inch of my shaft. "You good, princess?"

She nodded, her eyes glassy. "*You're* good."

I laughed. Then I lost all sense of time and place as her warm, wet channel swallowed me, driving me forward to a cliff. I thrust in and out, faster and more furious, feeling the throbbing and swelling that led to release.

"Oh, don't stop—I'm gonna come!" Her voice broke on a rising pitch.

I pounded her a few more times and then stopped, holding still, before rising and slamming deep inside her. She screamed, contracting into me and toppling me over into the abyss. I bellowed, letting myself fall on top of her, a spineless, limbless deadweight.

I'd never had such an intense climax.

We breathed heavily for a few moments before I rolled off, disposing of the condom. Then I rejoined her in bed.

While I didn't do pillow talk with every woman, something about Andrea made me want to be completely open, to know more about what made her tick. Supporting her head on my arm and draping my other arm over her belly, I gazed at her captivating profile.

"Which interests are most important for you to share with a man?"

She smiled. "You'd do better to ask which I absolutely *couldn't* share with a man. I can work with most men's interests."

"And the ones you can't work with?" I stroked her curls, savoring their tightness and heft.

"Collectors of anything. I don't see the point. It's just *things*."

"Most aptly put." I ran my fingers along her arm.

She stroked my chest, squeezing one of my pectorals. "Adrenaline junkies would worry me. I'd always suspect they're not going to come home from whatever rappelling or skydiving excursion they go on. And I sure as hell wouldn't join them."

"I share your sentiment." I traced her sinuous contours, resting my palm on her hip.

"And lastly—I know this is going to sound harsh—gamers. Videogames bore the bejeezus out of me."

I laughed. "I couldn't agree more."

We were silent a space, as I palmed her flat belly, swirling my index finger in her navel.

"Why are you still single, Guy Travis?" Her refreshing boldness took my breath away.

"High standards, enchantress."

"And what are those standards?" she pressed on.

"A woman must be independent, not clingy," I

began. "She must be career-oriented. Idleness like my mother's I can't abide. She must have a complex mind, a good heart, a sharp wit, a strong will, and a certain refinement. And, of course, she must be beautiful and sexy."

Andrea laughed. "Now I see why you're still on your own."

"Once more, you sell yourself short. If you look in the mirror, you'll see the woman I've just described." I cupped her cheek, pulling her down for a kiss.

****

We had gone four more rounds—one in the hot tub, one with Andrea kneeling face down on the mattress, one in the shower, and one with her riding me like a cowgirl—when we finally drifted off to sleep. I hadn't had marathon sex like this in several months, and never with such a total-package bombshell as Andrea.

I made a mental note to wake at exactly 8 a.m. That was a gift I had: I could tell myself down to the minute what time I wanted to rise, and my eyes would pop open at that precise time.

At 8, leaving my sleeping beauty deep in slumber, I padded out to one of the zen gardens to make my call. It was 4 p.m. Monday in New York.

"Promontory Press, this is Sheila speaking," a bright voice chirped.

"Hello, Sheila, this is Guy Travis. May I speak to Mr. Aansvort?" I took a seat on a stone bench, stretching my legs out.

"I'll see if he's free, Mr. Travis."

A minute later, a booming voice sounded at the other end of the line. "Guy Travis?" The same breathless excitement punctuated his words that much of the general public showed me. "*The* Guy Travis?"

"The one and only," I drawled, examining a fingernail. I must remember to have Char give me a manicure before she left. She was almost as deft a cosmetician as she was a cook. "Mr. Aansvort, I have a proposition for you."

"Yes, Mr. Travis. I'm all ears," he stuttered.

"You have an extremely gifted editor, Ms. Andrea Carpel. I'm interested in co-writing my memoir with her." I let this sink in. "Your press would have exclusive rights to publication."

"Your memoir, Mr. Travis? But that's...that's astonishing! That'd be a mega-bestseller on all the lists. They'd want to turn it into a movie. It'd be a goldmine. I—I don't know what to say." From the way he puffed as if he'd crested a high mountain, I'd guess he was a heavyset man.

"Say yes, Mr. Aansvort."

"Yes! We'll draw up a contract right away." He sounded jubilant.

"About that. I have certain stipulations."

Not even this could dampen his spirits. "Of course, Mr. Travis. Name them."

I smiled. This was almost too easy. "For starters, I'd want Andrea—Ms. Carpel—to work with me where I am right now."

"Ah. Yes, good. Where are you?"

"Verau. A small island off the coast of Fiji."

"Oh." That gave him pause. "Well, I'd have to ask her if she minds going so far, Mr. Travis."

I paused for effect. "As it happens, she's already here."

As he quieted, I could almost hear the wheels spinning. "That's handy then, isn't it, Mr. Travis? Any other conditions to mention now?"

"Andrea's—Ms. Carpel's—name would be the sole name on the cover. After all, she'll do the lion's share of the writing." I knew that the cover author made more money if she didn't share authorship with another writer. I certainly didn't need the money—or the fame. "And, she'll stay with me until the book is fully drafted."

His voice was warm and unctuous. "Not a problem, Mr. Travis. I'm sure she'd be delighted. I'll tell her supervisor to clear all her other projects so she can start immediately."

"And you'll email her all the details?" I pressed.

"Right away."

"Do be sure to tell her to stay put here in Verau." I stood.

"I will, Mr. Travis."

"Call me Guy."

"Guy, thank you. You've made my week."

I ended the call, satisfied with my handiwork.

Time to rejoin my sleeping lioness.

Chapter Twenty-Seven

Andrea

Awaking at 9 in Guy's arms, I felt sore all over—especially in my coochie. But that didn't mean I wasn't ready for another round. After priming me with his fingers, he took me from behind in my favorite position, spooning me. As a lover, Guy was just the right amount of overbearing and sensitive. He was dedicated to giving me pleasure and keeping me guessing while he was at it. I could've continued our sex marathon into next week—or next month, for that matter. But I knew the real world and packing awaited. I dragged myself out of bed, borrowing a kimono from Guy to return to my room to dress.

Before I left, he pulled me to him in a deep, sensual kiss, twining our tongues like vines as he caressed my breast. God, the man really could kiss. I fleetingly wondered if he'd like to hook up again in New York once he returned. But I would never mention it if he didn't. After all, he probably had hundreds of women on speed dial to cater to his whims. I doubted I was particularly special.

I sang Aretha in the shower as I soaped up—"You make me feel like a natural woman." I laughed as I realized it'd been months since I'd busted out a tune in the shower.

Clad in a white one-piece denim romper and blue strappy high sandals, I made my way toward the dining room, my stomach grumbling. I'd forgotten how hungry sex made me. Plus, I hadn't eaten anything other than bites of chocolate since the cake yesterday at the doctor's house.

As I entered the dining room, my phone chimed with an email from the press's owner, Geoff Aansvort. Reading it, I nearly dropped my phone. *What. The. FUCK?* Was this some kind of sick joke?

Ingrid caught my stricken expression, bounding over and coiling an arm around my waist. "What's wrong, D?"

Thank God she was here to support me, because I very well might've fainted. I passed her the phone, my hand shaking. "Read this. Geoff sent it a minute ago."

She skimmed it, her eyes bulging. "Wow. Is this for real, Drea?"

I nodded. "Geoff *never* jokes about shit like this. But there's only one person who can tell me what this is about." I narrowed my eyes at Guy, who was chatting with Bryn at the end of the breakfast table. Stomping over, I inserted the phone in midair between Guy's plate and his chin. "Care to explain the email I just received from my boss?"

Unperturbed, he salted his eggs, lifting a piece of buttered toast to his lips. "Ah, I see Mr. Aansvort works fast."

I snatched the phone back. "What do you know about this?"

"Take a seat, sorceress." He pulled out the empty chair beside him. "I'll tell you everything once you've got a plate of food before you. You need to replenish your glycogen stores."

I crossed my arms over my chest. "No. I want to hear it now."

He rose, seating me in his own chair and picking up an empty plate near the buffet. After filling it with omelet, bacon, sausage, pancake, and toast, he set it down. Then he slid his own plate to the side and sat in the empty chair. "Now, eat, princess. You need brain fuel."

Ingrid sat down across from us, listening intently.

"I called your boss this morning and arranged everything. You're staying here for as long as it takes us to knock out a first draft of my memoir." Guy bit into a strip of bacon, chewing thoughtfully. "I knew you wouldn't agree to it until all the details had been sorted. So I held off on telling you."

I gaped, not believing I'd heard right. "You went behind my back because you wanted to play God with my life? So you and Geoff could have a man-to-man talk to settle my future without any interference? So you could take all choice out of my hands?"

Guy met my gaze, unfazed. "This is everything you've dreamed of. You'll write a memoir and publish it. You'll be able to dedicate your time to your craft, and you'll gain the recognition you deserve as an author. You'll be able to stay here in Verau, as you wished to do, and—" he cleared his throat—"we'll have plenty of time together. I thought my solution was rather neat."

I threw up my hands. "You and Liam are unbelievable. You both think you can just snap your fingers and the world will do your bidding. You think if you want something—someone—you can just snatch her. Liam was incredibly lucky. He found someone who went along with the grab. But I'm not so easy, Guy. I'm not going down without a fight. I don't know how I'm going to fuck with your plan on this one, but mark my words, you won't win."

He looked genuinely puzzled. "Fight? Why should we fight, princess? We both agree on all the points I laid out. Perhaps our only source of disagreement is in the *how*. But what's done is done, and the ends justify the means. It's what I believe they call a win-win."

I slapped his face. To his credit, he barely flinched, though his cheek reddened. Tears hovered in the corners of my eyes, but I willed them back down. "Don't you get it, Guy? I want to have a say-so in my own fate. I don't want to be the pawn in someone else's chess game. I've worked damn hard to achieve what I've achieved, and this job means everything to me. When you come along and interfere with it on a whim, it makes a mockery of all my efforts. You're mocking *me*."

Now the tears fell fast, heedless of my attempts to hold them back.

Guy took out a perfectly clean white cotton handkerchief—of course he had one folded in his jacket pocket—and dabbed at my cheeks, snaking an arm around my back. "There now, fair damsel, please don't cry. Did you ever wonder why I went to such lengths to keep you here? I consider you a rare, priceless gem. I couldn't imagine you leaving so soon, and us not having time to get to know each other better. I thought I was doing what would make you happy, whichever way you looked at it. I'm sorry I upset you. That was the last thing I wanted—the last thing I'd ever want."

Ingrid set a chair down to my other side, hugging me to her. "Drea, take some air. I'll walk with you. After we've exercised a little, it'll all look clearer. But you really should eat something before we go. You must be starving."

Despite the hollowness in my chest and the stuffiness in my head, I still felt a keen hunger in my belly. I took a few desultory pecks at my food, as Ingrid filled my mug with coffee, fixing it the way I liked. I noted, in my peripheral vision, that Guy watched her closely, as though memorizing how I preferred my drink.

For the rest of breakfast, I tried to shove thoughts of Guy, Geoff, and the job to the back of my mind. These could all wait until Ingrid and I breathed in the fresh air.

After breakfast, Liam arranged his brother's departure for later that day with Josefa.

"Andrea, I take it you won't be joining Rory?" I could hear the smirk in Liam's voice.

These arrogant men were too much, slapping each other on the back when they made a score and supporting each other's criminal activities.

Ingrid's eyes jumped between me, Guy, and Liam. "Liam, please hold off on telling Josefa what Andrea plans to do. They still have another four hours before they need to leave."

Liam shrugged, his lips twisting into a grin. "Andrea knows how much I like her company. Far be it from me to send her packing before she's ready."

How on earth could Ingrid stand him? But she always did gravitate toward pricks. And now, it appeared, so did I.

****

"Drea, did Geoff say this project with Guy was important to your press?" Ingrid asked as we trekked along a dirt path skirting a mangrove swamp on the southern side of the island.

I scowled. "When I wrote him back to ask if someone else could do it, he said, if I didn't accept this assignment, I could consider myself terminated." I shuddered at the thought.

Ingrid took my hand. "So Geoff's determined to bring it about."

"Of course he is." I kicked a scallop shell along the path. "From his perspective, it's a dream come true. The famous Guy Travis handing his million-dollar life story over to the press, and requesting one of its editors to co-author it. It'll keep Promontory Press on the map for years to come, and drum up more business from other celebrities like him."

"Well, looking at it objectively, is it so very awful a proposition then?" Ingrid asked softly. "I mean, you did have marathon sex with Guy and wished you could stay longer. And you do want to hone your memoir-writing skills and get noticed for your own work. The bonus Geoff floated was pretty phenomenal. And I imagine Guy would be able to bump that up. Think of all the things you and I could do together if you were here longer. I'm sure you and Guy could hammer out a draft in two months or less, no?"

I laughed. "Ingrid, you could charm the stripes off a zebra. The bonus is the main attraction. I've never had that kind of money offered to me for anything. I guess selling my freedom for two months or so is a small price to pay for comfortably padding my savings account. Mom and Dad will be retiring soon, and Vanessa, Chris, and I will probably need to help support them at some point. And I've got to admit that the idea of having my name on the cover of a book I've co-written is a pretty awesome prospect. Especially if it makes it big. It'll open up all kinds of doors in the literary world that are closed to me now."

"Not to mention I'll get to see you, *and* you'll be able to get to know Guy more." She hopped excitedly.

"Guy can take his chocolates and stick them where the sun don't shine," I gritted.

She grimaced. "That sounds painful."

I gave a curt nod. "I certainly hope so."

Chapter Twenty-Eight

Liam

Later that afternoon, I sat on the terrace with my laptop, staring out at the violent dark waves whipping up and the grey clouds louring. The storm was due to pass through in the next few hours, right around the time when Josefa would return from Fiji after dropping Rory. I'd been tempted to leave my brother high and dry and let him hire a captain and boat of his own. But in the end, I'd taken pity on him. After all, he had come to my island on a fruitless mission, and left empty-handed.

My thoughts drifted to Monday, when I planned to fly out to help Ralph, Claude, and Rodrigo penetrate the cult compound in Indiana and rescue Gretchen and Katrina. Bryn had secured us a fake search warrant, on which I'd forged a judge's signature. We'd all wear FBI badges, carrying pieces. But if everything went according to plan, we wouldn't need to fire a single shot.

I would bring my sister and niece back here and, hopefully, get them both used to the world outside the compound. Island life was laid-back enough that here they could ease into normal existence. And I knew Ingrid would help them adjust. When her maternal instincts kicked in with that little girl in Suva yesterday,

I saw how compassionate she was. She'd be a perfect companion for Gretchen and Katrina.

Guy came out to join me, carrying a cup of tea in an actual saucer.

I slid him a sidelong glance. "Where'd you find a cup and saucer? I never ordered any for the kitchen."

"I brought them with me. Tea tastes foul in a mug," he clipped.

"Someone's in a bad mood." I clucked. "Andrea got you down?"

"She'll come round eventually." He sipped his tea, which smelled strongly of barley. "She's just in shock."

I sat back in my chair, placing my laptop on the table. "I applaud your skulduggery, my friend. I didn't know you had it in you to be such a caveman."

"Cavemen didn't have to face blowback for their stratagems," he grumbled.

I patted his arm. "It just forces you to sharpen your skills of persuasion. I don't imagine her holding out long."

He eyed me indignantly. "You set a bad precedent, old man. Your moral corruption has spread like a corrosive chemical through your immediate circle. And now here we are, with two captive women. Your capture can be justified through returned affection. But will mine fare as well?"

I sipped the tea in my mug. "If you want it to, Guy. Your will is at least as strong as mine—if not stronger."

"Of course I want it to," he said gruffly. "You know I'm big on follow-through."

I chuckled. "Nobody would accuse you of doing a half-assed job at anything." This was one of the things I loved about my friend. Like me, he never waffled or wavered with anything that meant enough to him.

Guy gazed out at a passing ship. "Will time alone bring her to my side, or ought I to help the process along?"

I fixed my eyes on a huge storm cloud hovering on the southeastern horizon. "Like any operational strategy, you need to have a general game plan you can modify as circumstances change. The key is to spot your opportunities and be adaptable."

****

Josefa made it back just as the rains began to lash the windows and doors. Battening down the hatches, the entire household remained indoors after dinner. The winds howled fiercely, as the whitecaps rolled into shore like advancing troops and the wind-tossed palms and pines swayed violently. Though Federico insisted on a chess game, my mind was only halfway on the moves. This was the biggest storm I'd witnessed on the island. I hoped the water purification systems, generator, and sewage treatment plant would hold up under the attack of the elements.

Thankfully, the latest delivery of food and supplies had come in yesterday, so we were set for a few days at least. Char, Jesse, and the other gardeners had brought in plenty of fresh produce earlier in the day. The fishermen had hauled in impressive catches from all the churned-up waters of the last day or so.

Guy, Bryn, Connie, Andrea, and Ingrid were playing rounds of poker at the oval table in one corner of the living room. A playlist of country music from the 1940s and 1950s on Guy's phone twanged from the speaker.

All evening, Andrea had studiously avoided talking

to or looking at Guy. She had occupied a seat at the far end of the table, near Jesse, leaving Guy's "corpse bride" spot empty for the first time since she'd arrived.

Bryn seemed to be wiping the floor with all the other players. I suspected he had a methodical system of playing based on his training in computer science. Ingrid, who was the true North on my compass, always pulling my attention back to her, was laughing at her own poor plays. I gathered she was running low on chips after folding several times in a row. I smiled, thinking she was the least likely person to carry off a bluff when she had bad cards. Nor did she seem to have a good poker face. I loved that about her. She was an open book and honest to boot.

Andrea, by contrast, elicited everyone's groans when she flipped over a low hand after making all the other players fold.

"Is there anything you can't do?" Guy's voice thrilled with admiration.

Ignoring him, Andrea raked in her chips.

Connie sighed, stretching her arms. "Does anyone want to play Scrabble? I'm much better at that than poker."

Ingrid brightened. "Yes! I'll fetch the box."

Connie and Ingrid dominated the five-way game from the get-go. When Federico checkmated me, I went to stand behind Ingrid, watching the plays unfold. While the other players formed words behind their holders, looking in vain for places to put them, Ingrid had a gift for working her letters around what was already on the board.

She looked up at me with a twinkle in her eye. "I think I'm mildly dyslexic, which helps in this game."

Sweet, modest Ingrid. She would never admit to a strength—only to what she perceived as weaknesses.

When she went out on a triple-word score with a seven-letter word that garnered her a fifty-point bonus for a total of ninety-five points, everyone made sounds of mock despair.

"I had a good draw with those letters." She pulled more letters from the bag. "And luckily that triple was still free to use."

Andrea sipped her hot chocolate, which Tima had made for everyone after dinner. "I could've warned you all beforehand, but chose to hold my tongue—when it comes to Scrabble, Ingrid is not to be messed with."

When Ingrid used up the last available letters, and points were tallied, she'd won by a wide margin. I had the urge to fling her over my shoulder and take her back to our room, fucking her senseless. But as the host, I had to make sure my guests were happy.

"Shall we all call it a night?" I proposed to the room at large. "It's past midnight."

"I'll be up a while longer to talk to a few clients in New York," said Stephen. "But don't anyone stay up for me."

Andrea stood, yawning. "I'm going to call my parents and sister. 'Night, Ingrid." She kissed Ingrid's cheek, her eyes flicking to mine. "If the bedbugs bite too viciously, let me know."

My lips twitched, as my eyes cut to Guy and then back to Andrea. "Try letting a bedbug do some biting, Andrea. It'll take the edge off."

She flushed, her eyes shooting daggers. "I'll be on edge as long as this house continues to be infested. I recommend fumigation."

Baiting her was quickly becoming my second favorite pastime, after fucking Ingrid. "Since your own fate is bound up with said bedbugs, I wouldn't advise exterminating them. You'd take yourself down too."

Guy gallantly came to Andrea's rescue. "A lady has every right to kill bothersome parasites. The instinct for survival trumps all else."

Andrea was still fuming from my comment.

"Perhaps," said Ingrid, ever the peacekeeper, "a parasitic relationship can become symbiotic over time."

"Yes, Andrea," I gibed. "Why don't you try sleeping with the enemy?"

Guy bridled at my remark. "Old man, you must've forgotten never to kick someone when they're down."

Andrea's chin lifted. "I'm quite certain Liam is unfamiliar with that expression. He obviously excels at putting a boot in someone's face."

With that she turned on her heel, storming out of the room, with Guy trailing in her wake like a hopeful puppy.

I chuckled, oddly glad that Guy had forced Andrea to stay. Her displeasure and pain appealed to my sadistic tendencies, and her animosity fueled my wit.

With no further obstacles in my way, I slung Ingrid over my shoulder to the sound of her squeals, and carted her back to our room. My dick was ready to go by the time I slid open our door.

I had just tied her to the four corners of the bed and begun to torment her with the falls of a flog, when the lamps went off.

Shit. The generator had failed.

In the pitch blackness, I untied Ingrid, thinking fast. I'd need a few of the staff to come with me to the area outside the northern outbuilding, where the generator was. But I didn't want Ingrid to be alone and afraid. I kissed her in the darkness.

"My sweet rosebud, I'm going to bring you to the living room, where other guests will soon keep you company. In the meantime, I'm going to fix the power. You won't be afraid?"

She shook her head. "No, Liam. As long as you're safe, I'm not afraid. It's not dangerous, what you're doing?" She clung to my neck, and my dick sprang to attention once more, as though the raging storm had no sway over my desires. "Can I help?"

"No, little lamb. I want you to stay inside with the others." I picked her up in my arms.

"Promise me you won't risk your life—or anyone else's," she said into my shoulder.

"I promise."

Using her phone as a flashlight, Ingrid lit our way to the living room, where I deposited her on the sofa, kissing her tenderly. On my own phone, I texted Bryn, Sione, and Mafu to meet me here.

Two minutes later, they arrived, ready for anything.

"Mafu, can you find the barbecue lighter in the workshop?" I asked.

Mafu nodded.

"Sione, can you bring an umbrella?"

Sione bobbed his head.

"Bryn, you've got the flashlights?"

"With fully charged batteries, boss," said Bryn.

"Let's go."

Chapter Twenty-Nine

Guy

At first, I thought the knocking was the sound of trees outside. But when I realized it was coming from inside, I sprang out of bed and strode to the door, sliding it open.

Andrea poured herself into the room, the darkness masking her features.

I held her by the elbows. "Are you all right?"

I cursed myself for not checking on her as soon as the lamps had gone off. Assuming she'd already turned in, I hadn't wanted to disturb her sleep for a power outage that would probably be resolved by the time she awoke. But apparently she'd still been awake.

She was trembling in my arms. "I—I can't stand being in the dark all alone, knowing there's no light. It makes me feel as if I'm drowning. As if the ocean has swallowed me."

Lighting the way with my cellphone flashlight, I led her to the bed, seating her on the mattress and sitting down beside her. "Fear not, princess. Liam will have the electricity back on within the hour."

"My cell phone was out of charge, so I couldn't text Ingrid. I just barely stumbled here to your room." In the glow of the flashlight, she still looked panic-stricken.

I wrapped an arm around her. "You did the right thing coming here. We'll talk until the lights come back on."

Relief washed over her face. "You'd do that?"

"I can think of no better way to spend the night than in your company." I meant every word. "Tell me why you fear the darkness so much."

She blew out a stuttery breath. "When I was eight, my family took a vacation to the redwoods near San Francisco. My older sister Vanessa wasn't there—she'd gone on vacation with a friend's family. My older brother Chris, my parents, and I were driving down the coastal highway late at night in a beat-up VW Rabbit looking for any place that was still open to sleep. We saw a motel that flashed 'Vacancy,' so my dad pulled down into the lot. But as soon as the motel owners saw who we were—a Black family who couldn't afford a better car—they shut off the vacancy sign and turned off the lights in the office."

I gripped her hand. I rarely swore, but were I the swearing kind, I'd be cursing like a sailor right now.

"My dad drove on, until we reached a park just north of Bodega Bay. By now it was so late, no motel would admit us. So he parked us off the road on the edge of the beach. We had plenty of room to sleep in the car—space wasn't the problem. But as the night progressed, I got colder and colder. The beach was a freezing place to park, and the engine was cut off, so there was no heat. Since I couldn't sleep, my thoughts swirled. What if the encroaching ocean waves swallowed me whole? The tide was rising the whole night, and the roar of the swell grew closer and closer. The black, cold, unknown was about to overwhelm me, and I wouldn't be able to breathe when it came. My teeth chattered, my nightmarish visions grew more graphic, and all this time, the rest of my family was snoring soundly as if impending doom didn't threaten us. Since then, I've tended to transform things at night into terrifying versions of themselves. But the worst of all is pure blackness, which reminds me of the advancing ocean from that terrible night."

She convulsed, as if reliving the moment. I held her firmly in my arms. "I'm sorry you experienced this trauma. If I could absorb it for you, I would. You're incredibly brave to speak of it now. Just as you emerged alive from that nightmare, you will emerge from other nightmares, stronger each time for having gotten through them and shared your story."

She turned to me in the dim light. "It's the *largeness* of everything that frightens me most. When I zoom in on a patch of Google Earth, it looks harmless enough. But when I gradually zoom out, I have a near panic attack, seeing how *much* there is of the planet— how everything that seemed immobile turns out to be alive and whirling." She shuddered again.

I cupped her cheek, gazing into her hazelnut eyes. "Then immobilize it. Whenever the world in movement frightens you, picture it as no more than a series of still frames that only together form a motion picture. Keep the frames separate, if you need to. You control your perspective on the world. You *can* draw out leviathan on a hook."

The glimmer of a smile on her lips told me she recognized the biblical reference. "My aunt Bridget would say you're blaspheming."

I gave a wry smile. "I'm known for that, princess."

She looked down at her hands. "Thanks for listening. You're right. It does feel good to talk about it."

"Putting words to things reduces them."

She reflected for a moment. "What do you want, Guy?"

I knew exactly what she meant. "I want to get to know you. I can't think of a better way to do that than having you co-write my memoir."

Her eyes were surprisingly open and soft. "But why me? You have hundreds of women fawning on you across the world."

I considered this. "Perhaps it's because you *don't* fawn on me. You have your own life, you know your own mind, and you give as good as you get."

"I'll continue to dog you, you know. I don't take lightly to having my freedom pulled out from under my feet." The fire returned to her eyes.

"Do your worst. I deserve it."

"Are you sure you know what you're getting yourself into, Guy Travis?" Since she only used my full name when she was teasing, I knew she felt better.

I returned her mirthful glance. "I have absolutely no clue, Andrea Carpel. And that's precisely what I like about the situation."

****

Liam

A combination of pine branches, palm fronds, and a fallen aluminum awning made it difficult at first to access the external casing to the generator. The torrential rains pelted down, while southeasterly winds whipped ferociously. With Mafu and Sione's help, I was able to clear the surface of debris, while Bryn trained several flashlights on our work. Bryn held up the awning as a shield from the winds, while Sione held a large sturdy umbrella and Mafu stood ready with the barbecue lighter. Prying off the case, I found that, sure enough, the igniter had gotten wet, preventing the generator from getting gas. Switching off the igniter, I proceeded to wipe down every surface I could with rags, under the shelter of the umbrella.

"Lighter, Mafu."

He handed it to me. Turning on the igniter, I lit the flame. Then I switched the generator back on. A few seconds later, several lights flicked on in the house, telling us power was restored. We carefully replaced the casing, before turning to the problem of remounting the awning.

"We could do it when the storm has passed, boss," Bryn suggested. "It doesn't really protect the generator."

Figuring the winds were likely to tear up the awning again anyway, I partly wedged it in between the generator and the low wall. "Fine. Let's go in."

Ingrid was busy serving tea to those servants who'd been alarmed by the electrical outage. She'd used her cell phone to light her way around the kitchen and found some candles. With the help of Epeli, she'd brought out trays of mugs to the staff gathered in the dining room.

I was flooded with a feeling I hadn't experienced in a while. Seeing her busying herself to calm other people's fears made my fondness for her grow. Rather than panicking, she'd put herself to work. I'd always suspected she was resilient and courageous, but this just confirmed it.

Sopping wet, I slunk my arms around her waist from behind, as she deposited a tray on the kitchen counter. "Weren't you afraid?"

"No." She twisted her beautiful face toward me. "I knew you would take care of it."

My chest expanded, and there it was again, that pang of something I couldn't pinpoint. The sense that small things didn't matter—that the bottom line was much bigger and more all-encompassing than anything in this moment, what went before, or what directly followed. I was being swept along in a current I couldn't fight, without knowing my destination. For once, my lack of control didn't faze me. I was ready to embrace the unknown.

Chapter Thirty

Ingrid

It was time to tell my parents everything. Well, not everything. But a watered-down version that would pave the way to their forgiving me. Once Andrea had arrived, Liam let me use my phone and send emails without supervision. Now, late Wednesday night, several hours after the storm had died down, I stepped onto the porch outside our bedroom, took a deep breath, and tapped the call icon next to *Mom*. Liam was in the living room with some of the guests, so I had complete privacy.

As the ringer sounded, my heart stuttered, and I paced across the porch, gulping in a few deep breaths. I had only a vague idea of what I was going to say, praying the rest would come to me.

"Ingrid, sweetie!" Mom's voice echoed down the line. "Let me just turn off this skillet."

A moment later, she came back on. "How are you, darling?"

"Mom, it's so good to hear your voice. I'm fine. How are you?"

"There's a lot happening here. But I don't want to bore you with it all just now. First off, how's Grigoriy?" She was so enthusiastic and supportive of anything I did, I winced at the thought of coming clean.

"I have a lot to tell you." I clenched my fist. "You remember those photos I sent of him and me on the beach?"

"Yes! Those were beautiful. It looks like a tropical paradise."

"Well, actually, we're not in the Maldives. We're near Fiji—in the South Pacific." I took a steadying breath. "I'm sorry I lied to you. I was protecting, uh…Grigoriy." *One thing at a time*.

"Not in the Maldives? But darling, why did you tell us you were?" She sounded deeply hurt.

I braced myself, gulping. "I was afraid that if you knew where I was, you might make me leave."

"Why would we do that, love?"

Good question.

"Well, it sort of felt as if we sneaked away. I didn't want anyone to think he'd kidnapped me." *Halfway true*.

Mom's smile seeped through her voice. "Dad and I know you, darling. You're impulsive and happy-go-lucky. But we trust your judgement. Before calling the police, we'd always double-check with you."

I closed my eyes. "Thank you, Mom."

"As long as you're happy and safe with Grigoriy, that's all that matters." She had to be the sweetest mom on earth, setting the bar high for sympathy, trust, and kindness.

"Yes. About that. I'm incredibly happy with, um, Grigoriy. I'm in love with him." I swallowed again, letting the words tumble off my tongue like coal scuttling down a chute.

She laughed. "We figured as much, Ingrid. After all, it's been almost five weeks since you first called from the island. And just the fact that you went there with him after knowing him for only two months—you must've trusted him."

Oh, what a tangled web we weave…

"Mom," I said in a small voice, "his name actually isn't Grigoriy. It's Liam. Liam Stauner."

"*Not Grigoriy*?!" Mom sounded more confused by this than any of the preceding lies.

"No. He's American—not Russian."

Mom breathed a sigh—was that relief? "Oh, thank God, Ingrid. We were so worried, Dad and I. We thought if he was Russian and had an island in the Maldives, he must be involved in something shady. Dad, especially, was prepared for the worst. But why ever did you lie to us, Ingrid?"

"He's a low-profile billionaire, Mom. He doesn't want to call attention to the fact that he bought this island as his second home. He's very reclusive. I was respecting his wish to keep under the radar." *Please, God, don't let me burn in hell for telling more lies to my mom.*

"Oh, I see. Yes, that makes sense." I could hear the wheels spinning in her head. "He's not a real estate developer, is he?"

Shit. "No. No, he's not. He's a foreign exchange trader."

"Oh, Ingrid." Disappointment leached through her voice, and I bowed my head, ashamed. "Was any of the rest true? Are you really working on E-Design projects for Simon?"

I scrunched my eyes shut, grinning and bearing my shame. "Not exactly. I'm working remotely still, but Simon wouldn't hear of my doing E-Design."

Mom's voice grew uneasy. "Did you really know Liam for two months before you left?"

Damn. My tissue of lies was truly untangling.

"Um, we actually met shortly before we left for his island."

"*How* shortly before?" Mom prodded.

I paused, as if I'd crested a roller coaster. *In for a penny, in for a pound...* "The night before."

Mom exploded. "*What?!* Ingrid, why did you go off with him after knowing him for only one night?"

"It was sort of love at first sight, Mom. I trusted him." *Another half-truth.*

"Oh, God, Ingrid. I don't know what Dad is going to say about all this. He's not here now—he had an early meeting at the department." I could almost see Mom brushing the hair off her face. "How long are you going to stay with…Liam?"

"Just a little while longer, Mom. I promise you everything is wonderful. Simon is…understanding, I love Liam, and life here is filled with art, good company, and exercise." I gnawed on a fingernail, deciding not to mention Andrea.

"I just hope you haven't let your heart lead you astray, sweetie." Mom sounded deeply skeptical. "For you to just up and leave your friends, family, and work, all for a man you just met…I know you say you love him. But love needs the test of those who know us—of hardship, work, and routine—to prove itself real. Above all, it needs time. Promise me you won't make any more rash decisions without speaking to me or Dad first."

My cheeks heated. "Of course not, Mom. I promise. I love you."

"I love you too, Ingrid."

I ended the call.

Large, warm arms coiled around my waist from behind, and Liam's sun-like presence filled the room. I jumped slightly, before settling my head into the beloved hollows of his chest and shoulder.

"So, you love me?" Liam caught the top of my ear lobe in his teeth, swirling his tongue in my outer ear.

How I long to tell him, with words and deeds.

"Haven't you heard the saying that those who eavesdrop hear only bad things about themselves?" I groaned as his tongue stabbed my ear canal.

"I fail to see how hearing that you love me is bad news." He pulled my head in closer to him by the throat. He knew I loved it when he toyed with choking me.

"I told my mom that to keep her from worrying," I hedged. "She said love needs time and the test of daily life and hardship to prove itself."

"I can provide plenty of hardship, my little captive. Time is also on my side." He cupped my crotch in his hand, lifting me slightly off the ground, while keeping his other hand on my throat. I loved it when he reduced me to his fuck toy, his sex doll, as he was doing now. Thoughts of home, Mom and Dad, and responsibility dissolved in the background as I ceded to the delicious sense of being controlled by Liam like his puppet. His low voice vibrated through my temple. "I'm going to treat you to a new form of hardship now."

What could he have planned? Would it be the bamboo cane? God, I hoped not the latter. My butt had been sore for days after that, even though he'd only given me a few strokes. But he said "new" . . .

237

Lifting me by the groin and throat, he carried me into the bedroom and laid me face down on the mattress. My sheath was already drenched from his manhandling. He removed my clothes, piece by piece, caressing my curves and praising me. Then, pulling me up onto my knees, he walloped my ass several times with his palm, gently rubbing out the sting. He repeated this on the other cheek. Whimpering, I leaked copiously, thoroughly primed.

I heard the swish of his own clothes being shucked. He wet his fingers with my leakage, working it into my anus. Oh, so he was going to plug his finger in my butthole while taking me from the back. *That* was always incredible.

But then I felt him applying generous amounts of a cold lube to my asshole. *Oh, no.* I clenched my butt cheeks and sphincter in response.

"No, little bird. Relax. You'll love it, I promise," he said in soothing tones.

"Oh, Liam, please. Not tonight." I knew in my heart of hearts he was going to have his way.

"Trust me. It'll be like nothing you've ever experienced. Breathe in." I did so. "Now breathe out." As I exhaled, he slid a finger into my anus, working the lube inside. Looking back, I saw him slathering his rigid cock.

Parting my butt cheeks, he directed me once more to inhale and exhale deeply. On the out breath, he slid his tip into me. I closed my eyes, thinking of the ocean and how relaxing it was to swim laps in the cove.

"That's right." He eased more of himself into me by degrees, until his balls tickled my perineum.

Excruciating pain erupted like flames through my

core. But strangely, beneath the hurt, pleasure lurked. I was so full, I thought I might explode. Pulling out halfway, he plunged in again, embedding himself in my ass. Millions of little sensors zinged all at once in my erogenous zones.

He leaned over, cocooning me with his solid heat. "How do you feel?"

"*So* good," I groaned. I had no idea pleasure could rise from these hidden parts.

"You'll feel even better in a moment." He grunted. "Fuck, you're tight. You feel so right."

As he pumped in and out, building me up to a pitch, I began to miss him when he withdrew and welcome his down thrusts. Before long, I became addicted to his steady rhythm. Bottoming out on a stroke, he reached around, sinking two fingers in my pussy and stimulating my clit. Hundreds of starbursts instantly shattered in my center. A scream tore through me as pleasure split me open. The orgasm seemed to last an eternity, all in one present moment. Liam shuddered and roared. My body jerked violently, and I collapsed onto the mattress, taking him with me.

If orgasms with Liam were like espressos, this was like speed. Tears rolled down my cheeks as I heaved with emotion.

Hearing my sobs, Liam kissed my cheek, brushing away my tears. "Are you okay?"

I nodded. "It was just very intense."

But he was right. The hardship was worth it.

Chapter Thirty-One

Ingrid

At last my present for Liam was ready. Working off and on for two weeks, I'd decorated the southern end of the main building. This section comprised Andrea's and Guy's rooms, and other guests' bedrooms. That Saturday morning, while I put the finishing touches on my surprise, excitement fluttered in my belly as I pictured how shocked Liam would be at the transformations I'd made to the bare rooms. I hadn't ever had this much fun on a decorating project.

I'd worked within most of the parameters Liam had set. I knew he wanted to preserve a certain minimalism. Wherever possible, he wanted to keep Asian accents. Since he'd collected a variety of pieces from non-Asian cultures, I had grouped these by region, so as not to jar the eye. I knew he preferred calming, understated effects to loud, bold ones. He loved dark browns, ivories, beiges, and rose colors—or, as I joked, the colors of a dog.

But one area in which I'd gone my own way and ignored Liam's conditions was in handling his family photos. He'd said he didn't want them to be displayed—that they were better kept locked up. But I disagreed. I knew I could make the borders and frames look fantastic by matching them to the surrounding colors of a room. His family were all very attractive, and I couldn't imagine Liam feeling ashamed of them. I also believed it would do him good to show pride in his ancestry by displaying them to visitors. I was sure once he saw the results of my work, he would agree they deserved to be showcased.

I remembered who everyone was from the time he showed me photos of them all and told me the story of his baby sister's tragic accident, his mother's descent into alcoholism, and his father's violent death in prison.

I'd dispersed the twenty-four family photos among four rooms, grouping them by era. The all-Asian room featured him and his siblings growing up, including members of his foster family, and the picture of his sister and her daughter. The Latin-American room displayed his grandparents and great aunts and uncles. The North-American room presented photos of Liam and his friends in the marines. And the European room showed photos of his parents. Another Asian room was devoted to friends Liam had made since the marines and Guy.

The rooms I'd decorated were all rooms guests used collectively, such as sitting rooms and common rooms. But I'd told everyone to keep the final touches a secret from Liam, who seldom came to this part of the house. I hoped he would now want to frequent it, once he saw what I'd done.

After breakfast, as Liam was rising to go put in a few hours of work on the market, I took his hand. "My present for you is finished."

He smiled his warmest smile, the one that made me feel I was sitting on a hearth by a roaring fire. "I'd love to see it."

I led him to the southern end of the building, guiding him down the broad corridor.

I slid the door open to reveal a spacious sitting room where I'd tucked a three-foot-high teak bookcase filled with Liam's engineering textbooks, histories of cycling, travel books, and other texts that meant a lot to him. Three jade pieces of different sizes and shapes graced the top of the long, low bookcase, and on a small table next to the sofa perched an ornately carved mahogany replica of a zen garden. On one of the walls I'd hung a large watercolor scroll with kanji calligraphy rolling along the sides.

His mouth hung open, and his eyes widened. "This is amazing, Ingrid. You really are talented."

He laid a kiss on the top of my head, advancing into the room to survey everything from different perspectives.

"You didn't overdo it at all. It's tasteful and enjoyable." After sitting a moment in a chair, he rose and went over to the bookcase. "I think I'll be spending a lot more time in the southern end now."

I beamed. "Wait'll you see the other rooms."

Next I led him to a large common room that overlooked the mangrove swamps and had southern exposure. Since it was flooded with light, I'd made it into the all-Asian room, placing the photos of him and his siblings and foster family on the walls and in two corners. At first, Liam's eyes traveled to the objects and art I'd arranged at strategic points. Then his gaze fell on the photo frames.

His face darkened like thunder and his brows cut furrows in his face. "You didn't do what I think you did, Ingrid?"

I laid a hand on his arm. "I devoted each room to a different branch of your family. This room is you and your siblings—and your foster brothers and parents."

This didn't seem to be going as well as I'd hoped.

Liam stormed over to each picture, one by one, tearing it off the wall or pulling it up from a table. Then he stalked over, pinning me with blazing eyes. "What did I tell you, Ingrid? I don't want anyone to see these photos. They're private."

I put my hands on my hips, frowning. "Why, Liam? They're beautiful photos of people you love. They deserve to have pride of place in these rooms, where guests can see your personal narrative, understand your roots."

His voice took on a dangerous edge, his gaze chilling me. "First of all, I don't have to give you a reason, Ingrid. If I tell you my wishes, you follow them. You've disobeyed me, and I'm angry. Second, the last thing I want is for people to 'see my personal narrative' or think they can 'understand my roots.' I control what people see and understand. If they have these photos, *they* will control the narrative—or they'll think they can. Third, some of these people don't even deserve to have their photos kept. Which is why I secret them away. Those people don't represent my roots at all."

I refused to give up. "But, Liam, it's good to confront the past head-on, to accept who you are and affirm the connections that have shaped your life. Erasing memories of the past makes you hollow inside. It creates a disjointed identity. Seeing the people who've meant something to you reminds you that others believe in you. It enables you to believe in yourself."

I hadn't realized until I spoke that this last reason was the main reason for my persistence.

His dark brows cut a groove above his nose, and fury rolled off of him in waves. "Ingrid, you're going to pull every photo you've laid down—or hung up—and I'm going to watch you do it. One by one. *Now*."

"No," I insisted, though my chin wobbled. "Think it over a little, Liam, before you undo everything. Or at least come see the other rooms before changing them. You may like—"

His mouth set in a firm line. "I'm giving you three seconds to follow my command before I punish you. And it'll be a punishment you won't like."

"I won't do it, Liam." I shook my head, a tight feeling gathering in my throat as tears threatened my eyes. "Please, just consider looking at the rooms first."

Dropping the photos unceremoniously on the floor, Liam slid the door shut, locking it. "Come here, Ingrid."

The authority in his command tolerated no protest. I took a few tentative steps toward him.

Wheeling me about so my back was against his chest, he spoke in sinister tones against my temple. His hand closed on my throat, and his other arm clamped my waist. "Take off your dress, bra, and panties."

I couldn't have shaken my head if I'd tried. There was no question of defying his orders.

"Did I hear a 'yes, Liam?'"

I swallowed. "Yes, Liam."

He released my waist, giving my hair a firm yank. "*Now*, Ingrid."

The menace in his voice made my whole body tremble. I hurriedly slipped my dress over my head, unhooked my bra, and slid my panties off. I was completely naked, except for my choker necklace.

He crooked two fingers under the necklace and pulled it toward him, dragging me with it, so I stood directly under his towering figure. His eyes were dark forests promising only danger. "Go to that chair and stand in front of it, facing toward the mangrove swamps."

He inclined his head toward a chair in the corner of the room. My heart jackhammering in my chest, I padded over, stopping at the edge of the seat. What was he going to have me do? What was he going to do *to me*?

I saw his next actions out of the corner of my eye, since I didn't want to go against his orders and turn my head. Unfastening the belt from his pants, he prowled over to me. He slid the flat part of the belt back and forth and down my back as if he were rubbing me down. Then he inserted it sideways into the cleft of my ass, sawing it up and down. *Ow*, that was a new one, and it wasn't so pleasant. When I reached back to stop the motion, he grabbed my wrists in one hand and pinned them over my tailbone.

Throwing his weight into the chair, he laid me over his lap, ass upwards, and palmed my butt cheeks. "I'm going to use this belt on your ass, Ingrid. It's going to hurt."

He began by spanking me with his hand, hard, laying six agonizing slaps on each cheek. Leaving them to sting a long minute, he caressed my reddened cheeks. My arousal seeped into his pants.

"You're going to count each stroke of the belt until we've reached twelve. Starting now."

He slapped the belt across my ass.

Searing pain traveled like wildfire through me, and I jumped in his lap.

"O-one," I whispered.

How will I endure twelve of these?

He walloped me again, this time harder.

I cried out. That one hurt like a mother. "Two!"

"Are you going to take the punishment you deserve? The *whole* punishment?"

I gulped. "M-maybe."

He whipped the belt across my rear again, and I yelped. "Three!"

"Are you going to obey me and remove those photos, in every room?"

I remained silent, as he cracked the belt over my butt again twice.

"Four, five!" I shrieked.

"You didn't answer my question, Ingrid."

"Please, Liam," I wailed. "Just look at them first."

Fwwapp! The belt stung like hell, and I squealed in agony, tears bathing my face. "S-six!"

"You either obey me or you get punished, Ingrid."

He belted me again. Hard. And again. Harder.

"Jackrabbit!"

He held the belt aloft for a moment and then threw it aside, blowing cool breath over my ass cheeks. The contact with the rush of air briefly made things worse, before the tingling dissipated. Then he surged up, bending me facedown over the armrest. Stripping his pants and boxer briefs, he stood behind me, his legs encasing my hips.

"I'm going to fuck the living daylights out of you. I'll show you no mercy."

Without preamble, he drilled into me, lifting and slamming with such force that it scooted the chair to the side. Pounding me relentlessly, he drove in and out, the slap-slap of our thighs alternating with the squeegie sound of my pussy milking his cock. It hurt like hell having his skin touch my flaming butt cheeks. But the internal burning was building, and I was about to climb into paradise.

Just then Liam pulled out, shooting his hot come all over my bare back and bellowing like a lion.

AARRGGHHHH!!!!

I struggled to stand up, furious at having been denied pleasure. But Liam pushed my hands against the opposite armrest, draping himself over my back and settling into me like a deadweight. His hot seed burned my backside over the welts of the belt.

Our hearts were racing, and our chests heaved against one another. My heart raced from rage, and his from exertion. My chest heaved with rebellion, and his with satisfaction.

"So you see, my little witness, you don't want to cross me." Raking his rough palm up through my hair, he pulled my head back till my scalp tingled. He pressed his lips to the shell of my ear, making me quiver. "I'd have you lick up every drop of my come, but you can't exactly reach around to your own back."

Fuck him.

"You don't think you actually deserved to come? After your disobedience?" His tone was at once vicious and mocking.

The sicker he was—in words and actions—the more desperate I was to get off. Since he'd captured my arms, I rubbed my clit against the armrest.

"Unh-unh." He leaned more weight into my hips, so I couldn't move. "No orgasms for you, little slave—not until you do what I say."

I fought back with my only remaining weapon, my spirit. "I haven't changed my mind, Liam."

"Neither have I, Ingrid."

Chapter Thirty-Two

Liam

Ingrid wasn't speaking to me, nor I to her. As soon as I'd released her, we dressed in silence, and she stooped to pick up the photos by the door, placing them on a low table. I had an urge to burn them, but I let them be for now.

I'd exorcised part of my anger by whupping Ingrid with the belt and fucking her like a ram in rutting season. The most cathartic part, of course, had been denying her an orgasm. But now the slow-burn anger settled in—the kind that sex couldn't help. We were at an impasse, each certain we'd eventually win the other one over and refusing to budge an inch. I was furious that Ingrid hadn't respected my wishes, that she'd been stubborn enough to continue defying me, and that she'd suggested I needed to face my past. Most of all, I was pissed that she had a personal-improvement agenda for me—or any agenda at all. If I wanted to change, I'd change. No woman was going to make me change.

What Ingrid thought she had to be mad at was beyond me. Nor did I have the bandwidth to care.

At the bar, where I helped myself to a drink, Guy caught my murderous expression.

"Pour me one, will you, old chap?" He slumped into an armchair.

"One what?"

"Whatever you're having."

I handed him a Scotch, taking a seat opposite. "What've you got to be down in the dumps about? I thought Andrea and you were on speaking terms again."

He took a gulp of whisky. "Today she's in a foul mood and won't give me the time of day. Apparently her niece's birthday party is in twelve hours and she's upset she has to miss it. She blames me for holding her hostage here, as she calls it."

I raised my glass. "Here's to not speaking to our women. We'll form a confraternity of mute celibates."

"Otherwise known as Trappist monks." He swirled his Scotch around.

"Celibacy is purer, nobler, than being ruled by libido." I leaned on my elbow, considering this idea.

Guy cough-laughed. "You stand about as much chance of remaining celibate for the next six hours as Marjorie Taylor Greene stands to gain the presidency in '24."

"Since when do you follow politics, Guy?"

"I don't. Which is rather my point, old man."

"Well, back to the other point, I may be celibate for longer than six hours." Not wishing to jinx myself, I didn't say *a lot longer than six hours*.

"I'll believe it when I see it—and maybe not even then." Guy tossed back a slug of whisky. "You and Ingrid love each other."

That startled me. "Says who?"

He scoffed. "Come, come, Liam."

"That's precisely what I won't be doing."

"Why so?" Guy tilted his head.

"Ingrid wants me to face my past, so against my express wishes, she went ahead and displayed my personal family photos in the rooms she decorated." I swigged my Scotch.

Guy arched an eyebrow. "Can't you just take them down?"

"That's the practical solution. But as a lawyer, you know humans are anything but practical creatures." I tipped back the rest of my drink. "No, I'm mad because she disobeyed me and is still disobeying me—all because she wants me to change. Fuck knows why *she's* mad. Probably because I denied her an orgasm."

Guy whistled long and low. "That is bad. But if she's digging in her heels, she must really believe in her cause. Ingrid's so good at picking her battles that I suspect this is the first she's ever fought."

"Trust you to take her side. I can see it'll be me against the three of you," I grumbled.

"Not at all, my good man. I see your point of view entirely. I only want to know more about Ingrid's position." He placed his glass on the side table. "It may be hard for you now, but think of it from her perspective. People she grew up with see photos as things you hang up for the whole world to see—and they proudly record everyone, down to the first cousins once removed. And don't forget that Ingrid's a designer; she sees photos as artistic statements as much as sentimental objects. Most importantly, she grew up surrounded by supportive friends and family. Of course, for her, photos capture only good things. With her sheltered past, she knows little of the sorts of traumas you went through."

"That still doesn't explain why she's so insistent." I

crossed my legs. "After all, the decorating was meant to be a gift to *me*."

He clasped his hands in front of him. "No doubt that's why. She probably put a lot of stock in those photos, on the basis of some underlying principle she stands by. And that principle now involves you."

"Well, maybe your legal training is good for something after all, Guy," I conceded.

"Reconciling two lovebirds?"

"No. Finally explaining why each middle-class household in America devotes walls to showcasing every person who's ever sneezed in their direction." I scrubbed a hand over my stubble.

"It's the same principle as Facejob and other social media. The more friends you appear to have, the easier it is for you to face yourself in the mirror." Guy's tone was withering.

I laughed scornfully. "If that's what Ingrid meant about believing in myself, I'll take my insecurities any day."

****

Ingrid

Taking a shower, I turned the water to lukewarm, but it still stung the belt lashes riddling my backside. Directly afterward, I went in search of Andrea. I could've done with a stress-relieving swim at the cove, but it would now be high tide, so the ledge would be flooded. Regardless, Andrea and I needed a catch-up.

We walked out the back of one of the zen gardens toward the southernmost point of the ring road, opting to stay on pavement. Fringed with colorful, fragrant wildflowers and bursting with birds, it offered just as many sensual experiences as the dirt paths.

Andrea carried a perfect coral murex shell she'd miraculously found far off the beach. I couldn't believe all the rounded parts and spikes were so intact. She could've sold it for a pretty penny online.

"What if this shell is a metaphor, Drea?" I mused, as Andrea displayed it in her flat palm.

"For what, sweetie?"

I led us westward. "For the way we hunt for things in the usual places and never find them. But when we're not looking, we find the perfect version of them in an odd place."

"You're thinking of Liam." She pocketed the shell.

"And Guy too." I gazed out at a cargo ship on the horizon.

She pursed her lips. "I must admit, I'm rather doubtful someone is my soulmate when he steals my freedom."

"But circumstance had a lot to do with that," I pointed out. "As much luck went into our being here now as went into your finding that shell. What if it is fate?"

She straightened her spine. "I view my situation as business only. I'm going to work with Guy professionally, get the job done, and go home."

"So you haven't slept with him since your marathon session?" I slid her a sideways glance.

She blushed. "No-o."

"But you made out." Her stammering response, flush, and slow blink told me everything.

"Well, yeah. The power was cut off."

I laughed. "Oh, then it doesn't count."

She nudged me. "It was an emergency measure. After all the systems tripped on, I went back to my room."

"But the sexual tension must feel like a tightly coiled spring when you two are working together?" I plunged my hands in the pockets of my rompers.

She shook her head. "We haven't gotten started yet. Since the storm I've had a lot of loose ends to tie up with my other projects—passing the baton to Rudra and Cleo, mostly, but also cleaning up my inbox and setting up an autoresponse to confirm I won't be reading submissions for awhile. And I've done some preliminary research for Guy's memoir."

I smiled slyly at her. "Wouldn't the best preliminary research be talking with him?"

Her lips quirked. "I wanted to have some leading questions ready for our first session, on Monday morning after breakfast."

"God help him when he sees you in work mode, with your sexy green glasses and your hair up. But, D, what will you wear? You didn't bring work clothes to the island, did you?" I had a brainwave. "What if you borrowed some of mine?"

Andrea inspected my backside dubiously. "What do you have that can accommodate my booty, honey?"

I chortled. "We're not *that* different! And we both have wide hips and narrow waists. We'll go through my stuff when we get back from the walk."

Andrea sobered. "What's going on with you and Liam, anyway?"

I lowered my voice. "How did you know something was wrong?"

She sloped an eyebrow. "Earlier, when I was working in the common room, he passed by wearing the face of a terminator, and then two minutes later you passed by looking like death warmed over. I put two and two together."

I heaved a sigh. "We had a fight. I put up photos of his friends and family in some of the rooms I decorated, even though he'd said he didn't want them displayed. I thought he would love the effect once it was done. And I was sure that having the pictures out in the open would help heal the wounds from his past."

She looped an arm around me. "Honey, I could've told you he'd react badly to that plan. He doesn't like to have people poke holes in his perfect armor. And exposing his past for everyone to see doesn't strike me as Liam's M.O. at all. He's a control freak. If he really does have a troubled past, he probably wants to keep it safely, neatly compartmentalized."

"But he cares about all these people—or cared about them at some point," I countered. "They make up who he is today. I want him to be proud of who he's become."

"What makes you think he isn't?" She followed me around a large shaded puddle in the road that still hadn't cleared from Wednesday morning after the storm.

I hesitated. "He's holding back, D. For some reason, even though he's slowly opening up, he's reserving a lot of himself from me. Time and again, he reduces his feelings for me to pure sex. Every time I mention love, he mentions ass fucking, or he fucks me in the ass—or, as in the dressing room in Suva, he takes me from behind. The night you came and we had a heart-to-heart about our feelings, he would only talk about long-term commitment in terms of what *I* wanted—not what *he* wanted. After I talked to my parents, when we came to the island, he said I was too good for him. And only when you and Rory forced his hand did he confess his murders to me. To my mind, it all adds up to him doubting his own worth and not daring to make himself vulnerable."

She nodded. "I agree with your assessment. So, what are you going to do about your fight?"

I ran my tongue over my lips. "I'm not backing down. I've done enough backing down with Liam. I mean to push him a little more. I have a plan."

Chapter Thirty-Three

Liam

I was talking to Bryn and Guy about Monday's trip as everyone waited at the dinner table for Waisake and Tima to bring out the soup course. Suddenly the whole room went quiet, and I swiveled to see what was causing jaws to drop, breaths to hitch, and eyes to round. Ingrid sashayed into the room, looking like sex on a stick.

Holy fucking fuck bunnies. She clicked in on her new black satin stilettos wearing the tight fawn leather mini-dress I'd bought her on Monday. Her silky hair hung in loose, fuck-me waves, and her long gold earrings dripped sex. Her shapely nude legs shone in the lamplight. Her tits were two round, smooth abiu fruits like what I'd eaten in Brazil. Her perfect ass made me—and probably every other male in the room—salivate. And her small waist drove me fucking insane. What drove me even more insane was her bare neck—specifically, the absence of the choker necklace. *My* choker necklace.

I had the temperature of a tropical fever victim, and fury zapped through my blood. My heart was doing suicide sprints. My throbbing dick had popped up like a jack-in-the-box. Rage and lust warred within me.

"You're fifteen minutes late," I ground out.

Completely ignoring me, she swished her way down to Warren, the nude leather hugging her hips exactly the way every man wanted to do right now.

"Is this chair taken?" she asked sweetly.

Warren was at the opposite fucking end of the table from me.

Looking like the turd in Edvard Munch's *Scream*, Warren stared at her for a beat, before giving a slight shake of his head. Damn right, he should be terrified. He was abetting the rebel.

She took. The. Fucking. Seat.

My fists clenched on the table, and an artery snapped in my neck. I wanted to roar so loud that the house would topple to its foundation. And I wanted to tie her up and whip her till her ass looked like a game of pickup sticks.

By some miracle I mustered the control to take three deep breaths.

Fine. If the mouse wanted to play with the cat, let her discover his claws.

"Ingrid, come sit in my lap." I scooted my chair back, planting my forearms on the armrests.

Waisake and Tima came out of the kitchen with trays of clam chowder, taking them around to each place. They seemed oblivious to the tension in the air.

Everyone's eyes ping-ponged between me and Ingrid like spectators at a Wimbledon match.

"I'm fine where I am." Ingrid calmly sipped her water, still not meeting my death glare. "I want to catch up with Warren about how the repair work on the drainpipes is going."

I fought to preserve my composure, lowering my voice. "You'll come to me, Ingrid, or you'll go back to our room, where Sione will guard you while we finish dinner. Which will it be?"

She crossed her tanned legs, stirring my dick to further heights. "Guy, won't you put on some music for dinner? Something that will loosen *some* of us up?"

Guy coughed, fumbling with his phone. "Um, certainly, Ingrid."

Having set out all the soups, Tima and Waisake returned to the kitchen.

"Ingrid, you must have a death wish tonight." I leaned in, my voice like a steel trap. "In ten seconds, I am going to carry you out of here. Unless you obey my order."

Andrea piped up. "Ingrid, if you need me to knee him in the balls, just say so. Nothing would give me greater pleasure."

"Thanks, Drea. But this is between me and Liam." Ingrid took an unruffled spoonful of chowder. *Her last meal for awhile. Enjoy it while you can, little mouse.*

"Ten. Nine. Eight. Seven." I paused to sip some whisky. "Your punishment will be far worse than the one you had earlier."

"I'm sure I don't know what the punishment would be for." Ingrid lifted her chin, finally meeting my eye. "I haven't done anything wrong."

"Six. Five. Four." I narrowed my eyes. "You're disobeying my wishes—again. And you're disrespecting me in front of others."*And looking like that, you need to be locked up until I can deal with you. While I have breath in me, you won't tease me without satisfying me.*

Fuck if her rebelliousness wasn't making me nut on myself. I didn't know this kind of game could turn me on so much.

"You can flex your muscles all you like, Liam. But I'm not budging from this seat." She poured herself a glass of white wine.

I drummed my fingers on the table. "Three. Two. Last chance, Ingrid."

She shook her head, sipping her wine while holding my stern gaze.

"*One*." I scraped my chair back and stood to a hushed audience, none of whom had touched their soups. Cracking my knuckles for effect, I rounded the table and stalked down to where Ingrid sat.

As I got closer, I noticed her fumbling with something under the table. Then, to my shock, she placed her hands on the table with two black feathers peeping out from under them. They looked just like the crow feathers taped in her journal.

How in hell had she accessed her journal? Was she threatening me? Was this a warning that she would talk to Andrea? If she did, that was as good as talking to Rory. I couldn't pretend I'd warmed Andrea to me over the last week.

But worse than being found out was the thought that Ingrid's heart had turned against me. All week long I'd felt assured of her love. The idea that it wasn't mine after all was so chilling that I froze mid-stride, my limbs congealing.

My throat worked on a swallow. "What do you want, Ingrid?" I said in such low tones that only those immediately around us could hear.

As her eyes locked with mine, I read determination, challenge, and something indefinable in their expression.

"Come outside with me, Liam. To the terrace." She stood, heading toward the open doors.

When we'd stepped out, she slid the doors closed. As she made her way to the balustrade, I followed. Thoughts raced through my head. Were we back to square one? But that was impossible. Not after all we'd been through together over the last five weeks. I was in deep enough that her anger unsettled me. I couldn't think clearly enough to wrest back control.

She leaned over the railing, and then twisted to me, her russet eyes shining like the bare back of a horse in the sun. "I want you to court me."

Inwardly I heaved a profound sigh of relief. I'd never been so glad in my life. So this was not a declaration of hostilities. Nor was her heart turning against me. Quite the reverse. "What do you mean, exactly?"

"I want more of the series. More episodes like our first night at the restaurant and our day in Suva. I want you to woo me." She crossed her hands over the stone rail. "I want you to make romantic gestures, plan dates with me. As if we're a normal couple."

"Or what?" I cocked an eyebrow.

She fingered the feathers, examining them thoughtfully. Then she looked back up at me. "I want you to do it in hopes of binding us together more strongly. In the hopes of keeping me forever, without crow feathers."

I leaned on the railing, admiring her profile in the moonlight. "If I say yes, will you sit on my lap for the rest of dinner?"

She laughed. "Of course."

The lead weight that had settled in my gut when

she showed the feathers eased up, and my chest swelled. "Then, yes, my little rebel. I'll court the fuck out of you." I looked down at her hands. "How did you get the feathers?"

"I found them by where the black petrels are laying their eggs, on the southwest side of the island. They look awfully like crow feathers, don't they?" Her eyes danced, and an impish smile curved her lips.

"Eerily similar." I traced her lips with my thumb. "Directly after dinner, we're going back to our room. My dick-meter has an hour tops on it while you're in this dress."

She grinned. "After we've fed the meter, can we come back and dance?"

"Just so long as you remember its time limit."

Chapter Thirty-Four

Ingrid

Liam's kiss was sweeter and more tender than any kiss we'd ever shared. Our tongues spoke of contrition, asking forgiveness for the mistakes of the day. Liam's said he was relieved I loved him enough to put the two of us above all else. Mine replied I would wait as long as he needed for him to feel as I did. Tangling, our tongues promised that love was bigger than any small squabbles we could place at its doorstep.

How I loved this man. Whether he was barking orders or cuddling with me after sex. Whether he was watching from across the room as if his heart was lodged in me, or holding me tight while we danced. Whether he was racing against me along a straightaway on our bikes, or working alongside me at our laptops. I loved all his moods, his quirks, his insecurities. When I caressed the back of his neck and ran my fingers through his hair as we kissed, my touch conveyed that I would take him as he was, without change.

Oh, Liam. Tears sprang to my eyes as I thought of the photos I'd insisted on displaying. Of course he had every right to keep them close and out of sight. I'd been wrong to foist on him a healing process that only he could begin, if and when he wanted to. I vowed to take them all down and replace them with the best of my own art pieces that I'd created over the last five weeks on the island.

My tongue told that story too. And his tongue said, yes, it heard and understood me. But forgiveness was a given. As our lives were bound up with one another, so too were our sins. Liam's hands pressed into the small of my back, and he slipped his tongue away, coating my lips with one final swipe. Already my mouth craved his warmth again, and my body dreaded separation.

When we strolled back inside hand in hand, tousled and red-faced, Guy, Andrea, Bryn, and Connie applauded.

"If we're going to be supporting actors in a Jennifer Aniston-Bradley Cooper flick, we might as well do it right," Guy said, explaining the ovation.

"Does the world-famous playboy Guy Travis watch rom-coms?" Andrea looked skeptical. "A memoirist has to know these things."

A blush crept up his cheeks. "If I confess I've enjoyed a few in my time, would you bow out of the contract?"

"On the contrary." She sipped her wine. "I'd say you're a man of impeccable taste."

Sitting in Liam's lap at the head of the table, I felt as if we were in a world of our own. He fed me steak and salad, sharing his whisky. While the rest of the table chatted, joked, and ate, Liam only had eyes and ears for me. We kissed, nuzzled, and whispered to each other, like two lovebirds.

I caught Andrea shooting a knowing glance at Guy, who gave her a jaunty wink in response.

"If I were a guy, Ingrid, I'd have fucked you by now." Andrea cracked a grin at me. "You're hot as sin in that dress. I'm surprised Liam is taking his sweet time about it tonight."

"It's called foreplay, Andrea." Liam nestled his lips in the area beneath my ear, his hand gliding along my inner thigh. "You and Guy should try it."

I came to my friend's defense. "Andrea invented foreplay, Liam. If anyone knows how to drive a man wild, it's her."

"I won't debate that," Liam remarked wryly.

"Liam's taking Ingrid with him on Monday and leaving us behind." Guy passed Andrea the cheese plate. "We'll have lots of time for work and…anything else you like."

"Work sounds good." Andrea gave him a pointed look. "After all, that's the sole reason I'm still here."

"I thought perhaps we might recline on the terrace loungers for our morning session, and then move to the southern porch in the afternoon." He slathered camembert on a piece of baguette. "In the middle, we'll enjoy a leisurely two-hour lunch in the manner of the French."

"I see you have a strong work ethic," Andrea deadpanned.

He quirked an eyebrow. "It is my life we're writing, princess. I believe it's customary that the autobiographical subject be comfortable during the proceedings."

She squinted. "I can see I'll be the taskmaster in this partnership."

Guy's eyes gleamed wickedly. "Task away, fair one."

It was news to me that I was going with Liam to Indiana. "What if we hadn't made up before the trip?" I murmured in his ear.

"All the more reason to take you with me." He turned to kiss my lips. "You didn't really think I'd be apart from you?"

"I thought women don't belong anywhere near gunfire." I threaded my fingers through his hair. I was privately delighted that he'd never meant to separate from me.

"During the actual operation, you'll be in the hotel. But Bryn will stay with you." He feathered my neck with his lips. "I'm relying on you to comfort Gretchen and Katrina. It will be strange for them to be on the outside, and having another woman close by could help them reassimilate."

"I hope they'll be okay." I had a foreboding that things weren't going to be as simple or straightforward as Liam predicted. "They may put up a lot of resistance to being rescued."

"The cult stole Gretchen's adulthood—and Katrina's whole life," he said. "It's time they both got their lives back."

No sooner had the cheese plate been cleared away, than Liam scooped me up in his arms and stood, speaking to the table at large. "Don't hold the dancing for us. We'll be back in a little while."

"Going to do a little spring cleaning, old man?" Guy refilled Andrea's wine glass.

"That's right," Liam shot back over his shoulder. "No better time than an autumn night when the cleaning staff have gone to bed."

When we got back to our room and Liam set me down, I held up my index finger for him to halt in his tracks.

"Sit here." I indicated a chair.

A puzzled crease indented his brow as he took a seat.

Still in my stilettos, I switched my hips, strutting slowly toward the porch door, and turned around in a leisurely way, kicking out one of my hips and resting my hand on it.

Liam let out a low, tormented groan. The tent in his pants was like the steeple of a country church.

As I lazily flounced back toward him, I stroked my curves with my hands. Stopping midway, I twisted to the side and jutted out a glute toward Liam. Lovingly, confidently, I sloped my hand around its globe, dipping my head to hold his gaze through my eyelashes.

"*Fuck*, Ingrid." Liam bit his knuckles. "I can't take much more."

I ran my tongue over my lips slowly, pouting, as I took one step toward Liam. Sliding my hands over my breasts, I used my forefinger to trace little circles in the exposed area of my cleavage.

"*Agghh*," he moaned, his eyes practically rolling in their sockets. "Have mercy, Ingrid."

Bending over slightly so my breasts were visible, I hooked one knee in front of the other to enhance my hourglass shape. Then I straightened and took two more mincing steps toward Liam.

The knuckles of his fists were ghostly white from straining to keep from touching me.

Standing four feet away, I gave him my back as I gathered my hair over one shoulder, unsnapping the back of the halter strap on my nape. Again I caressed my backside, swishing my shoulders back and forth and grinding my hips to accentuate my curves in movement.

Peeking over my shoulder, I puffed a kiss at Liam.

"*FUCK*. I'll give you two more minutes of this, Ingrid." His voice was abrasive and his tone bordered on desperate.

I chuckled breathily. Now I gave him a three-quarters view. With one hand on my waist, I teased the front zipper down two inches from my cleavage, pausing to reach under and play with my breast. Taking a step closer, I unzipped two more inches, holding his lust-darkened gaze. I nudged the hem of the dress up my thighs by two inches, slinking my hands along my outer legs, up my hips, and along my waist and ribcage. Then I did the classic pinup girl's pose, bending my elbows and poising my fingertips next to my cheeks to point toward my face as I held back my hair.

"One minute," he rumbled.

Sliding the zipper down at a glacial pace, I watched Liam's eyes following the movement like a jaguar preparing to pounce. When I reached the end of the zipper, I let the dress open by two teasing inches, so a vertical line of flesh and panties was visible through the crack.

Liam sprang from the chair, but when he was within half a foot of me, I took a large step back, holding up my palms. Draping the halter straps over my shoulders, I eased one down, shrugging my arm free, while holding up the main part of the dress. Then I slid the other one down my other arm. Finally I peeled myself out of the dress, letting it clump behind me on the floor. I did a leisurely turn, allowing Liam to view my near-naked body from every angle. Then I hooked my fingers in the upper band of my panties.

Suddenly Liam's hands were everywhere on my

body at once. Groping my breasts. Squeezing my ass. Sliding up my thighs. Palming my belly. Dipping into my panties. Cupping my cheeks and throat. Coiling my hair and tugging it. Sawing my hips against his erection.

"You are the most fuckable woman on the planet," he growled into my bellybutton as he pulled down my panties. While down there, he licked and swirled my navel like a lollipop. "I missed you."

"For ten hours?" I laughed throatily.

"It was torture being separated from you while we were fighting." He knelt, shunting my legs apart and opening my wet pussy with his fingers. I shivered from the cool air blowing into my channel and his thumbs moving over my mound. "But even when I was angry, I was committed to you. It's impossible not to be. You're too damn perfect."

"Perfect for you?"

"Perfect, period." He rose, carrying me to the bed and laying me down on my back, spreading my legs wide. Kneeling between my thighs, he kissed his way down my belly. I trembled with excitement and pleasure. "Now, where were we?"

Chapter Thirty-Five

Liam

We checked into the hotel on the outskirts of Sinclair, Indiana at 2 p.m. on Monday. I'd told the flight crew to be ready to take us back to Verau anytime from 5 onwards. It was a short turnaround for a flight crew that'd just done a sixteen-hour flight—but the co-pilot going out, Mike, had agreed to pilot going back, so Stuart didn't need to be so alert. At least they'd have three hours for a nap while we completed our rescue operation and the jet refueled. It was risky as hell, and in blatant violation of FAA regulations, but there was no way around it. The small airport didn't have much air traffic scheduled for that day, so the runways would be clear.

We'd rented two Range Rovers—one for Bryn and Ingrid to use to return to the airport, and one for me and Claude to drive Gretchen and Katrina. We didn't plan to linger in town, knowing anyone from the cops to the feds could be on our trail once we penetrated the compound.

In the hotel room, I changed into a bulletproof vest and raid jacket, together with dark jeans, even though it was eighty-two degrees out. Attaching a lapel mic, I inserted my earpiece. Claude, Rodrigo, and Ralph were dressed similarly. Just to look the part, I'd even fitted out my gun belt with a standard FBI cant holster. Pocketing one of the fake badges Bryn had arranged to have made for all of us, I looked at the search warrant again. Everything was in order.

When Ingrid saw me check my magazine and holster my weapon, she looked so frightened, that for a second I wished I hadn't brought her. But I remembered that the main reason for her coming was so Gretchen and Katrina would feel less at sea on the trip back to Verau.

"Don't worry, everything will be fine. We won't take any unnecessary risks, and we won't use our weapons unless we have to." I drew her close, kissing her warmly.

Her voice trembled. "Liam, I'll be willing you all to succeed and remain safe, every second you're gone. If I were religious, I'd pray. But as it is, I don't think the big guy would listen to me."

I brushed her cheek with my thumb. "Your will is as good as a prayer, for my money."

When Claude and I met Ralph and Rodrigo outside the hotel, we reviewed for the fourth time how we'd divvy up the tasks once we got to the compound. Ralph would cover one security guard and Claude the other. Rodrigo would case the compound, radioing Ralph, Claude, or me as he confirmed the alternative exits, suspicious activity, or attempts to block our rescue efforts. Meanwhile, I'd go in search of Gretchen and Katrina. If Rodrigo gave the all clear, he'd help me bring the two women to the entrance. We'd then race to the airport.

Claude's name in the field was "Scout." Ralph was "Dogtag," and Rodrigo was "Puma." I was just

"Captain."

Claude drove on the freeway for ten minutes to get to the compound, which was off of an exit outside of town. I noted that traffic was getting thick in the direction of the airport—probably because it was the way to the nearest city, Meerwood. By 5, rush hour would set in. I hoped we wouldn't be contending with that.

The compound was in the ugliest building I'd ever seen. It was as if a kid had slapped together five concrete slabs into a rectangle. My heart took a nosedive as I contemplated my sister and niece living in such a soul-sapping place for twelve years. It looked every inch a former car plant. Maybe the inside was better. We parked just inside a vast open parking lot, and strode toward the entrance.

"There are two security officers on duty, and they both carry," Ralph said for the fifth time, as though we were a surgical team relaying the procedure before and during the operation. I appreciated his thoroughness. "The cult leader and his subordinates may have weapons. And the place may have a landline."

We reached the entrance. I was pumped, the way I felt during a punishing weight workout. No time for nervousness or overthinking. *Here goes.*

I banged on the large metal door. "Open up!"

A beefy white security guard with a shaved head and fearsome jowls opened the door, his hand on his holster.

"FBI. Put your hands where I can see them!" Ralph shouted, covering the guard and disarming him.

Just for fun, I flashed my badge, shoving my way past the guard and opening the door wider. Another guard, even more hulking than the first and sporting a red beard, stood with his gun pointed at me. Weapons aimed at this second guard, Rodrigo and Claude cruised in shouting simultaneously, "Drop the weapon!" He did.

Ralph and Claude deftly ziptied the wrists and ankles of both guards.

"We have a warrant to search these premises for evidence of human rights violations," I incanted, producing the search warrant. "Offenses involving coercion of two members of this organization, Gretchen and Katrina Stauner. Will you assist us in locating these two members?"

My gaze jumped between the two security guards.

Jowls and Redbeard remained silent.

"Do you have information about their whereabouts in this compound?" I pressed.

More silence.

I nodded. Rodrigo held his gun to Jowls's temple, while Ralph aimed at Redbeard's.

"Talk now?" I prompted, leaning against a table and crossing my legs.

"We don't know." Jowls shook his head. "Members' rooms are on all four sides of the compound. The leader and his people are in the center."

"Where in the center?" I probed.

"We don't know," Jowls repeated.

"Does the leader or any of his team carry?" I asked.

Redbeard spoke up. "The leader has a piece. No one else."

"Are there any landlines here?" Once more, I addressed both.

Redbeard nodded. "In the leader's offices."

"Any other exits?" My final question.

Jowls offered, "There's an emergency door on the other side of the center block, on the ground floor. It has an alarm."

I turned to Claude. "You cover Redbeard here. Dogtag, cover Jowls. Puma, head up the staircase to the leader's room and watch for any activity. I'll search for Gretchen and Katrina. Puma, any important developments, radio in. Dogtag and Scout, same goes for this entrance area."

Everyone nodded. Rodrigo set out toward the central stairwell, which seemed to be fireproof.

"Bolt the front door. No one goes in or out." I turned and made my way to the left down a wide hallway toward a double door.

With luck, all four sides of the building connected on the second floor, so I wouldn't have to descend stairs all afternoon. And with luck, I'd find the two women sooner, and together.

The dismal grey concrete walls surrounding me, the sterile smell of ammonia and bleach pervading the air, and the bleak silence reigning downstairs thrust me back into the same depression I'd felt outside the compound. So far, my suspicions that this was worse than a prison were confirmed.

On the way to the doors, I noticed whiteboards on the right-hand wall announcing meeting times. I checked my watch. It was 3:30 on a Monday. Nothing scheduled was for this slot. I hurried through the double doors, scaling the stairs two at a time to the second floor.

Members shuffled past in both directions through the broad fluorescent-lit corridor that greeted me. Slim glazed windows lined the ceiling, all of them shut. The air was stale and dank. Everyone was dressed in sky-blue tee-shirts and black bottoms—slacks for the males and skirts for the females. I stuck out like a sore thumb in my fake FBI garb. Inmates here seemed to be either in their teens or over sixty.

I collared an elderly woman with a shock of white hair. "Excuse me, ma'am, can you tell me where Gretchen Stauner is?"

Her eyes grew large as walnuts, as she shook her head rapidly.

"Do you know where Katrina Stauner is?" It occurred to me then that my using their last names might confuse the old lady. "Katrina?"

Another quick head shake.

"Do you know who might know?" I tried one last time.

She pointed a shaky, wizened hand toward a closed door at the end of the corridor.

"Thank you, ma'am."

These people were short on words.

I stalked toward the door, ignoring the alarmed glances passing cult followers showered on me. I pushed the door open, prepared for almost anything, as I thought.

Shit. Not quite ready for this.

A group of about fifteen teenage girls were seated on their hauncheson the floor in a circle with their eyes closed, palms on their thighs, reciting in low voices some prayer or mantra. A young woman—maybe in her early twenties—stood in the center of the ring holding an open book. Was this their equivalent of school? If so, God help Katrina.

"Excuse me," I interrupted, clearing my throat.

The woman with the book trained her vague eyes on me.

"Can you tell me where Katrina is?" This time I omitted the last name.

The woman's eyes cut briefly to a girl with long straight black hair on the far side of the circle. I tried to resolve her features into Gretchen's. Yes, it was possible this was my niece. The nose and dark hair were similar.

When I stepped into the room, all hell broke loose.

The girls screamed and scattered like a flock of pigeons, flying out the door. I stopped the one who might be Katrina, placing my hands on her arms.

"Are you Katrina?" I tried to get her to focus on my eyes, but she wouldn't meet them head-on. She was shaking like a leaf. "Just nod if you are. I'm Liam, your uncle. Your mom's brother."

When she made no further move, I addressed the young woman again. "Please tell me if this is Katrina. I'm her uncle."

The young woman gave the briefest of nods—the sort you'd miss if you weren't paying attention—and then turned away, arranging books on a desk.

For now, that nod was enough for me to go on. I could always confirm things once I found Gretchen.

"Do you know where your mom is, Katrina?" When she said nothing, I turned to the young woman again. "Do you know where Gretchen is?"

She shook her head, busying herself with some papers.

"Okay, let's go, Katrina."

Now came the next hard part—getting her down to

Ralph and Claude. Once we emerged from the room, she tried to head left instead of right, toward the stairwell.

"Katrina, we'll pick up your mom and take you to a friend of mine named Ingrid. She'll help you," I cajoled in my most soothing tones.

She gave a quick shake of her head, her eyes black with fear.

I scooped her up in my arms and carried her along the corridor and out the doors, down the stairwell. I was saddened that she didn't fight my hold. She was too docile, by nature or nurture.

I hoped it was the latter, and that it could be undone.

Chapter Thirty-Six

Liam

After leaving Katrina with Ralph and Claude in the entrance area, I set off in search of Gretchen. Apparently no one had tried to enter or exit the compound since we'd arrived. Rodrigo would've radioed if anything was amiss in the central block.

On an impulse, I made my way down a corridor toward the opposite side of the building, climbing a corner stairwell. If the section I'd just visited was devoted to kids and elderly people, maybe this next section had adults.

When I entered the second-floor hallway, I heard chanting coming from what sounded like a large echoey room on the left with an open door. Sliding my back along the wall so I couldn't be easily seen, I listened. A man would call out and a group of at least twenty men and women would respond.

Man: "When the fire rolls in, where are we?"

Group: "We are by the lake of baptism, below."

Man: "When the bombs drop, where are we?"

Group: "We are in the caves of the saints, below."

Man: "When the waters rise, where are we?"

Group: "We are in the eagle's nest of The Seer, above."

Man: "When death comes, where are we?"

Group: "We are on the wings of the angels, above."

I remembered, as Ralph had told me and my own research confirmed, that this was a doomsday cult that believed in a combination of physical and spiritual escapes from the imminent end of the world. They lured members in by various forms of psychological manipulation, and then brainwashed and intimidated them into submission.

I decided to do this with little to no finesse. Stepping into the room, I closed and locked the door behind me. The chants abruptly ceased.

"FBI." I flashed my badge. "I have a warrant to search this place for Gretchen Stauner. Who here can tell me where she is?"

Scanning the room, I saw she wasn't among those present. Everyone was seated on the floor the way the teenage girls had been sitting, only in four rows of six.

One of the men, in his forties with a hawk nose, glanced at the woman next to him. I fixed my eyes on them. "Can either of you tell me where she is?"

"Why do you want to know?" the man asked.

"I'm here to take her away," I stated, baldly enough.

"She won't go with you," the man declared.

"Tell me where I can find her," I persisted, not arguing with his claim.

"She's teaching." The woman's eyes contained a spark of curiosity and interest. At last, some life and spirit in this godforsaken place.

"Silence!" barked the man leading the group in chants, who stood on a platform to the left of me.

I ignored him, giving a half-smile of invitation to the woman. "Can you show me where?"

The woman gave the man beside her an encouraging look. "My husband may show you."

Grunting, the man slowly rose.

"No," said the man on the platform. "No one leaves this room. And no wife gives an order to her husband!"

I examined him for the first time. Of medium height and build, he had longish blond hair and a square-shaped short beard. His ears stuck out like a monkey's.

The hawk-nosed husband paused in response to Monkey-Ears' command.

"We can do this peacefully or I can go another way," I said to Monkey-Ears. "I'm not leaving without Gretchen. One of you is going to lead me to her."

"No one leaves this compound," Monkey-Ears emphasized.

I strode over to the husband, whose eyes jumped between me and Monkey-Ears. "Come with me, sir."

A younger, heftier man leapt up and stalked over, fixing me with a glare I wanted to wipe off his face in an instant. "I wonder if you can fight without using your weapon."

"No problem." I stepped back, shifting my weight to my left foot and preparing to deck him with my right fist.

Somehow the pisser managed to clock me first, connecting his fist with the side of my jaw. After a second of reeling from the blow, I recovered enough to throw a jab to his nose. As he raised his fist to punch me in the eye, I jerked to the side so his blow glanced off my shoulder. He tried to hold me in a clinch, clamping his arms around mine. But I bent his torso to the side, shoving my head up against his neck and disengaging his right arm. Then I hauled off and slammed my left fist up into his jaw, knocking him off balance. While he teetered, I pummeled his midsection till he crumbled completely.

"Anyone else?" I asked the room, swiping the blood that oozed from my mouth and working my jaw back and forth.

"I'm going to tell the leader." Monkey-Ears stepped down from his platform and headed toward the door.

"I don't think so." I grabbed his elbow. "If anyone leaves this room before this man returns—" I jerked my chin toward the hawk-nosed husband—"there'll be shooting. I have people guarding your leader with weapons and instructions to shoot. If you want to avoid more violence, you'll stay put."

Noticing sudden movement to my right, I spun around, to find two other sizable thirty-something men lunging for my gun. The man coming from in front I seized by the wrist as he reached for my weapon, striking the side of his head with my left hand and knocking his hand off my piece with the same blow. I drew, pointing my gun at the other aggressor, who halted mid-stride.

"Everyone over to that corner," I said to the room at large. "Except for this man." With a nudge of my head, I indicated Hawk-Nose.

Everyone else, including Monkey-Ears, gathered in the far corner.

The husband sidled over.

"Stay there," I told him. Pulling zipties out of my pocket, I strode over to the group and bound the wrists and ankles of the annoying Monkey-Ears. "Remember, as long as no one leaves this room, there won't be any shooting." Holstering my gun, I turned back to the husband. "Take me to Gretchen."

I followed him down the corridor, past a large assembly hall full of empty seats, a dingy cafeteria, and a laundry room piled high with dirty clothes and sheets. The man led me to a bright, all-white room frighteningly like a hospital room. In it, an older version of the Gretchen I'd last seen twelve years ago was explaining something to a group of girls who looked to be about six. She'd written on a whiteboard various combinations of vowels and diphthongs, and was having the kids repeat the sounds after her. I felt a flash of pride that Gretchen was doing something as meaningful as teaching youngsters how to read.

But when I focused in on her, Gretchen looked old beyond her years. At twenty-nine she had crow's feet, frown lines, and slightly sagging shoulders. Rage seethed in me as I thought how this cult had stolen my sister's youth.

Hawk-Nose rapped on the half-open door. "Gretchen, someone's come to see you."

She looked astonished at that news, as if he was speaking in tongues.

I stepped into the room. "Gretchen."

"No. No, no, no." She shook her head, backing up against the board. I couldn't tell from her flaring eyes whether she recognized me or not.

"Gretchen, it's me, Liam. I've come to take you and Katrina away." I took a few steps toward her. "Everything's going to be all right."

She took me in more fully, her eyes dropping to my holster. "Leave me. I won't go."

"Please, Gretchen. Come with me. You'll be happier." I opened my arms in a gesture of friendliness.

Her eyes darted to the door, giving me a split second of warning before she tried to bolt. I caught her in my arms, hoisting her up over my left shoulder and hustling us out the door.

"Thank you for your help," I said to the man, before proceeding down the corridor toward the stairwell. Though Gretchen heaved with sobs, like Katrina she didn't put up a physical fight.

On my way down the first-floor corridor that led back to the entrance, Rodrigo's voice sounded in my ear. "We gotta go, Captain. Police are on their way."

Shit.

"Be at the entrance in a minute." I hurried as fast as I could with Gretchen slung over my shoulder.

No sooner had I reached the front door, than Rodrigo pounded toward us.

"The leader reached for a concealed gun and I disarmed him, but one of his subordinates saw us and called the police. When I reminded him I was the FBI and the police could do nothing to me, he called my bluff. He said, 'Then you have nothing to worry about when they come.'" Rodrigo tried to regain his breath.

Ralph whistled. "Trying to play the law against the law so they can watch from the sidelines, eh?"

Claude held up his phone. "I texted Bryn to leave now with Ingrid for the airport. And I texted Mike to put the crew on standby."

I nodded. "Claude, you take Katrina. I'll take Gretchen. Rodrigo, Ralph, you guys disappear."

"Bye, guys, it's been real," Ralph said to Redbeard and Jowls.

As we unlocked the door, a shot rang out and a bullet grazed the top of my shoulder, hitting the door just to the right of my head. I was so keen to get Gretchen out of there safely, I didn't turn to look back. "Claude, you with me?"

"Here, Liam."

"Katrina's okay?"

"Yeah, she's fine."

We hastened toward the Range Rover.

Another shot echoed in the air. Two minutes later, Rodrigo and Ralph tore out of the building, following with their backs to us, facing the compound. I was grateful for their protection.

Rodrigo said, "The motherfucker had another weapon."

Ralph laughed. "We separated, and he shot at Rodrigo and missed. That gave me enough time to tackle him and hit him in the head with his own gun."

"He's knocked out?" I placed Gretchen in the back seat next to Katrina.

"Yeah." Ralph fist-bumped me when I turned back to him. "I'll be in touch, Liam. Get back safe."

"You too, Ralph. Rodrigo, thanks." I clapped a hand on Rodrigo's back.

Claude climbed in the passenger's seat.

The wail of approaching sirens pierced the air. Our cue to move.

Locking all the doors, I backed up and sped out of the parking lot.

The cops turned the corner just as I drove toward the frontage road leading to the freeway entrance. Yep, they were on our tail. Time to hit the gas.

Ignoring the frightened looks of Katrina in the

rearview mirror and Gretchen's weeping, I focused on outrunning the two police cars. I entered the freeway, weaving in and out of a few cars to keep the cops guessing. It wasn't as easy to maneuver the Range Rover as my Maserati, but the engine had just as much horsepower. We played Smokey and the Bandit like this for almost ten minutes.

Fuck. Up ahead was a slowdown that had all lanes backed up at least a mile before our exit. Forcing my way over to the rightmost lane, I inspected the hard shoulder: big enough to crawl through at fifty. I charged into it, the police cars hesitating on joining me. But after a minute, they followed, now at a distance of about five hundred feet.

A chorus of angry honks blared as other drivers saw what I was doing—either because they envied me or feared I'd hit their car. I tuned it all out, zeroing in on making the off-ramp before the cops closed in.

After what seemed an eternity, I reached the exit, the shriek of sirens still clinging to us. Checking for movement on the immediate right and left, I ran the red light of a major intersection, heading toward the river. I looked back. After a pause, the cops ran the red too, putting them now a hundred yards behind. Upcoming was a drawbridge. I sped up, praying the bridge operator wasn't about to close the gate and switch the traffic signal to red. Relief flooded me as I made it onto the bridge.

I was the last vehicle they allowed on.

Fuck yeah. Someone *was* looking out for us.

On the other side of the river, I glanced in my rearview to see the police stalled at the bridge, its leaves canting in the air. Claude and I bumped fists.

285

That ought to give us the necessary ten minutes to ditch them. Still, I glued my foot to the accelerator as we raced to reach the airport. It'd be nice to put some distance between us and the po-po.

Five minutes later, we screeched to a stop on the tarmac. I helped Gretchen out, throwing her over my shoulder again, while Claude led Katrina to the jet stairway. The engines were already revving. After we'd seen the women onto the plane, I turned.

"Claude, thanks. Come to Verau soon." I half-hugged him.

"Get home safe, Liam." He slapped me on the back.

I flopped into a seat, taking my first full breath since lifting Gretchen onto my shoulder in the compound. Like a caffeine fix, adrenaline had kept me running for the last three hours, but now I came crashing down with a thud. I didn't want to move for a good long while. I was finally in a position to be grateful for all the luck we'd had this afternoon. At last I could think of seeing Ingrid.

She swamped me in a snug, loving embrace. Seeing the patch of blood seeping through my shirt on my shoulder—the bruises purpling my jaw, and the blood still flecking my cheek from my tussle with the cult member—she bustled off to find an ice pack, towels, and warm water. As she cleaned my wounds, I related a condensed version of everything that had gone down at the compound.

After giving me a slow, tender kiss, she left to look after Gretchen and Katrina.

I gazed through the window at the thick clouds shrouding the plane and blew out a heavy exhale. I hoped this had been the hard part.

Though something told me the real test was yet to come.

Chapter Thirty-Seven

Ingrid

Though their similar looks made it easy to tell that Katrina was Gretchen's daughter, you'd never have known it from the way they acted. Two people meeting for the first time would've shown more interest in one another than these two did. This was a mystery I wanted to get to the bottom of. Did Gretchen even know Katrina was her daughter? Did Katrina know Gretchen was her mother? Why were they so indifferent to each other?

For the first few hours of the flight, I couldn't get a word out of either. I brought them back to the dining area and served them tea, but they wouldn't accept any food. I put a jacket around Gretchen and wrapped Katrina in a blanket. While Gretchen had clearly been crying before she got on the plane, Katrina seemed shaken by the bullet and car chase.

Gretchen was tall, slender, and strong-jawed, with straight black hair falling to her shoulders. Katrina looked as if she was just about to shoot up any day. Still small-limbed, she had the darkest eyes I'd ever seen and long dark hair to match. She had gotten her attractive ski-slope nose from her mother.

Since neither was speaking, I did all the talking. I told them about Verau and the people there. I prattled about New York, where I came from, my family and close friends. I showed them pictures on my phone of the artworks I'd created, of New York, and Verau. Gretchen looked so stricken and overwhelmed that little I said or showed her made an impression. But Katrina gradually took an interest in the pictures, swiping back and forth among them as she saw me doing. I could tell from her hesitation and wonderment that this was her first experience with a cell phone.

So we sat on the sofa in the dining area, me babbling away as I sipped tea. Neither of them flinched when my arm or hand brushed theirs.

But when Bryn came back to pick up some food, my companions froze, their spines going ramrod straight and their breaths hitching. Liam had mentioned how the teenage girls had reacted to his stepping into their prayer room, how a man had shown him where Gretchen was, and how she'd been astonished at having the two men enter her classroom. I gathered that a certain segregation of the sexes had been the cult regulation. I vowed not to question Gretchen or Katrina on their former lives, as it seemed too soon.

When I heard Katrina's stomach rumbling, a knife twisted in my own belly. I had to find a way to feed them. Going through every item available in the refrigerators and shelves, I offered them chips, crackers, bread, cold cuts, chicken marsala with potatoes, filet mignon with rice and green beans, grapes, cheese, mango, and berries. Katrina finally accepted some cheddar cheese and grapes. I scored a major victory when Gretchen took a piece of bread and a slice of pecorino. I decided to keep plying them with food every hour, for as long as they were awake.

Three hours after take-off, I asked Gretchen if she'd like to go to sleep.

"Yes." Her voice was brittle and flute-like.

"Katrina, are you tired?" I asked.

"No." Katrina was scrolling through pictures of dogs I'd found on a New York City pet rescue site. Even though my apartment building didn't allow dogs, I often entertained the fantasy of rescuing one someday.

I was heartened by their vocal responses, even if they were monosyllabic.

"Katrina, if you wait here, I'll join you again in a few minutes after settling your mom into one of the beds in the back."

She nodded, enlarging a photo of a beagle mix.

After installing Gretchen in a bed and piling her with Alpaca blankets, I emerged to find Katrina dozing against the sofa back, her mouth open and my phone dropped to her side. I eased her down on her back, putting her legs up and nestling a pillow under her head, before covering her with blankets.

Fixing Liam some dinner and placing it on a tray along with a tumbler of Scotch, I closed the curtain to the dining area to give Katrina a bit of privacy as she slept.

While Liam ate, I shared my ideas for his sister and niece.

"The cult must've had set rituals everyone followed each day," I speculated. "I think the sooner they establish a routine on the island, the more secure they'll feel."

He grunted in agreement, wolfing down his steak.

"Until they get used to a mixing of the sexes, I suggest we change the seating at the table. We could place all the women at one end and all the men at the other," I went on.

He chuckled. "Ingrid, you live up to your French heritage. Have you ever heard the story of the French diplomat?"

I shook my head.

He sipped his whisky. "At a French ambassador's soirée, a newly sworn-in diplomat arrived wearing his insignia on the right side of his jacket instead of the left. Wishing not to embarrass the novice, the host instructed every other guest to switch their insignia to the right side of their jackets. In this way, he made the newcomer feel at home among his peers. Though the new diplomat later discovered his error, he'd had his first lesson in graciousness, tact, and hospitality."

I smiled. "You're saying I'm gracious and hospitable?"

He caught my hand up and kissed it. "In spades."

"I thought we could put them together in a room not far from ours. We'll need to take them to Suva for clothes. And it'll be important to find out what sort of work fulfills them—art, gardening, cooking, photography. . . or learning another trade from one of your people. Until they have a meaningful pursuit to replace the cult, they'll lack purpose."

Liam scrubbed his five o'clock shadow, which looked especially sexy and rugged now that he hadn't shaven since we'd left Verau, over a day ago. "What did you have in mind?"

I thought of Katrina's interest in my phone and Gretchen's teaching kids how to read. "Bryn might teach Katrina coding. And I could teach Gretchen French and German—if they're interested in these skills. They might like cycling, running, or swimming. Who knows—maybe even chess or poker would intrigue them."

He pulled me onto his lap. "Making our two guests feel at home may be your new passion, my sweet dove."

I brushed my lips to his. "And you may be proving that, contrary to popular belief, two wrongs *can* make a right."

****

We arrived on the island at midnight Wednesday. Because everyone but the exhausted flight crew had slept on the plane, the five of us were wired and hungry. I foraged in the kitchen, warming up two game hens Tima had earlier roasted for us with potatoes, carrots, onions, and celery. Having waited up, Connie helped me bring out the food, dishes, white wine, and a jug of water.

While Liam still sat at the head of the table, a break of a few seats separated Connie, me, Katrina, and Gretchen from Bryn and Liam.

Katrina took a tentative nibble of meat. I was jubilant when she took several more bites, trying a potato. Gretchen sat for a good twenty minutes without touching her food, as she watched us polish off our plates. I cheerfully explained that the vegetables all came from our own gardens, that even the game hens were raised by Heneli in a poultry yard.

"Gretchen, would you like something else?" I asked gently. "Maybe some milk, or cheese and bread?"

When she nodded, I rose and fetched her a glass of milk and a plate of different cheeses with fresh-baked bread.

She finished everything in a few minutes. I poured mugs of chamomile tea to wind us all down. Katrina scrunched up her nose at the bitter taste, pushing her cup aside. But Gretchen contentedly sipped hers, staring out at the wine-dark sea and the moonless sky.

"Tomorrow we can go for a walk," I suggested. "You'll meet my best friend Andrea. And we can collect shells at low tide."

Since both of them had started to shiver, I found sweaters, urging their arms into them.

"Maybe, Katrina, you'd enjoy it if I read you an Arabian folktale from a collection in Uncle Liam's bookshelf?" I proposed in an inviting voice.

As Katrina's eyes went wide, I saw the same enthusiastic glimmer she'd shown while looking at the dog photos on my phone. Though I didn't think she had a clue what I was talking about, my coaxing tone made the prospect sound like honey to a bear.

"Okay, let's draw you a nice hot bath, and we can all read together." I stood, taking Katrina's hand. "Gretchen, I'd love to run you a bath too." I was relieved when Gretchen followed us.

While Connie fetched the book, I fixed Katrina a bath in the bathroom off of her and Gretchen's room. I topped it off with bubbles, which awarded me Katrina's first smile—a beautiful, genuine, upside-down rainbow. Feeling as if I'd won the lottery, I helped her strip and settle into the water.

She purred like a kitten in a cat lover's lap, closing her eyes and letting the luxuriant soak in hot water relax her.

While she cleaned herself with lavender soap, I told her of all the things she could do on the island—

take pictures, learn from Warren how to fix things, learn how to garden from Jesse, and other ideas I'd suggested to Liam.

Mellow and sleepy after the bath, she looked so adorable in a terrycloth robe, that I instinctively wrapped my arms around her. Though she didn't hug back, she didn't pull away. I was already falling in love with this open, innocent flower.

Gretchen shook her head when I gestured to the bathtub, so I gave her a washcloth, towel, and soap, showing her how to operate the shower.

When I returned to her bedroom, I heard the sink running, so I suspected she was taking a basin bath.

Patting the place next to me in Katrina's bed, I opened up the Arabian folktales book. As she wriggled in next to me, I smoothed her wet hair, tucking it behind her shoulder. "Shall we read *Ali Baba and the Forty Thieves*?"

The same pot-of-gold smile arced across her face.

The story was long and intricate, but the shifts in Katrina's intent features told me she was following it. Katrina pointed at some of the watercolor illustrations as I read, showing her fascination at how the images captured the essence of the narrative—the murder of Ali Baba's greedy brother, the undying loyalty of Ali Baba's clever slave girl, and his eternal access to a secret treasure.

From her bed next to us, Gretchen seemed to be listening too. During the description of how the thieves cut up the dead brother's body and displayed its pieces outside their cave, she winced. Having grown up with these stories, I was of the old school of thought, that they toughened us up for the traumas of life and the evil in the world. They also contained a wealth of lessons about how the underdog could outwit the bully.

By the time I finished reading, Katrina's eyelids were at half mast and Gretchen was sound asleep.

"Tomorrow night, Katrina, we can read the frame story for *The Thousand and One Nights*. All about a clever woman named Scheherazade who saves herself by telling stories without endings." As she nodded dopily, I tucked her under the covers, turning out the lamps.

By the time I entered Liam's and my room, I felt tired again. Brushing my teeth and undressing, I slipped into bed, thinking Liam was asleep. But he edged into me, encasing my body from behind as I lay on my side. His fingers cascaded over my nakedness, making me drip with desire and rock into him. I felt his granite bulge pressing into the back of my thigh.

"You're a phenomenal woman, Ingrid," he murmured into my scalp. "Let me take you on a phenomenal trip."

"You're not spent after a day of shootings, rescues, and car chases?" I nestled my butt against his erection. I would never cease to feel at home in this position.

"Even if I were, you'd raise a man from the dead."

In the darkness, I smiled.

Chapter Thirty-Eight

Ingrid

The rest of the week was as exhausting as it was fulfilling. I still put in six hours a day of work alongside Liam, in our office or in the living room. The rest of the time I spent acclimating Gretchen and Katrina to life outside the compound. Whenever I was away from Liam, Gretchen and Katrina followed me around like the Pied Piper. When he and I were together, the two women hovered at a distance. I tried to find ways to occupy them while I worked. I had Tima show Gretchen how to clean and devein shrimp, cut up calamari, and shuck oysters the evening we had raw oysters and paella for dinner. I asked Jesse's assistant Leveni to teach Katrina how to plant cabbages, harvest sunflower seeds, and gather tomatoes. Even though Leveni was a twenty-two-year-old man, he was such a gentle, quiet soul that Katrina wasn't afraid of him.

Since Connie was an excellent seamstress, I asked her to teach Gretchen how to sew a dress or skirt. Gretchen became engrossed in making matching flowered cotton shirts for her and Katrina. Katrina loved taking my phone to capture photos of flowers, birds, and weather effects on the landscape. This she did sometimes for upwards of an hour, returning with stunning pictures of insects, clouds, and vegetation I didn't even know existed on the island. I showed her how to print these photos in my art studio. I also showed Gretchen and Katrina the bookcases in the southern end of the house, inviting them to read in the sitting rooms. Gretchen enjoyed reading for hours at a time—mostly dog-eared works of literary fiction that Liam had brought to the island as his favorites.

Andrea and I took the newcomers shelling at low tide every afternoon after Andrea, Guy, and I had finished our work. I told them the names of all the shells I knew, and pointed them to a website where they could cross-check what they found against a catalogue. Katrina was much more amenable than Gretchen to using the laptops Liam had provided. In general, Gretchen shied from technology.

Until we could get to Suva to shop, clothing was a challenge. One of the housekeepers, Ela, had a thirteen-year-old niece living on an island twenty miles north of Verau. By Friday morning, the supply boat had stopped off at her niece's place and collected some of her clothes for Katrina. A few pieces of my clothing fit Gretchen decently. She refused to wear shorts or slacks—only skirts and shirts, which seemed to be the uniform in the cult, judging from what she and Katrina had worn when they were rescued. Though I did manage to coax Gretchen into one of my white dresses, which looked stunning against her almond-tinted skin.

Every night I read Arabian tales to Katrina and Gretchen before they drifted off to sleep.

Katrina was now giving short answers to simple questions—"I don't know," "that one," and "over there." The why-when-how questions would have to wait until she opened up a little more.

Gretchen was a tougher nut to crack. She generally preferred to answer "yes" or "no," and then only when I asked a question while we were alone or with Katrina. Otherwise, she merely nodded or shook her head. I had the feeling she was observing our environment from a great distance, as if her own private world were inaccessible to us.

On Saturday morning, I took them both into the Asian-themed room where Liam had gotten so furious with me a week ago. I hadn't been in here since. I wanted to show them the beautiful light and the view of the tangled mangroves reflecting off the calm, green waters of the swamp.

Gretchen's eyes dipped to the photographs on the table beside the door. The photo of her holding Katrina when she was seventeen rested on top of the pile. She gasped, her hand going to her throat. Without saying anything, I watched her peer more closely at the picture, before deciding to pick it up. Her eyes slid to Katrina, giving me the first sign that she knew who Katrina was. Her glance was more penetrating and mindful than I'd ever seen it. But there was great pain behind her look, as though dredging up memories came at a great cost to her peace of mind.

"Gretchen, do you remember when that photograph was taken?" I approached to view it from the side.

Her eyes flicking up, she gazed into the distance out the windows. She seemed to be considering my question. "I remember where."

I waited. This was more than I'd gotten out of her in four days.

"My friend's backyard." Her voice had changed. Still like a flute, it was less fragile.

"How old was Katrina?" I ventured.

"Six months."

Katrina padded over, examining the photo. She regarded Gretchen with avid interest. I could see unasked questions popping up in her brain.

"Did you and Katrina ever see each other at the compound?"

Gretchen's features shut down as she dropped the photo on the table and turned to leave. Looking dumbfounded, Katrina cast one last glance at the photo and followed her.

"Katrina, wait." I trotted along behind. She halted, turning to me. "Did you know that Gretchen is your mother?"

She averted her eyes. "No."

"Were parents allowed to see their children?"

She cast a glance over her shoulder. "I don't know." Then she turned and jogged after her mother.

****

Liam

The mystery of the cult was clearly eating away at Ingrid. She was so troubled by her inability to find out anything from the taciturn Gretchen and Katrina that I leaned on Ralph, Claude, and Rodrigo.

On Saturday evening, in my office, Ingrid and I held a Zoom meeting with the three PIs. It was 4 a.m. in New York.

"What more have you got on the cult, Ralph?" I sipped my whisky, while the other men slugged coffee. Ingrid sat beside me drinking tea.

"On Thursday I located a man living in Crown Heights who made it out of the cult a year ago after being in it for thirteen." Ralph flipped a page in his notebook. Though his note-taking methods were crude, they worked for him. "Until now, he's stubbornly held off from talking to anyone about his experiences. But when I told him we'd rescued two members of the cult and wanted to understand them better, he agreed to talk. I met with him at a diner yesterday, and he opened up freely, in exchange for a tidy sum."

"Name of Stan Morrissey," Rodrigo chimed in. "I read a blurb about him online after he got out. Surprisingly lucid fellow, all things considered."

Ralph referred to his sheet. "Morrissey says the cult's leader, known to members as The Seer, founded the cult twenty years ago when he acquired the old car plant. The Seer was inspired by gnostic beliefs like the idea that everything in the material world is evil, including the human body and sex. Or the idea that the spirit seeks to rejoin a perfect realm of light after the death of the body. The only way to reunite with this spiritual realm is through a disciplined path of instruction that involves living a communal life, practicing sterility, and revering the revelations."

"What does 'revering the revelations' entail?" I slunk an arm around Ingrid's waist. I couldn't be near her and not touch her.

Ralph licked his index finger and turned a page of his notes. "That's where The Seer gave the creed his personal touch. He claims to have had a series of revelations from the Divine Entity. These revelations are such precious truths that they must be kept from the common herd. Only initiates to the cult are allowed to learn them, and then only by slow degrees. That's why the first stage of brainwashing—sorry, inducting—new members involves teaching them to keep everything in the cult secret from non-initiates."

"That explains why Katrina and Gretchen are so tight-lipped!" Ingrid exclaimed.

"Yeah, well," Ralph went on, "apparently each initiate undergoes an elaborate baptism in an underground pool, where The Seer also had a series of caves built. And, though no one but the longest-standing members see it, there's a high room at the top of the plant called 'the eagle's nest.' All of these locations are symbolic of various ends of the world that The Seer's vision protects his followers against. Fire, flood, bombs, global warming, even pollution—which The Seer counteracts by making the compound as airtight as possible."

I nodded. "All that squares with what I saw and heard on Monday."

Ralph slurped his coffee. "The Seer foresaw that the only way to lead a truly communal life was for no one to own anything—including children. So any members who enter the cult with children are immediately separated from their offspring. Parents and kids are thoroughly schooled not to miss family ties, since the cult is their true family. An elaborate hypnosis process makes members completely forget all former affiliations. The Seer's assistants schedule events in such a way that children rarely encounter their parents, and vice versa. This serves the double function of forcing all members to focus on the spiritual. According to The Seer, family ties are as evil as the body. Part of the discipline necessary for revelation is shunning the physical."

Ingrid looked as if a lightbulb had gone on. "That photo today jolted Gretchen momentarily out of her hypnosis."

I pulled my brows down. "But what about the wives and husbands I saw in that room?"

Ralph tapped his pen on his desk. "The sexes are separated—*but* if a couple enters the cult together, they're allowed to see one another during the day. Still, they sleep apart, since the cult practices celibacy."

Rodrigo piped up. "Hold up, how do you keep a cult going long-term without procreation?"

Ralph crushed his coffee cup and tossed it in an unseen trash. "You recruit. But it's a one-way ticket to the compound, since no one who learns the cult's secrets is allowed to leave to tell about them. Hence the aggressive brainwashing, restrictive routines, and security measures."

Claude leaned his jaw on his hand. "What's in it for The Seer? I mean, if it's not about money, power, or sex…"

Ralph shrugged. "He genuinely believes he was put on earth to shepherd a flock of people safely through doomsday—and to provide a revelation all other religions lack."

Rodrigo blew out a chuff. "Well, if he's so benevolent, why all the violence? He nearly shot me."

"He sees outsiders as demons trying to possess the spirits he's purifying," Ralph explained. "His shooting wasn't just self-defense, it was an attempt to exorcise demons."

Rodrigo tapped his mouth. "I remember Morrissey said he just walked out one day, unseen by the security guards—like a miracle."

"That brings us back to how I first saw Gretchen and Katrina," Ralph continued. "Each member is allowed out for half an hour to walk around the compound three days a week at complexly scheduled times. They walk in groups of six with supervision by The Seer's staff."

"Why no computers or cell phones?" I asked.

Ralph's eyebrows lifted. "They're further distractions from the true revelation."

Ingrid tilted her head. "Why does the cult render the women so docile? Almost as if they're drugged?"

"The Seer indoctrinates all members with the principle that two forces animate the material world— the masculine and the feminine." Ralph sneaked a peek at his notes. "The masculine represents all that is dynamic, violent, and restless. The feminine represents all that is static, peaceful, and submissive."

"Well, that's original," Claude snorted.

"The men I fought in that chant room seem to have soaked up the principle pretty well," I commented. "Sadly, so have Gretchen and Katrina."

"But why are the females so afraid when males are near?" Ingrid asked.

Ralph pursed his lips. "It's all part of the doctrine to separate them. Though previously married couples have a partial exception, since The Seer views marriage as a way to reinforce ordained gender roles."

"Yet he doesn't allow marriage in the cult," I confirmed.

Ralph shook his head. "Celibacy is superior, in his view. He'll accept married couples to the cult, but more precious and pure, to his mind, are the unmarried men and women, and single women with children."

"Damn," Rodrigo muttered. "Now I wanna go back and free everyone from that hellhole."

I tipped back my Scotch. "Why didn't those security guards know anything more about the cult?"

"Morrissey says The Seer employs six men to guard the entrance in pairs for eight-hour shifts." Ralph scrubbed his goatee. "They live on the same commune that foots the bills for the compound. So they're loyal to the cult, but they don't live in the compound or interact with its members." He added wryly, "Once I loosened the guy's lips, I couldn't shut him up."

"Commune?" Claude narrowed his eyes.

"Yeah." Ralph cracked a grin. "An agricultural commune that lives by The Seer's creed makes tax-free proceeds that support the compound. The commune is about ten miles from the compound. Equivalent doomsday procedures are in place there."

Puzzlement etched Rodrigo's brow. "What makes the compound members so special that they get to be supported by commune laborers?"

Ralph popped a stick of gum in his mouth. "Everyone at the compound is a religious leader, teacher, or scholar of The Seer's Book. That's why you saw so many classes and chant sessions, Liam. The commune members respect the members of the compound enough that they defer to them. And the compound doesn't cost much to operate."

I scowled. "No, judging from the rundown look of everything, the crappy AC, and the piles of dirty laundry, I'd say they don't splurge on necessaries."

"Does that cover it all?" Ralph met each of our eyes in turn.

I drained my whisky. "If I hadn't already dedicated my life to the material world and the ways of the flesh, I would now, just to spite The Seer and his creed."

Ingrid erupted in laughter. "There's not much of the spiritual about you, Liam."

I gripped her throat and bit her jaw. "I'm possessed by demons."

"Right, I'm off," said Claude.

"Me too." Rodrigo put his hand up over his camera as if to shield his view from our Zoom PDA.

"Sayonara, Captain." Ralph saluted me. "Be sure to indoctrinate Gretchen and Katrina in the cult of Liam Stauner. Do them a world of good."

Chapter Thirty-Nine

Ingrid

That Saturday evening was Liam's and my first date night. Well, second real date, but our first since he'd agreed to court me. Andrea had offered to watch Gretchen and Katrina. We began our date at 9. But it wasn't uncommon for weekend nights on the island to stretch into the wee hours of the morning. Liam wouldn't tell me what he'd planned, saying it was a surprise.

When I asked what I ought to wear, he said, "Something you can get dirty in."

Hmm. Okay. Taking him at his word, I donned well-worn denim shorts, a comfy tee-shirt, and sneakers, fixing my hair in a high, loose bun.

He told me to meet him on the porch of the southwestern outbuilding. *Very mysterious.*

Without a word, he greeted me with a kiss. Laying his hand on my lower back, he ushered me toward an empty wooden structure next to the poultry yard. I'd always wondered what he intended to do with this building.

"What do you have up your sleeve, Mr. Stauner?" I slid a sly side glance his way.

"Be patient, Miss Pellerin. You're about to find out." He threw open one of the huge wooden doors to the building, which was brightly lit inside.

"*What?!*" My jaw popped open, and my eyes jumped from their sockets.

Three lovely she-goats—their bulbous udders poking out from between their hind legs—greeted me. One was all white, a second beige-and-black-spotted over white, and the third brown with fine white mottlings. Each had soft fur, long perked-up ears, and bright eyes. The rustle as they chomped hay sounded like the rush of a distant river.

"They're darling!" I advanced toward the first, caressing her neck. "Mathilde, how are you this fine evening?"

Liam chuckled. "You've already named her?"

Scratching Mathilde's head and behind her ears, I smiled. "All three should have old-fashioned French names. This one will be…Toinette. And this one we'll name Zephyr." I pronounced it *zuh-PHEER*, in the French way.

He arched an eyebrow. "Zephyr? I was saving that for our daughter."

I laughed. "You can always rename the goat, in the event that you have a daughter." I stroked Zephyr's back. "How in the world did you get them out here without my noticing?"

"The supply boat made an extra trip this morning bringing just the goats and a Fijian goatkeeper, Jope." He knelt, petting Toinette's back. "We sneaked them back here when you were walking with the girls. You'll find we have all the supplies."

"Supplies for . . ."

"I got them for their milk." He stood. "Cue our second date."

"We're milking goats?"

"That and other goat-related things." His eyes sparkled. "Let's just say, the whole date is goat-themed."

"Wow." I stepped toward him, circling my arms around his chest and looking into his glittering, green eyes. "That is really romantic—and creative. I had no idea, Mr. Stauner, that you were so fond of goats."

"I like the fact that they eat anything." A devilish smirk tilted his lips. "And I like foods made from goat's milk. Let's get started. We have a half-hour's work before dinner." He dragged forward two platforms that were a foot high and had what looked like a pillory on one side and a feed box attached on the outside. "We'll start with Mathilde and Toinette."

As soon as Liam dropped grain into the feed boxes, the goats jumped up on the milking stands.

"Oh, aren't you clever, Mathilde!" I cooed, petting her rump.

Slotting their necks into the headpieces, Liam handed me a bucket while holding one under Toinette's udder. He pulled up two stools, taking a seat. I followed his lead.

"How do you do it?" I could barely contain my excitement.

Liam showed me how to pinch the top of the teat and roll my fingers down to squeeze out the milk. "You can do both teats at the same time, once you get the hang of it."

I laughed to see how much milk was streaming into my pail. "How did you learn all this?"

"Like so much else, the military. When I was stationed in Beaufort, South Carolina, one of my off-duty jobs was to keep hunters off a few properties in nearby Dale. One of them had goats, and the owners showed me how to milk them."

I was overcome with admiration. "Does the military pretty much teach you to do everything?"

He nodded. "Most of it's OJT—on-the-job training." He bumped his palm against Toinette's udder a few times, bringing milk down to the base, and continued milking.

I copied what he did. "Did you have a girlfriend when you were in the service?"

"Two of my three serious relationships were in the service. One for each tour." He freed Toinette from the headpiece, removing the grain box so she leapt down. After tying her up, he untied Zephyr and replaced the feed box. Zephyr bounded onto the platform, and he pilloried her head.

"What were their names?" I tamped down my jealousy, reminding myself this would've been anywhere from six to fourteen years ago. Meanwhile, I seemed to have milked the last out of Mathilde, halfway filling the bucket.

"Aileen and Ramona. I was with Aileen for two years, and Ramona for eighteen months." He made speedy work of Zephyr, emptying her udder to top off his milk bucket.

"Why did you and Ramona break up?" I tried to keep a measured tone, imitating Liam as I freed Mathilde from her headpiece.

He became grave. "She was pregnant with my baby."

My heart dropped to the base of my chest, as I turned stricken eyes to Liam. "What?!"

A glimmer of a smile played about his lips. "Just kidding."

I splashed him with goat's milk. "Not funny."

He dipped his chin. "You do realize, to even the score I'll have to come all over you."

"How do you figure?"

"I can't let a she-goat do my job for me."

I laughed. "Couldn't make it through a goat-themed date without that visual, could you?" I stared into my bucket. "The milk really does resemble—"

"Okay, let's move on." He took the buckets, heading toward the door. "Next to the kitchen."

When we got to the kitchen, we scooped out cups of the milk and drank it lukewarm and fresh. It tasted like a grassy version of whole cow's milk. I loved it.

Tima had left out various cookware items on an empty counter near one of the ranges.

"What are we doing now?" I was as thrilled as a kid carrying a water balloon to a fight.

He smiled. "We're making goat cheese."

"Don't tell me the marines taught you that too."

He ladled goat's milk into a large pan, setting the heat on medium-low. "This was self-taught. As I say, anything with goat's milk, and I'm hooked." He handed me a long wooden spoon. "Keep stirring to make sure it heats evenly."

While I stirred, he placed three layers of cheesecloth over a colander. Unwrapping a bowl of what smelled like freshly squeezed lemon juice, he brought out a bottle of white wine vinegar. Then he inserted a digital thermometer in the milk.

"Perfect temperature. Eighty-five degrees Celsius." He cut off the heat. "Keep stirring." As he added some lemon juice, I swirled the mixture around. Then he added vinegar, which I blended in. "All right. Now we let it sit for a half-hour."

"Are we going to feed our three sweet goats?"

He wrapped an arm around my shoulder, leading me toward the outside door. "We're going to feed us."

On the small terrace off the kitchen, he'd laid a small round table with champagne flutes, a bottle of bubbly on ice, and two place settings. On a side table was a large salad bowl filled with colorful fixings.

"Tima made us arugula, pear, and goat cheese salad with pomegranate vinaigrette." He opened his arm with a flourish.

My throat tightened. "It's beautiful, Liam. The thought that went into it is even more beautiful."

"Miss Pellerin, please take a seat." He pulled out my chair. After settling me, he helped us to salad and laid our dishes down. Sitting across from me, he poured our champagne.

"You're chef, waiter, sommelier, and date all at once." I beamed.

"When you smile, I wish I were an artist too." He held his glass up to mine. "To courting."

"You're such a natural at it, I suspect you've been holding out on me." I smiled into my fizz. "But even if you've forgotten Ramona, I haven't."

He laughed. "Ah, yes. Ramona. She turned out to be too reclusive for me. She loved to stay in remote places for weeks at a time, never missing civilization."

"Hmm, says the man who bought an island in the middle of the South Pacific."

His lips curved. "Well, yes. There's that. But she really sought to escape people. She preferred animals and plants to humans. And she coupled her solitude with extremely dangerous hikes and kayaking ventures." He sipped his champagne. "She would've hated staying a month in Paris or London. Not to mention living in New York."

"So you broke up with her?"

He put down his glass, gazing at its rising bubbles. For a long moment I thought he wasn't going to answer. "No. She broke up with me." He rubbed the back of his neck—the sure sign that he was nervous and reluctant. "She invited me home to meet her family, and I lasted all of two days before she called it off."

I was floored. "Why?"

He cleared his throat, his eyes flitting up to mine. "You really want to know?"

I pushed my dish back, leaning my forearms on the table. "I do." He was really holding back. I felt bad pushing him, but having come this far, there was no retreating.

"For her parents, there were two good reasons for her not to stay with me. I had no formal education beyond high school, and I still didn't know what I wanted to do when I got out of service. They saw me as a bad boy with no future." He took a gulp of champagne. "For her, I was too possessive. Her parents meant a lot to her, so her reason plus theirs meant I got the axe."

We were silent a space.

"Boy, am I ever feeling lucky tonight," I said quietly.

Surprise was splashed over his features. "Why?"

"Ramona's loss is my gain."

He flashed a warm smile. "Apparently *she* wasn't

impressed by my goat-milking skills."

Something occurred to me. "That was when you were twenty-six?"

He nodded. "Why?"

I was thinking of when he made his first kill. "No reason." I was putting a few pieces of Liam's past together. *After all, he was only living up to people's expectations of him. People he loved.*

I thought of how nervous Liam must've been sharing that with me, knowing I'd broken up with Adrian, my former fiancé, because he'd been too possessive. And then, for him to confess that he'd been dumped for being unworthy—that took courage from anyone, but especially someone who resisted making himself vulnerable.

His frown cleared. "You ready for the fun part of cheesemaking?" He rose. "Bring your bubbly."

Together we poured the curdled goat's milk into the cheesecloth, allowing the whey to drip out. After I'd salted the curds, we tied up the cheesecloth into a bundle, which we hung from the spigot of the faucet to drain further.

"We'll leave it for an hour before shaping it into logs and chilling them." He led me over to another stove unit, where a delicious-smelling curry was simmering. He stirred it with a ladle. "Goat's milk curry, anyone?"

I breathed in a deep whiff. "*Mmm*, it smells divine."

After serving ourselves plates of rice and curry, we brought them back out to the terrace.

"You know," I said as we sat down, "Tima is going to dread date nights. She'll always have to cook for us *and* the others."

"She may look forward to our dates." He smoothed his napkin in his lap. "I'm paying her double for tonight."

I hummed over the delicious curry, which tasted especially rich because goat's milk formed its base.

"Is Simon still mad at you for extending your remote work another month?" Liam forked some curry and rice.

I rolled my eyes. "Mad is a gross understatement."

"Have you thought any more about opening up your own gallery and exhibiting your works along with others'?" He sat back and sipped his champagne.

I laughed. "Ah, Liam, you say that as if twenty grand were a vine-ripened tomato you could just pluck and eat."

"It'll be my investment, so yes, it's mine to pluck and eat." His serious expression morphed into a wicked grin.

"Then it wouldn't be my gallery," I reasoned. "I'd just work and display there, paying you a commission for sales."

"No, sweet bird. It'll be your gallery. Call it whatever you like. Investment, gift. I'm investing in you. In us." He set his glass on the table, leaning in.

I fiddled with my choker, splaying my fingers on the table so my ring shone in the lantern light. "Haven't you already invested quite a lot in me?"

He burst into laughter, though I couldn't imagine why. "Yes, I have, Ingrid. But not in the way you think. Not through cash dropped at a few stores."

"Then how?"

The intensity of his gaze burned a fissure right

down through the center of my body.

"I've invested hope. Hope, my little rosebud."

At his words a tight lump clotted in my throat, my eyes pricking with tears. *Hope*. It was like faith. It blossomed directly into love. There was no mistaking his look. His heart was open and vulnerable and *hopeful*. He'd made it so. Or together we'd made it so.

I'd been wrong when Andrea had found that murex shell. The miracle wasn't in the shell's lying so far off the beaten path. It was in turning and stooping to pick it up.

Chapter Forty

Ingrid

I awoke early that Sunday morning, deciding it was high time I went swimming again at the cove. Not having been there in ten days, I sensed that many things could've changed—the rocks, fish, shells, even the feel of the water, since we were deeper into the islands' winter season. If I left on my bike and swam forty-five minutes, I could be back before Gretchen and Katrina were up. I couldn't wait to share the beauty of the cove with them, when they were feeling confident enough to try riding bikes or walk that far.

As I donned my bikini and shorts, Liam stirred. "I'll come too," he mumbled. "Lemme just get dressed."

Liam dressed quickly for his ride, which was longer and hillier than our ring road loop. The sun's rays burst like fire through the pines as we rolled northwards, giving everything gold and auburn haloes. Sweeping sunbeams swirling with insects and the dust of the forest tracked us until the hills blocked them. Birds I'd come to know as Fiji parrot finches—their bills and tails bright red and their wings forest green— undulated through the air, dipping down to the grasses or loose bark for insects. Breezy, dry, fragrant, and warm, the morning was perfect for whatever humans chose to shape it into.

At the edge of the dirt path that met the road, Liam kissed me goodbye. "Maybe I'll join you for a dip later. And a walk along the beach."

As always since he'd gone to the compound, I wanted to tell Liam I loved him. It had been on the tip of my tongue for so long, that I'd grown accustomed to reining it in. It didn't matter if he already knew it—I yearned to give voice to it. But I held back, knowing that when the time was right, I wouldn't hesitate.

I usually checked a webpage listing the low tides to time my cove swims. But today I figured if the tide came in while I swam, I would climb out, and if the tide was already in, I'd wait for it to go out. I liked the spontaneity of my visit.

Propping my bike against the external rock wall of the cove, I stripped down to my bikini, stretching my arms and shoulders. At the entrance to the cove, the tide was at a moderate height. I couldn't immediately tell whether it was flooding or ebbing. I would know in about ten minutes, using the ledge as my gauge.

Without further preliminaries, I slipped into the water, savoring the silky-smooth lapping of the current and the heft of the saltwater against my body. I did the breaststroke for a few minutes, advancing toward the open sea and the light. Before reaching the entrance to the ocean, I turned around, front crawling back toward where I'd started. I took a sighting of the tide when I came to the arching rock "door," as I called our entrance to the cove. It had risen. So I would need to watch for when it got six inches above the ledge and step out, to make sure I could still climb up to the "door" and exit. Otherwise, the only other exit was floating out to the open sea, which I hadn't yet tried.

Nor did I wish to. The currents around this part of the island were an unknown to me. But because it was a narrow strait, I suspected even a strong, able swimmer could get sucked under without fanfare.

Thinking about it made me shudder. I did four more laps back and forth in the gentle waves, noting how the breeze turned from cool to balmy in just the time since I'd arrived. I was on my way to the end again, doing the freestyle stroke, when I saw a white boat passing the oceanside entrance. As I paused to catch sight of it again, it was already gone. Had it turned into the inlet, or had it sheared off southeast along the main shore? In all the time I'd swum here, I'd never seen a boat pulling up to this stretch of the beach. Liam had once said all the good fishing was toward the end of the strait. These were small fish here, not worth the trouble of floating or motoring in and turning around.

I returned, doing another lap. By the time I reached the "door," I sensed it was now or never. I should exit. I'd overshot the mark already, since my foot couldn't easily grip onto the ledge. I made several attempts to catch the door by riding with the tide beyond it, swimming back, and hooking my arm around the rock framing the opening. But even when I successfully grabbed onto the rock, I couldn't pull myself up. I would have to do this the clumsy way—on my belly by slow degrees. Using all the upper body strength I'd developed in the gym, I hoisted myself up, flopping onto my chest and hinging at the waist. So far, so good.

Suddenly I was whooshed up and out by strong arms holding both sides of me under the arms. Oh, that was a timely save! I divided a smile between the kind men who'd helped me out. They must be the fishermen whose white boat I'd seen. A thank you hovered on my lips, when a large hand covered my mouth and a sizable arm clamped around my waist from behind, lifting me effortlessly.

Oh shit. These were not rescuers. They were marauders. *What do they want from me?* I came with nothing to the beach, except the bike. That's when I realized it was me they wanted. The way they were treating me, I didn't think they cared if I didn't want them. *Shit, shit, shit.* Straining against the solid arm that girded me and kicking back against striding calves, I screamed in vain into the palm of the man carrying me. A second man strode alongside my captor, talking to him in an Island language. I shook my head, as though by refusing to go I could get them to set me down.

Now I recognized we were at the high tide point of the beach, where the white boat I'd seen earlier had moored in the inlet. A third man, whose black close-cropped beard was cut at neat angles, gestured toward the boat and said something. When I realized he was encouraging his friends to put me in the boat, I vehemently shook my head, crying out into the hand that muffled me.

The boatman tossed two coils of rope and some cloths in the direction of my captor's companion. The next thing I knew, the hand against my mouth was replaced with a cloth stuffed into it to gag me and another cloth was wound tightly around my face to hold the gag in place. As fast as I could take all this in, my wrists and ankles were bound tight with rope.

I began to think from their perspective, not mine. If

they were going to kill me, surely they wouldn't go to all this trouble to secure me first. If they were going to kidnap me, why would the boat man have had to encourage his companions to bring me to the boat? The third possibility made my heart stop, before it tumbled forward at breakneck speed. Why would they bother to seek me out for that, when willing women abounded? No, it must be the first after all. I was going to die.

My legs gave out, as I collapsed onto the sand. All this time, the boatman had apparently been clearing a place for me in the boat, because my captor and his companion hoisted me up and laid me down on a tarp on the floor of the boat. *Fuck. Please God, don't let this be what it looks like. Please let Liam come back now!* I didn't want to look at what they were doing, but I willed myself to look so I would know. My captor had a gold tooth that gleamed whenever he opened his mouth to speak or grin. His companion had patches of black hair missing that exposed his bare scalp and burn marks on his cheek.

My last hope was that they wouldn't push out to sea, but would stay put, until Liam could get here. How long had it been since he'd left? Maybe half an hour? Maybe he'd come back sooner than he'd said.

The gold-toothed man unsheathed a fish-cleaning knife—long, thin, and pointed at the end. When I convulsed with fear, the patchy-haired man held down my ankles. The angular-bearded boatman rounded me and pulled my hands over my head, pinning down my wrists on the tarp. Closing my eyes would be worse than keeping them open—I'd imagine worse than what was happening. But what was happening was pretty horrific.

Gold Tooth smiled at me with hollowed-out pupils, taking his knife and slicing the strap that connected the front and back panels of my bikini bottoms. I heaved with panic, incapable of drawing one full breath. Then he cut the strap on the other side, ripping off what was left of my bottoms. Tremors passed from my chest down my quivering belly to my jumping thighs. But still the Patchy-Haired One immobilized my ankles and the Boatman held my wrists.

As Gold Tooth pointed his knife into my navel, I gasped, unable to look away. If I was going to bleed to death, I had to know how it happened. He used his knife point to excavate my belly button. Was he cutting? I couldn't tell, I was so numb, but for the tingling in my spine. He pressed the flat of the blade into my belly, sliding it to my crotch, where he used the tip to nudge open my labia one by one. I nearly blacked out from terror then. Dying by having my vagina sliced down the middle was one of my worst nightmares.

Gold Tooth raised the knife high and threw it down so the point lodged in the wood at a spot a few millimeters from my crotch. If I'd moved at all…! I spasmed from the thought, chills shooting up my arms and neck. He hastily pulled down his shorts and exposed himself. I turned away, refusing to watch.

****

Liam

Should I do the second southern hill or turn around and join Ingrid? I had more steam in me, so that wasn't the issue. But I'd had a strange feeling, when we said goodbye, that someone was watching. A foreboding of danger. My instincts had gotten me through eight years of service unscathed, just as they'd kept me from getting caught for any of my contract hits. I decided to follow them now and turn around, instead of extending my ride.

Suddenly, as I descended the northern hill, I knew beyond a doubt I had to race at top speed. The area felt eerily calm, as if a tornado was about to touch ground. Since my thin bike tires were no good on the dirt path, I laid my bike down at the roadside and ran down toward the entrance to the cove. Ingrid's bike was propped against the outer wall, and her shorts and small backpack were still there. I ducked down through the "door," as Ingrid called it, and realized the tide was high. Higher than I'd ever seen it in the cove when we'd swum before. The water reached to the base of the entrance. I looked to the right. No Ingrid. To the left…no Ingrid. *Fuck*. Had she been swept out by a current?

Don't panic. Don't assume the worst. One thing at a time. She probably knew to climb out before the water rose too far. I ran down along the edge of the cove rock face, tracing its curve to round the end as it gave onto the beach.

About fifty yards away I saw a white fishing boat in the inlet with two men on their knees facing each other and a third man in the middle kneeling forward. Something didn't sit right—literally. What were these men so intent on, why weren't they out fishing, and why were they kneeling as if they were at some sacrificial ritual?

And where the fuck was Ingrid?

Pounding toward the boat, I saw one of the men look up, a murderous glint in his eye. That's when I knew. *I knew*. These fuckers were in the process of…No, I wasn't going to let them. I'd kill them all first.

As I reached the boat, the middle cunt stood, pulling up his shorts and grabbing a long fillet knife. His gold tooth glinted as he jumped off the boat, advancing toward me with the knife. I tried not to let the scene in the boat distract me. In all my time in the military and as a hitman, my heart had never done so many acrobatics as now. More was on the line than ever before. I had to hope I wasn't too late. I let the cocksucker get to within two feet of me with his knife, and I slammed my right palm into his extended wrist, slapping my left palm into his knuckles, so his fingers whipped open and the knife went flying off to my right. I made a dash for the blade, stooping and grabbing it a second before he could.

I closed in on him, his arms bent at the elbows at waist level, his eyes psychotic and trained on mine. I wanted to stab the motherfucker in the heart and then cut off his balls—and I could have. But the two other men sprang from the boat holding larger daggers and backing up their companion as they approached me in a semi-circle. *One at a time.* I decided to deal with the unarmed man with gold teeth first. Slicing my flattened left hand into his right carotid artery, I followed with a backhand snap against his left carotid, knocking him down.

Kicking the dagger out of the hand of the guy to my right, I sent it flying. I gripped his right wrist and twisted, jabbing my knife into his veins. The third man charged me from the left, stabbing my upper left arm. I grabbed hold of his forearm and flipped him over onto his back, pulling the knife from my arm. The guy with the bleeding wrist was fumbling for his dagger on the ground, but I beat him to it, plucking it up so I now held all three weapons.

I could've slit the throat of every last one of them. But even in the heat of the moment, I realized that's just what Rory was waiting for me to do. Even knowing I could claim self-defense, especially since it was me against three and I was on my own property, I reined it in.

"Into the boat, everyone. *Now*."

I marched the three of them to the boat, where I found Ingrid tied up and gagged.

"Untie her," I ordered one of the pigs, who had bald patches in his hair. He started to unbind her.

"Lie down, hands above your heads," I directed the other two men, who instantly complied.

Focusing first on the guy with gold teeth, I dug my knee into his solar plexus while choking him with my right hand. All this time I held the knives steady in my left. He didn't even have the strength to fight my arm. When I heard him spluttering, I eased up, landing a final punch in his stomach that knocked him out cold.

The image of him on top of Ingrid flashed through my head. Grabbing his left hand, I lopped off the top joint of his middle finger. He came to, screaming.

"To mark you," I gritted into his squinting eyes, "and remind you never to return."

I was vaguely aware the Ingrid was standing on shaky legs, coughing, with marks on her ankles and wrists. The shithead who'd released her had started the engines.

Seizing the other pig who was lying down, I slashed his cheek with the knife, deeply enough to leave a scar and brand him. Then, snatching the arm of the guy starting the engine, I whirled him about and marked his cheek in the same way, carving a nice long gash down his face.

"For when we meet again," I snarled, bolting his eyes to mine.

Still clutching the three knives, I lifted Ingrid over my shoulder and climbed off the boat.

I turned, shouting, "Come anywhere near my island again and you're dead men! I'll put a bullet in you."

They hurriedly motored out of the inlet, disappearing around the end of the strait.

As I turned us back toward the cove, I caught sight of a woman—was that Char?—behind a wide pine in the grove that flanked the beach about thirty yards away. She darted out of view as soon as I spotted her. But I recognized the unmistakable figure and hair. What would Char be doing here at this time of day?

Nevermind. She would keep. I needed to attend to Ingrid. I carried her all the way to the entrance to the cove, sitting in the sand with her crosswise in my lap.

"Ingrid, are you okay?" I stroked her hair, holding her as close as I could.

She buried her face in my chest, her sobs starting out softly and growing more violent and uncontrollable as she gave in to them. Quaking all over, she howled as tears streamed down her red face. It was torture to see her like this and not be able to take her pain away.

Kissing her forehead, temple, and cheek, I felt the vibrations of her moans and bawling, and they terrified me. Her wails resounded through the air, echoing off the rock face. Her heaving frame in my arms felt like all the abandoned living things of the world rolled into one.

"I'm sorry, Ingrid. I failed you." I squeezed my eyes shut thinking of what might have been. "This is all my fault."

"No," she hiccupped on a sob. "No, Liam. He didn't do anything. You turned up just when I was praying most for you to come."

"You mean he didn't—" I couldn't finish it.

"I don't think he even cut me with his knife." She shivered.

Relief crashed over me like a tidal wave.

"Let's get you home, give you a bath, and put you to bed. I'll stay by your side for as long as you need me." Standing, I lifted Ingrid with me.

I called Sione to have him bring the Jeep around.

I never put down my precious cargo until I lowered her into the bathtub.

Chapter Forty-One

Ingrid

Andrea and Guy joined Liam and me in our room after my bath. While I'd bathed, Liam had directed Guy how to stitch up the gash in his arm, popping Ibuprofen to dull the pain. Now he had a bandage around the wound. Andrea smothered me in a loving hug, while Guy looked more concerned than I'd ever seen him. When Liam had asked me if I was okay with seeing them, I gladly agreed. Guy meant as much to Liam as Andrea did to me, and now was the time for everyone to come together. I felt safe surrounded by these close friends.

Liam paced, preoccupied. "Should I have ended those fuckers then and there?"

Guy folded himself in a chair. "Since they took Ingrid to the boat, and the boat was in the inlet, technically they attempted the assault off your property. You could've pleaded self-defense while they threatened you on the beach, but you wouldn't have been able to claim the same on the boat—unless they resisted your efforts to help Ingrid. Which they didn't."

Liam wheeled about, stalking back toward the door. "Still, should I have gone with my instinct and maimed them all?"

Guy turned to me. "I assume Ingrid will want to

press charges. You merely swapped one form of justice for the other. Either you maim the assailants or put them in prison for up to eight years, as I believe you could get in Fiji, considering they also assaulted you with deadly weapons."

I shuddered, remembering Gold Tooth's acts of terror with the knife. Andrea, who'd climbed in bed next to me, tightened her arm around my shoulders.

Liam paused in his pacing, running a hand through his hair and gazing at me. "I took the route of the law this time, Ingrid. I've never opted to do that before in my life. The one time I stood to lose someone I care about she made me abide by the law."

I thought of what might've happened to Liam if he'd gotten caught up in the wheels of the justice system. "I'm glad you didn't seriously harm anyone, Liam. We'll report the attempted rape and let the local police deal with them. I don't know what I'd do if you were sentenced to prison, even for a few months." An awful idea occurred to me. "They won't sentence you for cutting off the top of the man's middle finger, will they?"

Liam gave a mirthless laugh. "Let them try. If he's pussy enough to press charges, in the midst of being charged with attempted rape and assault, I doubt anyone—judge or jury—would have sympathy for him."

Guy crossed his legs. "Establishing your culpability would be an entirely separate case, Liam. The suspects will have to get over this hurdle first."

Relief flooded me. "We need to go to Suva anyway, to buy clothes for Gretchen and Katrina. We can file a report with the police then."

Liam's tense features relaxed somewhat. "We'll go tomorrow."

****

The next morning, Josefa ferried Gretchen, Katrina, Andrea, Guy, Liam, and me to Suva. We started with the serious business, filing our complaint at the police station in the city center. After Inspector Mani, a short, spry man in his early fifties, had written up a statement based on Liam's and my stories, he gave us his card and said he'd be in touch as soon as he'd located the three fishermen. Apparently Liam and I would be asked to identify the suspects in a lineup.

On our way out of Mani's office, Liam seemed to remember something. "Oh, we have a potential witness. A former cook whose last day in my employ was yesterday. Her name is Char Panthong. She may have seen the crime from where she was standing."

"Do you know how I can reach Ms. Panthong?" asked Mani.

Liam wrote down her contact information from his phone. "She told me she was staying with a cousin on an island north of Verau."

Mani nodded. "I'll call her. Let me know if you think of anything else."

"What was Char doing there?" I asked Liam once we'd emerged from the station.

"I don't know. I meant to ask her, but she left on her cousin's boat before I got a chance. I was surprised she didn't say goodbye." Liam's brow furrowed.

I reflected. "I've seen her out early in the morning gathering herbs for her aunt's medicines." Her aunt was an herbal healer of great renown around the islands. "I think it was a daily ritual for her. She had passing fishermen bring the herbs to her aunt."

As we walked the streets of Suva, Gretchen and Katrina were like visitors from another planet. They gawked at the traffic, jumped at the pop music blaring from passing vehicles, and shied at the crowds of tourists and locals. I held their hands, marveling at how different this trip was from our excursion two weeks ago. So much had happened since then. Once again, perspective was everything in transforming a person, place, or thing. Now, I was determined to put all thoughts of the assault behind me as I focused on fitting the women out with a wardrobe.

Guy and Liam chatted in armchairs in our first exclusive boutique, while Andrea and I pulled clothes for Gretchen and Katrina.

"Guy wants to buy me a few outfits," Andrea whispered as we selected items on a rack and held them up for Gretchen and Katrina's inspection. "He says I need—and I quote—'to find some covers for our book so he can inscribe them with his pen.' When I said that sounded like mixing work with pleasure, he said his pen does double duty."

I laughed. "I dare you to take him up on it, D. If you do, I'll perform any dare you have for me."

"*Any* dare?"

I nodded. "Do your worst."

She smiled. "All right. I dare you to take Liam up on his offer to give you a gallery. And show your art along with other artists."

I narrowed my eyes. "A shopping spree versus a gallery? I think I got the short end of the stick."

She shook her head. "Oh no, Ingrid. You got the *long* end of the stick."

We erupted in giggles.

By early afternoon, we'd fitted Andrea out with a whole new work, leisure, and lingerie wardrobe. Cheerfully handing over his black American Express card, Guy looked like the cat that got the cream. In the meantime, we'd helped Gretchen and Katrina find enough attractive shirts, skirts, shorts, underwear items, and dresses to make them comfortable on the island.

I caught a spark of genuine excitement in Gretchen's eye as we left the shop. Katrina actually bounced next to me, her hand squeezing mine. Ah, was there anything in this world a lavish shopping spree couldn't fix? It even helped to fix my anger at those who'd assaulted me—which said a lot.

"Before we tackle shoes, we must refuel," Guy declared. "There's a French bistro tucked away on a side street a quarter of a mile up this way. Its owner is charming."

Andrea rolled her eyes, though her smile said she was impressed. "Guy, how in the world do you know about this bistro?"

"Princess, can you know so little about me a week into writing my life story?" Guy feigned offense. "You'll recall I spent some time in Suva while island-hopping in the South Pacific four years ago on the yacht of an Egyptian heiress."

Andrea crooked a cynical smile. "No, Guy, we haven't quite reached that point in your meteoric rise to notoriety."

He sniffed. "Believe nothing you hear, unless it comes from the horse's mouth."

She snorted. "If I'm even a halfway-decent judge of character, you're guilty until proven innocent."

A roguish glint lit his eye. "If so, allow me to compound that guilt, enchantress."

I *had* to find out if they were sleeping together again. So after we'd ordered our lunch at the bistro, I invited Andrea to come with me to freshen up in the women's restroom.

Of course, Katrina and Gretchen tagged along. Oh well, they'd learn sooner or later the sexual politics of the island. But to protect Katrina, I decided to speak in code.

"Drea," I opened, as we rinsed our hands at the sinks, "have you and Guy had biblical acquaintance over the last week?"

Andrea laugh-spluttered as she dried her hands. "To answer in your PG terms, honey, we've had a few leading 'moments.' That's all. All systems on his end read 'Go.' My systems are slower to fire up."

"What's slowing your systems?" I probed.

"Oh, I don't know, maybe hearing about the trail of broken hearts he's left in his wake over the years? Maybe suspecting I'll just be another notch on his—" she hesitated, realizing Katrina's wide eyes and young ears were trained on her—"goalpost. Maybe remembering how he redirected my career as though shuffling the track of an electric train set."

I lowered my voice. "But don't you find his determination and resourcefulness hot?"

She applied lip balm, rubbing it into her lips. "Oh, no doubt. And the power that allowed him to do that is *steamy*. I just wanted to make sure he felt sufficiently punished."

My eyes flared. "Has he been?"

She winked at me in the mirror. "We'll see."

Chapter Forty-Two

Andrea

After lunch, we shopped for shoes for me, Gretchen, and Katrina. Then Ingrid insisted that she and Liam show Gretchen and Katrina the sea wall while Guy and I wandered off for a couple of hours on our own. We agreed to meet back at the boat at 6. Traipsing around the broad streets of Suva's city center, Guy and I headed toward Albert Park and the Thurston botanical gardens that housed the Fiji Museum. The museum contained a number of archaeological and cultural artifacts from the last four millennia, including an old Fijian raft, a double-hulled canoe, a collection of impressively shaped clay drinking vessels, carved wooden house posts, traditional apparel, and tons more.

In the hall that showcased traditional island jewelry, we passed a group of loud American tourists.

A twenty-something blonde woman squealed with delight. "*Ohmigod*, Guy Travis! *Ahh!*" A dozen cell phones were trained on Guy. I had never felt so exposed in my life. "Who's he with? Is that, like, his new *girlfriend*?"

"Shit, they're *cute* together," another woman proclaimed. *Flash!* "But she looks *shy*."

The blonde said, "I'm totally posting this."

Another woman cried, "Guy, give me your

autograph!"

Guy quickly removed his jacket, using it to shield my face from the cell phone cameras. Wrapping a defensive arm around me, he wheeled us about, leading us toward the exit. He escorted me out the door, keeping his jacket over me until we were walking among the roses of the botanical gardens. I'd never felt so protected, as if Guy's sole aim in life was to safeguard me from the world's prying eyes.

"Forgive me." He seated me on a bench facing the sea, keeping his jacket over my back. His amber eyes were filled with worry. "I didn't expect that onslaught, or that anyone would recognize me here. Are you all right?"

By way of answer, I pulled his face down to mine, brushing his lips. Withdrawing briefly, I dove back in, my tongue springing into action. Like a geyser gushing forth, he took over, daring me to respond to every movement he offered. He pressed my lower back into him, using the nape of my neck to control our kiss. *Shit*, this guy's assurance was hot. Judging from the way my sheath was like a sprinkler system run amok, it seemed to agree. Even if *I'd* forgotten how skilled he was at seducing, my pussy hadn't. I fused my body with his, draping my thigh over his knees and moaning into his mouth. He pulled my leg up by the back of the knee, running his fingers along my hamstring until I trembled.

"I suggest we repair below decks." He spoke hoarsely in my ear. "Now."

I nodded.

I soon found out that when Guy said "now," he meant *now*. Flagging a cab, he bundled us in, handing the driver a fifty. "The port. If you get there in under five, you'll get another fifty."

The driver sped like a Formula One driver to the port, reaching it in four minutes. Guy passed him the bill. "Drive safe, old man."

At the boat, Josefa looked surprised to see us. "Mr. Travis, Ms. Carpel!"

"Enough of the fanfare, Josefa." Guy handed me onto the boat. "It's Guy and Andrea. We'll be down in the berth."

I'd expected the berth to be stuffy, but it was surprisingly well-aired. Though far from roomy, it had enough space for a comfortable bed, chair, and small table. Guy locked the door. Taking a seat in the chair opposite the bed, he leaned back, propping his legs up on the bed's edge. He dropped a lazy, lustful, indulgent gaze on me.

"Take off your clothes."

I began with his jacket. "Is this Guy Travis, International Playboy commanding me?"

"It's the voice of your inner sex goddess, Andrea. Your shirt next."

Delighted at his authoritative tones, I pulled my shirt over my head. "Any further requests?"

"You have permission to choose the order in which you strip. I'll give you another minute to do so," he drawled, resting his hands on his thighs.

My heart raced as I removed my bra, noting the fire that leapt up in his eyes. Unzipping the back of my skirt and shimmying out of it, I said, "Isn't this rather one-sided?"

His voice was dark and sinful. "That's the point."

I held his eyes as I lowered my panties and toed off

my shoes. While getting naked, the floodgates of my pussy unloosed under the heat of his gaze and the intensity of his focus. Before Guy, I never realized just how much I loved a man to take charge in the bedroom. I was incredibly aroused by the power differential: he was ordering me to do things from an easy position in his chair, fully clothed, while I snapped to it, naked. My sex pulsed with expectation.

"Sit down at the edge of the bed and lean back on your forearms," he directed. "Legs spread wide."

When I'd assumed the position, he slowly rose from his chair.

"Wider."

I spread my legs as wide as I could.

He stood a few feet away surveying me like a tiger on the prowl. Fuck, he was hot. I mean illegal levels of hot. He carried a self-contained world about with him that sucked everyone else into it, whether they liked it or not. I enjoyed being drawn into his magnetic field. Its pull was all the stronger for my having resisted him for two weeks. Or maybe I was just weaker.

His Roman nose looked scornful, his nostrils flaring slightly. Gazing at his lips, I remembered a series of sketches Ingrid had done of them one night that had perfectly captured their shapeliness. His thick locks and razor-sharp cheekbones wiped all other heads and faces off the map. And his lithe body that elegantly contoured his clothes reminded me of the things he'd done to me while naked in bed.

In a flash he was on his knees, drawing his fingertips up my inner thighs. I moaned.

"So open and receptive," he murmured approvingly. He inhaled deeply. "Ah. I've missed that aroma."

Pulling my labia apart, he drilled his tongue into me, flicking my clit, before withdrawing like a tormentor.

"*Annhh*," I crowed, the stupor of arousal settling on me.

Fluttering his tongue against my throbbing nub, he dragged it down my divide in a zigzag motion, stimulating every nerve ending along the way.

"Oh, God, *yes!*" My hips thrust into his face.

He palmed my belly, riveting it to the bed.

I gave in to the exquisite torture and total control of this man, who knew his way around my girly bits far better than I did.

His tongue swooped into my sensitive parts again, working them into a tingly, tense, needy state that burned and wound me up at once. When his finger circled my clit, massaging and pinching it, I unraveled like the chain on a winch dropping anchor. As pleasure ripped through me, I cried out, arching my back and clawing the bed. How the hell did he *do* that? Even in my euphoria, I half resented his expertise.

But I needed this. *How* I needed it.

I heard the rip of foil as his teeth opened a condom. Somehow, in the midst of my release, he'd removed his pants and boxer briefs. He pumped his cock and sheathed it.

"You came prepared, I see." I cracked a lust-hazed grin.

"It's required equipment around you, sorceress." He pulled my legs onto the bed, rotating me so I lay flat on my back. Bending over me, he preyed on my mouth like the tiger he'd been since we'd entered the cabin.

Demanding as he was, I gave him everything I had. His tongue made me yearn for his length to fill me. At last, he inserted his tip into my pulsating heat. Then his crown and shaft, all the way to the base. *Ahhh*, nothing felt so right as this.

He lifted up and plowed into me, the muscles in his shoulders rippling with his movements. As he stroked and rocked me, I climbed higher and higher, feeling the vibrations from deep within travel outwards to my thighs. Shaking, I gave in to the earthquake rumbling through me. The tremors moved from my toes up my legs and core to my ribs. Guy covered my scream with a kiss. He groaned into my mouth as I clenched and drove him to his peak.

We lay a few moments, panting and slick, on the bed.

"That's a first for me," I croaked. "I've never done it on a boat."

"I'll give you plenty of firsts." He stroked my hair. "No place will be safe from your moans. Don't move."

He withdrew, getting up and disposing of the condom. Then he rejoined me, spooning me and draping a calf over my leg.

After a few minutes, the boat's motor started up.

"Oh! The others must've arrived." I twisted toward him.

"They won't miss us, fair one. Tarry awhile." He kissed his way along my jaw to my neck. "We'll make up for lost time."

Feeling his erection poking my cleft, I laughed. "That's you already? Are we headed into another marathon?"

"A two-hour marathon." His fingers roamed to my

soaking sheath. "Let's give the people on deck something to speculate about."

Chapter Forty-Three

Liam

On Wednesday afternoon, Inspector Mani called to say he'd arrested three suspects. He'd also taken a statement from Char. I had the feeling she'd been the reason the police had been able to locate the men so fast. Like all locals, she knew most of the fishermen from surrounding islands. I hadn't mentioned to Mani the distinctive marks I'd given the fishermen with the knife.

On Thursday morning, Ingrid and I returned to Suva to identify the men from a lineup. At the police station, I waited while an administrator led her into a room with one-way glass. After she'd finished, the administrator ushered me into the same room. I immediately picked the guy with a bandage on his middle finger and eyes like moon craters. I didn't need to see his gold tooth to remember his face. After I'd pointed him out, they assembled a new lineup. I saw the patchy-haired guy with the burn marks on his face and a tape on his cheek where I'd slashed him. When I'd identified him, they summoned the third lineup, in which I recognized the bearded guy with the ice-blue eyes, whose tape was on the opposite cheek, covering the knife gash.

As I rejoined Ingrid in the waiting room, for the

first time in a long while I actually had some respect for the justice system. The test would be if they could put these perpetrators behind bars for the maximum sentence.

Inspector Mani approached, asking us to come through to his office.

When we'd taken seats, he flipped through some pages, taking one out to look over. "Ms. Panthong states that she arrived at the scene of the crime when you were herding the three suspects toward the boat, holding three knives. According to her, you slashed the face of one of them. When the other two rose from the bottom of the boat, one was cradling his bloody hand and the other had a gash on his cheek. Is that correct, Mr. Stauner?"

Damn. "Yes, I did use one of the suspects' knives on them."

Mani went on. "She describes all your cuts as 'calculated.' When I asked her what she meant, she said they didn't look like self-defense, since none of the suspects were offering any resistance. Does that square with what you remember?"

I exploded a breath. "I was warning them not to come back. But the idea is the same—it was in the spirit of self-defense, and they weren't my knives."

Impassive, Mani continued. "Lastly, Ms. Panthong remembers you shouting that if they came anywhere near your island again, they were 'dead men,' that you would 'put a bullet in them.' Is that correct?"

Oh, for fuck's sake. "Yes, I did say that. And I'd say it again," I seethed.

"Might I ask why you didn't mention any of this in your original statement?" he put coolly.

"It wasn't important," I shot back.

Mani let a beat of silence follow.

"Thank you, Mr. Stauner." He replaced the paper in his file, standing.

"Has the prosecutor filed charges?" I demanded.

"Ovini Ioane is reviewing the report as we speak. He'll almost certainly take the case. The arraignment is scheduled for tomorrow afternoon." Mani rounded his desk, opening the door. "He'll be in touch."

When Ingrid and I left the station, I felt like punching something. Who the fuck was the suspect here anyway? Mani had made *me* feel like the perpetrator.

Ingrid wrapped her arms around me from the side, leaning in and tucking her head in the groove of my shoulder. "Remember what Guy said, Liam. Don't worry. Are you as hungry as I am?"

Leading her into a café near the station, I ordered us cappuccinos and Gulgula—deep-fried balls of batter with spices. Once we'd sat down with our dishes, I called Guy.

"Guy, who's our prosecutor, Ovini Ioane?" I tapped my fingers on the table.

"He's one of the state prosecutors who works for the ODPP—the Office for the Director of Public Prosecutions." I could hear the smile in Guy's voice. "Yes, he's a hard-ass. As you're no doubt wondering."

"Good. It's about time I enjoyed the *benefits* of a hard-ass prosecutor."

****

The next day at 5, Ovini Ioane called to tell me the results of the arraignment.

"All three suspects pleaded not guilty to the

charges," he informed me in bass notes. "They've been released on their own recognizance. The preliminary hearing is three weeks from now—Friday July first, at two."

"You're not afraid you're rushing things?" I tamped down my fury. "What happens in the meantime?"

"If the main defendant persists in his innocence, and evidence warrants doing so, I'll try to get his accomplices to cooperate," said Ioane. "If they're willing to testify in our favor, their sentences may be mitigated. The defendant may then plead guilty, in which case, we won't have to go to trial."

"That'd be nice," I clipped. "Did they offer any story?"

"No, but that's standard at this stage. We'll find out soon enough. I'll be in touch."

We ended the call.

I was no longer such a champion of the legal system. My support of it had been brief.

Ingrid wrapped her arms around my waist. "Come outside to the porch and tell me everything."

Seating her in my lap on a lounger, I repeated what Ioane had said.

"They're only going slowly to protect the innocent," she amazed me by saying.

"You really are incredible," I marveled. "Doesn't it piss you off that they didn't even post bail?"

"The judge probably deemed they couldn't afford it." She opened up the top buttons of my shirt, laying soft kisses on my chest. My dick twitched. "I'm sure they all have public defenders."

I groaned as she unbuttoned my shirt further.

"Tomorrow is our third date. Are you prepared for another surprise?"

Her face lit up. "Yes! I can't imagine what follows goat night."

Since I'd been distracted this week, I'd decided on something much less elaborate. "Wear your bikini and a kimono."

Now she was rubbing my abs, kissing my neck, and tickling my ear. *Fuck.* This woman would be my ruin. But what a delicious ruin.

****

Our date Saturday night was at the infinity pool, where we made out and played shark in the water, before eating a Fiji-style chicken stew with potatoes, carrots, bell peppers, and bok choy. I'd set up a table and two chairs at the water's edge. Ever since the assault at the cove, Ingrid had been swimming in this pool. The views of the palm grove and the inlet beyond were stupendous.

She looked gorgeous sitting across from me in the light of the waxing gibbous moon, her shoulders bare beneath her halter-top bikini.

"Gretchen asked me to put on music this evening." Ingrid sipped her wine. "It was the longest sentence she's ever spoken."

I smiled. "Katrina didn't move away when I sat next to her on the terrace earlier. She wouldn't answer any of my questions, but it felt like real progress."

"I heard them talking to one another in low tones in the southern sitting room." Ingrid helped herself to a second portion of stew. "I think Gretchen was explaining something to Katrina about one of your books. When I came in, they fell silent. But Katrina was smiling."

"Gretchen looks like a completely different person now from how she looked in that blinding hospital-schoolroom. Eleven days of island life plus a better wardrobe have made her younger by five years." I was so relieved at this change that I made a point of examining my sister every morning to see it unfolding, the way a plant-lover watches the blossoming of a hyacinth.

"When they're ready to go to New York, I think Gretchen will want to teach again." Ingrid bit a piece of chicken. "I caught her studying Epeli's philosophy and history books the other day and peeking at his notes."

"What'll be your first question to them when they finally open up about their experiences?" I spooned some soup and sipped it.

She sat back, turning her wine glass around. "What kind of love did the cult give them?" Her lush brown eyes met mine. "I can't imagine someone living long without love."

I held her gaze. "Once they've had a taste, they'll spend their whole life in search of it."

****

In the early hours of Wednesday, I awoke with a start. My watch told me it was 4:05. Had I heard something? Disconnecting from Ingrid's warm, soft body, I rose, stepping out onto the porch. All was quiet, except for the deep, two-toned swell of the crickets. I scanned the landscape. The full moon hung low in the western sky, and a light breeze stirred the trees, creating rippling shadows. Nothing seemed amiss.

But I couldn't get back to sleep, even once I held Ingrid close. Something was definitely out of joint. My feeling resembled my premonition on the morning of Ingrid's assault. It was as if a presence had crept onto the island. A malignant presence.

As soon as day broke and Ingrid stirred, I made love to her. Whether because her belief in humanity dwarfed her bad experience at the cove, or because her temperament was inclined to forgive, her trauma hadn't warped her view of men, sex, or society. Apart from avoiding the cove, she still rode the bike, swam in the pool, and walked about the island with the other women. She was more cautious though—she didn't venture out alone. I hoped that just as Katrina and Gretchen were coming out of their shells, so Ingrid would once more be able to enjoy her cove in solitude without fear.

Chapter Forty-Four

Ingrid

As Liam and I dressed for a bike ride around the loop road, a scream rang out from Gretchen and Katrina's room. We threw open our door and dashed down the hall. Mother and daughter had flattened their backs against the wall opposite Katrina's bed, though Katrina was turning her hand over and over.

"What is it?" I cried, advancing into the room.

Panting with fright, Katrina pointed toward her turned-back sheets.

Liam stepped over to the bed. I tiptoed behind him, gasping at what I saw. A large, brown, green-eyed cane toad—about seven inches long—crouched beside her pillow.

"It was under the sheet!" Katrina wailed.

Liam removed his sneaker and inverted it over the toad, forcing the creature into his shoe. "Ingrid, grab a stack of paper from our room."

I ran and found the scrap paper I kept around for drawing in the bedroom. Hurrying back, I handed them to Liam, who inserted them under the toad's body. Stalking out the porch door with the sneaker over the papers, he disappeared into the brush for a few minutes.

I examined Katrina's hand. "Did you touch the toad?"

She nodded. "I didn't know it was there. When I woke up it was by my head."

I shuddered. "Does it itch?"

"Yes. I also touched my face. My eyes burn." Tears brimmed in her eyes.

"Let's wash your hands and face." I guided her into the bathroom, where Gretchen joined us, helping to clean her up.

We emerged from the bathroom to find Liam bent over and examining the floor from the bed to the porch door.

"Nothing," he said in puzzlement.

"What are you looking for?" I asked.

"The marks that the toad should have left if it hopped in here. Katrina's sheet has several dirt marks on it. But there are none on the floor." He stood, shaking his head. "Strange."

"Liam, you go ahead and ride. I'll stay here with Gretchen and Katrina. They've had a pretty big shock." I wrapped an arm around Katrina, who was trembling all over.

"You're sure? I don't have to go." He looked doubtful.

"You'll feel better if you have your Sunday ride." I nodded my encouragement. "We'll go take pictures on the dirt path with my phone—shall we, Katrina, Gretchen?"

"Yes." Katrina gave a keen hop.

That's when I realized I'd gotten several whole sentences from Katrina! Toad or no toad, that was quite a feat.

"All right. I'll be back in a little over two hours." Liam started for the door.

"Be sure to change sneakers." I grimaced. "You've got cane toad toxin in one of those."

****

After breakfast, Liam and I put in three hours of work in our office. We had a quickie on the desk, before joining the others for tea in the dining room. Just as I was pouring Assam into Andrea's cup, Leveni dashed in, ghostly pale.

"Liam, come! Down by the mangrove swamps!" His usually mellow voice crackled with urgency.

"What is it?" Liam was already following him, with me close in his wake.

"I'll let you see." Leveni trotted ahead, muttering what I thought were oaths in Fijian.

I jogged to keep up with their long, rapid strides. What could it be that had the calm and gentle man so shaken?

It took us a good ten minutes to get to a point in the swampy inlet where we could see the upside-down mangrove roots branching into the water. Dense leafy tops crowned their central stalks. From the angle of our approach, at first I could see nothing out of the ordinary. But when we reached the dirt tract that stretched down to the swamp, I noticed an empty brown fishing boat camouflaged inside a tangle of roots. Following the way it pointed, my eyes journeyed to a patch of bare, dry earth.

Only it wasn't bare. A man's body lay three-quarters facing up to the sky, his split legs crossed on their sides and his arms splayed like an arrowhead. Even without the black blood that had seeped through his shirt, he looked very much dead.

"Over here!" Leveni waved to a point in the thicket

349

Kathleen Haley

where a person could duck under the spidery overhanging roots to access the flat expanse of dirt on the other side of the swamp.

Jogging after the two men, I pushed through the overgrowth. I halted ten feet away from the dead body, my limbs congealing. Staring unblinkingly toward the distant pine tops with hollow eyes was the man who'd tried to rape me.

Liam shot a wary glance at me. Leveni hung back, while Liam approached the body, examining it without touching.

"Bullet in the chest," Liam pronounced. "How'd you find it?"

Leveni pointed toward the road. "I was carting compost to the heap. I caught sight of the boat, and wondered who it could be. When I got to the point where we were just standing, I saw the body. I ran up to the house directly."

"Fuck," Liam muttered under his breath. "If it were up to me, I'd toss the body in the swamp." He cast a longing glance at the water, followed by a sideways look at Leveni. "But I guess it's time for another dose of the Fiji police."

****

Five long hours later—after extensively questioning everyone on the island and investigating the crime scene and related areas—the medical examiner, the coroner's technician, two forensic scientists, and a sergeant took seats at the dining room table. The inspector, Wije Lenoa, a good-looking man of medium build, remained standing at the end of the table, his shrewd dark eyes trained on Liam, who sat beside me at the other end. Guy, Andrea, and Leveni sat

350

on the other side of Liam. Lenoa flicked open the small notepad in his hand, taking out a ballpoint pen.

The M.E., a tubby, perpetually flushed man, cleared his throat. "Early indications show the victim suffered a gunshot wound to the chest. By the looks of things, the bullet damaged the aorta, and the victim would have bled out within minutes. I found no exit wound. If you were to push me, I'd say the time of death was between 4 a.m. and 9 a.m. this morning. I'll know more when I get him back to the morgue."

The forensics scientist, who was lanky with long black hair pulled back in a ponytail, reported, "The gun was fired from eight feet away. Extracting the bullet, we found it was a nine-millimeter NATO round. The lands and grooves in the barrel of a nine-millimeter M9 Beretta pistol we've removed from an arsenal on the property correspond to the land and groove impressions on the bullet. The body appears not to have been moved since the victim fell. We removed several short black hairs from the victim's chest and shoulder, which we're running through our QPCR DNA analysis. Since twenty-six of the island's thirty-seven inhabitants submitted to the DNA test, we won't have the results for another half-hour."

The other forensics scientist, whose birdlike nose matched his peering eyes, added, "We seized bootprints in the dirt near the victim's body that matched prints leading in both directions from the building containing weaponry. A chunk was missing from the rubber sole of one of the boots. Boots with matching tread and damaged sole were found inside the building, which was locked. We lifted latent fingerprints from the M9 Beretta and the boots."

The sergeant, who had curly brown hair and a perfectly round face, read off his notes. "We also lifted prints from a silencer in the arsenal. All thirty-seven island inhabitants we questioned denied having heard a gunshot in the suspected window for time of death. The victim's identity has been established as Penaia Vakameau, a fisherman living on Vanuavatu. Vakameau's usual routine is to leave with two other fishermen in the captain's boat at 3 a.m. According to the captain, one Filipe Dakuitoga, and the other fisherman, Cakobau Bari, Vakameau told them that this morning he was taking his own boat out—the boat found at the scene of the crime. We lifted latent fingerprints and footprints from the boat, checking them against the victim's. No evidence was found in the boat that Vakameau had caught any fish before arriving on Verau. Vakameau's sister, who lives a few houses down from him, called Samabula—around the same time that Mr. Stauner called Totogo—to report her brother missing."

Inspector Lenoa took that as his cue to begin questioning us. "Mr. Stauner, I understand you had a disagreement with Vakameau ten days ago, on Sunday, June 5. Is that correct?"

Guy interposed. "My client won't be answering any of your questions."

Liam straightened in his chair. "It's fine, Guy. I have nothing to hide. That is correct. Vakameau tried to rape my girlfriend." He looked at my hands on the table.

Lenoa plunged a hand in his pocket. "And apparently you roughed up Vakameau, Bari, and Dakuitoga with a knife, slicing off a joint from

Vakameau's middle finger and slashing the cheeks of Bari and Dakuitoga?"

Liam's brows cut a gorge above his nose. "They had far worse coming to them."

Lenoa lifted an eyebrow. "According to a report, you threatened the lives of the three fishermen, shouting that if they returned to your island they were dead men, and you would put a bullet in them. Does that sound right?"

Guy interrupted. "Don't answer, Liam."

I grew rigid in my own seat, fearing an outburst from Liam. I placed a hand over his balled-up fist under the table.

Liam's voice contained suppressed thunder, like the rumbling of a nearby storm. He growled back at Lenoa, "I said that in defense of my girlfriend, in the heat of the moment."

Guy addressed Lenoa. "Just how credible is your witness, Ms. Panthong, who had previously formed a romantic attachment to Mr. Stauner?"

Oblivious to the double onslaught of Guy and Liam, Lenoa checked his notepad. "Mr. Stauner, I take it from the servants that you do regular target practice with your M9 Beretta?"

"I do," Liam ground out.

"And you wear the boots that are in your arsenal?" Lenoa probed.

"Yes." Liam hissed, his eyes shooting fireballs at the inspector.

"Do you have an alibi for the entire window of time between 4 and 9 a.m. this morning?" Lenoa's voice was measured.

I spoke. "He was with me until 6:30 and after 9

a.m."

Lenoa cocked his head. "Can anyone vouch for you between 6:30 and 9?"

Liam narrowed his eyes. "I was on a bike ride, doing my usual exercise loop around the island."

The sergeant interjected. "The servants and other inhabitants I questioned have alibis for that window. No one recalls seeing Mr. Stauner after six-thirty. No one saw or heard anything near the scene of the crime before nine. It appears the area is one not usually frequented by staff and guests."

Suddenly I regretted that when I'd taken Katrina and Gretchen out for photos we'd gone north rather than south toward the mangroves.

Liam set his mouth in a grim line. "What if the murder took place much earlier? Your window of time is pretty wide. Does everyone have an alibi for the time between 4 and 6:30 a.m.?"

Lenoa's impassive eyes bored into Liam. "No. But then no one else has the weapon or the motive, Mr. Stauner."

Glancing at their watches, the forensics scientists rose. The lanky one announced, "We're going to call in for the results for the DNA analyses. The first batch, including Mr. Stauner's, went back on the boat a few hours ago."

In the ensuing tense silence, I gnawed my lower lip. "Can I offer anyone some tea?"

Lenoa shook his head, but the M.E., the coroner's technician, and the sergeant murmured yes. I hesitated over leaving Liam, but he gave me a slight nod. Andrea rose to come help me. Guy and Liam spoke in low voices about the interrogation Liam had just undergone.

I heard Guy say that Liam shouldn't have submitted to the DNA test until he had formal counsel from an attorney in Fiji.

In the kitchen, Andrea whispered, "Is Liam their prime suspect?"

When she suggested it, my heart ricocheted against my chest walls. "I don't know. Maybe the DNA results will prove something different."

But I was riddled with worries I didn't express to Andrea. Would Liam be arrested for a crime he didn't commit—just like his father? If Liam was arrested, would damaging evidence from his past come to light? Would Rory use this case to leverage his own ongoing hunt after his brother?

She squeezed me from the side. "Don't worry, sweetie. It's all going to be okay."

I prayed she was right. Wound tight as a spring, I used the simple, practical action of preparing tea to numb my anxiety.

We brought the jasmine tea out with trays of mugs, pouring it and passing them around.

The two forensics men returned, taking their seats. "The fingerprints and footprints in the boat as yet have no match to anyone on the island. The hairs found on the victim match the DNA for Mr. Stauner, which is the same as the fingerprints on the gun, boots, and silencer."

Liam stood, erupting like a volcano. "That's impossible. I didn't touch that body."

Inspector Lenoa gave a curt nod to the sergeant, who advanced, clapping handcuffs on Liam.

Lenoa said, "Mr. Stauner, you are under arrest for the murder of Penaia Vakameau. You have the right to remain silent…" He continued rattling off Liam's rights according to Fiji's legal code.

"Fuck this," Liam stormed, his face purpling as the sergeant held him. "You assholes are gonna regret fucking with me."

Guy stood. "Liam, I'm coming with Josefa in the boat behind you. I'll call the defense attorney I know in Suva, Devansh Patel."

"I'm coming too." I jumped up.

"Me too, Guy." Andrea scraped her chair back.

"Katrina and I want to come too." A voice I never would've expected to speak at this moment sounded from behind me. Gretchen stood with Katrina, her arm around her daughter. I was so shocked, I nearly lost my balance.

Meanwhile, the sergeant, the inspector, and the rest of the investigators bustled Liam out the door toward the pier. I called Josefa to let him know we'd depart in half an hour. Gathering everything we'd need for an overnight stay in Suva, I joined everyone down at the boat at 8:30.

As long as I had breath in me, the man I loved would never be wrongfully detained a minute longer than it was humanly possible to rescue him.

Chapter Forty-Five

Liam

My cellmate was a safecracker named Petero with a neck scrawnier than a turkey and a shuffling gait. But I soon found out he was smart as a whip. I guess you'd have to be to crack safes—or maybe not, since he got caught. Since Petero couldn't post bail, he'd been inside for almost three weeks. His prelim hearing was set for Friday morning.

I'd never had such strange conversations as Petero and I had that night. Nothing personal or practical—only philosophical shit. And I was no philosopher. I guess being behind bars makes philosophers of us all.

"You ever wonder why it's only when you break a man that he shows his greatest strength?" Petero mused, hunched over on the edge of his bed in the posture of Rodin's Thinker.

"That's news to me." I plonked myself down on the hard mattress of my bed, only half listening. "I take it you have an example?"

"A man by the name of Viliami in the next cellblock over has been in here for three months." Petero's voice had a twang like a bass harp. "He was an accountant who falsified financial documents for his company and then skimmed off the money he made. Great idea, really—if it'd been foolproof.

357

Unfortunately, his company got audited, and he got booked. Then suddenly everything bad happened to Viliami all at once. His wife had a miscarriage in her sixth month of pregnancy, he lost all his savings in a ponzi scam, and his family had to abandon their house because it was infested with termites. Some people would go all zen and say, 'I'm in jail. I can't do anything about that shit till I'm out.' Not Viliami. He's high-anxiety. He was driving himself insane with worry. So in order to survive, he flipped the script. He pretended that everyone wanted to get in the clink with him, where life was simple. He worked it up in his mind that everyone outside was better off without money, property, and worries. A jail cell was the place to be. Short of that, having nothing and no connections was the life. Call it a coping mechanism, but it allowed Viliami to sleep at night and rise in the morning. If that wasn't strength, I don't know what is."

Stretching out, I folded my arms behind my head. "Pushing through the pain."

"What's that?" Petero looked up.

"An expression they use in the military." I crossed my legs, thinking about Gretchen and Katrina living in the cult. They must've had to devise plenty of coping mechanisms. But *was* that strength? Or was it just lying to themselves? Didn't self-deception make us weaker? "Where Viliami sounds strong is in his adaptability and resourcefulness. He's got mental strength."

"That's everything." Petero lay down, crossing an ankle over his raised knee. "But even stronger than the man who adapts to bad circumstances is the man who learns from his own failures."

I chuckled. "My chess teacher says the same thing.

He insists that only by making mistakes do we progress."

Petero cracked a wistful smile. "As a young man in Germany I found I had to make a fool of myself to learn the language. Painful as it was to make mistakes, they were the only way to improve. The humbler I got, the better I spoke."

As Petero rambled on, I tuned out. I began to think about the ironies of my being here now. As a hitman I never made mistakes. Clever and careful, I never tripped up. In this way, I avoided the kinds of failures that Federico and Petero would say make a man stronger. I also avoided jail. Guilty as I was, I had my freedom.

Recently—especially today—I'd blurted the truth, thinking justice would be fair and my own innocence could protect me. Now, though innocent, I sat in jail facing a murder charge. I'd finally made a series of stupid mistakes. By Federico and Petero's logic, I should learn something and grow stronger.

What if, by some absurdity, I was proven guilty? What if the law *really* failed me? From that possible outcome, two thoughts crystallized. I *really* wanted my freedom. And I *really* needed to let Ingrid know I loved her. I wanted my freedom all the more because I loved Ingrid.

If she were still just an obsession, I might be reckless enough not to care about imprisonment. But since I loved her, I cared very much about being locked up. I didn't want to miss a moment with her.

Now, facing a stint behind bars, I realized I'd made yet another mistake in not telling Ingrid how I felt. But this was a mistake I could learn from. It taught me what

I stood to lose—the love of my life.

Restless, I jumped up, wondering if I could call her. Catching the attention of the guard, a corpulent, double-chinned man whose badge read "Kafoa," I asked to be allowed to make a call. Since I'd been booked at 10:45, visiting hours were long past.

Kafoa shook his head. "Phone hours ended at 11."

Damn. I wouldn't have made the curfew anyway. Now the endless night stretched before me. "What time do visiting hours start tomorrow?"

Kafoa scratched a zit on his forehead. "Eleven."

"What time is it now?"

"One-thirty." Kafoa yawned.

"Shut the fuck up, will you?" yelled a man in a nearby cell. "It's the middle of the goddamn night."

"Can it," another resident rasped. "No one wants to hear *your* pipes."

"Better them than your ugly mug," the first man quipped.

"I'll show you ugly when I flatten your beak," the raspy one snapped back.

Jail clearly produced first-class specimens of wit.

I turned and began to pace the short eight feet to the wall and back. Now my thoughts roamed to Rory, who would say it was accidental justice that I rot in prison, since I'd be paying the price for past sins. But was it fair to ask a man to pay for past crimes with present innocence? If I'd felt I was capable of committing those crimes again, I might say yes. Yet because I'd managed to get out of the business and stay out, I saw that earlier chapter of my life as separate from this one. I thought of myself as a different man.

But maybe I was wrong. Maybe, as Ingrid had said

the day she displayed my family photos, I saw my past too much as a series of discontinuities. The first era, when I was loved by my parents, until I was eleven, was scarred by my baby sister's death, my dad going to prison, and my mom's alcoholism. In the second period, of high school bullying and foster care, which lasted till I was eighteen, I'd had Guy. Rory and I were never close, since he blamed me for the three of us getting dispersed to different foster homes. In the third era, I'd found love with Aileen during my first grueling tour, and with Ramona at the end of my second tour. During the fourth, when I was a hitman, my girlfriend Morgan had loved me. Now, in the fifth era, I had Ingrid, Gretchen, Katrina, and Guy.

Maybe I needed the faith to recognize that people could and did love me *as I was*. I could love who I'd been in all my phases. And however I was now, I could let myself be loved again.

If all those eras were rolled into the same man—the man I was now—then, as Petero suggested, I could draw strength from past pain. Reliving my suffering, I could grow stronger by holding it in mind as still present within me. But it took courage to face myself, my failings.

That new courage came from Ingrid.

For some time now I'd trusted Ingrid fully. And for just as long I'd felt ready to sacrifice myself for her well-being. But only now was I prepared to admit my flaws to her. Or, rather, since she knew them already, I was willing to let her see me as *she* saw me—not as I wanted her to see me, not the curated, controlled version, but the sometimes-raw, sometimes-vulnerable me.

And I knew exactly how I was going to show her I loved her.

****

At 11 the next day, Kafoa's successor, a guard named Apolosi, unlocked my cell to bring me to the visiting area. Ingrid, Guy, Andrea, Gretchen, and Katrina had gathered around on stools on the other side of the bulletproof glass, ready to talk into the intercom. A wide grin split my face. This was quite the welcoming party. I drank in Ingrid's bright smile, her compassionate brown eyes, and her incomparable beauty. She had black shadows under her eyes, as though she'd rested little.

"Did you sleep at all, old man?" Guy asked.

"Not much." I rolled my shoulders back, remembering the springs digging into my back. "But on the plus side, I did a lot of thinking."

"Devansh Patel is arriving in fifteen. He wanted to give us a moment." Guy opened his jacket. Now, in the visiting room, I could tell it was a sultry day.

"Where did you all stay last night?" I clasped my hands on the counter.

"At a hotel nearby," Ingrid said. "We tried calling you as soon as we got in, but they said calling hours were over."

Andrea lifted the hair off her neck to combat the heat. "We had an incredible breakfast at a café Ingrid said you took her to a week ago, near the station. Only, Ingrid didn't touch a bite of food—though she drank two cups of coffee."

My sweet wood nymph.

"Ovini Ioane is now the prosecutor for the case against you." Guy looked apologetic.

"Seems about right," I remarked wryly. "Another hard-ass prosecutor riding me."

"With luck, the judge at tomorrow afternoon's arraignment will grant you bail," Ingrid submitted. "Then we can feed you Tima's delicious goat curry for dinner."

I smiled, remembering our goat-themed date.

A man I assumed was Devansh Patel sauntered over, greeting everyone in a cool but cordial manner, wearing a neat red bowtie, suspenders, and pinstripe pants.

His reedy voice pressed thinly across the intercom. "Mr. Stauner, I'm sorry we meet under these circumstances. Mr. Travis has told me great things about you. I hope to represent you in this case."

He took out a pad and pen.

"We'll focus on the arraignment for now," Patel commenced. "Of course you'll plead not guilty. The judge will likely take into consideration the fact that you notified the police directly after finding the body, that you didn't attempt to evade justice during the investigation, and that you pose no flight risk nor threat to the community. I'm optimistic that he'll let you out on bail."

My confidence in this man grew by the minute.

Patel went on. "It's unfortunate that because the murder victim was also the suspect for the assault and attempted rape, the latter case has been dismissed. Now the prosecution may use aspects of that case as weapons against you, particularly the testimonies of the other fishermen and of Ms. Panthong."

I'd been expecting that. My character profile had been shot to hell with how I'd dealt with Ingrid's attackers.

"Is there anything else you'd like to cover at this point, Mr. Stauner?" Patel rested his forearms on the counter.

"Only one question. Supposing no further evidence is forthcoming, will the possibility that someone off the island could've committed this murder keep a jury from being certain about my guilt? That is, certain enough to decide against me?" I wiped my clammy palms on my pants.

Patel nodded. "We'll work to keep them uncertain from the very start, Mr. Stauner."

Chapter Forty-Six

Ingrid

We all attended Liam's arraignment the next day at 4. The judge set a reasonable bail, adjuring Liam not to contact or interfere with prosecution witnesses, and to report to the Totogo police station every Friday. The preliminary hearing was set for three weeks later, Friday, July 1—the same date the assault trial had been scheduled for. When Liam was released, I caught the relief that washed over Gretchen's features, and the flash of joy in Katrina's eyes. They understood and empathized with him in his struggle, and they were rooting for him.

Carrying the discovery file under his arm, Devansh Patel joined Liam, making an appointment to see him in Suva the following Wednesday.

I hugged Liam fiercely, plastering my body against his to maximize contact. His belly rumbled with laughter. "Liam, I missed you dreadfully."

"However much you missed me, I missed you ten times more." He gave me a tender, lingering kiss. "You look as if you got less sleep and ate even worse than I did."

"I felt as if I was in jail with you—only worse, because I wasn't." I gave him a lopsided smile.

Guy proposed, "I know a charming Thai restaurant

not three blocks from here."

Andrea tucked her arm in his. "You're as good as a Suva guidebook."

"Hopefully not as out of date," Guy rejoined.

****

When we got home to Verau later that evening, Liam surprised me by suggesting we retire to the Asian-themed southern sitting room where my decorating gift to him had gone awry three weeks ago. Ushering me ahead of him, he flicked on the lamps and slid the door shut, locking it.

My ears pricked up at the sound. Was he going to do a reprise of that morning and punish me? He coiled his arms around me from behind, crossing an arm over my chest and cupping my breast. "I have a command for you."

"Anything, Liam." *I'm devoted to you.*

"I want you to replace all the photos you hung and set around the room." When I hesitated out of shock, he tilted my chin up. "Now."

What can this mean? I followed his order, taking the photos I'd left by the door and putting them in all their places.

"Come here, Ingrid."

I stepped forward until I stood three feet away.

"All the way."

I advanced until we were six inches apart.

"Are all the other photos still in the other rooms?" His tone was stern, but it contained a soft note.

"I hadn't yet gotten a chance to take them down . . ." I faltered.

"Leave them where they are, Ingrid. Touch them under penalty of severe punishment." Meeting his eyes,

I saw flaming irises. He gripped my nape, bringing my lips closer to his. "Do you understand what this means?"

My throat tightened, as tears distilled in my eyes. "I think I do."

"I love you." He brushed my cheek with his thumb. "I love you more than myself, more than anyone I've ever loved. There was a time when I wouldn't have thought this moment possible. That time is long past. Before you, I never dared hope someone like you could exist. You're the morning sun rays beaming through the pines, the freedom of the open seas, and the warm stones of a summer evening. In you I have a little world more precious than all the great wide world combined. I seek your spirit as a desert dweller seeks water. Your heart is my compass, your mind my mirror. You alone make me believe in eternity, for everything Ingrid exceeds the bounds of time. I'm yours, my lovely sylph, forever and a day."

Tears cascaded down my face. Liam caught them with his lips and tongue. Cupping my cheek, he leaned in and rolled his tongue along the parting of my lips. I marveled at how his mouth heated my whole body. His taste was like fine liquor. His tongue wove a spell about mine.

As our lips drew apart, I nuzzled his. *Liam loves me*. Were there any sweeter three words than these?

In the midst of my tears, I released a joyful laugh. "I love you too, Liam. But I'm so transparent, I'm sure you already knew."

He chuffed a laugh into my lips. "I love your transparency."

"Was this the result of being locked up for two

days?" My lips skimmed his.

"You locked my heart up long before, sweet jailor—and I threw away the key."

I buried my head in his chest. "Tomorrow can I show you the rest of the rooms I decorated?"

"Yes. But first, we need to redecorate this one." He arched an eyebrow.

At my questioning look, he nodded toward the famous armchair.

"Come sit on my lap and tell me stories of Gretchen and Katrina in Suva." He hoisted me in his arms and carried me to the chair. "And then we'll talk about whatever pops up."

Laughter rippled through me. "Is freed-from-jail sex as good as makeup sex?"

"Better, little kitten. Far better," he growled in my ear.

After I'd shared some tales from the last two days in Suva, I shifted so I straddled his hips, facing him in the armchair. Feeling his behemoth bulge boring into my crotch, I ground into it through his pants.

Moans escaped us both. Liam made short work of my panties, ripping them and tossing them aside. Undoing his fly and pulling his pants down, I freed his stunning cock, my mouth watering at the sight. He swiped two fingers through my dripping channel, groaning at my readiness and licking the juices from his fingertips.

I raised my hips, feeding his shaft into me. *Oh*, he felt heavenly, and his grunts told me he too felt the bliss of our rejoining. When he was fully seated inside me, I rode him, rising and falling on his taut dick as I slung one arm around his neck, the other around his powerful shoulder.

"I love you, Liam." I swiveled about his rigid length. "I always will." Sliding up his erection, I sank once more. "It's not that I'm easy, but that you're hard." I rocked up and down again. "Every day I thank the gods who smiled on my abduction." I climbed his girth, reveling in the solid, generous mass of man surrounding me. "I've belonged to you since the night we met."

I could no longer speak, as my thoughts spiraled out into general impressions of being captured, claimed, and owned by Liam. The friction of his dick against my walls and sensitive areas sparked burning and pricking that intensified each time Liam thrust up into me, adding pressure to my movements. Feeling him on the edge undid me. He shoved his cock to the bottom. I began to howl as I came apart, shattering into smithereens. Our orgasms met head-on, his shudders and groans joining mine.

"Did you mean I was physically hard?" Liam asked into my hair.

"That too," I panted. "But I meant uncompromising, unyielding, difficult in all the ways I love."

"You may be the only person to appreciate those qualities, Ingrid."

"I only appreciate them in you."

****

I'd thought Liam would have a chip on his shoulder for the wringer he was being put through. But he took everything with surprisingly philosophic calm. Over breakfast on Sunday morning, I delved more into this mysterious stoicism.

"Liam, was your cellmate a follower of the Dalai Lama?" I swallowed a spoonful of oatmeal. "You went into jail a roaring lion and came out a lamb."

"I second that." Andrea buttered her toast. "Personally, I prefer post-jail Liam."

"Remind me to revert to old ways," Liam postured. "But I guess you could say I had a come-to-Jesus moment of sorts."

Guy frowned. "I hope you'll remain keen for freedom, old chap. If you become too Buddhist before the trial, the jury will smell the whiff of resignation."

I sipped my coffee. "Is it that you know you'll be acquitted? Or do you trust that further evidence will surface to preclude a trial?"

"The latter." Liam refilled his coffee mug. "I have a plan."

"You'd better run it by me." Guy sounded wary.

"It's nothing to do with tampering with the prosecution's witnesses. Or at least, not directly." Liam poured cream into his coffee. "I'm entitled to form a defense. I was thinking, why not put Claude, Rodrigo, and Ralph on the case? Bring them out here and have them comb the islands, interviewing fishermen and their families and friends—keep their ears to the ground. If, as I suspect, the murderer is someone who came to the island that night and left after the murder, then the three of them could suss him—or her—out."

Guy nodded. "That's fine. All three men are skilled at gathering evidence that's admissible in court. They'll have a lot of legwork—or boat travel—among islands. But if they spend a full day or more on each island, they may dig up something we can use."

"I'll fly them out tomorrow." Liam polished off a

sausage link. "And I'll buy more boats and captains to put at their disposal."

Bryn perked up. "I smell hacking opportunities. Say the word, boss."

"That'll be phase two, once the boys have done their work." Liam took a bite of omelet.

"You'd damn well better not get caught," Guy warned. "Or you'll be thrown back in the slammer sooner than you can say 'shared toilet.'"

Bryn laughed. "On my watch they'll never know what hit them."

****

That afternoon, in the art studio, I decided to work on a clay bust of Katrina. Katrina, Gretchen, and Andrea joined me, all of us with tea mugs in hand. I put on classical music from a Fiji radio station, since I always sculpted better to music. After making some preliminary sketches of Katrina from various angles, I carved out a large chunk of clay from a slab, using my knives to pare off pieces.

"Gretchen, Katrina, if you'd like to paint or sculpt, I'd be happy to set you up," I offered. I knew neither activity would interest Andrea, who enjoyed gossiping and watching.

"I'm going to draw from my photo of the stork I took earlier." Katrina reached for a sheet of paper and pencil.

Three weeks after being rescued, and Katrina was on track to be loquacious!

"Gretchen, did you ever do art with your young students?" I shaped an edge into a round.

"It wasn't permitted." Gretchen leaned back in her high stool. "My lessons were aimed at getting kids to read The Seer's book of revelations."

I'm batting a thousand today!

"Was any art allowed in the compound?" I used my thumb to smear the clay into a smooth curve.

"No visual representations of any kind." Gretchen sounded so sad, that I opted to switch topics.

"Gretchen, which would you rather see—a Katrina with painted colors that mimic her actual skin, hair, and eyes? Or a Katrina with natural clay-fired colors like mauve, maroon, burnt sienna, and amber?" I asked.

Gretchen considered this. "I think natural clay-fired ones."

"Good, because I prefer that too." I looked over at Katrina. "Do you agree?"

Her rainbow smile emerged. "Yes."

"Drea, tell us how work on the memoir is going." I sipped some tea.

"Guy's childhood in the Bronx is pretty interesting." Andrea traced a wood whorl in the table with her index finger. "Since we spent the whole first two weeks on his parents, we've only just gotten to when he was five and had his first memories."

"Do you two still follow the sun as you work, and take two-hour lunch or tea breaks?" I looked up to find her eyes darting over to Katrina. "Oh, I'll bet your breaks involve a lot of *eating*."

Andrea's lips twitched. "Yes, Guy and I are always very hungry. And we work much better together after we've both filled up."

I bit my lip. "Does Guy like a lot of condiments with his dishes, or just plain fare?"

Andrea cleared her throat. "He brings out all the extras. Though on occasion he enjoys a simple meal too."

I tilted my head. "I can't imagine he's one for lingering at the table after eating."

"On the contrary," Andrea corrected. "I was surprised at how long he likes to digest his food before rising from the meal."

"And of course, that often gives *rise* to another meal," I pointed out.

"Of course." As Andrea tittered, I giggled with her.

Gretchen knew something was up from the get-go, but Katrina only realized it then, her eyes jumping between the both of us.

I shifted gears. "Katrina, which dog do you think we should rescue if I move in with you and Uncle Liam in New York?"

I don't know why I said *if*, since last night Liam had announced that I was moving in with him, not leaving any room for doubt. He told me before slamming the final thrust into me that would bring me to climax, so naturally I said yes. Or shouted it, over and over. Not that his tone permitted dissent. And I was over the moon with the idea of living with him. He used the same tactics to convince me to accept his offer to buy me an art gallery.

But first things first—we needed to get over a major hurdle here in Fiji.

"The Jack Russell Terrier!" Katrina chirped.

"They need lots of attention. Will you help take care of him?" I dipped my head, looking at her through my lashes.

"Yes. I'll walk, feed, and play with him." She clapped her hands.

I smiled. "Then we'd better hurry up and exonerate

Uncle Liam so we can get back to New York and bring that terrier home."

Chapter Forty-Seven

Liam

After the assault, Ingrid had asked me to show her some self-defense moves each morning after our bike ride, in hopes of regaining her confidence when she ventured out alone. I kept the moves simple, using techniques I'd learned in the marines. On Wednesday morning, before we took the boat to Suva, I showed her the choke hold.

Besides Josefa, it was just us two going to Fiji that day. Andrea and Guy were swamped with work—and other things. I wondered if Guy was going to toss her aside as he'd done to countless other women. He invariably started out expecting a relationship, and then over time grew bored. But with Andrea, Guy seemed different. I could tell he liked the way she knew her own mind and pushed back when he teased. He respected her independent projects and writing chops. It was entirely possible that Andrea could dump Guy—a show I wanted a front-row seat to. For all I knew, she was using him for sex while she was stranded here on the island. Only time would tell.

Ingrid wanted to catch the produce market, but it closed by the time my appointment with Patel would be finished. So I reluctantly agreed to let her go on her own and meet her afterward at our café by the police station. I walked down the main road across the creek toward a side street where Patel had his practice. He was running late, so I read a bicycling magazine while waiting.

After twenty minutes, Patel ushered me in, pouring me a cup of coffee and seating me opposite his desk.

"Let's start by poking holes in a few of their arguments, Mr. Stauner." Patel propped his elbows on the armrests, steepling his fingers. "Starting with the motive. Though Ms. Panthong's testimony will be admissible as an admission by a party opponent, Bari and Dakuitoga's testimonies may be discredited on the basis of their character profile. After all, you and Ingrid did file a complaint against them as accomplices in the assault."

"A complaint which should've been kept confidential," I muttered.

"And words are just words—they are not deeds." Patel's chocolaty-brown eyes held mine. "Now, for the murder weapon. Does anyone have access to the key to your arsenal—or does anyone have a copy?"

"Hell, no. I keep it in a safe in my bedroom. No one knows the combination—not even Ingrid." I crossed my legs.

Patel's brow furrowed. "Well, we'll park the weapon temporarily. Now, as for those hairs found on the victim's body. They're highly suspicious. If there was no struggle before the perpetrator fired the gun, why would there be trace evidence on the victim's body? The only plausible explanation would be that the murderer touched the victim with gloved hands and somehow conveyed the hairs onto the torso. The fact that they're *your* hairs only proves that the murderer had access to your dwelling."

My eyebrows jumped. "You mean it was a frame-up?"

"Quite possibly." Patel pursed his lips. "Last but not least, the point you mentioned the other morning. The fact that any number of suspects who don't reside there could've decided to use your island and Mr. Vakameau for target practice."

I nodded. "I've got three PIs investigating the other islands for any indication why Vakameau opted not to fish with his companions that day, but instead to go out alone—and then had no fish at the scene of the crime."

"So I take it you know of no one off the island who might have had a motive for killing Vakameau?" Patel confirmed.

"None that I can think of."

"The island issue relates to the time-of-death question," Patel continued. "Just because you couldn't account for two-and-a-half hours out of five doesn't mean the murder didn't take place at a time when you did have an alibi."

"As a matter of fact, Patel, I woke up a little after 4 that morning sensing an ominous presence nearby," I confessed. "Not that such a feeling would be admissible in court. But I'm usually right about my instincts."

Patel tapped his pen on the desk. "Is there anything else you remember about that morning?"

I went through the sequence of events in my head. "Yes. A cane toad somehow found its way onto my niece's bed. It scared her so much that Ingrid stayed back from our ride to comfort her. What struck me about the toad was the way it seemed to have been *placed* in the bed. It hadn't hopped there, so far as I could tell."

"Fascinating." Patel scrawled a few notes. "Does everyone on the island know your and Ingrid's riding routines?"

"I'd say so. We're pretty regular. Mondays, Wednesdays, and Friday mornings we always do our flat loop together for a little over two hours. We often do a variation of it on Sunday." I picked a piece of cotton off my pants.

Patel jotted something down. "The Prosecution has already interviewed everyone on Vanuavatu who might know where Mr. Vakameau went that morning. No one knows. That in itself is a red flag. Fishermen are creatures of habit, Mr. Stauner. Especially around the islands. For a man to break his routine, well, I'm thinking a good deal of money was offered."

"What was the payer's interest in him?" I wondered aloud.

"Precisely, Mr. Stauner."

****

I came out of Patel's practice feeling much better about the state of my case. I hoped evidence was about to start pouring in that would bring to light another suspect. I just had to be patient. Again, not a virtue I generally boasted, but one I was learning by being a prime suspect.

I was whistling as I rounded the corner toward the café. Then I stopped dead. Through the café window, the jeweler who'd attended to Ingrid and me a month ago was standing next to a seated Ingrid, his fingers on her choker, as if he had a right to touch her. As his lips moved in speech, Ingrid was smiling, but I could tell her smile was forced. Her body was rigid, as though she couldn't wait for him to give her some distance. The toad slithered his fingers along her neck and shoulder as he released her necklace. White-hot with rage, I pushed through the doors, storming up to him.

"What do you think you're doing? Get your damn hands off of her!" I gave him what I thought was a small shove, but he ended up careening across the floor and crashing into a table by the door. "Leave!" I pointed to the door.

Picking himself up and ironing himself out, he stumbled in a daze through the door onto the sidewalk.

I wheeled on Ingrid, who'd stood. "What was he doing touching you?"

"I told him I was waiting for you, but he said he just wanted to admire the necklace he sold me. Then he started fingering it, and said it was clearly made for my neck." Ingrid paused for a breath. "He said he hadn't realized how much value it had until he saw me modeling it—that he should've charged us more for it—and other banter."

I ground my teeth. "Ingrid, why didn't you shout for him to get the fuck away?"

She blushed a deep crimson. "I don't have it in me to be unkind or impolite—at least until a person forfeits all right to my respect. I thought he'd get the message that I was uneasy. Or that he'd see you coming, and scram. He insinuated himself into my area politely at first."

"I'll bet the fuck he did," I gritted. "Sit down, Ingrid. We're going to have a talk." Blushing, she sat back down, and I pulled the other chair around so I could sit beside her. "Ingrid, you've got to get a little more Brooklyn in you. You're too Upper East Side right now. I'm not asking you to change your nature drastically. I'm just saying, the world's a rough place, and I won't always be by your side to fend off the pervy jewelers. I need to know you can do that for yourself— that you *will* do it. Use your lungs, your self-defense moves, your instincts about people—more than your mind, your heart, or even your spirit. Tamp those down a little when you're among people you don't know. And just remember that if I catch any bastard touching you, I'll lop his balls off and use them to make chop suey."

She nodded.

I cupped her chin in the crook of my forefinger and thumb. "Say it, Ingrid."

"Yes, Liam."

I kissed her possessively and hungrily, cupping her ass and tugging her hair. Fuck, how I loved this woman. The day she realized she could snap her fingers and I'd jump under a train was the day my backside looked like a grilled panini.

Chapter Forty-Eight

Ingrid

In those days, meals were filled with talk of Liam's case, the progress of the PIs' investigations, the findings of Patel's team, and the prosecution's evidence. Tension was generally high. It was now six days before the preliminary hearing. Everyone on the island, down to Jope the goatkeeper, was keenly aware of the calendar: we all knew Saturday, June 25 was D-Day.

Seeing Rodrigo step through the terrace doors at noon took me back to the rescue operation in Indiana, where I'd seen Liam meet with him outside the hotel, and to our Zoom meeting later that week. He was a middleweight wiry man with medium-length curly locks, a strong nose, and honey-kissed skin.

Liam brought beers out for Rodrigo, Guy, Bryn, and himself. Andrea, Connie, and I had glasses of white wine, even though it was midday. We didn't have to work in the afternoon.

"Liam, you should call everyone in here, because we'll need all hands on deck." Rodrigo tipped back his beer.

Liam sent Seru to find all the servants. We chatted about soccer until everyone had assembled in the dining area, some taking seats at the table, some in free chairs, others standing.

"As you know, Ralph, Claude, and I have been scouring the islands all week picking up tidbits wherever we could." Rodrigo pulled out his iPhone, consulting notes. "Ralph got a tip-off about a party of drunk fishermen on Vanua Levu two days after the murder. The fishermen were in a pub they frequent, and one of them bought a few rounds for the rest. When the others commented on it, he said he'd come into some extra cash. He wouldn't say how he got it, except one sentence—'An American wanted me to pick him up.'"

Chills shot up my arms. *An American!* Just that one detail made me feel as if the murderer was around the corner. Rodrigo's approach was so methodical, I couldn't imagine whoever killed my attacker hiding much longer.

"I hunted down this fisherman—a guy by the name of Kamisese Gaunavou. His price was high, but he finally spilled that the American, who went by John Smith, wore dark sunglasses, was about six feet and lean, with moderately broad shoulders, slightly bow legs, and large feet. He carried a black backpack. He'd called Gaunavou five days before the job he had for him, which was to pick Smith up at a point on the southeastern side of this island at 5:30 a.m. on the morning of June 15. The pickup spot was about half a mile up the beach from the place where our body was found. Gaunavou picked Smith up, taking him back to Vanua Levu."

"Where he no doubt took the next flight from the airport," Guy commented. "Time to employ Bryn's hacking skills."

"On it," said Bryn, tapping frenziedly away at his

laptop. "If you can give me a name, so much the better."

Liam's eyes flared. "Bow legs...six feet and lean...large feet. *Fuck*, I wonder." He sprang up, raking his hands through his hair, and starting to pace. "Just supposing—for the sake of argument—that this Smith was Rory. Let's open up the field of discussion to everyone in this room. Andrea, Guy, Ingrid, and I went to Suva all day Monday. Does anyone else remember seeing Rory do anything suspicious?"

Heneli cleared his throat. "Boss, I saw him coming up from the mangrove swamp around the early afternoon. I found it weird, because he wasn't really dressed for walking. He had nice pants and shirt on, and leather loafers."

Liam halted, frowning. "Now I recall seeing him talking to Char the day before, and they exchanged something in their hands. He looked as if she was giving him directions."

Remembering something, I spoke. "That same Sunday, Andrea and I found a chunk of clay missing from my new slab. It was precisely cut out to a six- by four- by three-inch block."

Liam sat down again and propped his elbow on the table, leaning his forehead on his fingertips. "What could Char have to give to or receive from Rory?"

Bryn said, "Score! I found Rory Stauner's name on the flight list for Fiji Airways, arriving in Vanua Levu at eleven p.m. Tuesday June fourteenth, and returning to New York-La Guardia on Wednesday June fifteenth at twelve p.m."

"*Motherfucker*," Liam muttered, blowing out a long breath. "My own brother framed me. How did he get into my arsenal?" Then something seemed to click, his face turned white as a sheet, and he fell back against the chair. "Oh, shit. I gave a copy of the key to the arsenal to Char when we first erected the house. It was the first building I had put up, to house the weapons. She and I would meet in there…" He trailed off, shooting an embarrassed glance at me. "Anyway, she had a key. She must've kept it all this time. I don't know why it slipped my mind when the police questioned me. But how did Rory copy it, and why did she let him?"

Bryn ruffled his hair. "I wonder if he tried that gallium key trick, where you make a clay mold of a key and then pour gallium into the mold and congeal it. It only takes a half-hour to do right, so you have a key that should open aluminum locks a few times before it breaks off. The size of the clay required is more or less the same as what Ingrid said was missing from her studio."

Liam continued musing. "He had all day Monday to gather hair samples from our bathroom that he could plant on the body. He must've been hell-bent on pinning a murder on me and bided his time for a motive and an opening."

I shuddered. "You don't think he put that toad in poor Katrina's bed, do you?"

His eyes widening, Liam looked as if a megawatt lightbulb had fritzed his face. "It *was* him. He knew our riding routine. He must've known Katrina and Gretchen were staying with us, and that unsettling Katrina would make you stay behind from our ride so I wouldn't have an alibi."

"But how did he know Katrina and Gretchen were

staying here?" I asked.

Liam stared at me with wild eyes. "Same way he got the key to my arsenal—Char. Same way he heard about the assault on the beach and what I called out to those fuckers—Char. He may have been planning all this before he even got to the island back in late May. He saw an opportunity to get the inside scoop from Char because she'd been fired and was probably glad to get a payoff—and a chance to stick it to me."

Bryn volunteered, "I can hack into his cell phone and see what calls he made in the days leading up to the murder. Maybe we'll see if he called Vakameau."

"Do that." Liam's lips formed a tight thin line.

Only the tap-tap of Bryn's flying keyboard sounded in the ensuing silence.

"So he had the victim deposit him in the mangroves and then went up to your arsenal and put on your boots." I worked through the scene of the crime. "Putting a silencer on your gun and loading it, he clomped down to the swamp, shot Vakameau, planted Liam's hairs, returned to the arsenal, replaced the weapon, swapped out shoes, brought a cane toad to Katrina's bed, and walked up the shore to get picked up by Gaunavou."

"And then jumped on a plane back to New York a few hours later," Liam added.

"Your brother *really* has it in for you," Andrea remarked. "I never thought he could do something like this. I mean, it seemed as if he had only justice in mind. Well, and political ambitions. I guess his obsession to bring you down cut across bloodlines and blinded him to his whole identity as a prosecutor. To *murder* someone just to pin the murder on your own brother!

Damn, he must *really* hate you."

"Thanks for the recap, Andrea," Liam said drily. "I think we all get that Rory's off his rocker. I always thought he was capable of shit like this. But now that he's finally showed his hand, it still comes out of left field."

Bryn straightened in his chair. "Okay, I've got his call log with several island numbers, starting five days before the murder—June 10. I just need to match these numbers to names. Gimme a sec."

Tap-tap-tap, sounded the flurry of keys.

"Bingo," said Bryn. "We have him calling Gaunavou first, and then the victim, Vakameau. Each call lasts for about twenty minutes."

"How did he know whom to call?" I shook my head.

Liam looked me dead in the eye. "Char."

"But isn't Char obstructing justice by not speaking up?" I put.

Guy clarified. "Not unless she offers up false information. If she merely withholds it because she's not asked the right questions, she's not guilty of obstructing justice."

The possibilities flashed through my brain. "So Rory had Char on standby, feeding him relevant tidbits of news from the island. He must've paid her handsomely. But did he tell her how he planned to use the information and tools she gave him? Did he swear her to secrecy? Was she in on the murder?"

Guy tipped an eyebrow. "Likely not. Rory probably wanted to keep her in the dark as much as possible. Less of a mess in the long run."

"I'm wondering what Rory said to Vakameau to

get him to return to my island, even at the relatively safe hour of 4 a.m." Liam scrubbed his stubble. Then he switched tacks. "Guy, of all this evidence, what can Patel use to petition the judge to issue a warrant to force Rory to send his DNA samples to Fiji? Because I have a feeling little of the evidence we've got so far will hold up in court."

Oh, Liam was talking about the unclaimed DNA found in the boat! I got excited thinking of nailing Rory with his own DNA.

Guy held his chin in his hand, resting his arms against his chest. "For starters, the defense can ask Char some leading questions that she can no longer avoid without outright lying. They can question Gaunavou, whose testimony would go a long way toward establishing an alternative suspect and probable cause. They can request that the judge subpoena the flight lists for Fiji Airways on those dates. If all of this points to Rory, a judge is likely to order the DNA test."

"I'll call Patel right now and sum up everything we've discussed." Liam reached for his phone.

Guy reflected. "Depending on how fast Patel's team work, we may not even have to hold the preliminary hearing."

I prayed he was right. It would be incredible if Liam didn't have to stand trial and none of us had to go to court.

Chapter Forty-Nine

Ingrid

Andrea and I sat at the edge of the infinity pool in our bikinis on Wednesday evening after swimming in the sweltering heat. The shadows were lengthening as the sun prepared to set behind the house. Waisake told me these last two weeks had been several degrees warmer than usual for this time of year. Katrina was making bread with Tima, and Gretchen was reading in one of the southern common rooms. Liam and Guy were having pre-dinner drinks on the terrace, fifty yards up from the pool.

I slid a sidelong glance at my friend. "D, you're bubbling with happiness. What's going on?"

The quick curve of her lips told me I was spot-on. "You'll call me a fool."

"Never." I swished my lower legs in the cool water, not taking my eyes off her.

"Well, feel free to call me one." She met my eyes, her lips parted. "I think I'm falling for Guy."

My smile widened. I'd suspected her irrepressible joy might have to do with Guy. "Tell me everything!"

She threw back her head, groaning. "Someone must've put a contract out on my heart. Of all people to fall for—a renowned playboy who goes through women like a pile of junk mail."

I became sober. "Do you know, D, two things about him really strike me. The fact that he loves Liam and Liam loves him speaks volumes about his character. And with his good taste and judgement, he's bound to have fallen for you. You're funny, brilliant, talented, strong, loyal, and kind-hearted. Not to mention drop-dead gorgeous. Plus, you guys have undeniable chemistry."

Her eyes sparkled. "That's true." She paused, reflecting. "But then, I have the feeling a lot of women have great chemistry with Guy. That's why I want to run a few things by you. I'd really value your opinion."

"I'm all ears." I leaned back on my hands, appreciating Andrea's beautiful profile, the way her high cheekbones gleamed in the pool lights. I looked across at Guy, catching him stealing glances at Andrea every couple of minutes.

"So one night we were watching rom-coms in the movie room." She gazed out at the illuminated sea-green pool. "We started doing that a lot after I discovered he likes them. We came to the point in a film where the adopted heroine reunited with her biological parents." She sat forward, splashing water on her arms. "Though it was supposed to be a happy moment, Guy rose from his seat and headed out the door. When I followed him, he said I should go back and keep watching the film. But he was clearly upset. I talked him into sitting with me on the bench on the porch. After a few minutes of silence, he said in a tight voice, 'I was really angry at my parents from the age of nine to eighteen. But I bottled it up, because anger wasn't cool, and I didn't want them to win by getting to me.' His fists were clenched. I asked, was he mad because they'd put him in the care of his aunt Helen? He said, 'That, and the way they treated me as an afterthought the whole time I was growing up.' I had the feeling he was sharing this with me because we'd been writing about his parents that whole week. Guy doesn't just blurt this kind of thing to anyone—and he rarely sounds so raw. I've never seen so much emotion from him, Ingrid." She gave a half-shrug, shaking her head. "Do you think he opened up because he feels I understand him?"

I stared at the darkening seas that tapered to a smear of colored clouds in the east. "I think he picked you as his biographer for a reason, Drea. He trusts you. Even putting aside the intimacy of writing his life story together all day, you have a connection that allows him to be vulnerable around you." I covered her hand with mine.

"Wow." She blew out a breath. "I'm always afraid, when I feel a man gets me, that it's one-sided. Especially in the case of Guy, who's so detached and suave. I guess you could be right." She hesitated. "But there was this time the other week, when we were in the sauna. Guy brought massage oil and had me lie on my belly on the bench. Of course we were both naked. *Jesus*, that man's hands are God's gift. I was halfway to coming five minutes in when, out of the blue, he asked, 'Do you often sleep with a man on a first date, princess?' That killed my mood, and I sat bolt upright. 'What the fuck, Guy?' I said. 'Isn't your question a little hypocritical? I was here on the island for a few days, and you had a reputation for playing the field. It was going to be a one-night stand. You made sure it wasn't. You reaped the benefits of my adventurousness.

What's your problem?' 'Lie back down,' he said. 'I haven't finished your lovely glutes. I only want to know how easily you give your heart away.' I was still touchy, but I wanted his hands on me again, so I stretched out and let him continue his massage. 'Have you ever been burned?' he asked. 'No,' I said, 'I guess I've been lucky. I'm usually the one to break up with men, and I've never been seriously hurt. Have you?' 'Once, I discovered a woman was seeing someone else alongside me. I was just beginning to care for her. It hurt my pride as much as my heart.' He didn't seem to want to talk about it any further, so I let it drop. What do you think that was about?"

"I think he wanted to protect his own heart. He may have been trying to wrap his head around your instant physical attraction and deep connection. He wanted to find out if you could easily have that kind of rapport with someone else—or if he's unique." Drea's expression was somber as she absorbed my words. "The fact that you know your own mind and heart enough not to stay with a man beyond the point when you discover he's not right for you shouldn't scare Guy. It should reassure him that you're serious about him."

She mused. "So you think he's just as nervous as I am about free-falling into love?"

I laughed. "Love is a risky business. But if you both jump together, you increase your chances of surviving."

"There's just one more scene I want to share." She pulled her legs out of the pool and folded them on the cement.

"Share away. There's nothing I'd rather be doing, no place I'd rather be than right here with you now."

Pulling my own legs out, I sat facing her.

"One night Guy and I were having nightcaps on our southern porch, listening to Brazilian samba music." Andrea shifted so she was facing me. "He told a hilarious story about a potbellied pig that belonged to his aunt Helen in the Bronx. The pig got drunk one night on beer out of a keg in the backyard that it somehow managed to open. The pig got loose, going on a rampage around the neighborhood, picking a fight with a cock that belonged to a house down the street. Those who saw the fight said it was a close call who got the better of the other. Just when I was looking forward to hearing the fight's outcome, Guy snapped his mouth shut and became quiet. When I asked him what was wrong, he said, 'You must be sick of hearing my stories. Forgive me for bending your ear all day and night.' I couldn't get him to talk about what upset him or why he clammed up. And he wouldn't tell any more anecdotes that night. For the life of me I can't figure out why."

I thought about this a moment. "Liam mentioned that Guy is always the entertaining raconteur of every social gathering. For the most part, he wears that badge with pride. But he may hesitate at being typecast like that around you. He may want you to see him as more. I'm just extrapolating from what you and Liam have said, and what I know of Guy after ten weeks."

Andrea nodded slowly. "Yes. That makes sense. Honestly, I love it when he shares stories about his world. He's had so many experiences, and he's really clever at bringing them to life through words. But I can see how he'd be sensitive about his public face, if he's baring his soul to me."

I angled my head. "I think no one falls harder— when he falls—than a man with his defenses up who has sensitive inner layers. Guy strikes me as that man. From all you've shared, it sounds as if he's girding his loins for giving his heart to you. You both spend a lot of time together, during work and off the clock. But the sooner you can get in the habit of communicating on a deeper level, the more you can trust each other with your hearts."

Andrea gave a half-smile. "I think what sometimes stands in the way of my communicating is my self-reliance. And what stands in his way is pride."

"That's interesting. What stands in Liam's way is his slowness to trust and his urge to control everything around him. And what stands in my way is my desire to avoid confrontation."

As Andrea slid back into the pool, I joined her. We were both getting goosebumps, and it was actually warmer in the water than out of it.

Andrea submerged herself up to her neck. "How much do you wanna bet that the men up on the terrace are discussing either the murder case or their latest financial investments? The furthest thing from their minds is relationships."

Following her gaze to where Liam and Guy were absorbed in conversation, I had to agree.

****

Liam

Half my mind was on the case, and the other half was on Guy, who was talking about an investment he was pulling out of, on Stephen's advice. Deciding that neither Friday's trial nor the stock market was calming my nerves, I veered off topic.

"Are you wooing Andrea for the long term?" I caught Guy's expression, which was that of a rabbit frozen in the underbrush. "I'm only anticipating what her father and brother are going to ask when they meet you—if your intentions are serious."

Guy expelled a long breath. "All I think about all day long—when we're not focusing on your case—is Andrea. It scares me, old man. As Cole Porter says, I've got her under my skin, in a bad way."

"Why bad? Why does it scare you?" I poured more Scotch in our empty glasses.

"I've never had it this bad for a woman." Guy gazed out toward the infinity pool, part of which was visible from where we sat. We could just see the heads of Ingrid and Andrea as they floated in the water. "What if it all goes south?"

"Your insurance against that is everything that makes your relationship strong. Humor me—tell me what binds you together."

"We have fun together." He swirled his glass of whisky. "We love talking about trivial things, watching films, relaxing in the sauna and hot tub, working out in the gym, playing cards, and shelling. In New York I can see us going out to dinner—she's a foodie—seeing shows and live concerts, attending parties, and traveling."

"What else?" I prompted.

He blushed. "When she's not a lady, she's quite a siren."

I laughed, clapping him on the shoulder. "I thought as much. What else makes the two of you strong?"

"We make a good team." He swigged some Scotch. "Not just when we're working on the book, but in everyday matters. Where I'm weak, she's strong. And when she's vulnerable, I try to support her."

"All this sounds like a promising foundation for a relationship." I paused. "Does she get you—and do you get her?"

He nodded. "Fundamentally, yes. We have occasional misunderstandings, all of them my fault. As you know, I'm an entitled, snobbish prick who sometimes speaks his feelings too indirectly."

"Sometimes?" I chuckled. "You're a bundle of contradictions, Guy. You can be direct about so many things. But when it comes to your own feelings, you beat around the bush."

"Like Hamlet, I'm one part wisdom and three parts coward," he conceded. "Were I to act as I should, I'd declare my feelings to Andrea and put our shilly-shallying to rest."

"Does she feel the same?" I stretched my legs out in front of me.

"A few things make me think she's rather partial to me." Guy leaned back in his chair, a smile playing about his lips. "On the night you were jailed, we were all on edge at the hotel. I decided to go on a walk to clear my head. Andrea was talking to her parents, but she ended the call to keep me company. She somehow managed to hunt down vegetarian takeout especially for me—past midnight in Suva—just to make sure I ate something. And she found a sleep mask at some shop on the street, since I'd forgotten to pack one in the rush of our departure. Thanks to her, I actually slept a little.

"On another occasion, we had a Zoom meeting with a potential photographer for my memoir, a New Yorker named Jonathan. When he started mocking me for being out of touch with how regular people live and outlandish in my tastes, Andrea rushed to my defense and snapped, 'Are *you* in the loop about classical literature and history? Are *you* in personal touch with high-profile Tunisians, Croatians, and Colombians? Are *you* consulted by celebrities on how to throw parties and madly sought after to attend them?' When Jonathan gaped, speechless, she went on. 'No? Then I suggest you keep your criticisms to yourself and give a vote of thanks to people like Guy for keeping the world interesting.'

"On a third occasion, I happened to walk in when her laptop was open to an email from her sister Vanessa, and Andrea had gone to the bathroom. I couldn't help catching the phrases that jumped out before I could look away. Her sister had written scathing words about me and the way I'd kept Andrea on the island. In reply, Andrea had enthusiastically defended my 'wicked sense of humor, loyalty, sophisticated taste in music, clothes, and food, and cosmopolitanism.' I must admit I was floored by her high praise."

I matched his smile. "It sounds as if she's on the same page with you. I wouldn't have pegged either of you as bashful. What's stopping you from committing to each other beyond the island?"

"Probably our reason is one and the same: we don't trust me. *I* don't trust myself not to hurt her—and she, rightfully, doesn't trust me not to hurt her. When my reputation precedes me even in my own rationale, how can I expect her to discount it in hers?" He drummed his fingers on his lap.

I tossed back the rest of my Scotch. "There's a first

for everything, Guy. Andrea may be that one woman who makes you want to settle down. But you'll never know until you give it a go. You've got to tell her your feelings. Trust me, I learned the hard way. As soon as you do, you'll free yourself. Find the perfect moment and seize it."

His brow creased. "I think I have an idea. If you're game."

I waved a hand. "After losing my heart to Ingrid, I want everyone else to lose theirs too. It feels fucking fantastic. Whatever you're planning, I'm all for it."

His eyes danced. "Even if it involves a bagpipe band, twelve strippers, and a pop-out cake?"

I rubbed the back of my neck. "If that's what you want, Guy, I'll help you. But Ingrid and I are taking a boat to another island for the night."

He chuckled. "No need. I just wanted to see what your limit was."

Chapter Fifty

Liam

The preliminary hearing was scheduled for today at 4. I got up at 7 to make coffee and calls. Ingrid followed me into the kitchen to fix breakfast. As I waited for the water to boil for the cafetière—into which I'd dumped extra scoops of coffee to give myself a good jolt—I mentally reviewed what Patel and the defense team had accomplished over the last five days.

"Share your thoughts, Liam," Ingrid urged as she cracked eggs to poach.

I was relieved to have her to unburden myself to. It'd been six years since I'd had the benefit of being in love with someone. But Ingrid was more intensely focused, sympathetic, and selfless than any of my previous girlfriends. She was an ideal confidante.

"The defense questioned Char, confirming that she did indeed lend Rory the key to the arsenal for an hour that Sunday." I turned off the whistling kettle and poured water over the coffee grounds. "She also confessed that he'd paid her to keep him informed about things on the island, and that she'd told him about the assault, my attack on the fishermen, and my parting words to them. She also told him about Gretchen and Katrina—how you only leave them when we go riding together and how they rely on you for emotional support. She said Rory didn't tell her why he wanted this information, nor, she claimed, was she suspicious of him, since he was my brother. Still, you've got to wonder how she could've thought we were friends, since Rory paid her for the information."

"So she won't be considered an accessory to the murder?" Ingrid slid the eggs into the boiling water.

"No. But she also told Rory the names of the three fishermen who assaulted you, and put him in touch with Gaunavou for transport between other islands and Vanua Levu. She confessed to being disaffected after I fired her." I pushed down the filter of the French press, bringing it over to the bar counter along with two mugs.

"Did the defense team question Gaunavou?" Ingrid ladled hot water over the poaching eggs.

"Yes. He described in detail the man who hired him. Patel looked at security footage for Fiji Airways, along with flight lists. Not only was Rory's name on the list for June 14 and 15, but he matched the description of the man Gaunavou ferried from Verau to Vanua Levu on the morning of the 15th. Further, a gait analysis revealed that Rory's bow-legged, supinated walk matched the tread of the boots outside the arsenal and near Vakameau's body." I cut up slices of bread and placed them in the toaster.

"And did Patel include in his argument the fact that Rory had a strong motive for the murder? That he wanted to frame you?" Ingrid mixed cream and sugar into her coffee.

"Yeah. The motive didn't by any means fit the standard mold, but Patel included it." My tone was grim.

"Was all this enough for probable cause? Did the

judge order a DNA test from Rory?" Ingrid plated the eggs and brought them to the bar counter.

I looked at my watch. "Yes. According to Patel, he ordered it yesterday at noon. Rory had twenty-four hours to send it into the lab. The lab will then send the results to the prosecution and defense."

She placed a hand over mine. "Will it be in time for the hearing?"

I shook my head. "We'll see. We'll probably have to leave for Suva at 1, just in case the results don't come back before the hearing."

"Supposing the DNA matches the prints in the boat. Will Ioane drop the charges against you?"

"We can only hope." I gave her a half-smile.

"Would Rory be extradited to Fiji for arrest and trial?"

"He would. And that will be a moment I don't want to miss." I sipped my coffee. "I also don't want to miss the moment when he's sentenced to life imprisonment for first-degree murder."

I may have committed nine kills myself, but I hadn't betrayed and framed my own brother.

****

As the morning crept onward, everyone in the house was tense. Tima dropped a plate when she served breakfast to the rest of the servants. Bryn made a major mistake on the Sydney forex market and spent hours trying to recoup his losses. Katrina accidentally bit down hard on her tongue and needed Ingrid to give her some ice and paper towels. Even Ela tipped over a bucket of soapy water in one of the rooms she was cleaning and needed help sopping it up. In short, it wasn't the day to try to accomplish anything of value.

Since my arrest, I'd fallen into the bad habit of tapping my front teeth with my index finger. Guy pestered me to stop on the grounds that the dentist would have a field day fixing my teeth, and that it was seriously irritating to those around me. Guy wouldn't know a nervous habit if it bit him in the ass. The man was coolness personified. But under his composed exterior, I knew he too was worried.

As I paced the terrace at midday, my thoughts turned to the many ironies of Rory's being the murderer. Here we both were, sons of a man who'd been framed for arson by a policeman. Now Rory had attempted to frame his brother for murder. Further, Rory was a prosecutor. He was supposed to uphold justice, not commit crime. Moreover, he had chased me down for years trying to catch me for murder. Now he himself had killed someone. Finally, in trying to frame me, he had incriminated himself. I couldn't wait to see his reaction to being foiled at the eleventh hour, after all his elaborate plans had been thwarted.

All the PIs called to wish me luck in the hearing—if we should have to go through with it.

Half an hour before we left for Suva, Gretchen approached me in the dining room. She had never sought me out, especially not for a one-on-one, so I was stunned. We stood next to the table, a few feet apart.

"Liam, I wanted to say thank you." Gretchen cleared her throat. "Thank you for bringing me and Katrina back together, and bringing us to live with you. We're both very happy."

She produced a soft gift wrapped in tissue paper. I realized she was marking the seriousness of the moment.

"For me?" My eyebrows shot up, and I took a breath to steady the emotion that swept over me.

She nodded.

I opened it and found a short-sleeved button-down cotton shirt in a muted yellow.

"Did you make this, Gretchen?"

"Yes. Connie showed me how." She fidgeted, looking a little awkward and embarrassed, but her eyes met mine. That was all I needed to know that my sister was on the way back to me.

"Wow. You even knew my size. Thank you, Gretch." I reached out and touched her shoulder.

She didn't flinch.

I was moved by her words and gift. Apparently two Stauner siblings had learned how to trust others over the last month.

At 1, Guy, Andrea, Gretchen, Katrina, Ingrid, and I piled into Josefa's boat and headed toward Suva.

At 3, as we disembarked, Patel called.

"The DNA was a match, Mr. Stauner." The slight charge to Patel's voice suggested he was mildly excited. "The prosecutor is reviewing the entire case as we speak, in light of the new overwhelming evidence against your brother."

"How long will it take him to make a decision?" I tapped my teeth again, and then, catching Guy's head shake, stopped.

"We're hoping he'll decide in the next hour. I'll let you know as soon as I hear."

After we'd ended the call, I gathered everyone to walk slowly toward the courthouse. I had the superstitious belief that if I pretended the trial was still happening, it would get called off—but that if I assumed it was going to be called off, it would still happen.

We all filed into the courthouse, taking seats on the benches in the large entrance room.

After a few minutes, I couldn't sit still any longer. I sprang up and paced, my pulse spiking. I hated how everything was out of my control. I also hated watching the lawyers, judges, and court officials filing into the courtroom as if the trial were going forward.

Fucking call already, Patel.

At 3:58, as I stood near my group of supporters, he called.

"Yes, Patel?" I tried to keep the anxiety out of my voice, but my heart was knocking at my ribcage. Ingrid stood beside me, watching and listening intently. I squeezed her hand, not sure whether I was trying to reassure her or myself.

"Ioane has dropped the charges." Patel's own voice had a barely controlled thrill to it.

I blew out a deep, long breath of relief, my face relaxing. Ingrid looked ecstatic. I summoned the strength to ask, "What about Rory? Will he be charged?"

"Yes. Ioane has requested that Rory be extradited. It'll take a few months for him to be handed over to the Suva court. But he'll be arrested and tried here for murder." Patel's voice grew warm. "Mr. Stauner, allow me to congratulate you on the outcome of this case."

"Thank you. I'm grateful for all your hard work and support." I ended the call. Everyone except Guy was on the balls of their feet with anticipation. "They called off the trial. Ioane dropped the charges. I'm a free man."

"Yay!" Andrea hugged Guy.

Ingrid hugged me. Gretchen and Katrina hugged each other. Then we all came in for a group hug, which I never in my life would've seen myself doing. A Marine hitman in a group hug was like an ogre among a bunch of Pollyannas. But I went along with it. This was a pretty spectacular day.

"Do I have the green light to go ahead with our plans?" Guy murmured under his breath as we walked back to the boat.

I laughed. "Yeah, Guy. If everything can be prepared on such short notice."

"Not much to prepare, old man. I was expecting your acquittal."

****

As Gretchen, Katrina, Andrea, and Ingrid headed off on a long walk around the island, everyone else prepared for the blowout party Guy had planned. The four women didn't know about the shindig, as I'd told the servants and guests not to mention it. The main surprisee—if that was a real word—wasn't myself, but Andrea.

I had to hand it to Guy. He was a master party planner. In less than two days, in a special room where none of the women went, he'd prepared festive streamers, magic-lantern-style tissues, fairy lights, candles, and other paraphernalia, which he guided the servants in setting up on the terrace. He directed them to bring out tables, chairs, tablecloths, and place settings. During the preparations, he played mood music—an eclectic mix of Latin dance numbers that got most of the household grooving before the party even started. The crescent moon rose like a fingernail clipping low in the eastern sky as the staff put the finishing touches on the terrace.

With Ralph, Claude, Rodrigo, the three new boatmen, Dr. Leong, and his wife, the guest list stood at forty-five. According to Guy, this was an extremely modest head count for his parties. Apparently four hundred was more his style. Everyone planned to stay the night on the island, since much drinking was in order.

Speaking of drinking, Guy had ordered two boatloads of supplies, which bartenders and caterers hauled in—gallons of liquor, ingredients for twelve different appetizers and three entrées, and several cakes from a boutique bakery in Suva. Guy wanted Tima and Waisake to have a night off from cooking and everyone to focus on socializing and dancing.

By the time the women returned from their walk, their surprised looks as they saw the festive set-up and spread were worth a few pictures on my phone.

"Is this to celebrate your freedom, Liam?" Ingrid asked.

"That, and other things." I pulled her in for a deep kiss.

"Hmm. You're very mysterious." She looked laughingly up at me.

From Katrina's wide eyes and slack jaw, I knew this was her first real party. Gretchen reached up with wonderment and touched a magic-lantern tissue hanging in front of one of the lamps. The pattern it cast on the terrace was full of diamonds and spirals that twisted and reshaped themselves as the breeze blew.

Once everyone on the island had gathered on the terrace, Guy directed the caterers to pour champagne before bringing out the appetizers. Epeli and Katrina drank sodas, but everyone else, including Gretchen, accepted a glass of bubbly.

Stepping onto a small stool, Guy raised his glass. Everyone took the cue to stop talking.

"We have so many things to celebrate this evening, that we thought we'd consolidate them into one blowout. On the top of the docket is the exoneration of my dear friend Liam, our generous host and employer. Let us raise our glasses and drink in honor of his freedom." Cheers went up, as servants and guests drank. "Our next cause for celebration is welcoming home Gretchen and Katrina, Liam's sister and niece. Long may they both thrive under the nurturing love and care of Liam and Ingrid." Cries of "hear, hear" went up all around, as everyone sipped their champagne. Tears rose in Gretchen's eyes, and a smile bloomed on Katrina's face. "Let us also toast our gracious mistress and hostess, Ingrid, whose love for Liam has transformed him from Goliath into David." I burst out laughing, and everyone joined in, swigging their fizz. "Last but far from least, I would like to honor Andrea, the writer of my memoir and the woman I'm in love with." Cheers swelled the air once more, as people tipped back their glasses. Andrea's eyes widened, and a generous smile spread across her face. She too looked transformed by Guy's words. "Now let us all eat, drink, be merry, and dance with abandon!"

On that note, Billy Joel's "All You Wanna Do Is Dance" sounded from the speaker, and everyone sought out appetizers, beer, and cocktails. Andrea cruised over to Guy, murmuring something in his ear that made Guy break out in a broad beam. Then they kissed as if there were no one in the world but them.

Ingrid watched their exchange too. Smiling and lifting her head to mine, she pulled me down for a passionate kiss that could give Guy and Andrea a run for their money.

We never stopped touching that whole party. If my hand wasn't on her lower back, it was on her nape or ass. If her arm wasn't tucked into mine, it was around my shoulder or neck. We were like a pair of marionettes joined at the hip. We chatted, drank, and ate. Then we danced for hours, as the moon arced above our heads and set in the west. Even Gretchen and Katrina danced, linking hands and laughing as they surprised themselves with their joyful recklessness.

Guy actually got drunk. I'd never have believed it if I hadn't seen it. The man's tolerance was through the roof. But tonight, flushed, he swayed, told racy stories about Polish countesses, and slurringly compared country houses in England, Portugal, and France. His ridiculous dancing was especially worth recording on my phone—so I could hold the video over him in the future, any time I needed something he was reluctant to give.

Around 5 in the morning, when the party was still in full swing, Ingrid's soft voice sounded at my chest. "Are we going back to New York soon, Liam?"

I smoothed her hair. "Do you want to, my little blossom?"

She smiled at my endearment. "I do, and I don't. I love Verau and its people. And I love the rhythms of life here. But I know all good things must come to an end. My parents are dying to meet you, I want to put in my resignation in person at work, and we'll need time

407

to get Gretchen and Katrina settled before school starts. Now that Andrea and Guy are an item and you're free to leave, it seems like the natural moment to say farewell to the island until next time."

"Then we will, sweet Ingrid." I kissed her nose. "Until next time."

"Do you see that upside-down Big Dipper low in the sky over there?" As she pointed, I nodded. "That's the way we did things. We moved in together before dating. We took our honeymoon before saying 'I love you.' We committed to each other forever before you met my friends and family. I wonder what else we're going to do upside down."

I leaned in to speak low in her ear. "I'm going to carry you upside down to bed. And I'm going to do it now."

Epilogue

Ingrid

I didn't think it was possible to love Liam any more than I did when we left Verau. But as summer passed into autumn, and we placed Katrina in a private school in Brooklyn Heights and enrolled Gretchen in childhood education courses at Hunter College, my love grew daily stronger. He was so attentive, patient, and loving with his sister and niece, that it tugged at my heartstrings every time I saw them together. He helped Katrina with her homework, made Gretchen a built-in bookcase in her bedroom, and played with Errol, the inexhaustibly energetic Jack Russell terrier Katrina had rescued.

The building Liam owned was on the Upper West Side, overlooking Central Park. Our family—Liam, Gretchen, Katrina, Errol, and I—occupied the top floor, which Liam had designed as an open-floor plan with few walls. Liam and I rode the park loop on our bikes three days a week, and I swam in the pool Liam had installed in the basement of our building.

By mid-October, I'd put the finishing touches on the gallery Liam had bought for me in Chelsea. It was everything I'd dreamed of: exposed-brick walls, hardwood floors, loft ceilings, plenty of natural light streaming through the picture windows, enough space to house the exhibits of three artists at once, and a large office area in the back. To open the gallery, I was doing a Verau-themed exhibit of my own works—those I'd made on the island—together with the works of two artists I'd gone to school with at Brown.

My assistant, Charlie, was a reedy woman with tortoiseshell glasses and a natural Marilyn Monroe beauty mark above her lips. Having done a degree in business, she helped me price all the artworks, hired a web designer for our website, and marketed the gallery. Together we picked frames, display cases, pedestals for sculptures, and other necessaries for showing the art.

The grand opening was Saturday, October 22. Gretchen and Katrina, Andrea and Guy, my parents, Armen, and other friends would be there, along with specially invited members of the art world and wealthy buyers.

Two weeks ago, Andrea had moved into Guy's penthouse overlooking the East River. Though they'd completed the final draft of Guy's memoir, Andrea wanted to start a new project with him so they could work together again. The project had been rewarding for them both. Marketing for the memoir already had filmmakers sniffing around Promontory Press for film rights, and Andrea had been promoted to associate editor for her work on the book.

A week ago, after his extradition, Rory had been arrested and charged with first-degree murder in Suva. Liam and I would fly out in a month to testify at his preliminary hearing. But Liam's and my life was so rich and full now, that we had little time to think of Rory.

On the afternoon of the opening, realizing my last period had been more than six weeks ago, I began to suspect something was amiss. I went out to buy pregnancy tests, and both came out positive. Privately, I was jubilant. I had wanted to have kids ever since my previous boyfriend Adrian, but the time had never been right. Now, it seemed as if everything was coming into place, career-wise, housing-wise, and man-wise. Liam had told me several times he wanted to have a large family, but his time frame had always been vague. What would he think of having the new addition to our family pushed up—to now? There was so much on my plate with the gallery, that I decided I would figure out how to tell Liam afterward.

Before the opening, Guy, Andrea, Liam, and I met for drinks at a bar down the street from the gallery. Gretchen and Katrina would come directly to the gallery at 7.

When Guy and Andrea arrived, it was the vision I'd had in the cove that Sunday back in late May. They cruised into the bar like celebrities in black tie, wafting sophisticated auras of confidence. Everyone kissed and hugged, ordering cocktails.

It had been over a week since I'd spoken to Andrea, so we had a lot of catching up to do. As I was midway through a sentence, Liam leaned into me, reaching around for his cocktail, and knocked my small blue purse off the barstool.

"Allow me." He knelt down to pick it up. I followed his movements absently while still talking. But instead of rising, he opened the purse and pulled a black jewelry box out of it like a magician.

He looked as surprised as I was at this feat, as if to say, "What do we have here?"

But when I studied his eyes, I saw a telltale twinkle

of mischief. My breath hitched, and my heart stuttered.

Still on one knee, he lifted the box, cracking it open. All the air left my lungs in a swoosh. Nestled inside the box a ring perched with two brilliant round blue sapphires flanking a diamond center stone.

The buzz in the bar lowered, as everyone zeroed in on us.

"Ingrid, your blithe spirit has caught me in its spell, and I don't want to break free. Before you, I never would've believed something so good could come from something so bad—that love could be born out of death like a phoenix rising from ashes. But now that I know these things are possible, I want to witness more miracles with you by my side. I want you to be my wife, bound to me by love, even though you'll always remain my little crow feather. Will you, Ingrid—be my wife?" His voice cracked a little on the question.

I took his free hand, pressing my palm to his as we had done that night in Verau. "For as long as you're bound to me, I'm bound to you."

"Is that a yes, my sweet torturer?" His eagerness was palpable.

"Forever and a day, Liam. Yes."

He slipped the ring on my finger, standing and melding me to his body as we kissed. Applause sounded all around us, but every particle of my universe was concentrated in us two.

I whispered in his ear, "Liam, are you prepared to witness another miracle with me by your side?"

"What miracle is that?" He looked down at me lovingly.

"We're going to have a baby." I swallowed the lump in my throat.

In a split second his face went from overjoyed to over-the-moon. "*Really?*"

I nodded.

He swooped me up in his arms and spun us around, crying out, "You've outdone me again, Ingrid! Nothing can top that!"

I thought of our party in Verau. "Once more we've done things upside down. Unless we get married first…"

"We can be married tomorrow, if you like!" He laid another fevered kiss on my lips. "I'm going to be a father!"

Andrea winked at me. "Looks as if tonight's party, like the one in Verau, will consolidate a few celebrations into one."

Guy smiled. "Congratulations, old man—you've just created a third category of abduction. The one with a happy ending for everyone."

A word about the author...

A former academic, I took up writing romance recently and quite by accident. In early 2022 the right elements conjoined—my love of villains, my taste for high comedy, and my pull towards strong women. Now I can't stop cooking up plots and drawing new characters. Though I write mostly dark romance, I invariably weave plenty of reality into the fantasy. My preference for lone wolves, quirky characters, and intense plot results in what my reader and author friends call *romance with teeth*. I live in Berkeley, California with my dachshund-Chihuahua, Pooh-bah. When I'm not writing, I love traveling, cooking, playing piano, and cycling in the nearby hills.

Find me on my website:
https://kathleenhaley1.wixsite.com/my-site-2
or on Instagram:
https://www.instagram.com/kathleenlotthaley/